D1474603

To the Color

TO THE COLOR

A NOVEL OF THE
BATTALION OF ST. PATRICK

Book Two

RAY HERBECK, JR.

FIVE STAR
A part of Gale, a Cengage Company

LIBRARY OF CONGRESS CATALOGING-IN-PUBLICATION DATA

Names: Herbeck, Ray, Jr., author.
Title: To the color : a novel of the Battalion of St. Patrick / Ray Herbeck, Jr.
Description: First Edition. | Waterville, Maine : Five Star, a part of Gale, a Cengage Company, 2022. | Series: Battalion of St. Patrick ; book 2 |Identifiers: LCCN 2021048045 | ISBN 9781432891367 (hardcover)
Subjects: GSAFD: Historical fiction.
Classification: LCC PS3608.E7263 T6 2022 | DDC 813/.6—dc23
LC record available at https://lccn.loc.gov/2021048045

First Edition. First Printing: June 2022
Find us on Facebook—https://www.facebook.com/FiveStarCengage
Visit our website—http://www.gale.cengage.com/fivestar
Contact Five Star Publishing at FiveStar@cengage.com

Printed in Mexico
Print Number: 01   Print Year: 2022

TO THE COLOR

To the Color

PROLOGUE
A DIGEST OF
Changing Flags,
PREQUEL TO *To the Color*

In late summer of 1845, charismatic, cocky Irish immigrant John Riley swaggered into the frontier military town of Fort Mackinac, Michigan, for the last time. With a wink and his winsome grin, he told his benefactor and protector of Irish immigrants, Judge O'Malley, his "brilliant plan": he would enlist in the U.S. Army there for a unique purpose—to desert.

It was behavior not unfamiliar to Riley. In his youth, he had deserted a wife and child in Ireland by enlisting in the occupying British army. He buried guilt beneath arrogance and occasional money sent them while fighting Queen Victoria's "little wars" in distant lands. He rose in the artillery to a proud if calloused master gunnery sergeant. Riley more recently deserted the British in Canada for what seemed brighter monetary promise in the United States. But "native born" prejudice doomed him for the last two years to drinking, brawling, and digging ditches for O'Malley. Now he would bank on his military professionalism for quick promotion and resulting higher pay. Then he could afford to "go missing" yet one more time. Wizened O'Malley thought his plan daft and told him so in his inimitable biting brogue.

But Riley turned a deaf ear and gawked at patriotic locals. The crowd cheered as pristine troops marched to rousing music from the log fort down to a wharf and waiting steamship. They would embark for Texas, newly admitted to the Union. The U.S. policy of expansion by any means necessary, labeled "manifest destiny," demanded a show of force to settle a boundary dispute with Mexico. Riley scoffed at the rowdy throng's clamor for conflict. He was a charming but cynical soldier of fortune who looked and felt older than his twenty-eight years. His jaded blue eyes saw this as mere politics, no prelude to war.

But happily, it was a handy means to his personal end. He planned to enlist and then desert in Texas with money enough to sail back to Ireland. There he hoped to find something he had lost. Exactly what that might be, he was not yet sure. He knew that it was not his long distant "family," which he dismissed as a youthful indiscretion. But whatever it was, Riley sensed that he must try to find it. He believed the place to start looking was "home." O'Malley warned that his dream would become a nightmare. Inside the bustling stockade, Riley observed more well-trained, mostly immigrant U.S. troops preparing to leave. The sergeant of the final company appeared gravely ill. Riley seized upon this unfortunate fact. He demonstrated mastery of the drill manual to Captain Moses Merrill, the West Point graduate who headed Company K, Fifth U.S. Infantry.

Merrill was under pressure to bolster numbers with more recruits. And he needed experienced soldiers. Though he suspected Riley was a British deserter, and he could not knowingly enlist such a person, Merrill swore him into the U.S. Army anyway as an infantry private. They shared an unspoken understanding: Riley would be promoted to sergeant when the opportunity arose. Riley was ecstatic: his "brilliant plan" was off to a grand start.

But three agonizing months later, Riley remained a private. Encamped with thousands of U.S. troops in a muggy, flea infested tent city dubbed "Fort Texas," he felt trapped on the Rio Grande across from Matamoros, Mexico. And Riley bridled at the harsh corporal punishment of comrades that made the "bloody British" look like pacifists. Still, he proved an exemplary soldier. So, following an exhibition of his military prowess, the honorable Captain Merrill recommended Riley as the next sergeant. But anti-immigrant upper officers denied him promotion. Instead, they gave the stripes to a less worthy but "native born" candidate, seen more trustworthy in the event of war.

Angry and frustrated, Riley was a prime candidate for a clever Mexican plan to decrease the number of U.S. troops it might face in that war. Mexico knew that half the U.S. army was immigrant Irish and German Catholics seduced into ranks by economic need. And Mexico was a Catholic nation. Since there was no war yet, Mexican food and trinket vendors still were allowed in the U.S. camp on Sunday, "market day." On the Sunday that he was denied promotion, a beautiful, young Mexican girl named Luzero slipped Riley a flyer. Then the stunning, mysterious young woman vanished into the crowd. After recovering his lust laden senses, Riley read the flyer: it promised three hundred-twenty acres of land, bountiful cash, and higher rank to U.S. soldiers who deserted and joined the army of Mexico. Riley seized upon this as his salvation.

He eagerly presented the plan to his best friend, Sergeant Patrick Dalton, a combat veteran of the Seminole War in Florida. In his late forties and another brawny Irishman, Dalton was digging latrines in the camp jail for cursing a hard-nosed native-born Dragoon officer, Colonel William Harney. Riley pleaded that the flyer could make them both "landed gentlemen."

Unlike Riley, Dalton was a ten-year U.S. Army veteran who felt a certain loyalty. Almost a father figure to Riley, Dalton saw the offer as an insult in the face of the coming war, the possibility of which Riley still refused to accept. They parted in bitterness.

At sunset, after the camp flag was lowered to the bugle call of

"To the Color," Riley secured a pass from Captain Merrill to attend evening Mass. It would be held outside camp by a Mexican priest from across the river since Catholic priests could not accompany the U.S. Army. Though suspicious, Merrill had to obey the standing order of commanding General Zachary Taylor that all requests for Mass be granted: Taylor wanted to reduce desertions, then at epidemic proportions.

While waiting anxiously for the pass, Riley watched a Southern officer's servant hand Merrill some coffee: Sandy was an aging, crafty slave who subtly let Riley know that he recognized him as a potential "runaway." But Sandy kept quiet. Riley grabbed the pass and left.

Following Mass that night, Riley hid in the rowboat of the returning priest and crossed the river to Matamoros. Small but tough Mexican soldiers seized him. At six-feet-two inches tall, he appeared to them to be a giant. Through a haze of alcohol, Riley joked that he was seeing leprechauns. He shouted, "Take me to your pot of gold!" They did not laugh.

Weeks later, Riley languished in a Mexican jail with forty-two other Irish U.S. deserters, all lured by the same flyer. Its author was steely Captain Francisco Moreno, a case-hardened yet refined veteran of Mexico's frontier battles, including the Alamo ten years earlier. Moreno manipulated events to surface a leader among the U.S. deserters: it was Riley, no surprise to himself. But rampant Mexican prejudice against Anglos foiled Moreno's original plan to integrate them into Mexico's serried ranks.

A resulting riot pitted Riley and his men against not only Mexicans but runaway slaves from Texas: Mexico had outlawed slavery years before. But seeing blacks as soldiers held "equal in ranks" surfaced explosive bigotry on all sides. Riley received surprising empathy from Sandy, now a fellow "runaway." Too old to soldier, he was making his way to Mexico City to start life over as a free man. Sandy warned Riley that war was coming, and he should find a way to "go missing" yet again. But Riley remained skeptical. He would pursue his "pot of gold."

That night, Moreno shattered Riley's dream. Moreno and Riley had discovered a mutual bond of military professionalism. But Moreno informed him that, since they could not meld into Mexican ranks, they no longer had a purpose. Therefore, Riley and his defectors must be shot.

Desperate, Riley hastily contrived a proposal to forge a unique artillery company from the disparate elements of his deserters. To avoid more racial conflict, they would serve as a separate unit under bilingual Moreno. Riley, of course, would be lieutenant and second in command with a high rate of pay. Moreno agreed. He looked more relieved than surprised.

Through impressive powers of persuasion comprising brawn and "blarney" (Irish for embroidering truth until it teetered on the brink of a lie), Riley created his outfit. But in a move that stunned only Riley, a unit of the Mexican army attacked U.S. troops across the Rio Grande, triggering war. Moreno knew all along this was going to happen. Riley was furious at having been duped: he understood that he was more trapped than ever.

War had made them all not merely peacetime "flogged deserters," as he put it to his men. Now they were wartime "hanged traitors," if captured in enemy uniform and convicted in a court martial. And if caught trying to desert Mexican ranks, they simply would be shot on sight. As a test, Moreno ordered Riley and his men to fire their cannons at the U.S. fort across the river or suffer fatal consequences. Riley had never bargained on this. He wondered in agony if Dalton and former comrades fell victim to the bombardment. His "brilliant plan" had lost its sheen.

Elsewhere in Texas, superior U.S. forces defeated the main Mexican army, which then fell back to Monterey. During the retreat from Matamoros, Riley realized that the Mexican army was undermanned, poorly equipped, and comprised mostly ill-trained conscripts. He believed it had no chance.

And that meant Riley and his band of deserters had no chance. So, Riley determined to recruit from recently captured U.S. prisoners using false promises, blarney, and outright lies. He believed that the more U.S. soldiers he persuaded, with their better training, the better chance they all would have of escaping the hangman. And if he survived long enough, maybe he could yet desert and return home.

But that which Riley considered a character flaw, his pesky need to help the underdog, combined with romance to undo his plan: during the subsequent grinding siege of Monterey, Riley found himself irresistibly drawn to young Luzero, the patriotic "soldadera" ("soldier woman") who first gave him the desertion flyer. Uncomfortably, she would force him over time to confront his ingrained prejudices and question his selfish motives.

Within the deadly trenches around Monterey, Riley and his band fought not only their former comrades but hostility between themselves and Mexican soldados. Still looking for a chance to "go missing," Riley experienced unusual pangs of guilt when young Richard Parker, one of his first "recruits," was killed. Parker had doted on Riley's tales of glorious military adventures. Riley realized for the first time there could be an unintended, tragic price to his "brilliant plan."

After several thirsty weeks of starvation, the Mexican army admitted defeat but did not surrender. So Riley and his company escaped the hangman's scaffold. Under terms of an armistice, Mexican troops departed Monterey by marching past crusty General Zachary Taylor and U.S. troops. Former U.S. comrades recognized Riley and his deserters. They pelted them with vegetables, fruit, boos, and insults, to his men's outrage and Riley's professional shame.

Furious Colonel Harney watched the humiliating spectacle

beside amused General Taylor. Harney judged these "Poper Irish traitors" a threat, a palpable incentive for more desertion. Taylor shrugged it off and said to ignore them as a small, pitiful nuisance. But intransigent Harney vowed a terrible vengeance.

The retreat from Monterey proved grueling. Depressed, angry, and hungry, Riley's grumbling deserters all blamed him. Bitter at their disdain, defeat and dismal prospects, Riley refused to "snare more recruits for the damn hangman" from the newest batch of U.S. prisoners. Moreno implied that those not recruited would be killed.

Riley saw among them his friend, Dalton. Thinking he was saving Dalton's life, Riley persuaded him to join by lying about Mexico's military chances. Dalton later found comfort from his plight in the arms of earthy Belarmina, "Bel," a saucy cantina dancer and friend of Luzero who joined the soldaderas.

Riley's lies came to haunt him, though, even as he and Dalton molded a unique artillery battalion of gritty, fatalistic Irish and German turncoats, each seeking an elusive dream. Their initial prejudice against Mexicans, mirrored in Mexican prejudice against them, gradually was replaced by mutual trust and respect:

Sergeant Henry Ockter, a prim former Prussian artilleryman who fell in love not with the soldaderas, but with four ancient cannons with which he must "make do," like all Mexicans;

Sergeant Dennis Conahan, a five-foot-tall rollicking fiddle player more minstrel than military, who found Irish humor in any grim situation;

Corporal Auguste Morstadt, Conahan's fierce, towering Teutonic friend, who encouraged Conahan to play music more classical than contemporary;

Private John Price, a beefy Britisher who was bested in an early row with Riley and then became a prickly thorn in his side;

Private Tobacco Chewer, a nameless caustic Irishman and Price's best friend, whose loftiest dream was to grasp an ever-full tobacco pouch;

Sergeant Enrique Mejia, staunch leader of the Mexican guards, who kept the despised "gringo" deserters in line, then found in them a way to rise above his class;

Lieutenant Camillo Manzano, aristocratic commander of the guard company, whose hatred of the "gringos" was inflamed even more by the attraction between Riley and Luzero.

While Riley cobbled this command together, events two thousand miles away conspired to confound his efforts. Obsessed with completing "manifest destiny," President James Polk had manipulated Mexico into starting this war, which triggered ongoing protests and the birth of "civil disobedience." In the halls of Congress, former President John Quincy Adams and his protégé, young Representative Abraham Lincoln, led staunch opposition. After delivering a speech supporting a bill that requested more money and troops, commanding General Winfield Scott privately told them that a vote for this bill would, in effect, be a vote for peace. To Lincoln's amused disbelief, Scott explained that Polk had arranged for a former disgraced Mexican leader to be secreted from Cuba through the American naval blockade to take command. In exchange, this "new" Mexican supreme commander would end the war and give Polk the land he wanted in the West—all for the right price, of course.

But upon receipt of that fifty thousand dollars in U.S. gold, General Antonio Lopez de Santa Anna promptly re-discovered his patriotism, broke his word, and vowed to fight. Impressed by Santa Anna's professional military demeanor, Riley saw the hand of Fate giving himself and his seemingly doomed followers their best chance. Dour Moreno knew better, though, having served under the mercurial, vain Santa Anna at the Alamo and elsewhere.

14

Nonetheless, Santa Anna created a dazzling new army with Napoleonic uniforms, military protocols, and improved arms and equipment. And he instilled hope in Riley and his men, singling them out for special treatment with the biggest artillery guns in the army and garish, unmistakable uniforms. Santa Anna saw in them an anti-war propaganda weapon he could wield in the American press.

In January 1847, captured U.S. Army dispatches revealed that Taylor's victorious army in the north was losing half its numbers. His crack regulars were being withdrawn for General Winfield Scott's planned invasion in the south.

Santa Anna decided to seize this opportunity and attack Taylor's weakened force of unreliable volunteers. Riley and his band of rogues joined in feverish preparations for a hard march north to Saltillo from Santa Anna's base at San Luis Potosi, all in the dead of winter.

But before the campaign began, Riley yearned to find something beyond new uniforms to inspire his men. He needed to assuage the guilt that now constantly gnawed at his soul. In the past, he always had managed to outrun what he saw as the bony fingers of Fate trying to enfold him. But now he felt weighed down by these comrades whom he had persuaded to follow him. A rising sense of foreboding nagged at him like a harping banshee. Riley believed that he must create an exceptional unit identity with a peerless symbol, something around which they might rally should things go badly. Then, possibly, they might survive and even obtain their promised three hundred-twenty acres. Or, he mused, would they merely just spit in the eye of Fate?

Chapter 1
San Luis Potosi: The Flag
January 1847

When Moreno and Riley arrived at Santa Anna's headquarters, the complex was alive with hurried preparations for an imminent campaign. The captured dispatches from only a week ago revealed that Taylor's weakened U.S. Army up north lay unsuspecting and vulnerable. Inside, they found Santa Anna confronting his three brigade generals. His chief of staff, aristocratic General Micheltorena, pleaded their case. Micheltorena had the dour appearance of a lawyer, Riley thought: obviously, not to be trusted. Maps of the Saltillo region rested on easels.

"Excellency, General Lombardini begs to point out that his new troops have no shoes yet," Micheltorena said in Spanish.

"Give them sandals," Santa Anna snapped, busying himself at a map of the route north. Lombardini looked disgusted but bowed his head in subservience.

Riley, of course, did not understand the Spanish but thought it rude that Santa Anna never even faced the general. He and Moreno remained stoic.

"General Pacheco would remind his excellency," Micheltorena continued delicately, "that his men have no blankets, and we are marching north in winter."

"Issue them canvas undergarments," Santa Anna replied, "and remind him we surprised the rebels at the Alamo by just such a winter march." Pacheco stiffened at the rebuke but bowed his head. Santa Anna continued to ignore his top generals as he fussed with his maps.

Arrogant bastard, Riley thought. He did not need to speak Spanish to detect the insulting condescencion he had known in the British army.

"General Ortega reports his men well equipped, Excellency," continued Micheltorena, "but famished from hunger."

"Let them chew on their new and very expensive muskets!" Santa Anna yelled. He ceased plotting his route north and sighed in his patented, long-suffering fashion. He broke the chalk in his hand with a dull crack. Ortega looked incensed but smart enough to swallow his pride. "It will inspire them to capture food from the norteamericanos!" Santa Anna whirled around with a maniacal fury and waved them all out of the room.

As a nervous adjutant ushered Moreno and Riley forward, Riley thought that Santa Anna's face for one terrifying instant resembled the twisted, unrecognizable countenance of battlefield dead after three days. Riley shivered.

"We march north in one week!" Santa Anna roared after the departing generals. "Be ready! Or be shot!" Shaking from rage, he quivered unsteadily on his bad leg.

Micheltorena passed Moreno on his way out and rolled his eyes. Moreno smiled. Both had seen this before, Riley realized. He grew anxious as they stood at attention and waited. Santa Anna recognized them and calmed himself far too quickly. Was this all an act? Riley wondered. Perhaps Santa Anna was better suited for the stage than the battlefield, he thought.

"Ah, my friends," Santa Anna said, almost in relief. "It is an honor to see officers whose battalion, I know, is already prepared." He limped to a washstand in apparent pain, opened his gold snuff box, and dabbed white powder on his tongue. "Opium?" he asked, as if it were an hors d'oeuvre. Both begged off. "It eases pain of the body and frustration at such incompetence."

"The captured dispatches have helped you, Excellency?" Moreno asked.

"They have saved our country," Santa Anna said solemnly. "So, in a singular honor, I send your companies north with the engineers in three days to pave the way for the rest of our army." He walked to a map and pointed out the route. "Along the way, locate caches of norteamericano food and ammunition we can seize." He looked at the nearby painting of the new uniform for the deserters, then looked at the result as worn by Riley. He nodded in approval. "But what shall we call this unique battalion of reformed gringos?" he asked playfully.

"The Battalion of Saint Patrick," Riley blurted out, "who drove all the snakes out of Ireland, your grace." Riley had never believed the old Irish folktale, but now it surely seemed to him a fortuitous act of faith.

"But all are not Irish," Moreno pointed out. "Some are German, and there are a few British . . ."

Santa Anna frowned, silencing Moreno with a wave of his hand. He seemed to be enjoying a vision, possibly induced by the opium. "Your Irish saint will drive the norteamericano snakes before him," he expounded, gesturing dramatically with his arms as he paced the tent, "into the waiting talons of our Mexican eagle!" He paused to face Riley and Moreno. "And as we know, the eagle eats the snake." He pointed to his gold embroidered Mexican flag on which an angry, defiant eagle held a snake in its beak. "Viva el Battalon de San Patricio!" he shouted.

As Riley and Moreno walked back to the compound, they saw an endless column of superbly equipped Mexican cavalry. Regiment after regiment trotted out of camp, each wearing new and brightly trimmed uniforms. Most carried lances with red pennons fluttering above the dust.

"The cavalry leaves already to screen our advance from prying gringo eyes," Moreno said.

"These gringo eyes see too many lances," Riley said, an edge to his voice. "Ain't enough carbines."

"None sit a horse or wield a lance better than a Mexican vaquero, in or out of uniform," said Moreno.

"That may be true, Major, but tell me," Riley taunted, "what's the range and caliber of a lance?"

"Carbines might be more practical," Moreno admitted begrudgingly. "But do these caballeros not look magnificent?!"

" 'Tis a blessing we outnumber th'Yanks four to one," Riley said. "We'll need every damn one."

"We can do nothing about the rest of our army," said Moreno. "But we must do something to give our men heart, to unite your men and mine in a shared purpose, a unique military pride."

Riley nodded thoughtfully to agree, but something else was on his mind. "Tell me plain, Major," Riley said. "When we were forced to bear down on one another, would you have fired?"

"I would do what I must for Mexico," Moreno said immediately, then softened slightly. "But I would regret it."

"Ah, Major darlin', 'tis plain that Irish blarney is slowly filling your black heart," Riley said with a laugh.

"As Mexican bravado has hardened yours," Moreno countered.

Suddenly struck by an idea, Riley cocked his head toward Moreno. "Back at the butchering of the late Lieutenant Richey," Riley said, "you mentioned something about all Yanks, good or bad, being guilty 'under the same flag?' "

Moreno instantly saw what Riley meant. "We can unite our battalion the same way!" he said. They picked up their pace, firing ideas back and forth as if exchanging musket volleys.

"Green with something gold for old Ireland!" said Riley, looking at his flask after he took a swig.

"An eagle and a snake for Mexico!" said Moreno, for once taking a swig from Riley's offered flask.

"The silver cross of your cathedral here for Holy Mother Church," said Riley, pointing at the edifice. "That'll make Ockter and his Dutchmen happy!"

"And an image of your Saint Patrick for General Santa Anna!" Moreno exclaimed. For the first time, they enjoyed a good laugh together.

For those few moments, Riley realized he had not looked at Moreno and first seen a "greaser." Riley felt oddly refreshed, like after taking a bath in a cold, rejuvenating mountain stream.

At the end of the day in golden twilight, Riley and Moreno led Luzero, Bel, and six more soldaderas to an ancient Spanish convent. Ornately carved and painted wood statues nestled in alcoves; tapestries hung on walls; and stone and plaster decorations graced the ceilings.

Riley looked around in awe, crossing himself. Bel remained with the others in a courtyard as a Mexican nun took Riley, Moreno, and Luzero down a long corridor. Luzero carried her sewing basket and a burlap bag. Riley and Moreno's boots tramped heavily on the tiled floor, sounding to Luzero like the drums of war intruding into a sacred place.

In a tiny office, they confronted the sister superior, a pale, wizened fifty year old with fiery dark eyes. In Spanish, Moreno had just introduced Luzero, who looked devout with her respectful curtsy and clad in her rebosa shawl.

"My mother enrolled me at the convent school of your order in Mexico City," Luzero said. "At sixteen, I had to leave for the army," she added sadly. The nun nodded with an understanding smile.

"Our hope, Sister, is to recruit your holy seamstresses in

what might seem an unholy, violent cause," Moreno pleaded.

"This damnable invasion is what is unholy!" asserted the spunky nun in English. Her heavy Irish brogue surprised all but none more than Riley, who laughed out loud. "These thirty years this land has been my home," she continued. "My sacred duty now is to help it fight for its life. And no good Irishman ever shies away from a proper fight."

"I am John Riley, Sister, late of County Galway," he said, kissing her hand. She arched an eyebrow in wary recognition.

"Sister Superior Marguerite O'Gara," she said smiling, "late of County Cork. Legends seem smaller when you look them in the eye, I must say," she added. "I see now you've got neither the horns of a devil nor the halo of a saint."

Riley laughed, showing her a crude sketch. She looked puzzled.

"Each side of the flag, it is different," explained Moreno.

"Yet united in the flag itself," Luzero said.

"I'm blessed if it won't be truly glorious in the sight of God!" the nun exclaimed. She frowned slightly at Riley. "Sure and 'our side' needs something a bit grander, though," she observed.

Riley pulled out his flask and offered it to her. She looked stunned and Luzero shocked. Moreno seemed mildly amused.

"I do not imbibe, kind sir," O'Gara replied sternly.

" 'Tain't for the content, Sister, but the sentiment," Riley explained. She looked at the engraving and smiled in pleased understanding.

In a dusty archival room, Sister Superior O'Gara pulled out drawer after drawer of ancient Spanish silk vestments heavy with gold and silver bullion and intricate, handwoven lace. "When the Spanish were booted out, they left us these," she said.

"Getting good at making do with their castoffs our own selves," Riley said, thinking of his ancient cannon. "We're still a bit shy of green cloth, Sister."

"Not with this," said Luzero, handing the nun her burlap bag. Sister O'Gara carefully pulled out and unfolded Luzero's beautiful gown made of raw green silk, perfect cloth for a flag.

"No, darlin'! 'Twas your sainted mother's!" Riley protested. She put a finger to his mouth.

"It is a sacred thing, now," Luzero whispered. "She would want it so." Late that night, nuns worked with camp followers in a candlelit dining hall with large tables as Riley and Moreno walked the aisles. Luzero patiently sewed silver bullion into the shape of a cross. Others carefully cut up the old vestments and sewed bits of gold bullion onto a six-foot-square green silk banner comprised of sections of Luzero's gown. Nuns carefully painted words onto silk "scrolls" cut from white vestments.

One elderly nun sat at a table across from Bel, who smoked a cigareet. The nun was carefully painting a full color image of St. Patrick onto a green panel, copying it from a leather-bound book of scripture. Bel, looking especially buxom in a low-cut camisa blouse, was painting a large, gold image of the Irish harp. She copied the engraving on Riley's flask placed on the table. Her naked winged maiden had even larger breasts than the harp maiden on Riley's flask. And her face looked more Mexican, with high cheekbones.

Riley and Moreno stopped by Bel when Riley noticed her well-endowed interpretation. His eyes grew wide as Moreno chuckled. Riley picked up his flask. He took a drink, looked at the engraving, then at Bel and her painting.

" 'Tain't like it's not a self portrait!" Riley laughed.

"He thinks the harp maiden looks more like you than the flask," Moreno said in Spanish to Bel. She giggled.

"Do you not want her to look good?!" she joked. The old nun across from her burst into laughter.

" 'Tis plain this voyage is making for odd shipmates,"

observed Riley.

"The usual crew for a ship of war," said Moreno dryly, "saints and sinners."

"Gringos and greasers," replied Riley.

Moreno smiled as he lit a cigar. "No more," Moreno countered, holding out something in his hand. "Irish Mexicans." Moreno dropped a gleaming brass lapel pin of an Irish harp into Riley's open palm. Riley looked touched.

In early dawn light, the flag was unfurled for the first time in the brawny hands of Morstadt, now the towering color bearer for the San Patricios, as the deserters now were called. Morstadt wore the Irish harp pin on the left side of his red barracks cap. He also sported two new yellow, fringed epaulettes as color sergeant. Price and the tobacco chewer, both with cap harps, flanked Morstadt and, as color guard, wore angular yellow slashes on each sleeve as new corporals.

This color guard stood between the two deserter companies, with the Mexican guard company at one end, all braced at attention in double ranks. Every barracks cap of the San Patricios bore the gleaming Irish harp as did every black shako of the Mexican guards. Moreno had made them his personal gift.

Mejia and Manzano stood in front of their company of riflemen—Riley, Moreno, and Dalton—in front of the color guard. The flag fluttered easily above them in the brisk morning breeze.

"Present . . . arms!" Riley bellowed. Ockter, Conahan, and Mejia echoed the command, Mejia shouting in Spanish. All three companies snapped their firearms forward with a singular crack of palms against wood stocks. Riley beamed as he eyed his beautiful new flag. It looked almost spiritual as it wafted in the breeze, he thought, much like a prayer. Or was it more of a hope? he wondered.

Silver bullion lace scavenged from the Spanish vestments glittered in a cross on both sides of the massive, six-foot-square green banner. A pure white shamrock edged in gold bullion perched joyously in the uppermost corner of each side, nearest a sharp brass spear point atop the staff. Painted and embroidered at the crux of the cross on one side was the bearded image of Saint Patrick, holding the key to everlasting life in one hand. In the other, he held a staff whose bottom was crushing a wriggling snake. A painted scroll beneath him read, "Battalon de San Patricio."

On the other side, a gold embroidered and painted Irish harp maiden centered on the cross. Surmounting the harp was a gold Mexican eagle eating a snake. Above it flew a white and gold scroll with painted red letters that said, "Libertad Por La Republica Mexicana." Beneath the harp stretched another scroll reading, "Erin Go Bragh."

Santa Anna and his staff faced the San Patricio Battalion across the road leading north. Micheltorena and some junior officers surrounded Santa Anna, insulating him from Pacheco, Ortega, and Lombardini, still smarting from yesterday's tirade. On one side of them stood a brass band; on the other, massed regimental battle flags and a color guard of grenadiers. The army itself stood regiment by regiment in ranks along both sides of the road, twenty thousand men stretching to the horizon of the nearest hill and well beyond. Eerily silent crowds of expectant townspeople stood behind the soldados. The only sound was the flapping of battle flags until the music of Latin chanting approached. Acolytes and a cross bearer appeared, slowly walking over the hill followed by the local priest. He was blessing the departing troops with incense.

"They pray for victory over godless invaders," whispered Moreno piously, "deliverance from death, strength against evil."

"The Good Lord must tire of both sides praying for the same damn thing," Dalton said, crossing himself as the priest passed with his blessing.

" 'Tis plain that He must find it confusing," Riley mused, crossing himself, "having to choose sides in any good fight."

"I fear that this new army of conscripts has but one good fight in it," Moreno said.

"One good punch can end any fight," Dalton asserted.

"And, Major darlin'," Riley said, "Dalton and me never been ones to pull punches." Dalton and Riley exchanged rueful looks, cracking grins.

The San Patricios marched past Santa Anna's reviewing party as the band played "Adios," a traditional Mexican air. They followed the elite Zapadores regiment of combat engineers. They would blaze the trail for the army.

Luzero and Bel stood at the roadside and waved along with hundreds of other soldaderas. Trying to maintain decorum, Riley managed a wink while Dalton blew a kiss as they passed. The ladies smiled through their tears.

The gathered Mexican regiments shouted, "Viva San Patricio!" "Viva Santa Anna!" and "Viva Mexico!" over and over in a vocal wave that rolled up and over the hill. Santa Anna removed his red, white, and green feathered fore-and-aft hat, sweeping it in front of him graciously as Moreno gave him a sword salute from horseback. Santa Anna nodded approvingly at the new flag as Riley approached.

"Eyes right!" Riley commanded, giving his own sword salute. All three companies snapped their heads forty-five degrees to the right as they marched past Santa Anna. Townspeople cheered as if they were at the bullfight.

Santa Anna looked imperial, confident but a bit detached. His eyes gleamed as he surveyed the passing troops. "Micheltorena, does it not consume you?!" he confided in Spanish, leaning across his saddle.

"How can it not consume us all, Excellency?" Micheltorena replied. "The appetite of war sadly is insatiable."

"Not the war," Santa Anna frowned petulantly, "the power."
He handed Micheltorena a written decree, which would be
hand-copied and distributed to every regiment. "See to this," he
added curtly. Micheltorena read the document:

"Today, you commence your march through a thinly
settled country, without supplies and without provisions.
But you may be assured that very quickly you will be in
possession of those of your enemy, and his riches.

"And with them, all your wants will be abundantly sup-
plied. But until that time, my soldiers, do not wander in
search of food more than half a league from camp, or you
will be taken to be deserters and shot."

With the words of Santa Anna ringing hollow in their ears, the
San Patricios and Zapadores marched north hungry and
parched, followed in a week by the rest of the ponderous army.
Vivid moments of misery forced their way into Riley's mental
footlocker:

As they stumbled through dust storms in barren deserts, Riley saw hungry soldados kneeling by pear blossom cactus, raven-
ously eating its juicy fruit with deftly wielded pocket knives;

As they pushed through driving snow, Riley saw troops pull
thin, tattered blankets around themselves while passing a small
group of ice encrusted soldado corpses, huddled frozen in a
shallow ditch;

And Riley saw one ravenous soldado stumble too far away
from dusk campfires to chase a rabbit, when a volley cut him
down. He dropped dead in the snow, his blood spreading a red
stain across the white ice.

Two wretched weeks later, the San Patricio companies
trudged wearily past a grisly sight on the outskirts of a small village. The ground was soaked dark red under six odorous corpses

of young women, hanged from trees amid swarming flies and pesky vultures. Stripped to the waist, they had been whipped to the bone and stabbed many times. And their ears had been cut off. Crude signs dangled from their necks reading *"Yankedos."*

Price, the tobacco chewer, and Morstadt traded looks of disgust as they passed with the colors.

"Bloomin' waste of fine female flesh, if you ask me," grumbled Price.

"Despised are traitors in any sex," Morstadt said sadly, "and on any side."

"It gladdens me heart to be a hero, it does," the tobacco chewer cracked, spitting toward the corpses. They forced a grim laugh and marched on.

Riley, Dalton, Manzano, Moreno, and a few guards with Mejia walked up to the corpses. Mejia's guards fired a few rifle shots to scatter the vultures. Moreno looked worried. "Cut them down and bury them, quickly," he snapped in Spanish.

"Sí, mi major," Mejia replied with a salute.

Mejia barked commands. The guards cut the ropes and the rotting, bloated bodies fell with a sickening thud. Mejia spit on the corpses as the guards began digging a common grave.

"Any dead are worthy of respect," Dalton groused, outraged.

Mejia frowned at his tone, though not understanding his words.

"These women gave themselves to occupying gringos," said Manzano in disgust. He glared at Riley, who knew that Luzero was on Manzano's mind.

"Some occupying gringos are Mexican citizens now," Riley retorted. "Or are Mexican wenches reserved just for the native born?!"

"The army is close behind," Moreno said. "They should not see this." Dalton and Riley exchanged curious looks. "In the Mexican soul, compassion fights revenge," Moreno explained.

As the digging continued, he lit a cigar.

The San Patricios entered the quaint, tiny village warily with arms ready. Though it appeared deserted, the few streets were littered with debris, furniture, and personal possessions from ransacked houses and businesses.

One dying peon sat in a pool of his own blood against a wall. He clutched a rosary in one hand and his own bloody scalp in the other. He had been shot several times. Moreno, Manzano, and Riley walked up to him.

"Where is everyone?!" Manzano asked in Spanish. "What happened?!"

"The church," the peon barely whispered. "In the church . . ." His brains suddenly splattered against the wall as a shot exploded. Riley glared at Moreno, holding the smoking pistol.

"With no surgeons, it was my duty to answer his prayer," he said sadly.

"Whatever rules your soul, it surely ain't compassion," replied Riley.

Manzano led Riley, Moreno, Dalton, Ockter, Conahan, and a squad of San Patricios including Price and the tobacco chewer to the small adobe church at the end of the main street. Sounds of weeping and moaning came from inside. As they entered, Price gagged from the stench. The dirt floor was covered in pools of soaked blood surrounding dead Mexican men and boys, all scalped. The white walls were spattered in blood and bits of gore. Women and girls, some apparently raped, wept over the slain and tended to the dying. One bloody scalp hung draped over the gold cross on the altar.

"Get rid of that thing!" Riley roared, pointing at the scalp. Ockter crossed himself and gingerly used his bayonet to pick it up and toss it to the floor.

"Heathen Apaches?" Dalton growled to Moreno.

"Apaches do not scalp," Moreno said. "And Comanches do

29

not raid this far south."

A woman screamed in hysterics when she realized that most of these men in uniform were Anglos, not Mexicans. Other frightened women wailed as Manzano and Moreno walked among them, trying to calm them.

The tobacco chewer found a white buff leather sling and black cartridge box. The sling was inscribed "1st Ark. Vols."

"Arkansas rackensackers," he spat in disgust, handing the evidence to Conahan, who gingerly hopped over bodies to take it to Riley.

"Lieutenant Richey should've seen this," Conahan said, handing it to him. " 'Tis a blessing at least to know why you die."

"Gringo bastards! Murderers!" screamed a distraught woman in Spanish. She kept pointing insistently at Riley and the others and shrieking.

"Why are they blamin' us?!" Riley yelled at Moreno, on edge from the ongoing hysterics.

"They think all Anglos are under the same flag," Moreno said.

"Not anymore!" Riley snapped. He slammed down the cartridge box and stormed outside. Riley was pacing, feeling as if he could explode like a flaming bomb from burning frustration and anger. Moreno walked to him.

"Professionals soldier against the color and cut of uniform, not the color of skin!" Riley raged. He looked searchingly at Moreno.

"This war . . ." Moreno said, trying to find the right words, ". . . it grows beyond merely us, beyond just the soldiers." He lit a cigar. "Sometimes, I think we were all at the Alamo, and we are all here because none of us could ever leave it behind." Riley offered, so Moreno drank from his flask. "We have done all we can here."

"We'll move out," Riley said. "But I doubt we can ever leave this sorry place behind." Riley had seen much horror in his career, all kept safely out of mind in his mental footlocker. He doubted if this would remain hidden.

Hours later, huge clouds of billowing smoke and sparks ascended into a black sky chased by towering flames. The entire ranchero of Agua Nueva was burning, and with it went tons of U.S. Army food and ammunition. A few explosions of black powder punctuated the loss as hungry, exhausted Mexican soldiers sat and sprawled along the roadside. They stared pathetically at their promised food and ammunition as it evaporated before their eyes.

"I would say supper was a might overcooked," Dalton said, lighting his pipe.

Dalton and Riley sat at the head of the weary San Patricio column, the men lying everywhere. Moreno walked up with Manzano.

"This surely means victory," Manzano asserted. "The gringos burn their supplies and retreat."

"They're only denying us what they can afford to lose," Riley said, Moreno nodding in agreement. "Same thing happened to that other 'Napoleon' in Russia," he added, "or so I heard."

A bugle call turned all heads down the road. Santa Anna and his staff arrived, trailed by a glittering squad of Hussar Guards of the Supreme Powers. With black fur busbys, red jackets, and ice-blue pelisses, trimmed in silver bullion, they cut a rich and distinctly Napoleonic air of imperialism. They galloped into an open space between the burning barns and the halted San Patricios.

Santa Anna looked ecstatic. Within earshot of Riley's group, he turned to Micheltorena. "Norteamericano hysteria, General! Surely, the sign of a frightened army!" he exclaimed, surprisingly in English, Riley noted. Even Micheltorena looked at his chief curiously. "Speak English, so fewer can understand us," he said. Santa Anna handled his frantic black stallion with superb horsemanship as the frightened creature pranced nervously near the flames.

"Perhaps, Excellency," Micheltorena replied, "unless they merely fall back quickly to secure a stronger position." Santa Anna scowled at this negativity, but the sudden clatter of cavalry distracted him.

Young, excited Colonel Andrade and two companies of lancers herded a dozen captured Kentucky cavalrymen. Clad in grimy gray battle shirts, the sullen volunteers stumbled along afoot. Andrade rode to Santa Anna and saluted.

"We should have snared more, Excellency," he said breathlessly, "but they ran faster than rabbits!" Santa Anna laughed, joined by Micheltorena. "We would not have caught any had we stopped to fight the fire they set." He looked penitent for his failure.

"It is not important," Santa Anna replied casually. He dabbed his finger into his opium box and touched it to his tongue. Micheltorena looked worried by this, Riley thought.

The Kentucky cavalrymen recognized the San Patricios as they shuffled past, pointing first at the new flag, then at the obviously Anglo men and drawing the right conclusion. They unleashed catcalls, boos, and jeers. One particularly crusty Kentuckian pointed at Conahan and Ockter.

"You boys a bit far north ain't ya, for Irish traitor scum?!" he yelled.

"Sure an' we've come two hundred miles just for to view your backside, at the first volley!" Conahan shouted gleefully.

"And I will have you know," added Ockter, "that Germans make as good a scum as Irish!" The Irish deserters burst into laughter as Morstadt's Prussians shouted *"Javol!"* while shaking their fists.

Conahan pulled out his fiddle and began playing "The

Rogue's March," traditional air for criminals drummed from the ranks, as the Kentuckians filed past. He fell in beside them to strut a minstrel cakewalk as he played, pulling peals of laughter from the San Patricios.

"Don't feel lonely, lad," Riley shouted to the Kentuckian. "Your pals'll join you soon at San Luis Potosi—as prisoners!" Riley's men cheered.

"And soon ya'll gonna be catawamptiously chawed up," the Kentuckian shouted back, "at Buena Vista!" He spat tobacco juice at Riley. The glob landed near his boots. The captured Yanks cheered.

"His mother never learned him proper," scoffed the tobacco chewer. He fired a glob of juice that splattered the Kentuckian's flannel shirt. The San Patricios roared in laughter as the sullen prisoners finally left.

"Buena Vista! Did you hear?!" Santa Anna exclaimed. "That is but fourteen leagues more and very near the pass at Angostura!"

"After a night of rest and some water," said Micheltorena, "our men can march there easily by midday."

"General Micheltorena," Santa Anna snapped, looking at him as if he was insane, "pass this order: no troops stop here to fill canteens or to rest. Resume the march at the double-quick. We will surprise the norteamericanos at dawn!" He dabbed more opium.

Micheltorena looked over at Moreno and Manzano, who looked dismayed. Riley and Dalton traded worried looks, as if doubting Santa Anna's grasp of reality. Riley knew Santa Anna suffered little in the way of dissent.

"But, Excellency, they marched thirty-five leagues today across desert," Micheltorena pleaded. "And after this night, the norteamericanos can hardly be surprised. They certainly know that we are here."

"To gain final victory," Santa Anna asserted haughtily, "the Mexican soldier is known for his frugality and his capacity to suffer." He abruptly wheeled his horse and departed with his Hussars. Soldados rose to cheer him as he passed. Santa Anna grandiosely waved his hat to them as he trotted into the night.

"Resume the march, Major," Micheltorena sighed to Moreno as he rode slowly past. "We must not deny the gringos the 'surprise' for which they surely must be waiting." He headed back down the column to pass the order.

Manzano walked back to Mejia and the guards yelling orders to get the column on its feet and moving again. Riley nodded at Conahan and Ockter, who proceeded to roust the San Patricios.

"Company, form ranks!" Ockter bellowed.

"Off your arses and onto your dogs!" shouted Conahan, strutting down the line. Moans, the usual groans, and curses greeted him as the men stirred.

"Faith we can get fat eating his worship's words," Dalton said. He fired up his pipe.

" 'Tain't words we're gonna be eating, I'll wager," Riley said. He drank long from his flask but felt the bile of doubt rising in his belly. Still, Riley comforted himself with his notion that Fate had at last come over to his side, supplying this golden chance to win at least a truce, if not the entire war. Either way, he would keep his new commitment to his comrades. And Luzero might be made proud of him.

As the San Patricios slowly rose and reformed, thick black smoke and glowing embers rolled up into the night sky. They covered the blanket of brilliant winter stars in what at first seemed to Riley to be a billowing shroud of mourning. But he fought to convince himself that it was, instead, a victory bonfire. Riley shrugged a laugh: he hated it when he slipped into believing his own blarney.

CHAPTER 2
BUENA VISTA
FEBRUARY 1847

A brawling cloud of smoke wafted across the high desert plateau known as Angostura, near the village of Buena Vista at the base of a mountain of solid purple rock. The rays of a mournful mid-day sun revealed a short, thin line of dull-gray U.S. volunteers, battling for their very survival. They were strung out across gullies and ridges. They appeared to Riley through his spyglass to be straining to the breaking point against massive onslaughts by dark-blue columns of Mexican soldados.

Batteries of horse artillery manned by regulars bolstered the sagging U.S. line between each brigade. Their guns belched orange fire in lethal barrages of exploding shell and clattering, shotgun-like canister. Masses of Mexican infantry and cavalry drove toward them in deep columns, one company in line of battle behind the other in the Napoleonic fashion of human battering rams. Shattered, bloody corpses and writhing wounded littered the barren landscape, already fought over for hours. Thick white smoke from the horrific battle seemed to choke the ground into shaking spasms and amplify the din of the rattling musketry, booming cannon, beating drums, blaring bugles, whinnying horses, and screaming soldiers. And Riley loved it more than he cared to admit.

The four lumbering guns of his San Patricios thundered from a small hill on the left of the Mexican line, overlooking the entire battlefield. The grimy, sweating crews immediately rolled them back into position and began to re-load. Just behind the center two cannon, the brilliant green flag flew surrounded by four stacks of arms, the gunners' muskets.

At one end of the battery, Riley and Moreno directed fire and observed the effect with a spyglass. At the other end, the San Patricio infantry company and that of the Mexican guards lay on the ground in ranks. Nervous yet eager, they kept popping their heads up to watch the battle. Dalton and Conahan walked calmly among the Irish to steady them and keep them down, as did Manzano and Mejia among the Mexicans. Suddenly, a salvo of U.S. shells exploded with thumping booms and orange flame on the downward slope ten yards in front, showering them in dirt, rocks, and cactus.

"Don't tempt Fate, lads!" Dalton shouted barely above the roar of battle. "She is a faithless slut!" Nervous laughter rippled as he dusted himself off, continuing to walk among them. He lit his pipe.

"We're just out of range," Conahan warned, "but hug th'ground anyway, tight as you would a whore!"

Another salvo of U.S. shells exploded on the slope closer to the Mexican guards. Dirt and debris rained on them.

"Be patient!" Manzano yelled in Spanish. "And stay alive!" he added, standing and dusting himself off. "Mexico will need you today!"

"Stupid donkey!" sneered Mejia, pushing down one curious soldado with his foot. "The brave man lives only as long as the coward allows him!"

Dalton and Conahan met Manzano and Mejia in the interval between their companies. They crouched in a huddle.

"I do not like this long-distance fighting," Manzano groused, nodding at the roaring battle spread out below. He looked frustrated, anxious.

"The more distance you got," Dalton advised, "the longer you can fight."

Conahan tried his canteen. It was empty. Mejia offered his gourd canteen. The incessant pounding of massed drums drew their attention to the center of the fight, enshrouded by smoke.

"Lookee there, comin' out of that gulley!" Conahan gasped, drinking. He pointed, handing Mejia back his canteen with a grateful nod.

"General Lombardini surely will pierce their center!" Manzano cried.

"Viva Mexico!" Mejia shouted to his men, pointing. All strained to see.

Magnificent, grim, and irresistible, a Mexican infantry column twenty companies deep emerged from a dry wash through thick smoke to tramp past Santa Anna, Lombardini, and their staffs. Shouts of "Viva Mexico!" and "Viva Santa Anna!" resounded as drums pounded and bugles blew the advance.

Lombardini saluted, drew his sword, and trotted to the front of his column. Six shells exploded near Santa Anna. Several of his staff were blown from their horses and a dozen passing soldados were killed, their dismembered bodies unnerving surrounding comrades.

Santa Anna fearlessly mastered his terrified black stallion, drew his sword, reared the horse onto its hind legs, and pointed his blade toward the U.S. line. Passing soldados were inspired. They closed ranks, shouted "Viva!" and moved forward over the bloody corpses at the double quick.

"Santa Anna's got sand, he does," Dalton said admiringly. He hoped the assault would succeed but he harbored some doubts.

"This attack may win the day . . . but before we have been able to be part of it!" Manzano complained, unable to hide his disappointment.

"This day we have got to win," Dalton warned. "But you

don't let fly your best punch without first a blow to the belly."
Dalton looked across the line of San Patricio guns just as they
fired again, the ground trembling from their roar. Dalton located
Riley and stood. "If the lads get restive, Conahan," he said,
"play them a lullaby." Connahan nodded a grin as Dalton trotted toward Riley.

"Load!" Ockter bellowed behind the battery. The sweating
gunners, faces encrusted with black powder, rolled the guns
back into position. They worked with quick precision, the
months of incessant drill in evidence.

"Still falling short," Riley said, lowering his spyglass.

Beside him, Moreno frowned and took the glass. "We must
try again!" Moreno insisted, looking. He could see Colonel Andrade leading his cavalry forward at a walk with flags, lances,
and sabers held high. Red-jacketed Hussars and Jalisco Lancers, sky-blue Tulancingo Curassiers and dark-blue heavy cavalry
of the First and Fourth Regiments rolled grandly toward the
U.S. line.

Riley eagerly grabbed the spyglass and saw Andrade look
over his shoulder at his magnificent troopers, raise his saber for
all to see, then point the blade forward. Bugles blew and the
five lines broke into a trot. Riley had never seen even the crack
British cavalry do better.

Double ranks of lean Mississippi Volunteers faced the oncoming cavalry with new, fast loading percussion rifles of longer
range than smoothbore flintlock muskets. Clad in dusty, white
duck trousers and bloused red shirts, these tough Southerners
appeared cool under fire in their broad-brim straw hats. With a
confident air, they loaded their brass trimmed rifles and waited.

Riding behind their line atop a gray stallion was their iron-
willed commander, young Jefferson Davis, elegantly clad in a
dark-blue officer's frock and plantation straw hat. Something
about him reminded Riley of the slave catcher he had seen back

in Mackinac. How long ago that seemed now.

"Maximum elevation!" Riley commanded. "Gotta help our pony soldiers!" He tossed Moreno a look of hopeful futility.

"Depress screws completely!" Ockter yelled, strutting along the line.

Morstadt began turning down the screw beneath the barrel of his gun, allowing the muzzle to rise. At the gun beside his, Price did likewise until it stopped against the wooden trail of the huge carriage. The tobacco chewer stood by Price holding a smoking slow match. He saw Dalton walking past briskly, on his way to Riley. He stepped to Dalton, just beside the flag between the guns.

"The corporal is out of chew, sir," the tobacco chewer said urgently. Dalton paused to stare. "Sure an' he ain't never fought a fight without it."

"All I got is smoke and dry at that," Dalton said with a helpless look, continuing his way.

The tobacco chewer stepped back to his gun looking uneasy. "Then it's bad luck to me," he muttered, blowing on his match to keep it lit.

"I am obliged to point out," Dalton said breathlessly, reaching Riley and Moreno, "that you are eating cold soup while Lombardini is serving hot meat and potatoes at center table!" He pointed at the rising dust cloud from Lombardini's two thousand tramping, dusty, dark-blue infantry. Their leather shakos shimmered in the sunlight like scales on a slithering black snake, wending its way toward the center of the U.S. line.

"Right now, them pony boys need us," Riley said, looking through and seeing the opportunity. "But all things comes to him what waits his turn."

"Ready!" Ockter snapped.

"Fire!" Riley yelled. The four guns belched orange flame and recoiled twelve feet with a throbbing roar. The gunners rolled them back into firing position.

Four huge explosions erupted just in front of the Mississippi line, showering the volunteers with more dirt than destruction but scattering some. The Mississippians dusted off, re-formed ranks, and raised rifles, all to the shouted commands of Colonel Davis.

"Range is too damn far," Riley muttered, hating to admit defeat. He lowered his spyglass.

"We must help Andrade!" Moreno pleaded, grabbing the spyglass.

"Against those Mississippi rifles," Riley predicted, "he'll need more help than we can give, I'll wager."

"To win this fight," Dalton urged, "we had best help Lombardini, at the damn center!" He looked pleadingly at Riley, who understood.

"Besides, sir, what cavalry's ever won a battle?!" Riley said, agreeing with Dalton. "In the end, 'tis infantry what rules the field."

Frantic, Moreno looked in urgent desperation through the spyglass.

"Viva Mexico!" Andrade screamed. "Ataquen!" His one thousand horsemen shouted "Viva!" almost in one shrill, thrilling, throaty voice. They lowered their lances and pointed their sabers straight ahead, spurring their horses into a thundering, ground-shaking full gallop.

For an instant, Riley remembered tales told in Ireland of the battle that ended the grand era of knighthood at Agincourt. The brilliantly plumed French knights lowered their lances and charged massed ranks of English and Irish infantry armed with long bows, the Mississippi rifle of their day. Chivalry died with an armor piercing arrow through its heart. Riley held his breath.

The Mississippians opened fire in a series of crisp volleys

unleashed company after company and rolling down their two lines, arranged in an inverted *V.* Andrade's troopers were charging into its apex. Each company re-loaded so quickly that by the time the last company fired, the first could fire again. Clusters of Andrade's cavalry disappeared in clouds of dust as horses tumbled and troopers fell. The volleys seemed never ending. The cavalry closed the wide gaps and kept coming on, but the Mississippians fired too rapidly. More clusters fell until only a few squads staggered to a stop short of the Mississippi line and fired their flintlock carbines. Andrade led his shattered survivors back to the Mexican line. The Mississippians whooped and hollered. Jefferson Davis removed his hat and wiped his sweating forehead, relieved and thankful.

"They looked magnificent," Moreno sighed, lowering the spyglass. "We did all we could."

"The most we did was dirty their white trousers," Riley griped.

"But we can still make the others shit in theirs!" Dalton urged, puffing his pipe furiously. He pointed with it at Lombardini's assault column.

At last, Moreno nodded at Riley to agree. "Trails right!" Riley bellowed at Ockter.

"Bearing two-hundred fifty yards, dead center!"

"At last!" Ockter hollered. "We can be hitting something!" The weary gunners managed a spirited shout. They inserted wooden handles into the trails of the two thousand-pound guns and pushed them to the right, making the muzzles bear to the left. "Hold!" Ockter yelled, raising his arms. "I do the rest!" He personally adjusted the elevation screw on each gun, running quickly from one to another.

"Prussians are plainly mad," Riley said, "but they're so damn good with the heavy iron, you just gotta smile and join the asylum."

"As we are good with the bayonet," Moreno said, handing Riley the spyglass. "And perhaps just as mad."

Through the rolling white smoke, Riley saw nervous volunteers firing ragged volleys, cutting gaps in the Mexican ranks. As the soldados re-formed and pushed closer to the U.S. line, their bristling bayonets and blood curdling cries of "Viva!" unnerved some volunteers. They broke and started running for the rear. A line of mounted Dragoons turned them back wielding sabers. Volleys kept dropping scores of soldados, but more from behind stepped over the crumpled bodies to keep advancing. Many fired from the hip as they marched.

"They're cutting our lads down like scythes in a wheat field," said Riley, looking through the glass. Then he lowered it, looking at Moreno surprised. He had never thought of "greasers" as "his." "But our lads keep comin' on!"

"Like the bull," Moreno said softly, "remember?"

"Ready!" Ockter cried, at last finished with adjusting the guns.

"Fire!" Riley bellowed. The guns roared and recoiled.

Four huge explosions ripped along the entire front rank of Indiana volunteers, killing, dismembering, and maiming an entire company. The survivors panicked when they saw a line of shiny Mexican bayonets emerge through the thick smoke. They broke ranks and ran for their lives, pushing past the Dragoons trying to stop them. Screaming Mexicans poured through the gaping hole in the center of the American line.

Suddenly, Riley saw a section of U.S. horse artillery race across the entire front of the advancing Mexicans. The two guns and two-wheeled limbers, each pulled by six wildly plunging horses, careened away from the Mexican line at ninety degrees and stopped with the muzzles facing them. The gunners dismounted, quickly unlimbered the guns, loaded canister, and fired a shrieking salvo point blank into the cheering soldados. The front company evaporated in a cloud of blood, screams, and dust.

"Damn the Irish bastard!" cursed Riley, watching through the spyglass. It seemed the nightmare of Monterey had returned to haunt him.

"Must be O'Brien again," Dalton said smiling, packing his pipe.

"Ockter!" Riley yelled, pointing at O'Brien's guns.

"I am correcting for the problem already!" Ockter shouted, saluting.

"Then eliminate the damn problem!" Riley ordered, punctuated with a return salute.

"Fire!" Ockter commanded. The guns roared.

Four shells burst among the gunners of O'Brien's section, killing and wounding many. Captain O'Brien himself fell wounded, but he personally touched off a gun one more time into the face of the advancing Mexicans.

The surviving gunners picked up O'Brien and retired, leaving the guns. Jubilant Mexican infantry cheered and stood atop the captured guns waving their tri-color battle flags in victory.

The San Patricios cheered just as jubilantly, some standing atop the carriages, others dancing jigs, slapping backs, sharing flasks. Conahan arrived and embraced embarrassed Ockter in an awkward, stiff hug. Morstadt waved the dazzling green flag back and forth, to be seen by the U.S. line.

Riley's elation faded when he saw Mexican infantry bayonet O'Brien's wounded gunners lying among the captured guns. As the Mexicans swept past to push forward into the wavering volunteers, they took no prisoners.

"Savagery!" Riley snapped, thrusting the spyglass at Moreno.

"Revenge," Moreno explained, looking. He handed the glass to Dalton.

"Victory," Dalton surmised simply. He lit his pipe and gave Riley a look.

"How could I sink to this?" Riley agonized aloud, nodding at the field. His British-instilled professionalism always had covered the brutality of battle with a civilized veneer, giving it a comforting sheen of martial pride.

"You are under the same flag," Moreno reminded softly. He pointed at the green banner being waved by Morstadt standing atop a gun carriage.

Riley stared at the rippling green flag, its silver and gold trim sparkling in the intense sunlight. Flags to him had always been important symbols of civilized warfare, rallying points for right over might. He had fought uncivilized hordes with the British but never fallen to the level of the savages, he thought. But perhaps, Riley wondered, it was all nothing but savagery.

One side merely drugged its own conscience with a potion of military honor, training, and decorum. Perhaps his entire life had been devoted to nothing more than a sham. He dared to think that perhaps, just perhaps, the murderous savages were in fact the only honest warriors. This chilling realization momentarily unnerved him. He felt he needed to cling more desperately now to his sense of professionalism.

Across the field, General Zachary Taylor sat on Old Whitey and stared at the distant green flag perched atop the gently sloping hill. On one side of him, ten blazing artillery guns in line were keeping the oncoming Mexicans at bay. On the other side, his routed volunteer infantry slowly re-formed.

Thick white smoke rolled in waves across his front. He had just thrilled at the sight of his former son-in-law, Jefferson Davis, coolly repelling that gallant Mexican cavalry charge. Taylor's beloved daughter had died of a fever while married to Davis only three months. Taylor still bore him a grudge, though if asked why he would not be able to answer. Some feelings were beyond the reach of mere words.

Colonel Harney suddenly interrupted Taylor's reverie by arriving with two companies of Dragoons, halting behind the guns. He trotted to Taylor.

"What Mexican battery is that?!" Taylor snapped, pointing at the green flag. Its silver cross glistened in the now dusky sunlight.

" '*Battalon de San Patricio*,' " Harney read in clumsy Spanish, looking through his spyglass. His cheeks flushed red. "They're not greasers, sir," he smirked. "It's Riley and his damn Irish deserters."

"No wonder they can shoot!" Taylor snapped. "We damn well can't allow that," he added. He rose in his saddle to survey his shaken troops, still rallying behind the roaring artillery. "Them shameful volunteers ain't ready yet," he grumbled. He remembered bitterly advising President Polk against counting on volunteers to do any heavy lifting when it came to fighting. Taylor's gaze fixed on the fresh, eager regular Dragoons just brought up by Harney.

"Well, Harney, it seems you've been served up a hasty plate of your favorite soup," he cracked. Taylor whipped off his straw hat, rose in his stirrups, and waved it at the Dragoons. "Take out them damn deserter guns!" he roared.

"Huzzah!" the Dragoons shouted, punctuated with cheers.

Across the valley, Riley had been watching all the while. He was certain that he knew what was coming—exactly that for which he had pepared. "Now we can end it!" Riley bellowed, pointing at the rapidly forming Dragoons with his spyglass. He stood at the gun served by Price and the tobacco chewer. He personally turned the gun's elevation screw slightly and checked the aim. "We can send up Harney, Taylor, and even Taylor's horse, Old Whitey!" he yelled. "Then we can baptize Price so's he gets land with the rest of us!" Crews laughed.

"Me a bloomin' Papist?!" Price muttered. "Who'd figure?"

" 'Bout as likely as meself with no chew," said the tobacco chewer. "Saints preserve us." They both laughed.

Conahan finished personally aiming the gun to the left of Riley's. He had to stand on tiptoe to see over the barrel. "Taylor's short of hat size ridin' that white target," he joked.

"Target their guns," Ockter urged, sighting Morstadt's, "so their guns will not target us in return!"

"God in heaven," Morstadt mumbled in German, crossing himself, "bless us with victory and peace." His German crew crossed themselves.

"My target is Colonel Harney's flaming red hair," Dalton yelled as he adjusted the fourth gun. " 'Tis shaggy and in need of a hot trim!"

"The honor be entirely yours, sir!" Riley shouted at Moreno.

Moreno nodded gratefully for the privilege of ordering what could be the winning salvo not only of this battle, but the entire war. He marveled that the infectious confidence of Riley and his men had somehow seeped into his usual dark outlook. Manzano walked up to Moreno as he was lighting a cigar, feeling ever so slightly better about their situation.

"They think they can end the war with one barrage?" Manzano asked incredulously in Spanish.

"Maybe they can," Moreno replied, "or, maybe, we can." He raised his sword. *"Fuego!"* he commanded, slashing the blade down.

Riley, Dalton, Ockter, and Conahan touched off their guns. As they roared with what seemed one deep, resonating boom, the crews shouted, "Viva!" Moreno and Manzano exchanged surprised looks at the spontaneous burst of Spanish. Riley tossed a quick nod at Moreno, then peered through the spyglass.

46

Four huge explosions burst around Taylor. One blew a field gun apart with a metallic clang, scattering bloody pieces of its crew. Another hit within yards of Taylor, wounding some staff officers, spooking his horse, and showering him with dirt. Two slammed on either side of Harney, whose horse dumped him.

"Damn sons o'bitches!" Taylor shouted, dusting himself off. Junior officers rushed to see if the general was all right. He shooed them away with such a blistering tirade that Bliss was red faced in embarrassment.

Harney rose slowly to his feet, aware of the chuckles among his Dragoons behind him. He dusted himself off, glared across at the green flag, and remounted.

Riley lowered his spyglass with a frown of disappointment. It could have been so much easier, he thought, if the big guns had done their work. Now, he knew, his original fear would become fact. Well, at least he knew his battalion was ready. He heard distant bugle calls precede the expected deep rumble of pounding horse hooves. Riley climbed atop his gun.

" 'Tis bad luck to us!" he bellowed at his men. "We only shook their damn nest! Now the hornets are buzzin' our way!" The sweating, grimy gunners exchanged frowns and quite a few curses. Riley looked over his shoulder at the rising cloud of dust just as Dalton joined him at the gun. "But since they're gonna come all this way just to ask for our damn guns . . . ," Riley suggested, forming an idea.

". . . 'T'would be rude not to give them what they want!" Dalton cracked to complete Riley's thought.

"So it's like we drilled all those months," Riley shouted, his voice rising with his anticipation for a good fight. "Give 'em the damn Waterloo jig!"

The San Patricios answered with a shout so mighty that it startled Moreno and Manzano, just approaching. Riley sidled up to Moreno.

"Major darlin,' " Riley confided, "got us a new brilliant plan, been working on it a while. 'Tis a surprise, you might say. But we got to be quick about it!"

As Riley explained in a blistering rush of brogue, Moreno's face at first registered surprise, then satisfaction, and, finally, hope. Manzano looked stunned.

Across the valley, one hundred Dragoons in a column four horses abreast trotted toward the San Patricio hill with Colonel Harney at the head. Sabers held upright and tucked into their right shoulders, they guided toward the fluttering green flag.

"Front into line," Harney bellowed, "march!" His bugler sounded the call. Officers and sergeants echoed the command. Without breaking speed, the two companies flowed from a column into two long lines trotting forward.

"Fire!" Riley bellowed. The four guns roared amid orange flame and white smoke. The gunners rolled the recoiled guns back into position. "Ockter!" he shouted. "Cut the range in half!"

"Load!" Ockter bellowed. He started to elevate the screws on each gun.

Four shells exploded just in front of the first line of Dragoons. A dozen horses and riders tumbled amid plumes of flying dust, cactus, and shrapnel. The others kept coming and closed ranks to shouted commands.

"Forward at the gallop," Harney bellowed, "march!" His bugler sounded the call as officers and sergeants again echoed the command.

The Dragoons broke into the faster, rolling pace while maintaining their lines. To survive, they knew they must close the distance to the guns as quickly as possible, getting beneath the lowest elevation to which the cannon barrels could be depressed.

"Ready!" Ockter screamed.

"Fire!" Riley yelled as he looked through the spyglass.

Moreno stood beside him but was more absorbed with the frantic infantry activity behind the guns. As the cannon again roared, he looked at Riley. "I should go back and help," he said, drawing his sword and walking away.

Riley merely grunted a nod as he peered through the glass. If his plan worked, Riley thought, the battle could still be won. If it did not work, he knew that this could be his last fight. And he knew that all his San Patricios felt the same way. "Aint' life grand!" he marveled.

Four explosions ripped into the second line of Dragoons, tumbling eight horses and riders. The lines continued to gallop forward undaunted, finally approaching the long slope up the San Patricio hill.

Harney could see the cannon muzzles protruding atop the crest. Suddenly, he saw the gunners fall back out of sight, leaving the guns but taking their flag.

"They're runnin', boys!" Harney yelled. He pointed his saber straight ahead. "Charge for the guns!" he bellowed. The bugler blew the call.

Shouting "Huzzah!" and cheering, the Dragoons pointed their sabers to the front and spurred their horses into a full, breakneck, heart-pounding run. They swept up the hill irresistibly toward the looming, silent, smoking guns. The lines dissolved into a horse race of squads thundering up the steep, cactus-strewn slope.

Thirty yards behind the abandoned guns, the San Patricio Battalion had formed a line of battle two ranks deep. They stood waiting for the Dragoons. Riley's gunners had grabbed their muskets as they fell back from the guns and formed up between Dalton's company on one side and Manzano's on the other.

Side by side, the three companies created a human wall capped with gleaming bayonets pointed skyward, muskets held at order arms with butts on the ground. Grimy faces looked fearfully anxious as the yelling Dragoons and thundering horses drew nearer, ever nearer, their dust cloud rising above the crest of the hill in front of them.

Last to fall back, Riley strode briskly from his guns with Price, the tobacco chewer, and Morstadt, carrying the flag. They hurried toward Moreno, Manzano, and Dalton, waiting in the interval between the Mexican guards and Riley's men.

Morstadt planted the flag there, flanked by Price and the tobacco chewer. As he arrived, Riley saluted Moreno, who arched an eyebrow and gestured at the formidable looking line. Riley gave a cocky nod.

"Hell ain't half full, or so's I hear," Riley said. "With a bit of the luck, the devil can have his fill this day." Riley had learned this bit of British trickery from some of Wellington's Waterloo survivors. They had broken a massive French cavalry charge with similar tactics. Riley prayed as usual for success when teetering on the brink of disaster.

"To your posts!" Moreno commanded. Manzano and Dalton saluted. As Manzano left, Dalton lingered by Riley and removed his pipe.

"No friend of mine calls 'luck' what surely must be pure skill," Dalton whispered, grabbing Riley's flask. He downed a healthy swig. Riley yanked it back in mock outrage. Dalton laughed, re-fired his pipe, and exhaled a small cloud of smoke as he trotted to Conahan and Ockter behind the deserters.

"Sure and they're a noisy lot," Conahan complained. He

pointed at the smoke wafting skyward from the main battle, still roaring across the valley.

"I almost cannot hear those beasts thundering down on us!" Ockter joked.

"We will soon make our own thunder," Dalton mused as he arrived.

"Fire by battalion!" Riley bellowed. "Ready! . . ." Dalton, Conahan, and Ockter split up to echo the command behind the deserters. Manzano and Mejia sang it out in Spanish. The three companies raised their muskets chest high with a solid snap. The pounding hoof beats grew louder.

"We cannot miss when they crest the top," Moreno said, staring at the guns. He lit a cigar.

"We'll wait 'til even your lads can't miss, sir," Riley joked. Moreno grunted but then, slowly, let a smile trace across his lips.

Manzano waited fitfully with Mejia behind the Mexican guards. Mejia walked the line, checking equipment and offering encouragement. Manzano watched the crest intently. He fidgeted with his sword. To him, the passing seconds felt like hours.

"Will gringos fall for such a stupid trick?!" Manzano scoffed, sounding a bit hopeful.

"He who would be a tamale will see corn husks falling from the sky," Mejia joked.

"Sergeant, we will win this day!" Manzano replied. "I feel it here," he added, thumping his heart.

"I know I have won only if I am breathing when it is over," Mejia replied grimly. "Feelings are nothing but fantasies."

Shaken, Manzano stared at him as the sergeant calmly checked his rifle.

"Aim! . . ." yelled Riley, raising his sword as the command was echoed in English and Spanish. The companies raised muskets and rifles to their shoulders. Riley saw that Moreno also raised his sword. "Should be your call, sir," Riley said breathing hard, his blood pumping as the horse hooves grew louder.

"I have the patience to wait as long as you, Captain," Moreno exhaled, eyes on the crest.

"The closer they get, the bigger targets they make," Riley observed, taking up Moreno's challenge. "Got all th'damn time in the world."

"They can open this bloomin' ball anytime now," said Price, nervously sighting down the barrel of his musket, sweat beading his forehead.

"But I would have plumper dance partners," joked Morstadt, holding the flag, "and less ponderous music."

"For old times," growled the tobacco chewer, sighting down his barrel, "sure an' a Dragoon's gonna spot me some chew." He cocked his musket.

"Bloody well right," Price snapped, cocking his. They eyed each other grimly as the cheering Dragoons and thundering hoof beats grew loud enough to be right on top of them.

Yelling at the top of their lungs, the front line of Dragoons charged up and over the crest of the ridge and into the looming silent cannon.

"The guns are ours!" bellowed Harney over his shoulder, riding between the guns with his men. He looked ahead and saw something that unnerved him.

A solid glittering phalanx of one hundred muskets was leveled right at him. He reined up and pulled behind a gun, waving his men forward. The Dragoons kept charging right past the guns to bear down on the San Patricios in line.

Riley looked at Moreno nervously as they thundered closer. "You can damn well fire anytime now!" Riley yelled.

52

Moreno exhaled smoke and smiled slightly: he had won the bet. *"Fuego!"* Moreno bellowed, slicing his sword down.

The San Patricios fired a massive volley so crisp it sounded like one crackling, thunderous musket shot. It blanketed the ridge in a swirling wave of white smoke rolling toward the oncoming Dragoons. Almost the entire front line of Dragoons disappeared in a bloody bedlam of whinnying horses and screaming men, tumbling and falling on one another between the guns and the San Patricios.

"To your own wake you'd be tardy!" Riley shouted proudly at Moreno, who looked smug. Riley pointed his sword to the flat hilltop behind the line.

"Battalion to form square!" Riley cried. "At the double quick, march!"

With well drilled precision, the three-company line trotted into a compact, double ranked square, the front rank kneeling with musket butts down and bayonets angled up to stop horses. Commands were yelled in English and Spanish. Both ranks reloaded quickly. Morstadt, Price, and the tobacco chewer planted the flag in the center of the square near Riley and Moreno. Dalton, Conahan, Ockter, and Manzano commanded the four sides.

The second wave of Dragoons thundered up the hill and into the swirling debris of the first line, whose survivors were struggling to remount. Harney and his officers rode among the troopers trying to regain order from chaos.

"Draw pistols!" Harney shouted. The Dragoons sheathed their sabers and pulled one of the two single shot percussion pistols each carried in holsters slung on their saddles. Harney watched anxiously as his men rushed to execute the command before Riley's men finished re-loading. "Charge!" Harney bellowed.

The Dragoons shouted "Huzzah!" and rode toward Riley's

square. They encircled it, firing at point blank range as they rode. Deserters and guards were blown backward with gaping, bloody .54-caliber holes in their heads and chests.

"Independent fire!" Riley commanded. Moreno echoed the command in Spanish. "Commence firing!"

The deserters and Mexicans began firing and loading as fast as they could, every man picking and choosing his own target. Dragoons tumbled as others pulled their second pistol, fired, and returned to the captured guns to re-load.

"Close ranks!" Riley yelled, the command echoed in English and Spanish. The tight square grew even smaller as the men stepped closer together to take up space created by casualties. Moaning, writhing wounded were ignored as San Patricios loaded and fired three times a minute, keeping Dragoons and their terrified horses back by the guns.

Musket balls whizzed past Harney and slammed with dull thuds into the dirt. He pointed his sword. "Rally on the downward slope!" Harney bellowed.

Officers ushered troopers to cover beneath the brow of the hill behind the abandoned guns, where they re-loaded and re-formed.

As the Dragoons left the guns, Dalton spotted Harney with his staff. Dalton nudged Conahan beside him, handed the sergeant his sword, and took Conahan's musket.

"Colonel darlin'!" Dalton bellowed, taking aim and cocking the hammer.

Harney turned in his saddle at the cry. His eyes grew wide when he saw he had been targeted.

"For Florida!" Dalton shouted as he squeezed the trigger and fired.

Harney had spurred his horse to avoid the shot but grimaced as the lead ball ripped through an arm. He tumbled to the ground. Staff officers rushed to him and propped him up. "Went through clean," Harney gasped gratefully, gripping the arm. He glared at the defiant green banner. "Get me that damn flag!" he ordered as they carried him below the crest and placed him among a row of writhing wounded.

With pistols drawn, half the Dragoons charged again over the brow of the hill and around one side of the guns. They encircled the square and peppered the San Patricios with more pistol shots.

Two squads carrying breech loading Hall's carbines emerged from the other side of the guns. They formed a line in front of Dalton's company and fired a volley at one section of the square. A dozen San Patricios crumpled and fell.

Another squad with drawn pistols charged that weakened sector with a yell. Their terrified horses careened headlong onto the bristling bayonets. Deserters knocked Dragoons from the saddle using their muskets as clubs. Dragoons fired point blank into their faces. A wide gap emerged in the square.

"Plug that hole!" Dalton yelled, pointing his sword.

"Follow me!" shouted Ockter in German. From Riley's company, he took off with a squad of German gunners at a run toward the gap. Dalton and Conahan joined them.

They slammed into the remnants of the first bunch of Dragoons, mostly fighting on foot now and hand to hand in the gap.

"Charge!" bellowed a Dragoon captain. He led his second platoon into the breach. They jumped their horses over those fallen even as surviving Dragoons struggled with Dalton and his men.

"Save the colors!" shouted Riley as the fourteen-man platoon bore down on himself, Moreno, Morstadt, Price, and the tobacco chewer.

Dalton, Ockter, and Conahan turned at the cry and saw the threat, but other Dragoons swirling around the square pressed the attack on the gap. Manzano saw and ran to Mejia on the Mexican line. He pointed at the flag.

Riley jabbed his sword into the dirt and picked up the musket of a dead deserter. He fired and blew one Dragoon backwards off his horse. He lunged with his bayonet at the crotch of a second charging Dragoon, lifting him screaming off his saddle and dead to the ground. Riley immediately jerked his bloody bayonet free, just as a passing Dragoon swung his saber at Riley's head. He ducked at the sound of the slicing blade but took a glancing blow, his scalp cut. He dropped to his knees, touched his head, and stared amazed at the blood on his hands. It looked almost foreign to him, as if it must belong to somebody else.

Moreno faced a charging Dragoon cooly, as if in a duel. As the trooper rode at him yelling like a demon and twisting his saber point down to skewer him, Moreno took deliberate aim and fired his pistol, flipping the Dragoon backward and off his saddle.

Another Dragoon riding past fired his pistol, hitting Moreno in the arm and knocking him to the ground. Moreno sat up, picked up his pistol, and struggled to re-load while bleeding profusely.

The Dragoon reined up, drew his saber, and circled back to finish Moreno, who did not see him coming. He raised his saber to strike but his eyes suddenly looked vacant as a large red hole exploded in his forehead. He tumbled to the ground beside Moreno, who turned to see Price lower his smoking musket to re-load. Moreno nodded quickly in thanks.

The tobacco chewer and Morstadt each fired beside Price, dropping two more Dragoons. All three began re-loading.

A Dragoon captain saw their vulnerability and pointed his sword. "Now!" he yelled. "Take the colors!" He spurred his horse. Six troopers followed him.

The tobacco chewer clubbed one Dragoon off his horse and

bayoneted him. The dying man spewed tobacco juice down his jaw. The tobacco chewer spied a tobacco pouch peeking from the dead trooper's jacket pocket. As he reached for it, the tobacco chewer took a pistol shot to the head. The side of his face exploded. He dropped dead across the Dragoon, still grasping the pouch.

Infuriated, Price thrust his bayonet up and into the belly of the guilty Dragoon, lifting him off his saddle and screaming onto the ground. The Dragoon captain fired his pistol from behind and blew out the front of Price's chest. He tumbled over dead beside the tobacco chewer.

Now Morstadt stood alone, grasping the flag in one hand and his musket in the other. Circling Dragoons, their pistols empty, slashed at him with sabers and grabbed at the flag. The Teutonic giant fended them off with his bayonet but would soon be overwhelmed.

Mejia and Manzano arrived at a run. Mejia fired his rifle, killing the Dragoon captain's horse and tumbling the officer to the ground at Manzano's feet. Mejia let loose a blood curdling *grito* or battle cry and charged the Dragoons circling Morstadt. Manzano engaged the captain in a clanging sword duel.

Dalton arrived with Ockter and Conahan, who stopped and fired toward Morstadt. Two Dragoons toppled from their saddles. Mejia grabbed the horse reins of a third with one hand and thrust his rifle upward with the other. His sword bayonet pierced the trooper's throat. Mejia yanked him to the ground and bayoneted him again. Morstadt swung his musket at the fourth and crushed the man's skull with a mighty blow. He fell but his foot caught in the stirrup. The terrified horse dragged its dead rider away through the cactus.

Manzano fenced expertly with the clumsy Dragoon captain, quickly disarming him after slicing both his cheeks. Backing up from Manzano's deadly slashes and thrusts, the captain tripped and fell. Manzano glared at the glowering officer as he lay on the ground, Manzano's sword point touching his throat.

"I would be pleased to take your surrender, señor!" Manzano announced breathlessly.

"Go to hell, greaser!" spat the Dragoon. He jerked a small single shot pistol from his boot and fired.

Manzano clutched his heart and crumpled to the ground. But as he fell, he managed to thrust his sword entirely through the neck of the Dragoon captain. The sword jutted into the ground and prevented the dead officer from falling back flat, sightless eyes staring skyward in surprise. Manzano lay dead across him.

Dalton helped Riley to his feet. He impishly picked up Riley's barracks cap and dusted it off. Riley yanked it from his hands as Dalton laughed. Conahan and Ockter stood protectively beside Morstadt and the flag. Mejia had helped Moreno up and was tying a bandanna tightly above his bleeding wound.

Riley looked around and watched the encircling Dragoons fall back in disorder toward the line of guns. He pulled on his cap at a jaunty rake. "Formation be damned," he gnarled ominously.

"Katy bar the door!" Dalton roared in delight.

"Battalion!" Riley bellowed. He picked up his sword and pointed toward the cannon. Surviving deserters and guards, battered, faces blackened and bloodied, turned to stare at him. "Take back our guns!" he yelled. "Charge!"

"Push them off our hill!" Moreno yelled in Spanish, pointing his sword.

With a shout, the square dissolved into a running, screaming mass of angry Irishmen, manic Germans, and passionate Mexicans, surging straight at Harney and his tired, bloodied Dragoons as they tried again to re-form behind the guns. Riley,

Dalton, Moreno, Conahan, Ockter, Mejia, and Morstadt led the charge, the fluttering green flag at the apex of a flowing, ragged *V.* The irresistible mob screamed "Viva San Patricio!" and "Viva Mexico!" amid wild, careening Celtic yells and Mexican *gritos.*

Harney was helped onto his horse. He glared at the bugler beside him. "Retreat," he snarled, and turned to ride back down the hill as the bugler blew the call repeatedly. Surviving Dragoons followed him and passed back through the guns. A few turned in their saddles to fire parting pistol and carbine shots. Others pulled wounded up to ride double in the saddle in jarring agony.

The ragged line of San Patricios and Mexican guards stood shoulder to shoulder across the brow among their re-claimed guns. They cheered over and over, "Viva San Patricio! Viva Mexico!" Some fired parting shots at the Dragoons as they galloped back across the smoky valley. Morstadt stood atop one of the guns. He waved the green banner defiantly as the roar of the battle across the entire smoky plateau began to wane, gradually decreasing.

Riley marveled at how battles never ended cleanly, but slowly sputtered out like a steam engine running out of fuel; but instead of wood, it was men. He and Dalton stood on the brow of the hill at sunset and gazed at the spectral aftermath. Smoke drifted like ground fog enshrouding hundreds of ghastly, contorted corpses bloated and blackened by the intense sun. A soft breeze chased thousands of bits of white cartridge paper across their bodies and the debris strewn plateau. Pitiful cries of *"Agua por favor!"* and *"Madre de Dios!"* from Mexican wounded between the lines rose above the thin, tinny sound of a U.S. brass band playing "Hail, Columbia" in the distance.

"Damn if the blaggards don't think they won," Riley observed in astonishment, nodding toward the music. He took a swig from his flask but Dalton yanked it out of his hand as he spied blood trickling down Riley's forehead.

"You had best tend to that," Dalton chided, pulling off Riley's cap and pouring the whiskey on his scalp before Riley could resist.

"Yeeowch!" Riley hollered, grimacing. " 'Tain't the wound what hurts," he snarled, "but the waste!"

Riley grabbed back his flask as they turned to leave but paused at sight of the carnage behind them. Dead deserters, Mexicans, and Dragoons lay entwined with dead horses stretching from the line of guns across the entire hilltop. Fierce expressions of rage, terror, or surprise remained etched on their grimy, blood-encrusted faces. Ockter, Conahan, and Mejia walked among them with burial details. They gingerly separated Mexicans and deserters, picked up the corpses, and carried them toward the backside of the hill. Dragoons were left where they fell. Riley had seen this many times before, he thought, but it had never seemed so personal as it did now. He looked on all his men as if each one were poor young Parker, the first to die among the pathos of Monterey. Somehow, the first face to be lost sticks with you the longest, he thought.

"Winning don't nearly seem worth the price," Dalton grumbled.

"Losing is worse," Riley countered, "th'damn price being the same." Riley gestured at an area now cleared of dead San Patricios. "Leastwise the quartermaster's doing a brisk business," he said. Dalton looked.

Surviving Irish and Mexican San Patricios scurried among the dead Dragoons. They rifled pockets, haversacks, and saddlebags for tobacco, food, watches, pocket knives, and other usable items. Several Mexicans removed broghans while others tried them on to replace their worn-out sandals.

★　★　★　★　★

"When the Florida swamps rotted my own broghans," Dalton mused, "I took Paddy Doyle's boots, him no longer needing them being dead three days." Riley stared at him expectantly. "His feet put up a terrible fight."

"In an icy Afghan pass full of frozen blood and bodies," Riley recalled bitterly, "the red coats of two dead mates once saved my arse. Leastwise here, there's no damn snow." Both smiled in wry weariness. Moreno arrived. Riley nodded and gestured with his flask across the valley. The band had begun playing "Yankee Doodle." " 'Tis a grand wake for themselves they're throwin'," he said.

Moreno stared thoughtfully across the valley as he lit up a cigar and inhaled deeply. "They celebrate George Washington's birthday," he said quietly.

Dalton and Riley exchanged looks of surprise. "Sure and it somehow escaped my mind entirely," Dalton joked. Riley laughed.

Moreno merely kept staring, lost in a grim, haunting memory. "The Texian rebels so celebrated in San Antonio eleven years ago this night," he recalled. "The next morning we surprised them. We drove them into the Alamo."

"His worship knows how to spoil a good party he does," said Riley.

Dalton looked amused by the jest, but Moreno just stared. "We won that battle too," Moreno observed, "and then everything began to go wrong for us."

Riley thought his voice seemed to drift off. He and Dalton traded anxious looks. "If that bunch don't retreat tonight," Riley said, trying to sound cheerful, "I'll wager history repeats itself on the morrow." Riley suddenly looked concerned when he noticed lights flickering on the battlefield; perhaps, a surprise attack. He pulled out his spyglass.

"We should go now," Moreno said, pointing toward the backside of the hill with his cigar. "The burial trench is nearly full." Dalton bowed his head and made the sign of the cross. They started to walk away but Riley held up his hand.

"Hold," he said ominously. Through his spyglass, Riley could see dozens of dark shapes in the twilight moving among the dead in a ravine with lanterns. "There might be a night raid afoot," he added. He shifted his view to a more brightly lit plateau. Hordes of Mexican camp followers were methodically removing rings, watches, eyeglasses, flasks, and usable clothing from the U.S. dead, stripping many to their white underwear. Some gave canteen water to the Mexican wounded. " 'Tain't nothing but the female vultures," he said, "picking clean the carcasses." He kept looking.

"Our women do not waste on the dead whatever may help the living," Moreno said.

"Not unlike soldiers," Dalton replied in a matter-of-fact tone. He saw Riley scowl in disbelief at something. Dalton nodded at Riley. "Sure and someone pinched the whiskey afore himself," he cracked. Moreno smiled.

"Herself is among them!" Riley gasped, unable to put the spyglass down. He saw Luzero and Bel struggle to pull a fine pair of black and maroon boots off a dead volunteer infantry officer. They seemed to be enjoying the grisly tugging match. Bel puffed at her cigareet. Riley finally tore himself away from the scene and lowered the spyglass in disgust. Dalton and Moreno looked confused. Riley glared at them fuming, taking a stiff drink.

" 'T'wouldn't be the pot calling the kettle black now, would it?" Dalton said.

"Wouldn't pick her out of the gutter now with a pair of tongs," Riley said bitterly. He knew he was being a hypocrite but could not contain his loathsome feelings. He could not explain them. He would not even try.

"You false tongued little parasite!" exclaimed Dalton. " 'Tain't like we ain't two sides of the same damn coin!"

"Thought I'd found someone above my own sins," Riley muttered and stalked away. He knew Dalton was right. But he also knew that he would never again see Luzero high atop that perch he had built for her in his mind, his perfect little world where at least one thing was not tainted, bruised, battered, and bloodied. He knew it was a fairytale but, after all, he was weaving this story.

Riley ambled toward the glow of torches and bonfires illuminating the backside of the hill. He could hear Conahan fiddling the haunting melody of an ancient Irish lament, "An Coolin." Battered and bloody, their uniforms torn, San Patricio survivors stood at attention around a deep trench. They bid farewell to the blackened, twisted faces of fifty comrades stacked like cordwood, Irish, German, and Mexican lying together, at last equal in ranks. A few Mexican guards prayed softly aloud in Spanish beside Morstadt and his crew praying in German. Ockter and Mejia flanked Conahan as he played, staring particularly at Price, the tobacco chewer and Manzano, lying on the top layer of corpses.

Riley, Dalton, and Moreno gathered at the head of the grave. When Conahan finished, they drew their swords, placed the hilt in front of their faces in a salute, kissed the hilt, and then slowly lowered the point toward the grave.

"Their fire was the spirit of Mexico," Moreno said reverently. "We are smaller men for their loss." Mejia echoed the same words in Spanish.

They replaced their swords and turned to leave just as the soldaderas arrived, Luzero and Bel among them. Many carried bundles of battlefield booty. Bel carried the officer boots. Each woman scurried to find her special man. Some found them in the pit and burst into tearful wailing, falling to their knees.

Bel was smoking a cigareet when she spied Dalton. She broke into tears of joy as she ran to him, flew into his arms, and squeezed him in a bear hug. Still gripping the tall boots in one hand, they slapped his back. His pipe fell.

"Lookee there!" Dalton cried in mock outrage. "You've spoilt my smoke entirely!" She handed him the boots. As he beamed while inspecting them, she picked up his pipe, stuck it in her mouth, and lit it with her cigareet. She plopped the pipe into his mouth with a sexy smile. "Gracias, my darlin'," he whispered, "and for the grand boots." They walked off together arm in arm.

Luzero knelt by Manzano's corpse at the grave. She crossed herself, stood, and finally saw Riley when he stepped into the light of a bonfire with Moreno. He saw her but when she started to run to him, he turned away. She stopped in her tracks, feeling confused. She had not seen him in weeks, since the army left San Luis Potosi. What had gone wrong? she wondered. Luzero stood alone, staring at Riley and feeling hurt.

Riley walked with Moreno to greet a lieutenant of Hussars who had just arrived. The Hussar handed a written order to Moreno. He read it, looked stunned, then crumpled it and threw it to the ground in disgust.

" 'Tain't a victory decree, I'll wager," Riley said.

"His excellency orders us to retire from the field tonight," said Moreno flatly. "We won the battle but have no more food, no more ammunition."

"One bayonet charge would crumble their whole damn line!" Riley roared. "Then we'd have all th'damn food we could eat!" Moreno nodded to agree as Riley darted a look at the burial pit. "Staying in this confounding land ain't nothing but a grand wish to die," he surmised. He saw Luzero staring at him near the grave, her tears glistening in the firelight. She turned and walked away, crestfallen. "And now for nothing," Riley added, more softly.

"The flower of our army has died here," Moreno said bitterly, peering into the roaring fire. "And with it our best chance to end this war," he added. "But our soldiers covered themselves with glory."

"Like the damn bull?!" Riley asked, disgusted. Moreno glared at him. "They ain't managed nothing but to cover themselves with quicklime," Riley snapped, "and take half my poor lads with them!" He nodded at the grave as he strode away. San Patricios were emptying bags of the white powder onto the corpses. Others began shoveling dirt.

Later, Riley stood alone watching his gunners hitch the heavy guns to limbers, pulled by strong oxen; others, carrying wounded to wagons and ox carts. Luzero saw him and glided up behind him. Taking a chance, hoping to fix whatever might have gone wrong, she gently slid her arms around him and squeezed. But he stiffened at her touch. She pulled back when he turned to face her, his face crestfallen in pain and disbelief.

"I understand," she said tenderly, thinking she at last knew why. "Women may weep together, but a man must grieve alone."

"Only for women what rob the dead," Riley said in a dull monotone.

"Like you, we only do what we must to survive," she replied, feeling irritated that she had to explain herself.

"Thought you different from them others," Riley muttered. "Seen corpse pickin' for years and done it myself a few times, but I . . . I never thought that you would . . . that you weren't above . . ." Riley could not find the right words to finish his thought. He knew he was a hypocrite but did not care.

"How can one such as you condemn me?!" Luzero lashed

out, her sudden burst of temper taking Riley by surprise. "What I do hurts no one. What you do filled that grave!"

"How could my angel fall to the level of just another greaser?!" Riley blurted, instantly regretting his words. But they were out of his mouth before he realized what he was saying, a reflex reaction like ducking from a right cross.

She slapped him hard across the face, whirled, and stormed away toward the oxcart of wounded. Bel was perched atop and reached down to pull her up.

Riley touched his stinging cheek and stared stunned as a whip cracked and the cart creaked away. He took out his flask, drank it empty, glancing at the engraving in the flickering torch light. Tears traced down his grimy, stubble-covered cheeks. "Gone an' stuck your foot in it," he muttered. "Sotted fool."

Hours later, thunder boomed and lightning crackled to illuminate the darkest of nights for the betrayed army, trudging back south through biting cold in a windy winter rain. Cavalry, artillery, and wagons labored on the muddy road while the soldados sloshed doggedly on either side.

Bel and Luzero huddled atop their cart full of moaning wounded. They tried to keep the shivering men covered in wet blankets while clutching rebosas tightly around themselves. Bel caught Luzero in a sad look back at the troops. "You must take him as he is," Bel advised. Luzero looked at her and Bel smiled. "Then you can change him!"

"He would first change the world," Luzero said with a sad little laugh.

"It is no longer his world to change," Bel said.

"Maybe that is why he says such hurtful things?" Luzero replied. She looked again at the column. "Now he must come to me, show me some respect."

A short distance back, Moreno rode his horse at the head of his surviving Mexican guards. Mejia slogged along doggedly beside him.

"Young Manzano's pride, his spirit," Moreno mused, "stolen from us like precious jewels, like gold coins we can never replace."

"At least, he died fighting," Mejia replied. "What more can a man ask of life?" He looked up at Moreno, who stared down at him curiously.

"Like the bull?" Moreno asked. Mejia nodded in simple certainty.

Behind the guards, Riley and Dalton sloshed through mud side by side at the head of their forty remaining deserters. Ockter and Conahan trudged glumly a few yards back, followed by Morstadt carrying the furled flag. Conahan stepped out, stopped, and checked on the others, strung out in a ragtag column.

"Close it up, lads!" Conahan yelled. "If we're goin' to hell," he said, "let's get there at the same time and afore th'damn beasts!" Curses and moans flew at him as the men quickened their pace. Teamsters cracked bullwhips above the oxen struggling to pull the big guns on the road beside them.

Riley looked behind him and saw nothing but a losing situation. He tugged at his collar, feeling tighter than usual. "Keep trying to wrestle a reason," Riley said. "Soon as I got it pinned, it comes at my blind side and throws me."

" 'Tis too simple for the likes of you," surmised Dalton. "The army won its match. 'Twas Santa Anna his own self what cried 'uncle.' "

"As did those wounded Yanks what got bayonetted," Riley asserted.

"I'm blessed if the Yanks can parade their halos either," Dalton said. "Damn!" His pipe finally went out in the rain. Riley lifted his poncho for Dalton to duck under as he struck a match and fired it up. "Least the greasers got something the gringos don't," he whispered, grinning. "We got Confession."

"So it's 'we' now, is it?" Riley said aghast as they resumed marching. "The newest 'sacrament' must be this damn uniform," he scoffed, "a sacred shroud what changes blood and bone into greaser." Dalton glared at him, pipe smoke billowing. "Or would the miracle's name be simply . . . Bel?"

" 'Tis easy finding something to cling to in this land," Dalton mused, nonchalantly agreeing. "Maybe because the damn land is so harsh, you got to find that 'something' just to survive." He stopped to hold up one of his new black and maroon boots, admiring it.

"Maybe for some," groused Riley, nodding at Luzero just ahead atop the oxcart. She saw him stare and pointedly looked away.

"Some would fight to keep it," Dalton said, "like the rest of us 'Irish greasers.' "He laughed.

"Spent too many years livin' hard to end up here, hardly livin'," said Riley bitterly, "like just another greaser."

"Comes a time," Dalton advised, "when you got to belong to something." He puffed his pipe. "And that's best when your time is running out."

"With this backsliding army, it's room we're running out of," Riley insisted. "And then where will you scold me?!" he teased.

"On the porch of my adobe hacienda," smiled Dalton, "looking out over my three hundred and twenty acres."

"I'll be reading your black hearted insults, I will," said Riley, "on the porch of my mudball cabin back in County Galway." The thought of deserting once again had roused itself, as if from a long nap in his besotted brain. It now seemed to him the only course left: he had done all he could to help his comrades survive. It was Santa Anna who had betrayed them all.

"No friend of mine leaves me his dirty laundry," said Dalton, an edge to his voice.

Riley noted the tone but forced a light laugh. Dalton could read him like a post office circular for criminals, Riley thought.

The long column wound at an agonizing pace up a mountain trail. Rain and darkness slowly engulfed them, leaving only the fading sounds of creaking wagon wheels, sloshing feet, cracking bullwhips, and moaning wounded to mark their passing.

Days later, the weary San Patricios entered a farm community spread across gently sloping hills. Many of the grizzled survivors were walking wounded with heads, arms, or legs bandaged. They ambled warily in a strung out, dusty column. Vacant adobe houses, wooden barns, and stone corrals lined a road that wound up to a hacienda atop the ridge.

The village overlooked fields ready for spring planting. But the neatly hoed rows lay collapsed from boot heels. Castoff muskets, cartridge boxes, belts, canteens, and shakos littered the area. Flocks of vultures fed on the rotting carcasses of mules and horses. The sickening sweet-sour stench of death floated upon the nuance of a chilly morning breeze.

The vultures paid no mind to the intruding soldiers. Conahan leaped at one bunch and waved his arms, yelling like a lunatic. They merely fluttered their wings and stuck to their grisly work. He looked at the amused men in ranks and shrugged, drawing a tired laugh from a few.

Riley pointed at the birds when he arrived with Dalton at the side of Moreno, who had beckoned them over. He sat on his horse beside the porch of an adobe house a stone's throw from the road. "They stand to like veterans, these greaser birds," Riley said. He and Dalton both grimaced at the acrid smell that suddenly had grown stronger. Moreno held a handkerchief to his face.

"They never lose in any war," Moreno said. He nodded at the porch. Under its brush arbor lay six soldados frozen in grotesque death and partially eaten by vultures, coyotes, and wolves. Riley deftly pulled out his flask.

"Ockter!" Dalton yelled. "Send in the diggers!" He lit his pipe and wafted the fragrant smoke around the pungent porch. Swarms of flies took flight from the purplish, blackened, and bloated corpses.

Ockter sent Morstadt with six brawny Germans carrying picks and shovels. They began digging a burial pit at one end of the porch; no surprise, no outrage, no sadness. Horror had become an insensitive routine.

"We will await our cavalry at the hacienda," said Moreno, pointing to the hilltop complex with Mexican sentries atop the walls. "Mejia is already there."

"Don't like being separated from our guns," groused Riley. "This rear-guard action ain't nothin' but a burial detail." Santa Anna had sent the cannon south separately with the main army, assigning the San Patricios and other reliable units the task of protecting its back.

"Sure and it is an honor," said Dalton, gingerly stepping over a corpse as he wafted more smoke. "In all the blessed army, Santa Anna knows we will not be traipsing across to the other side for to get a square meal."

Riley and Dalton mustered weary grins. Moreno was stoic, staring at the dead men. They ranged in age from a smooth faced teenager to a gray headed, grizzly bearded veteran in his sixties.

"They crawled here to die in the small dignity of shade," Moreno said, "like old and exhausted beasts, when they know it is their time."

Morstadt's men carefully tied ropes around the feet of the corpses. Rather than touch the putrid flesh, they dragged them across the porch. At the end, they prodded and pushed with shovels until the stiff figures fell off the edge and thudded into the adjacent pit.

Moreno made the sign of the cross. "I have told you that my wife's name is Esperanza?" he asked of no one in particular, lighting a cigar. He shifted in the saddle and pulled his gaze to Riley and Dalton, who looked at him. "Her name means 'Hope,' " he continued. "At times like this, thoughts of her sustain me." He nodded at the bedraggled column waiting in the road. "What sustains them?"

"For us, it is past thinking about," Dalton surmised. "It is just getting through another damn day double quick and ahead of the hangman."

"Dalton waxes a bit eloquent, he does," Riley scoffed. "He likes the sound of that word 'martyr.' " Dalton scowled. "The lads are staying for th'blessed land," Riley insisted, "not a thing more. They still believe Mexico's gonna stand and deliver three hundred and twenty acres, like the victim of any good 'highwayman.' " Riley smirked.

"You no longer believe?" Moreno asked, knowing the answer.

"Did he ever?" asked Dalton. Riley frowned.

Moreno took an overly long drag on his cigar. "Captain Riley, when the darkness looms," he said with a flick of his cigar at the corpses, "every soldier wants to run. We must cling to something of the heart to make us stay."

"Been soldiering goin' on fourteen years and seen piles of corpses deeper and riper than these," Riley confessed. "Through all that blood and smoke, ain't never seen a flag what wouldn't be held higher, a politico who wouldn't sink lower, or a woman who wouldn't do any damn thing, just to make me 'stand to' between their own hides and that." He nodded at the last corpse being dragged across the porch.

"A curse on you!" Dalton snapped with a puff. "We know two darlin' women who put the lie to that crock of blarney."

"You're blinded by 'love' your own self," Riley retorted. "In women or war, you can't put your faith in matters of the heart.

71

'Tain't tangible."

"Things that matter most seldom are," cautioned Moreno. "In the end, what does matter to you?"

"Payday," Riley said flatly. He pointed angrily at Conahan and Ockter. "Form the company!"

Minutes later, the San Patricios marched through the open gates of the hacienda courtyard. They gawked at more than a hundred mangled, miserable Mexican wounded lying sprawled across blood drenched tiles and leaning against adobe walls. Some were dead already and stared with vacant eyes. Flies covered their faces and maggots crawled in their open, clotted wounds. Rats scurried in the shadows among both living and dead. Mejia's guards carried corpses to a pile at the far end of the courtyard where they were stacked in a pyre. Wood and brush were laid between layers of bodies. A half-dozen soldaderas fluttered among the wounded, frantic for water. Weak voices pleaded, *"Agua por favor!"* Moreno halted the column and dismounted.

"Help them, Captain," he said to Riley.

"Break ranks and break out canteens!" Riley shouted. "Do what you can for these poor bastards!"

Conahan and Ockter waded into the pool of casualties with their men, sharing canteens and binding open wounds with bandanas. Mejia bounded down from the wall, leaving the sentries. He reported to Moreno, Riley, and Dalton.

"We found them like this," he said in Spanish, saluting. "Left behind with no food, no bandages. The village was abandoned."

Moreno looked disgusted. "General Santa Anna had no more room in his wagons," he said. "Those who could not walk would slow his retreat."

"Can fill their vacant ranks easy," said Riley. "There are plenty more in the same jails where these 'patriots 'come from."

"I'm blessed if I ain't seen those women around our camp,"

72

observed Dalton, staring at the soldaderas tending the wounded.

Mejia got the gist. "Señorita Belarmina?" he asked, pointing to the gate.

Dalton's face lit up when he saw Bel struggle into the courtyard carrying heavy buckets of water. With her were Sister Superior O'Gara and two other nuns from the convent at San Luis Potosi. The nuns had their sleeves rolled up and were staggering under the weight of more water buckets. Their habits and Bel's skirt and blouse were stained with smeared blood.

"Morstadt!" Dalton yelled. The big German had just planted and unfurled the green banner beside the hacienda porch. "Lend the good sisters a hand." Dalton was already trotting toward them.

Morstadt stepped to Sister O'Gara, taking not only her two buckets, but those of the other nuns. Dalton himself took the sloshing pails from Bel.

"Very much thank you," Bel said in halting English, out of breath but beaming. Dalton smiled in surprise. Sister O'Gara looked on proudly.

"Sure and de nada," Dalton said, giving a quizzical look to Sister O'Gara as Moreno, Riley, and Mejia arrived.

"We have been here five days, doing what we can," O'Gara said. "Señorita Bel asked me to begin teaching her English. She learns quickly."

"Tell me, sister," asked Riley, "any more army ladies drawing water down at the creek?" Moreno and Dalton looked knowingly at Riley, who saw. "They might need a hand," he explained.

"They left with the main army," O'Gara replied, "to tend injured officers, the only wounded General Santa Anna seemed to have room for."

"Luzero to Mexico City she is going," Bel said, with a sly smile.

"Some people surely go to great lengths to put great lengths

73

'tween their own selves and some people," Riley groused.

"Sure and you have again found the long way around the truth," snapped Dalton, firing up his pipe.

"Sister, are you sure Señorita Luzero left with the main army, not with some detached group like ours?" asked Moreno, obviously concerned.

"We were taking vestments and altar candles to the cathedral in Saltillo," O'Gara said, nodding, her Irish accent rising more to the surface, "when this blessed flood of soldiers engulfed us, all going the other way. We took refuge here and found these poor sufferers, abandoned. Señorita Luzero and the others went on. General Santa Anna was insistent. He was in a hurry, he was."

"Gracias, sister," Moreno nodded, barely suppressing a smile. She and Bel took a pail each from Dalton and led the other nuns into the courtyard. They joined Morstadt in distributing water. Moreno now looked plainly worried. "Perhaps our cavalry will bring better news tonight," he said. "For now, we must think that we may be in the same plight, abandoned."

Riley and Dalton traded grim looks, saluted, and walked back to their men. Mejia remained. He stared scornfully at Bel as she walked away with Dalton. "That camp woman has learned some English," Mejia said in Spanish. Moreno nodded, looking at him with amusement.

"It will help her get what she wants," Moreno said, "Lieutenant Dalton."

"If a mere camp woman can learn, so can I," said Mejia.

"You find in her accomplishment a challenge?" Moreno teased.

"Perhaps it will help me get what I want," Mejia replied, frowning. Moreno nodded at him, understanding.

That night, blazing bonfires illuminated the courtyard. The San Patricios spread their blankets over some shivering wounded

while the nuns covered others with brilliantly embroidered vestments. The hapless men smiled cheerfully at this, comforted to
be warmed beneath the shimmering sign of the cross. Some
pointed to the silver cross that shined in the firelight from the
green flag.

Conahan had broken out his fiddle. He sat among a circle of
Mexicans around a fire. Conahan picked at the strings, searching for notes to a sad Mexican tune hummed weakly by a
wounded Mexican corporal. Other Anglos slowly wandered into
the circle, Ockter and Morstadt among them.

"Faith I got it now," said Conahan, nodding at the corporal.
He applied his bow and began playing the entire Mexican
melody. The gathered soldados started to sing in Spanish. The
Anglos hummed along in harmony. Riley and Dalton were walking their rounds when they were drawn to the music. Dalton
hummed.

"Irish and greaser is speakin' the same language this sad
night," Conahan said, playing all the while.

"Irish, greaser, and Dutchman," insisted Ockter. Morstadt
nodded fiercely.

"My father he run a tavern near Baden," Morstadt said.
"Travelers sit and play Bach, Beethoven at our piano." He stared
into the fire. "I fall asleep thinking as a child, there is no worry
music cannot make go away." The other San Patricios stared at
Morstadt and then into the same fire as Conahan kept playing.

"Songs in the key of lonely," said Dalton. He turned to Riley,
who was staring out the open gate.

"Never see th'likes of her again," Riley admitted. " 'Tis just
as well. The last thing a drowning man needs is more water."
He had begun to comfort himself by looking at Luzero as just
another complication to be avoided.

"Faith you are thick even for a stupid sot," Dalton snapped.
"You are leading the choir but don't know if you yet like the

song!" Riley glared at him. "By the time you decide, the last note shall be sung and you left standing alone, wishing you could remember the damn tune."

Riley merely grunted, knowing that Dalton was right, though it galled him to admit it. But he would be damned before he said it aloud. Dalton and Riley walked to the roaring campfire. Dalton tried to sing along in Spanish with the other gringos, as they joined in the chorus with wounded Mexican soldiers. Their efforts were rough and sounded comical, but the Mexicans appreciated them.

As Bel helped Sister O'Gara spread a vestment over a dying young soldado, she heard Dalton singing with the rest. She looked questioningly at the nun, who merely smiled and nodded. Bel walked to Dalton and slid her arms around him in a grateful hug.

"Something for you I have been making," Bel said, pulling a small bundle from her skirt pocket. Dalton took it and unrolled a coiled silk hat cord of brilliant green. The ends were the head and tail of a snake hammered from tin. They shined in the glow of the fire. "The snake of Mexico with the snake of Ireland is joining as one," she explained, "like your flag."

Dalton was touched, almost teary. "More like you and me, darlin'," he managed to croak hoarsely with a warm smile. Bel could not hide her blush without a giggle, shying away. Dalton held out the hat cord for Riley to see.

"Lovely," Riley frowned. " 'Tain't regulation."

Dalton looked incredulous. "Neither are we!" he snapped. Turning to Bel again, he said softly, "I shall be needing an appropriately grand sombrero."

"You'll soon have the whole outfit speaking greaser with an Irish brogue," Riley said disgusted, rolling his eyes. He turned and walked to the open gate. Riley paused just inside the courtyard and stared out into the opaque blackness. The howl of coyotes and wolves seemed to beckon and grow louder. He lingered to take a long drink. He had never felt so alone in a crowd of his own making.

"There is nothing out there but death," Moreno warned. He stepped out from the shadows of the other side of the gate. "I have been contemplating the same view now for some time."

"Thought I'd take a walk down by the river," said Riley, a slight smile tracing his lips. "The view might be brighter from the other side."

"You did that once before," said Moreno. "What did it get you?"

Before Riley could answer, both became aware of the sound of approaching horse hooves, jingling harness, and rattling sabers.

"Ours or theirs?" wondered Riley, turning to the courtyard. "Take arms!" he bellowed. The San Patricios rushed to their stands of muskets, grabbed them and hurried to slip on their belt equipment. Ockter and Conahan barked orders all the while to form ranks.

"Horses approaching!" a Mexican sentry called out in Spanish. Mejia was checking his guards at another point on the walls. He ran to the sentry and peered into the darkness. Dalton trotted up beside Moreno and Riley.

"Lanceros!" Mejia yelled down.

"Yanks don't carry them pig stickers," sighed Riley, relieved.

A company of dusty Mexican lancers clattered into the courtyard. Some horses narrowly missed the sprawled and now scrambling wounded. The horses had been ridden hard, with frothy sweat dropping from their heaving flanks. The troopers were worn. They almost fell to the ground when a lieutenant ordered them to dismount. At the head of the column rode Colonel Andrade. He strode briskly to Moreno, Riley, and Dalton, who saluted.

"Please speak English, Colonel," Moreno said, "as a courtesy to my staff." He nodded at Riley and Dalton.

"As you wish," Andrade said, but he sounded as if it was beneath him. "All rear-guard detachments must fall back to San Luis Potosi immediately," he continued. "Force a night march or be cut off."

"Do we rejoin the main army?" Moreno asked.

"By the time our scattered units get there," Andrade said, "the main army will have left for Mexico City. We are told they will march from there to stop the gringo invasion from the sea, from Vera Cruz."

"Then ain't Mexico City where we belong?!" Riley blurted.

Andrade and Moreno exchanged subtle, knowing looks, even as Riley and Dalton's hopes began to rise. Moreno noticed.

"What we are not told, because he does not want it known, is that his excellency must first put down a revolt by the people against him in Mexico City," explained Moreno patiently. "The Assembly has turned against him."

"But how did you find this out?" Riley asked.

"Word of mouth," Moreno explained, "listening to the talk among refugees we have passed."

"One more reason to learn the language," observed Dalton.

"And so we have been given the 'honor' to hold San Luis Potosi," Andrade continued, "as much against our own people as against the gringo General Taylor." Andrade spat out the words in disgust.

"And Taylor is too mauled to mount an offensive," Moreno said. Andrade agreed with a sharp nod.

"Lunacy!" growled Riley. "How can you lick th'Yanks if you're fighting amongst yourselves?!"

"Then it is possible," said Dalton, seizing a slender ray of hope, "we will end this war marooned, as it were, in the backwaters of San Luis Potosi?" Moreno and Andrade nodded.

Dalton looked over at Bel in the courtyard. " 'Twould surely be better than up the long ladder and down the short rope."

"Quit your dreaming," Riley said. "You got more chance of finding leprechaun gold." Dalton reluctantly agreed with a nod. "And I suppose his worship traipsed off with our big guns to boot?"

"He took all the artillery," said Andrade, "but none of the wounded."

"No wagons are coming for these men?!" exclaimed Moreno. Andrade looked surprised by Moreno's outrage.

"Thousands have been left behind, intended for the care of the norteamericanos," Andrade explained, "since only they have doctors with them." A slight smile crossed Andrade's lips. "Our men in ranks joke that this is maybe the only way Santa Anna can slow the march of the gringo."

He turned and walked back to his column. Moreno stared after him, angry and depressed.

Riley shook his head with a grim laugh. "Unlike some we know," he said, "th'Yanks won't bless the other side's wounded with merciful murder."

Dalton shook his head to disagree. "Santa Anna's doing a grand job of that his own self," he said, "and on his own lads."

"It is disgrace enough to leave them our wounded," said Moreno, "but I shall not leave them our dead." He strode into the courtyard and waved Mejia over to him.

Shortly before midnight, the glare of a funeral pyre illuminated one end of the courtyard as Andrade's cavalry trotted out the other side. Moreno followed on his horse with Riley, Dalton, and the San Patricios marching behind. Bel and Sister O'Gara led the nuns and soldaderas, some weeping and waving sadly at the abandoned wounded, who stared in despair. Mejia's Mexican guards were last to leave. Sparks soared from the crackling flames and acrid, curling black smoke.

Riley and Dalton stepped beside the shuffling, serried ranks to look back at the hacienda. They watched spiraling embers race into the overcast sky, cheerless with no stars.

"I'm reminded of when the Yanks burnt their food," Dalton said wistfully, "back when victory was just up the road and around the bend at Buena Vista."

"Santa Anna's got to pull us down the road a bit to the coast, sooner or later," Riley asserted, "if only to man our blessed guns. Nobody else can work them."

"By then, I shall be speaking greaser like a native born," Dalton vowed, clenching his pipe.

Riley could not believe his ears. "Even rats got sense enough to jump a sinking ship," he said.

" 'Tis but one rat on this voyage," said Dalton, falling back in with the column. "And he will be going down with his 'impressed' crew, if that's what is in the cards."

Riley glared at him as he strode away, then looked back at the inferno of dancing sparks above the funeral pyre. It seemed that all his grand dreams were going up in that burning smoke. He thought about an old Irish maxim taught to him by his grandmother: if you want to hear God laugh, tell Him your plans. He took out his flask, raised it in a silent toast to her, and took a drink. Then he turned and fell in behind the column as it kept marching steadily, inevitably he felt, into opaque darkness and eventual oblivion. And he could no longer escape the hard truth: he alone was to blame.

CHAPTER 3
JALAPA
APRIL 1847

Two months later, Riley and Dalton led the weary San Patricios up a rugged mountain trail at dawn. Fingers of rose, lavender, and orange crawled like a claw across a blue-black sky as palm trees, tropical plants, and succulents crowded the roadside. To Riley it seemed a welcome, refreshing, and stunning contrast to the stingy, sparse high desert foliage of San Luis Potosi, where to him all had been pine trees, prickly plants, and boredom. The cacophony from an army of insects assaulted them from every side as a building chorus of wild bird cries announced their arrival. They had marched four hundred fifty miles south into the lush, tropical highlands midway between Mexico City and the Vera Cruz coast.

Uniforms were tattered and dusty but muskets remained polished, Riley felt proud to observe. The men sported a cockeyed, jaunty air of fatalism now that showed in rakish bits of civilian Mexican attire. Some wore broad-brim felt poblano hats; others, low-crown straw sombreros, but all with the Irish harp. Serapes and ponchos draped over uniform coats. Some had traded army broghan shoes for comfortable sandals and wore their trouser legs rolled, as did veteran Mexican infantry. Mejia's guards tramped just behind.

Riley, predictably, remained strictly regulation. Clinging to rigid military protocol was the only thing that Riley felt he could count on anymore. He wore nothing that revealed any melding with the Mexican culture, just army issue and the gleaming gorget given him by Luzero. He had not seen her since his regrettable outburst at Buena Vista.

On the other hand, Dalton sported a huge, battered felt sombrero. Dalton had wrapped the green snake hat cord from Bel several times around the base of its crown. Oddly, Riley felt jealous; not for the hat cord but for Dalton's comfortable relationship with Bel. Riley never knew that he could feel so alone and vulnerable. He pondered if this was his lot in life.

Near the crest of a ridge line, Riley heard horse hooves approaching slowly. At a spot where the road bends back on itself as it descends into a valley, he could see Moreno loping up.

"Let's wait here," Riley said to Dalton. "Give th'lads a rest."

"Batallon de San Patricio!" Dalton sang out in Spanish. *"Alto!"* He grinned devilishly at Riley, who cringed.

"Better off speaking Gaelic," Riley observed. "Leastwise the damn accent wouldn't grate." Dalton grunted a laugh.

The serpentine column ground to a jerky stop, its former crisp efficiency gone. The men relaxed in ranks. Riley studied Moreno as he drew nearer.

"He's riding slow," he whispered to Dalton. "Bad news."

"Could not be worse than being ordered to wave goodbye to darlin' San Luis Potosi," sighed Dalton.

"Thought her name were Bel," teased Riley.

"Only a week since the ladies been sent on ahead," said Dalton, "and it already feels like a lifetime."

"Certain ladies, what shall remain nameless, sent themselves ahead eight weeks earlier," Riley said. He had grown to accept his ingrained prejudice as a natural outgrowth of his chosen profession. But Luzero had forced him now to confront its cost. He fantasized about what delights he might have enjoyed with her, had he not allowed his bigoted ways to surface.

"Speaking of the light of dawn, as it were . . ." Dalton said. He nodded at a veil of palms beside the road silhouetted by rising sunlight. Dalton walked over and parted some fronds to peer at whatever awaited them below. His eyes grew wide in wonder. Dalton pushed back the brim of his sombrero and waved to Ockter and Conahan, lounging beside the column. They trotted over.

"God in heaven," exclaimed Ockter in German. He dropped to his knees, staring reverently. "Morstadt must be seeing this." Conahan nodded as he stared himself in awed disbelief.

"Sure and the condemned ought to know what they're dyin' for," Conahan said, turning to the curious ranks. He looked at Dalton, who gave a nod. "Battalion, break ranks!" bellowed Conahan. He waved them to the tree line.

By ones and twos, the fatigued men straggled to the roadside and peered through the palms. Morstadt joined Ockter, Conahan, and Dalton. Tears welled in Morstadt's eyes. Mejia and his guards gazed in more wistful silence, as if seeing some long-lost treasure again found. Riley stood alone in the middle of the road, waiting for Moreno. Dalton stared at Riley in frustration, muttered a curse under his breath, and strode over to him. He physically pulled him to the palms.

"I shall be dead afore I ever make you drink," Dalton grumbled, "but it will not be for not dragging your arse to the damn water." He held back a branch and revealed the view. Riley caught his breath.

Nestled against the base of the mountain was a walled town that shimmered dreamlike in morning sunlight. Two-story brick and stone homes with red tile roofs were linked by small green gardens. None of the pestilential mud, stick, and adobe structures common to the northern frontier were evident. Most houses were covered in white plaster; some, in pastel shades of yellow, blue, and pink. Streets were paved with cobblestones and lined with palm and banana trees. A domed cathedral fronted a wide plaza that surrounded a stone fountain splashing with sparkling water. Young women, modestly wrapped in colorful rebosas, gathered there with earthenware pots. Neatly manicured fields stretched to the edge of the valley like patches sewn into a colorful quilt.

" 'Tis like seeing a woman for th'first time with no clothes on," Riley said, staring. "An entirely different girl, this Mexico."

"Now that he is standing there at attention, as it were," Dalton said, "herself don't want him."

"Sure an' it's plain to see why," joked Conahan. "But she must be blind turning down th'likes of me!" He puffed up his chest like a rooster, drawing chuckles from everyone except Riley.

"Even I can see we are not wanted here," said Ockter, with a tug at his eyepatch. The others laughed at Ockter's rare jest.

" 'Tain't but one woman for me," Riley admitted, "and she don't want me no more than that lady called Mexico." He had unscrewed his pocket flask.

"Ah, the heartless bitch," crooned Dalton, knowing better, "and after himself making such a grand show of his tender affections too." Riley shot him a hard look, even though he knew that Dalton was right. Dalton smiled innocently.

"In San Luis Potosi, I try making Mexico my own," said Morstadt, nodding at the town. "She saw me as something to be jailed, not as a suitor."

Riley stared at them warily as they fell quiet. "One year ago this week, I divorced another painted lady," Riley admitted. "She betrayed me as will this one. If you think otherwise, you're a damn fool courting a lonely, forgotten grave." He took a stiff drink.

"If my three hundred twenty acres were down there," Dalton sighed reverently, "it would be worth the dying for to just be buried in it."

Riley felt a sharp pang of guilt when he saw them eye one

another in fatalistic agreement. Had he created a company of martyrs?! he wondered. He turned at a whiff of sulphur and sound of a striking match. Moreno stood just behind them, re-firing a Cuban cigar. Mejia was with him, holding the reins of Moreno's horse. Obviously, Moreno had been listening for some time.

"As young men, we all took women we did not want. We simply needed them for a passionate moment. Mexico is a young woman," Moreno said with a weary smile. "She does not want you. But she needs you."

"And ain't Mexico about to break our hearts," Riley said, "just like we done to them other fair maids?" Moreno returned his glare with an unnerving stare, slowly exhaling cigar smoke.

"Mexico is it?" joked Dalton, breaking an impasse with an accusatory nod at Riley. "Faith if I ain't died and gone above."

"When th'likes of us goes," said Riley, "we'll be heading in a different direction than up."

"And will you promise to again be leading this sorry lot?" Dalton added.

Moreno did not join the rest in laughter. He was holding something back, Riley thought, as always. Well, he mused, leastwise we have that in common.

"She is proud, spiteful, and hot blooded," Moreno admitted, "so if you win her heart, her pleasures are more rewarding." He drew his sword and idly caressed a roadside cactus with its blade. "Like this prickly pear," he said, "you must fight past its thorny exterior to reach the sweet fruit." He suddenly slashed the cactus to bare its insides. He looked down at the lovely town below. "Our city of Jalapa is among our sweetest."

"Begging the major's pardon, sir," said Riley, "but just where might be the thorny hide protecting this darlin' bit of fruit? Where is the damn army?!"

"If that is all what's left of the army," Dalton added, pointing to a small row of tents beside the city walls, "we will be taking up residence afore the devil's readied our rooms."

"The army is four miles west, fortifying the pass at Cerro Gordo, 'The Devil's Jaws,' " replied Moreno. "His excellency just told me our cannon await us there. That is where Santa Anna believes he will stop the norteamericanos." His words dripped with sarcasm. "That small camp below is ours for tonight."

"Considering his worship's newest vision," said Riley, "wouldn't Cerro Gordo be the proper place to perch?"

"The lads could make another four miles without breakin' a sweat," added Conahan. Ockter and Morstadt nodded.

"More to the point, four miles and Bel could be firing my pipe," mused Dalton. He caught a look from Riley. "And you could square accounts with herself, you could."

"She ain't interested no more," Riley muttered.

"General Santa Anna requests our presence here," Moreno said with a rueful smile, "at a fiesta." He crushed the stub of his cigar with his foot, grinding it with care into the moist black dirt.

Riley and Dalton looked dumbfounded as Ockter, Conahan, and Morstadt registered confusion. Oddly, Mejia seemed to understand, unleashing a grin.

"Ah! We must be celebrating our heroic advance to the rear!" said Dalton.

Riley choked on his whiskey in laughter, joined by the others. Moreno merely offered a sad, knowing smile. Riley had seen that look too often by now to feel anything but uneasy. When it came to Santa Anna, Riley had learned, you could only expect the volatile, the bizarre, or the dangerous. It suddenly dawned on him that someone could say the same thing of what lay buried at the bottom of his mental footlocker. He hoped to keep it there. That would depend on Luzero.

A short march later and the raucous noise of an enormous crowd and brass band music engulfed the marching San Patricios as they swung down the streets of Jalapa. The tune was Irish, "Rising of the Moon," but played with plodding unfamiliarity to sound oddly "Mexican." Beautiful fair skinned, upper class señoritas in Spanish finery flirted with them from balconies, tossing down flower blossoms as the weary troops passed beneath. Nearly every house on the main street was two stories with a balcony, all linked by gardens of banana trees, roses, carnations, and pumpkin vines.

Crowding the curbs were working class women equally beautiful but more careworn, some with young children. Their skin was darker and their clothes less stylish, though clean and colorful. They ran out to the soldiers in ranks and gave them flowers, food, and drink.

The only men in evidence were either ancient or very young. Those few of military age were rich dandies on the balconies. But they all cheered the ragged troops with shouts of "Viva San Patricio!" and "Viva Mexico!" Banners spanned the street and read *"Viva Heroico Batallon de San Patricio!"* Red, white, and green bunting abounded. Confetti flew in clouds. The mood was joyous.

Riley eased into a wistful smile when he saw young boys tagging along and marching with the troops, just like young American boys at that parade so long ago in Fort Mackinac. He nudged Dalton. "Little boys are the same on all sides," he said. "Reminds me of that 'wedding day' a year ago to that other woman, as it were," he added, enjoying the memory. Riley shook it off. "But then I am too easily led astray."

"Careful, now," warned Dalton in jest, "else you shall be pledging yourself to every painted lady what flaunts her charms."

Riley tossed Dalton a frown, then turned to check the column's formation. He saw Sergeant Mejia's rigid demeanor wither under a kiss from a pretty girl, who encircled his neck with a wreath of roses and carnations.

"The locals must be confused," Riley said. "We lost that fight at Buena Vista or rather Santa Anna threw away our damn victory. But they're treating us grand like heroes!"

"I'm blessed if we ain't as daft, though, just by being here," mused Dalton, blowing smoke fiercely. He had difficulty marching to the Mexican version of the Irish song. "They can pick a good tune they can, but it needs a bit of the old sod. Conahan!" he barked over his shoulder. "Give it a bit of a lilt!"

Conahan paced directly behind on one side of Morstadt, who carried the brilliant green flag. Ockter marched in stiff Prussian formality on Morstadt's other side. Conahan slung his musket and pulled up his fiddle, carried on a sling of its own. As he ripped into a lively riff, Dalton started singing loudly. The spirits of the San Patricios rose with every word of the song that celebrated a losing fight against impossible odds. They joined Dalton on the chorus.

A young woman ran out from the crowd, grabbed the flowing green silk of the flag, and kissed it tearfully. Then she gave the startled Morstadt a simmering look that could melt the bronze of their cannon. To the great glee of Conahan, Morstadt blushed and looked away from her before she ran back to the crowd.

Finished playing, Conahan doffed his cap to a flirtatious, buxom young girl on the curb who had clapped loudly to his fiddling. He had seen that with each clap, her full, unfettered, nubile breasts trembled beneath her flimsy camisa. She ran out, threw her arms around the leering, cocky little fiddler, and almost pulled him over with a sensuous if hurried kiss.

"Rosarita loves you, my little one!" she declared in Spanish. Her grandmother and chaperone sternly grabbed her and yanked her back into the crowd. Now it was Morstadt's turn to guffaw as Conahan blushed.

"Just think on how they'd welcome us had we but won!" Conahan blurted breathlessly. Riley and Dalton joined the others in a hearty laugh.

"Were I a black hearted rogue, I'd be recalling that heroic bull being herded toward the arena!" Riley said to Dalton.

"And like the bull at that blessed moment," Dalton replied as he blew smoke, "there is precious little left to do about it!"

Riley's look let Dalton know he did not agree. Somehow, he felt, he would find a way out, as he always did. He would just give it time.

They rounded a corner, entered the plaza, and marched around the fountain. The army brass band played on the steps of the cathedral behind a mounted line of Hussars of the Supreme Power. With drawn sabers, they scanned the crowd as if expecting trouble. Beneath their black fur busbys, they looked to Riley like Russian Cossacks of the Czar, loyal and deadly. As citizens surged into the square cheering, Moreno, Riley, and Dalton shouted orders to guide the San Patricios and Mejía's guards into line facing the Hussars. The band stopped. A hush fell on the crowd. A bugler blew the call "Attention."

"*Altas armas!*" shouted Moreno. The San Patricios presented arms smartly, with the sound of a single crack as palms slapped wood and leather. The band struck up the regal Mexican military air "Sangria de Patriota," which Riley now knew to mean, "Blood of the Patriots."

General Santa Anna made an entrance through the center of his Hussars, appearing to Riley much like Moses parting the waters of the Red Sea. Resplendent in full dress uniform, he flourished a floor-length blue cape heavy with silver embroidery. At his elbow was a sycophantic adjutant with a gold tray bearing four medals, each a white enameled cross hanging from a tri-color ribbon.

The crowd cheered wildly as he walked to Moreno, Riley,

Dalton, and Mejia, and personally pinned on each this "Angostura Cross of Honor." Santa Anna hugged them and kissed their cheeks. They saluted. Santa Anna then turned to face the assembled masses. He raised his arms and the band stopped.

"Fellow compatriots of Mexico," he declared in Spanish, drawing cheers as Moreno shouted out the English translation to the San Patricios. "I give the Cross of Honor to the leaders of our brave Irishmen who left an unholy American cause to join us!" More cheers resounded. "Their cannon helped us turn the terrible carnage in the north into our great victory at Angostura, which the norteamericanos call 'Buena Vista!' "

Jubilation erupted as Moreno finished his translation. When the words were at last understood, looks of amazement and confusion crossed the faces of the San Patricios. Riley and Dalton stared at Moreno in stunned disbelief. But Moreno had made himself distant from it all. He had experienced the subtle treachery of Santa Anna in the past. To him, it was nothing new. He stared straight ahead in stiff military formality, ignoring their astonishment.

"But now a new American army marches on Mexico City from our coast at Vera Cruz," Santa Anna continued, the crowd falling silent on this sour note. He nodded at his adjutant who unrolled a proclamation and held it up.

"But even as I turn our army to face them, I shall weaken their numbers. I shall circulate this tract among them. It offers two hundred acres of land to every man who deserts them and joins our valiant San Patricio Battalion!" Cheers returned.

"The going rate to go missing has gone down," Riley whispered to Dalton as Moreno finished his translation.

"So you would think we were winning, you would," said Dalton. "Has he started to believe his own blarney?"

"Can get a man into trouble, it can," admitted Riley. Dalton smiled.

"Perhaps the American hordes may tread haughtily on the capital of the Aztec empire," Santa Anna concluded reverently, again hushing the crowd with his eloquent Castilian Spanish. "But I shall not have to witness such infamy, for I am determined before that to die fighting!"

The crowd went wild as Moreno finished his translation. The band broke into a Mexican polka and some of the citizens began dancing in the plaza as others cheered. Santa Anna vanished behind his wall of guards, leaving the nearly hysterical crowd in a frenzy and wanting more. Riley and Dalton looked at each other plainly worried.

"If we are the bull," Riley growled, "then he's the damn matador."

Moreno overheard and turned his head slightly to stare at Riley with new respect. A thin smile curled his lips as if to say, "At last, you understand."

That night, paper lanterns and luminarias lit the inner courtyard and fountain of a large, U-shaped hacienda. A roaring bonfire blazed in the adjacent walled horse corral that completed the fourth side of the compound. Officers and the upper class of Jalapa mingled in the courtyard. The enlisted men and working class celebrated together in the corral. A Mexican string band played folk tunes for dancing. It was obvious to Riley that the upper class were light complexioned; the working class, a darker hue. Riley and Dalton navigated through the adoring elite to an arched gateway between the two areas.

"Plain as the difference 'tween night and day," said Riley, gesturing at the two groups with a crystal punch cup. "Your new home ain't no different from them others I've knowed, where the cream is what rises to the top."

"Only for lack of a proper stirring," argued Dalton. He cast an arched eyebrow at the approach of Santa Anna, Moreno, and Mejia, now sporting a single gold epaulette on his right shoulder. Riley and Dalton snapped to attention.

"I trust you are partaking of the pleasures afforded by 'El Encero,' " Santa Anna said, "my hacienda of 'pleasant confinement.' "

"Must be one of them twists in the lingo, your worship," said Riley. "Never knowed confinement anywhere to be 'pleasant.' "

"Sorry, Excellency," Dalton joked. "He has managed to confuse 'confinement' with 'commitment.' " All but Riley and Mejia laughed.

"I am pleased to announce a promotion, gentlemen," Santa Anna said with a practiced smile. "Sergeant Mejia is now a lieutenant, replacing the brave and lamented Capitan Manzano."

"Begging the general's pardon, sir," ventured Riley, "but ain't it more practical to elevate one who speaks the lingo of all the lads, not just the native born, as it were?"

"I am learning the gringo, capitan," Mejia announced proudly. His reply in English surprised Riley and Dalton. Moreno merely smiled. "When you will be learning the greaser?" Mejia asked. Riley looked suspiciously at Moreno.

"Not 'til I find myself a private tutor, I'll wager," Riley observed. Moreno bowed slightly at the compliment. He handed Riley his now dog eared copy of "Scott's Infantry Tactics."

"My thanks for the loan of General Winfield Scott's book," Moreno said, smilng. "His English is quite eloquent, for a gringo."

"So would be his cursing if he only knew," Dalton said, to laughter.

"Please be excusing me, my general," Mejia said. He snapped to attention, bowed to Santa Anna, and strutted proudly into the adjacent corral. His Mexican riflemen, waiting and watching, cheered him like a hero.

"War forces change," sighed Santa Anna, as if to apologize.

"Class lines at times must be crossed."

"You got to fill th'vacant ranks any way you can, sir," offered Riley, an eye cast at Dalton.

"Yes, but at this level it must be done carefully," said Santa Anna, "so as not to upset the social order." He stepped toward his upper-class guests and nodded. "We are 'creoles,' descended from the Spanish, the natural rulers," he explained. "The Indians of dark skin are, of course, the ruled."

Riley, Dalton, and Moreno exchanged uncomfortable looks. Santa Anna turned and saw. He gestured with a nonchalant wave of his hand at the mottled masses mingling in the corral. "They are 'mestizos,' half breeds of Spanish and Indian," he continued. "Each class distrusts and fears the other, until they are forced to unite," he paused with a tight, thin smile, "by war." He held both fists to his heart and looked to the heavens religiously. "My mission, my duty, is to keep them united, for Mexico!"

Santa Anna walked away to rejoin his upper-class guests. Moreno watched in a curious blend of respect and contempt. He lit a cigar. Riley tossed down his punch glass, pulled out his flask, and downed a healthy swig.

" 'Tain't like I ain't heard that blarney afore," Riley recalled. "Seemed less the lie, though, coming from a Yank preacher back in Mackinac."

"Seems to me," observed Dalton, "that Santa Anna's got to keep this war, any war, going just to keep his damn job."

"And that is why we are here; do you not see?" Moreno insisted, gesturing at the elite fawning over Santa Anna. "These are the wealthy, the politicians, the clergy, all from Mexico City. They take holiday here each spring to escape the heat. He courts their support, their money, to raise more troops."

"We are the proof of his pudding, as it were," said Riley.

"In this war, Mexico must take her heroes wherever she finds them," Moreno said too sweetly, "even if that is with you."

"Like I was saying, Dalton," Riley said, "the cream rises to the top." Moreno gave a little laugh, looking at Riley.

"Not always," Moreno quipped. "You also are promoted, Major Riley."

"Ah, well then," Dalton laughed merrily, "sure and that proves the well-known theory that shit floats!" Riley glared.

Moreno smiled. "You have been elevated as well, Captain Dalton," Moreno said. Dalton's smile faded and he uttered a curse. "And I am now Colonel Moreno," he said wearily, "of a regiment with fewer men than a company."

Moreno seemed lost, thought Riley, as he ambled off into the corral. Moreno stood in the shadows just outside the bonfire light. He watched his Mexican enlisted men drink and dance with the lower-class women of Jalapa on one side of the bonfire; the Anglo San Patricios doing likewise on the other side.

"Even when the best horses are harnessed," observed Dalton, "something can still keep them from pulling together."

"Different breeding," said Riley.

Dalton shook his head. "Different drivers," Dalton quipped. "It will take more than a bit of the luck for any of us to ever get that land."

"You'll more likely become a part of it," said Riley. Dalton looked at him. "Afore I let some peon plow these old bones under, I'll call myself a greaser." Riley wandered toward the enlisted men's party. Dalton held back, watching him. Then he followed, surrendering to his cynicism.

They found Conahan relishing his natural element, playing his fiddle while dancing a flamboyant jig. The flustered object of his attentions was young Rosarita, the well-endowed teenage girl who had run up to him at the parade.

"Aye, my darlin' Rosie," Conahan bellowed. "I wrote down this song just for you," he lied, drawing chuckles from the gathered San Patricios who knew better. "My little Rose, my 'Rose of Alabama.' "

"But this is Mexico," argued Ockter in his ear.

Conahan frowned. "Geography ain't th'blessed point!" Conahan said through his smiling teeth. He knelt before the giggling girl. She chattered away excitedly in Spanish to several gathered girlfriends. "Her grandma has gone," he whispered, rising to his feet. " 'Tain't the words what matter, but th'romance." He ripped into the rollicking tune about the seduction of a dark-skinned girl.

At the suggestive, bawdy lyrics, the San Patricios hooted, howled, and cheered, while innocent Rosarita and her friends, ignorant of the language, smiled and clapped, drawing yet more guffaws.

As Conahan played and sang, Riley wandered among the troops. Riley shook their hands, slapped them on the back, and shared his flask as he went. Dalton watched him, but from a distance. Riley offered his vial to Morstadt, who looked surprised.

"Thank you, sir," Morstadt said. "To the regiment!" He raised the flask and downed a mighty swig. Riley took back the flask with a frown; empty.

"The regiment is running dry," Riley observed.

"Morstadt bring up reserves!" the big German replied, taking the flask to a table heavy with earthen bottles of Mexican liquor. Dalton had been quietly puffing his pipe, staring in awe at Riley. At last, he joined him.

"My new rank is the darlin' silver lining to this dark cloud," said Riley. "If ever they pay us, my purse'll be heavy. I'll have ship's passage and bribes both." Dalton looked disgusted.

"How can you drink with them, laugh with them, fight beside them, and then leave them hanging in the wind, from a noose of your own making?!" Dalton asked.

"Because I'm their damned officer," Riley snarled. "It's my job!"

"You are still cut from the same cloth," said Dalton icily.

"Not anymore," replied Riley. "How else could I order them to die?" He added bitterly, "Or so says Luzero."

"Don't go laying your shame at her fair feet," Dalton growled. "She didn't tell you to skip out afore you pay the piper." Riley stared at him sullenly. "But sure and you would leave me behind to clean up your droppings."

"All of you've found something here, whatever you were looking for," Riley grumbled. "You've latched onto that something to keep you here, no matter what. Whatever I thought I'd found, I've now managed to lose."

Morstadt returned and handed Riley his re-filled flask. Morstadt bowed, turned, and grabbed two tiny Mexican women. He lifted them and carried them like two sacks of corn meal a few whirls in a dance to Conahan's song.

"Then damn well go and look for it!" urged Dalton. " 'Tain't complicated. All she wants is respect and to know that you need her."

"Ain't never needed nobody," asserted Riley. "If I'm gonna be let down, I'd best be doing it my own self."

"Then alone you have been and alone you shall stay," snapped Dalton. "Faith the stench alone will see to that!"

Riley glared at him, taking a swig from his flask. He turned and walked into the night as he had done all his life, quite alone. Riley comforted himself with the thought that this way, he would owe nobody anything. When the time came, he felt he could leave with as clear a conscience as he had ever known.

CHAPTER 4
CERRO GORDO
APRIL 17, 1847

Early the next day, Riley observed with a wry smile that the San Patricios showed the effects of a long, drunken night. He watched them with almost fatherly affection filing wearily into earthen fortifications at Cerro Gordo. They were built on a plateau in a narrow mountain pass almost impenetrable with lush, tropical growth except for the main dirt road to Mexico City. A steep slope rose from the right of way to the Mexican line, which loomed above it like a jagged scar of dirt cut through dense, entangling jungle. Bristling bronze cannon protruded with a deadly dull shine atop massive ramparts twelve feet high. The Mexican camp was pitched across a wide plateau behind this line at the base of a steep, wooded mountainside. Santa Anna's red-striped headquarters tent was prominent at the rear. Riley felt the position could be impregnable if manned with experienced, committed troops.

While some of the Mexican infantry carried themselves as tough, proud veterans in the tattered remains of once gallant uniforms, many more recruits wore simple, white canvas militia outfits as if nothing more than a fiesta costume. Veteran guards hovered near these "fresh fish" as they dug earthworks and filled sandbags. They eyed the San Patricios nervously as Riley's men passed. It was obvious to Riley and his men that few of these recruits wanted to be soldiers.

At the far end of the line to anchor the right flank sat the four hulking San Patricio guns, already entrenched. Riley felt a

97

warm glow of soldierly pride. "Battalion halt!" he bellowed. "Stack arms! Re-acquaint your sorry selves with our lonely ladies." He pointed toward the guns with a sweeping bow.

Ockter and his Germans immediately took to the big guns, inspecting and embracing them. Morstadt planted the brilliant green flag beside Ockter's gun. The Irish immediately took to the camp ladies beside the road, inspecting and embracing them. Bel greeted Dalton with a warm kiss and long hug.

Riley looked about furtively, then wilted like a weed in the blazing hot, humid heat. He stood alone, as he expected, watching. Then he spotted Luzero across the field in the tent camp, also alone and watching. Their eyes met for a moment. Then she turned away to continue hanging wash.

Moreno walked up to Riley, having seen this exchange. "Tomorrow, fourteen thousand veteran norteamericanos will march up that road," he said, jerking Riley back to reality. "To stop them, we have barely eight thousand soldados, mostly untested." He nodded toward the shaky recruits. Riley could not miss his meaning.

"Stalwart lads, one and all, I am sure," Riley cracked. "But bravery will only get 'em killed if they ain't yet been taught how to shoot properly."

"Miserable conscripts from Mexico City," Moreno sighed, lighting a cigar. "They will do their duty and die only to forestall the inevitable." He nodded toward Luzero across the field. "I have found it best to mend matters of personal strife before such a battle," he observed. "It clears my mind for the fight."

"In a fight, my mind's always clear," Riley snapped. "It's the blessings of peace what get me muddled." They shared a sardonic smile.

For several hours, Anglo and Mexican San Patricios worked together to depress the elevation angle of the big guns. As one detail chopped down saplings and stripped the bark, another installed the rough-hewn logs beneath the rear portion of the gun platforms. The effect was to rake the gun muzzles downward.

"It is perfect!" exclaimed Ockter, having checked the first gun finished. He had compared the downward tilt of the muzzle to the road and field below.

"We'll blast 'em to doll rags 'til they reach the base of this mountain," predicted Riley almost joyfully. Then he felt that old pang of guilt. These would not be the unruly, despicable volunteers they fought at Buena Vista but, instead, regulars and former comrades. His demeanor flagged. "Well, maybe the Fifth Infantry ain't even down there," he hoped aloud.

"It is too late for any to be worrying about that now," Ockter observed primly, "most especially, you."

"So I been told," Riley replied. Ockter at times seemed worse than a nagging woman, he thought, and more like a nagging conscience. He and Dalton had that in common, he mused.

Suddenly, the shrill call of a bugle echoed across the crowded plateau, alive with companies drilling, cavalry squadrons leaving on patrol, and more recruits arriving. Riley and Ockter turned to look. Santa Anna's maroon coach pulled by six handsome mules galloped across the plain with a heavy escort of Tulancingo Cuirassiers, breastplates and helmets shining in the sunlight almost as brightly as their cherry-red trousers. The coach rolled to a dusty stop at Santa Anna's tent, where the bugler stood beside a tall flagpole. A huge Mexican tri-color floated bravely above it all. Riley thought it a gallant if futile gesture.

"Officers call!" yelled Riley. Dalton, Mejia, and Moreno each left their respective work details to start walking toward the headquarters. "Ockter, you're in charge!" Riley yelled. "Try not to get too 'depressed,' " Riley joked as he trotted to catch up with the others. Ockter rolled his eyes and groaned.

Riley saw two Cuirassiers carry a large strongbox from the coach into the headquarters tent. His eyes grew wide. "If that's his new brilliant plan," Riley said, "it may at last be worth something."

"If it indeed is payday," said Dalton with an edge to his voice, "sure and I'll see you put your pesos to a worthy cause." His intent was clearly a warning.

"My blessed retirement?" Riley asked sweetly. If he got his owed money, it seemed to him that the time to make himself "go missing" might be now.

"A dandy wake," Dalton replied. Riley knew that he suspected.

Moreno overheard and turned to look at them suspiciously. He eyed Mejia, who frowned. Could they still not trust these norteamericanos?

Inside Santa Anna's tent, General Micheltorena presided over a meeting of the field officers. An adjutant counted shining gold United States dollars into their palms. Santa Anna watched in agitation. He paced in front of them. Last to be paid were Moreno, Mejia, Dalton, and Riley. The adjutant stepped to Riley. Gold coins clinked into his outstretched palm with a merry jingle, drawing a hostile look from Santa Anna.

"This is the last of my personal wealth, gentlemen," Santa Anna said in English, "the final dollars secured in early negotiations with the norteamericano pirates in Washington." He smiled. "The price of victory can go no higher."

He limped to a large map on an easel. It detailed the fortifications and projected American attack up the main National Highway. A small trail could be seen up the backside of the plateau. It connected with a smaller road to Mexico City behind the mountain.

"As you can see, even if the norteamericanos surround our

front, cutting us off from Mexico City," he pointed to the trail, "we can still save the army by retreating on this hidden path. It dates to the Aztecs. It is known only to us," he warned, "and a few unimportant Indians and bandits."

"When may we pay our men, Excellency?" asked General Vasquez. A stocky aristocrat, he stared hard at Santa Anna with the steely resolve of a tough campaigner. "Veterans have not been paid in six weeks and the recruits, never."

Santa Anna was imbibing opium, barely listening. He was unconcerned. "I pay my officers to restore your faith in me," he said, "and in our ultimate triumph. The soldados will be paid after the battle," he snapped the opium case shut, "when they will regrettably be fewer in number." Vasquez exchanged a look of disgust with Moreno, who merely sighed.

Outside the tent, the glum officers dispersed quietly. Vasquez stood with Moreno, Riley, Dalton, and Mejia, watching. Other officers spoke among themselves in hushed tones as they left, obviously depressed and angry.

" 'Tis a compliment to his grace," Dalton smiled, "to hold his little wake in English and still leave the mourners so touched."

"Were it in Spanish," snapped Riley, "the walls might've growed ears." He nodded at grenadiers posted at intervals around the outside of the tent. "Too many unpaid mourners might've stormed the funeral parlor."

Riley, Dalton, and Mejia saluted the senior officers and walked away toward the fortifications. Vasquez gave an approving look to Moreno. "Your Irish gringos everyday become more Mexicano," Vasquez said in Spanish. "Perhaps they will survive long enough to die proud and not merely paid."

"Some have yet to learn the difference," Moreno said, eyeing Riley.

That night, San Patricios huddled in blankets by their guns

and in the earthworks, waiting, wondering what the morrow would bring. Conahan idly fiddled a lonely, melancholy Celtic tune. Morstadt, Ockter, and others sat lost in thought around him. Several camp women cuddled with a few playing cards by campfire light, simply drinking themselves into a stupor.

Dalton walked the length of the line with Bel beside him. He checked on the men, offered encouragement with a pat on the back here, a cheerful wink there. Bel gave each man a handful of musket cartridges. Dalton lingered at Conahan's group to light his pipe. He also lit a cigareet for Bel while waiting for Conahan to end his sad little dirge.

"And where is little 'Rosarita of Alabama'?" Dalton asked. The group laughed tenuously. Much was on their minds.

"Grandmother," Conahan shrugged. He looked out at hundreds of U.S. campfires flickering like fireflies in the darkly wooded slope across the narrow valley. "This'll be the first time we fight our own," he mused, "the regulars, I mean. The Seventh is out there, somewhere." He looked at Morstadt.

"Maybe we must kill old friends," Morstadt said, "old regiment."

" 'Tain't like they are friends no more," Dalton warned. "And when the blessed regulars get to firing those volleys fast, crisp and clean like a perfect killing machine, that wall of flying lead ain't gonna have no sentiment."

Dalton squeezed Conahan's shoulder and walked on with Bel. He came to Mejia with a squad of his Mexican riflemen playing dice. Mejia was on his knees smiling after rolling a winning combination.

Dalton saw Riley standing alone at the end of the line, looking out across the valley. He looked at Bel.

"Stay here, my sweet," Dalton said in Spanish. He said it slowly, awkwardly, but it communicated. Bel smiled and squeezed him as Mejia looked up, surprised.

"You are learning the greaser, capitan," Mejia said, surprised.

"He has the very private tutor," Bel replied with a sexy smile. Dalton laughed and swatted Bel on her perky rump. She squealed as he walked to Riley.

"Faith I say this only for the sake of Luzero," Dalton said flatly. Riley turned at his approach. "You had best be going to her."

"I'd best just be going," Riley said, jingling the coins in his trouser pocket. "Hate sad endings to any story." Riley felt he had done all he could for his men, given them the best chance for their survival. If they chose to stay, fight, and die in a hopeless cause, that was now their choice. He had made his.

"Sure and the weaver of this tale owes his listeners the grace to finish the story," insisted Dalton. He nodded toward camp. "Go to her. At least keep faith with one of us."

"Faith ain't exactly my strong point," Riley said. "Never seen it pay off."

"Don't dish me up your self-pitying blarney, boy-o," Dalton snarled. "I know what is in the pot by its smell."

"I know what I am," Riley snapped, "a professional." He thrust his palm at Dalton full of the gold dollars. "Got my shilling. I'll stay the fight." He pocketed his money again. "But when the smoke clears, you'll find me among the missing."

"If I find your sorry arse humping over a hill, it is as a deserter I shall be taking you," warned Dalton, his eyes narrowing into slits as if taking aim.

"And when you sight me down the barrel of your greaser musket," Riley smirked, "will you pull th'damn trigger?!" Riley tasted a twinge of revenge as he wielded Dalton's old words in what he hoped was a cutting wound.

Dalton merely grunted, turned, and walked away, as Riley once did. As he strode angrily toward Mejia's group and Bel, Dalton saw Moreno step out of the shadows of the last gun embrasure. Dalton paused to salute. He was unsure if Moreno had heard. Moreno slowly puffed on his cigar. Dalton fired up his pipe. Moreno looked over at Riley, who stood taking a long drink from his flask.

"Our simple pleasures seem more pleasurable the night before the battle," Moreno said with a gentle sweep of his cigar.

"Leastwise smoke don't cloud the mind, Colonel," Dalton replied.

"Neither does truth," Moreno said, a sad smile emerging. "But for each of us, the truth of why we are here can be different. What is clear to one can be cloudy to another."

"And some stay lost in a damn perpetual fog, sir," Dalton said. He nodded in respect to Moreno and walked away.

Riley gazed across the valley. As he stared into the darkness punctured by dots of lights from U.S. campfires, Conahan began playing another tune. It was the romantic, haunting waltz to which Riley and Luzero first danced at the Christmas fandango. Riley found himself idly fingering the gleaming gorget hanging around his neck. He slowly turned away from the U.S. campfires to look over his shoulder at the Mexican camp and focused on Luzero's tent.

"It is a short walk, Major," said Moreno, stepping up on the gun platform beside Riley. "And you have long legs." He smiled and puffed his cigar.

"If I took that little walk," Riley sighed, "wouldn't know what to say to her once I got there." Moreno looked as surprised as Riley by this admission.

"It is not important. Words from a man mean nothing to a woman," he said. "She knows such words are worthless, what you Irish call 'blarney.' " Moreno nodded with a complimentary smile. "You are good with such words."

"Thank you kindly, sir, for such a grandly insulting compliment," Riley said, his smile quickly fading. "Can't trust myself to say what I truly feel. I'm too used to spewing what I think somebody else wants t'hear." Riley could not believe he had uttered those words but somehow he suddenly felt clean, as if he had just washed off the grime and filth of this entire war.

"If my lovely Esperanza were such a short walk away, she would want to hear the language of the heart," Moreno advised.

"I speak that about as well as I do the greaser," blurted Riley, quickly adding, "as Lieutenant Mejia might have put it."

"You see, Major," Moreno said, "the truth of your, well, 'gringo state of mind' betrays how you truly feel about us."

"Meant nothin' by it," Riley said, surprised that he felt a bit ashamed, and even a bit proud of his regret.

"You cannot help it, Major," Moreno said. "All 'gringos' are not norteamericano." Riley stared at Moreno puzzled. "When the British invaded your Ireland," he said, "were they not 'gringos'?"

" 'Bloody lobsterbacks' were the popular phrase," Riley said.

"And when you became a 'bloody lobsterback,' " Moreno continued, making Riley even more uncomfortable, "to the people of Afghanistan, were you not a 'gringo'?"

"And didn't I have the good sense to desert all them bloody gringos?!" chirped Riley, still missing the point.

"You cannot desert a state of mind," said Moreno, smiling patiently. "As God made man in His own image, so the gringo would make the world in his."

Riley leaned heavily against the parapet and took a drink. "There be one too many in th'world the likes of me," he said, "and not enough the likes of her. She makes me feel as if, someday, I might become th'kind of man she deserves."

"Let her know—but without the words," Moreno said.

Riley stared at Moreno as he disappeared into the night with a puff of cigar smoke. He picked up his candle lantern and walked to the Mexican camp.

Inside her tent, Luzero knelt in front of her personal shrine in prayer. Head bowed, hands clasped, she prayed softly in Spanish. On the table was a crucifix, the miniature of the Virgin of Guadalupe, and the portrait of her parents. The small clay tray in which the remnants of Riley's rose once lay was empty but for one lit candle. To her, it represented hope.

Riley stood outside her tent, watching through the narrow slit of the tent flaps. He frowned at sight of the rose tray now bearing just a candle. He shrugged and looked away with a sigh of profound regret.

Luzero finished her prayer, crossed herself, stood, and began to disrobe for bed. She pulled her camisa over her head. At the sudden sound of rustling in front of her tent and scuffling feet, she turned bare breasted.

She stared at the tent flap defiantly with a small dagger pulled from her skirt waistband. She was used to lustful soldiers lurking around her tent with prying eyes.

"Who is there?!" she demanded hotly in Spanish. "Are you a man or a sneaking pervert?! Here! Is this what you want to see?!" She warily approached the tent flap and flung it open. No one was there. But Riley's candle lantern sat on the ground. It threw dim light on a freshly cut red rose lying beside it. Touched, she picked it up and held it to her breasts. She stared across camp at the San Patricio earthworks. She shivered in the cold and went back inside.

The next day dawned with the now familiar, unrelenting, and smoky litany of battle: roaring cannon, crackling musketry, drumbeats, bugle calls, whinnying horses, screams, cries of anguish, and shouted commands. In the San Patricio battery, the muzzle of one cannon belched orange flame and white smoke with a thudding boom. The heavy gun rolled slowly back ten feet from recoil.

The shell burst just in front of a line of sky-blue U.S. regulars, felling six with surprised, wailing cries as the earth seemed to swallow them up. Ockter's German gunners shouted in exultation. They pushed the recoiled gun back into place and reloaded as the other cannons boomed in succession.

Each explosion took a heavy toll among regulars as they emerged from the distant tree line. But the U.S. veterans bowed their heads against oncoming fire as if in a hailstorm. They kept coming in their straight lines of battle as their drums beat a steady attack cadence.

Two batteries of smaller Mexican cannon fired salvos as the U.S. lines came within their shorter range. Shells burst in the air above the Yanks. More fell in bloodied sky-blue clusters. They closed ranks and kept coming.

Three U.S. batteries comprising eighteen field guns in a long line fired gun by gun, from one end to the other in a smoky supporting barrage.

Shells burst above and among Mexican infantry as they hunkered down in the trenches waiting for the enemy to march into musket range. Dozens were killed and wounded. Some raw recruits panicked at the carnage and ran for the rear. Veteran Mexican soldiers turned their muskets on the deserters and shot them down mercilessly. The rest remained, now too afraid to run.

Riley and Moreno stood together beside Riley's gun in the center of the battery, observing effects of their fire to correct range as needed. The smoke of battle swirled heavily and cut visibility. Moreno extended his spyglass and handed it to Riley.

"Identify the units!" Moreno shouted above the din. "It will ease the mind of some and test the will of others!" With a curious look, Riley climbed atop his gun carriage and peered through the smoke.

He could barely see flags and color guards marching near the center of each line as they swept across the field. Fife and drum musicians marched with them and played the familiar "Green Grows the Laurel," which grew louder.

"The First is present!" Riley shouted. A dozen San Patricios cringed at the call of their old unit. "And the Fourth Artillery, as redleg infantry!" He turned to see Ockter straighten to attention, give a slow, respectful U.S. salute, then touch off his cannon with a roar. Riley tossed a sharp nod to approve.

"The Second is comin' on, as well," he added, turning to Dalton, "to roast Captain Dalton's arse!" Rough laughter broke the tension at Dalton's expense. He stood to his gun.

"They shall have to see it first," Dalton growled, loud enough for Riley to hear. "And I for one will not be showing my backside!" Dalton fired his gun.

Moreno took back his spyglass and peered into the smoke. "They have reached the road," he said with a sigh. "We cannot bring our guns to bear on them much longer."

"Range, seventy yards!" Riley yelled. He personally depressed the muzzle on his gun to lower the elevation. Dalton, Ockter, and Conahan did likewise at their guns. Each shouted "Ready!" in turn.

"Coming they are into range!" Mejia yelled at Riley. The eager veteran urged his riflemen onto firing steps in their trench.

"If I get sent up today, by God, John Riley won't be alone no more," Riley vowed. He stepped atop the trail of his gun and shouted at the entire command, "Fire by battalion!"

"*Preparen! Apunten!*" Mejia yelled at his Mexican guard company. They raised, cocked, and aimed their rifles. Mejia awaited final command from Riley.

Dalton, Ockter, and Conahan stepped beside the breeches of their loaded guns, slow matches in hand, also awaiting final command from Riley.

"Colonel darlin'," Riley smiled as he handed his slow match to Moreno, "for possibly the last time, the unit is 'united,' sir.

108

The blessed honor be yours."

"*Fuego!*" Moreno shouted, putting his match to the firing hole on Riley's gun.

All four cannon and the Mexican riflemen unleashed a massive volley that resounded across the valley as one throaty, crackling boom. Their end of the line was awash in a rolling shroud of white smoke.

The entire front rank of an advancing U.S. regiment dissolved amid exploding shells, rifle balls, smoke, flame, dirt, blood, and screams. The second rank recoiled from the slaughter. A few regulars broke ranks and ran for the rear, but were pushed roughly back into line by sergeants and offiers.

"We've stopped them!" shouted Riley. The San Patricios gave a shout as the rest of the Mexican line opened fire with their shorter-range smoothbore muskets. More U.S. troops hesitated under heavy casualties. But Riley frowned as he held the spyglass to his eye. "Damn!" he exclaimed. "Maybe nothin' can stop them." He saw U.S. troops again close ranks, step over the dead, and keep coming. They responded to someone shouting through the thick, swirling smoke. Riley searched with his spylass: animated, agitated, red-headed Colonel Harney emerged through the fog like an enraged apparition, urging onward the battered infantry with the dedication of a demon. His left arm was still in a sling from his wound at Buena Vista. As the guns were being re-loaded, Riley shouted to Dalton. "That arrogant gamecock Harney has rallied them!" he exclaimed.

Dalton looked, cursed, and kissed the breech of his gun. "Send Satan's own back to hell," he snarled, touching off another blast.

Mejia expertly led his riflemen in firing rapid, crisp volleys that cut down more U.S. troops. But they kept coming. Then the soldados began calling for more cartridges. Their volume of fire was slackening.

Luzero, Bel, and other women dashed under fire from camp to the line. They carried canteens and canvas bags bulging with cartridges. The women spread out along the entire line. A few more raw recruits broke and ran for the rear. Women pushed past them tossing looks of disgust. They passed out ammunition and water under intense fire.

Bel and Luzero crouch-walked through the dead and dying in Mejia's infantry trench. Riley turned and watched them fill cartridge boxes from behind each soldier.

As Luzero knelt to hold one wounded rifleman in her arms, giving water, Riley could see that she was wearing his rose in her hair! He felt as if his heart just leaped into his throat, throbbing like a bass drum and preventing the shout of joy he wanted to unleash. Just as her eyes met Riley's, a shell exploded behind the trench. It killed the man in her arms and hid Luzero and Bel in a cloud of smoke and debris.

"No!" Riley roared; his face twisted in horror. He started to leave his gun and run down into the trench, cloudy with smoke and dust. Moreno grabbed him and spun him around.

"You will stay!" Moreno snapped. "It is your duty!"

"All that matters to me is in that trench!" Riley spat back.

Then both women emerged coughing from the cloud of white smoke, their white camisas drenched in blood and brains from the dead soldado. Moreno and Riley saw they were unhurt. Riley silently crossed himself at the sight of Luzero. She saw this act of thanks and looked touched. Then Bel shoved her to the ground when another shell exploded nearby.

"Send 'em back where it's safe!" Riley urged.

"They will be safe nowhere unless all do their duty right here!" Moreno insisted. Moreno's eyes narrowed. Riley squirmed in his gaze.

Ammunition replenished, the Mexican line fired heavier volleys. The women made their way back toward camp. Riley saw

Luzero and Bel among them and looked relieved, giving a nod to anxious Dalton.

U.S. troops reached the base of the slope but then stalled. They huddled together under intense Mexican small arms fire. The rank and file formations dissolved among piles of bodies. The flags of three U.S. regiments fluttered above the mass of struggling, confused men. Harney dismounted and walked among them, trying to regain control.

Mexican soldados stood and leaned over the breastworks to shoot down the slope at the groups of Yanks. Grenadiers of the Supreme Power in their bearskin shakos lit fuses on hand grenades and hurled them down the slope. They burst among U.S. troops with bloody effect. Shouts of "Viva!" cheered their bravery. But this heroism exposed the Mexicans to fire from the Americans. U.S. volleys blew grenadiers off the ramparts, followed by Yank shouts of "Huzzah!"

Moreno stood beside Riley and studied the U.S. troops. He was almost hit by musket fire, dirt spitting up around him from a volley. But he did not flinch. "If they stay where they are our infantry will kill them all," he said. "If they fall back, our cannon will again be able to hit them. To survive, they must come up."

"Take arms!" Riley bellowed. The San Patricios dropped their now useless cannon implements and grabbed their muskets. Riley and Dalton reached for muskets from the same stack of arms.

"Ain't never had much use for these wrist breakers," Riley said, sheathing his officer sword.

"Officer blades are for leading the way," said Dalton, taking his musket. " 'Tis plain we have both lost ours."

Riley and Dalton each gave a slight nod in pleased surprise, glad to find something on which to agree. Riley peered over the slope just as Conahan trotted up, breathless, looking happy as a loon.

"Faith my conscience rests easier!" Conahan panted. "The Seventh ain't nowhere below!"

"Nor the Fifth," noted Riley, studying the U.S. troops on the slope. Riley frowned suspiciously as Dalton walked up to peer over the breastwork. " 'Tain't likely they'll be breaking," worried Riley. He wondered why two of the very best U.S. veteran regiments were not taking part in this massive assault.

"They must be rallying down below, with them others," Dalton said. "We just can't see them from here."

Riley exposed himself, standing and leaning over the breastworks. At the base of the slope, clusters of U.S. infantry gathered and knelt by each regimental flag. As sergeants shouted orders, the men huddled by the banners, loading and priming their muskets. They looked calm, grim, and determined even as more fell to Mexican fire. "What are they waitin' for?!" Riley groused. "Let's get it over with!"

Moreno and Dalton frowned suspiciously, each suspecting something, neither knowing what it might be. Riley felt as if he had heard one footfall from a house intruder, and was waiting for the next.

The precipitous, familiar thunder of drums beating an incessant attack cadence intruded, mingling with repeated shouts of "Huzzah!" But it was coming from behind the Mexican fortifications! Riley and the rest whirled around to see lines of U.S. infantry charge out of the thick woods behind the Mexican camp at the base of the wooded mountain. The flags of the Seventh and Fifth Infantry flew high above the rippling sky-blue waves of troops shimmering with ribbons of gleaming steel bayonets.

"That hidden trail ain't hid no more!" Riley shouted at

Moreno, who pulled his pistol. "Expecting a little close work, Colonel?!"

"Some must be held to their duty," Moreno said, staring hard.

Riley grabbed Moreno's spyglass to take a closer look. He could see Major Rains, the southern officer who dined with Merrill the day he deserted. Rains rode a prancing charger near the color guard.

"Major Rains is leading your blessed Seventh, Conahan!" Riley yelled above the roar. "They're comin' on in grand style!"

"Huzzah! For th' Seventh!" shouted Conahan gleefully. Then he caught himself and looked at his dumbstruck comrades sheepishly. "Sorry," he shrugged. "Can lose myself in the old glory."

Then Riley saw Captain Merrill, leading his own Company K behind mounted Colonel McIntosh, who had turned down his promotion. "All the banshees of my personal hell flying right at me!" he muttered, lowering the spyglass.

Dalton saw and stepped up to Riley and Conahan, both staring transfixed. "Faith I am touched," Dalton said. "But this ain't no time for a blessed reunion! Hadn't we best turn the guns!" They shouted orders and two crews struggled to turn their guns in the embrasures and face the new threat.

At the base of the slope, the huddled U.S. troops gave a shout at the sound of the expected surprise attack. Harney pointed his sword toward the top.

"Charge 'em to hell, boys!" he roared. At the sight of the San Patricio flag fluttering above, he bellowed, "Rip down that damn traitor rag!"

They began to scramble up the slope like ants formed into inverted vees following their regimental flags at the apex.

In the Mexican lines, confusion was rampant. The raw recruits, fully half the army, threw down their weapons and ran for their lives, trampling officers and sergeants who tried to stop them.

The advancing lines of the Fifth and Seventh Infantry fired rapid volleys into the panicked Mexican recruits, dropping them by the score.

Veteran Mexican units formed ranks bravely and fired delaying volleys in return as the U.S. troops swept into the Mexican camp. The women streamed away from the tents just in front of the surging U.S. troops. Some of the women crossed the fire zone of the Americans and were shot down in the exchange of volleys.

Mounted Curaissiers quickly wheeled into line and fired a volley with their musketoons into the advancing Fifth Infantry, buying time for the mules to be harnessed to Santa Anna's coach.

"Fire by company!" Merrill commanded, seeing the coach. "Ready, aim, fire!" he yelled, gesturing with his sword. Company K's eighty muskets fired a crisp volley with a crackling boom just as the coach began to roll. One side was shredded into flying splinters; the braying mules killed. The Curaissiers wheeled about and trotted away.

Santa Anna and his staff commanded the battle line from a small knoll on the plateau. They saw the coach destroyed and U.S. troops charging through the camp. They saw more U.S. troops streaming over the rim of the plateau and into the trenches. Deciding all was lost, Santa Anna turned his horse and left the battle at a gallop. His hapless staff followed.

"Leave the guns," Moreno quietly commanded, ashamed of Santa Anna's flight. "Our army is destroyed. If we do not retire now, we will be cut off."

"And captured," Riley added grimly. "Leave the guns and fall back!" he bellowed, pointing the way with his upraised musket. At least, he felt, he could save as many of his men as possible by leading them away right now.

Mejia ordered his Mexican riflemen out of the trench and into line. They fired a volley, then retired only to turn and fire again, buying time for the others.

"I cannot leave my guns!" wailed Ockter, agonizing. He planted himself beside his gun and the flag, waiting with musket in one hand, slow match in the other, ready for the horde of Yanks storming up the slope.

Ockter touched off his cannon in the face of the first U.S. squad over the top. They disintegrated into a pink cloud of gore amid agonized wails.

Morstadt fired his musket, taking down a Yank charging Ockter, who now was busy in a bayonet fight with two others. Morstadt let loose a blood curdling roar and charged into another, impaling and lifting him with the bayonet. The other German gunners followed and hit the oncoming Yanks with brutal force in a hand-to-hand melee. They held their own long enough for Morstadt to pick up Ockter under one mighty arm like a sack of grain and heft him out of the trench. He swung his musket, knocking down another Yank, grabbed the green banner, and carried it back to the surviving San Patricios, booting reluctant Ockter to move along. "I cannot be leaving flag or you!" he yelled.

The San Patricios trotted along the road behind a trench filled with desperately struggling men. General Vasquez roared like an enraged lion on the ramparts. He screamed curses in Spanish at the Americans storming up and at the Mexicans running away. Those who fought beside him were inspired to stay by his bravery.

In hand-to-hand struggles with swarming Yanks, Vasquez and his men bought time for the San Patricios and other Mexican units to scramble out of the trenches and join the retreat, fast becoming a rout.

Moreno led the way at the front of the strung-out column. He pointed to a mass of refugees just ahead. Riley, Dalton, and Conahan were at the rear.

They saw Vasquez and his brave band suddenly overwhelmed. Vasquez thrust his sword into a Yank to the hilt but was then cut down by a volley fired at point blank range.

Riley, Dalton and Conahan paused to fire a parting shot at the squad that killed him. They dropped three and started to reload.

"Leastwise he went down fighting!" exclaimed Dalton, tearing open a cartridge with his teeth.

"Not dangling from a damn rope!" added Conahan, shoving a ball down his barrel with a ramrod.

Riley loaded his musket and started trotting back to join the mass exodus. Dalton and Conahan looked fatalistic. Conahan shrugged, Dalton nodded. They turned in the other direction to rejoin the lost fight in the trenches.

"Hold!" Riley yelled. He ran back to bar their path with his musket. "You'll not be killing yourselves on my watch!"

"No friend of mine lets another die in my place!" said Dalton, his pipe fuming.

Mejia's ever thinning rear guard had backed into them, firing a weak volley. As the remaining few stalwarts re-loaded, Mejia correctly surmised the situation. He stepped beside Riley with his sword drawn.

"Do not be going back!" Mejia warned.

"I'll not be turnin' tail!" Conahan insisted. "The jig is up. May as well end this ball on a note o'grace!"

"They dying for us to be living!" Mejia explained in halting English. He struggled to find the right words in his new second language. "By dying, how you say, you shaming their sacrifice. I am not letting you!"

Dalton and Conahan paused to reconsider. Musket balls

whizzed overhead and spat up dirt all around them. Riley looked and saw the sky-blue wave rolling toward them across the plateau after cresting through camp. On the other side, more sky blue swelled over the breastworks. Soon this irresistible tide would sweep them away.

"Put your feet to their duty, lads!" Riley urged. He turned and fired his musket in what seemed futility. "Ain't ending my days a dead greaser patriot!"

"For once you are right," Dalton mumbled. "Sure and they deserve better than the likes of you."

They fell in with Mejia's company and tried to maintain an orderly, dignified retreat. But the last Mexican troops fighting a delaying action were overwhelmed, killed, and captured. Survivors broke into a full speed foot race and ran for their lives. Riley's band was caught up in the rush and swept off the field.

They disappeared into a motley flow of broken humanity surging toward the distant mountains in the west, behind which lay Mexico City. The sun hung low. The broken army looked like a legion of phantoms filtering through a mournful, glowing cloud of dust and smoke.

Cheering U.S. troops flooded across the plateau in absolute victory. Throngs of dejected Mexican prisoners were herded through their own camp even as it was ransacked for souvenirs by jubilant Yanks. More than a few U.S. infantrymen removed swords, daggers, and engraved belt buckles from fallen Mexican officers. Captured Mexican flags, stands of muskets, and dozens of artillery pieces were gathered into a large munitions park in the center of the plain.

One gleeful squad emerged from Santa Anna's tent laughing and joking. Each man wore a different article of the general's finery. One sported a cocked hat with plumes; another, the blue cape with silver trim worn at Jalapa. A third carried an engraved silver chamber pot. The man wearing the cocked hat carried a walnut box. He opened it and discovered one of Santa Anna's spare wooden legs. He strapped it onto his knee, held back the lower part of his leg and hobbled about in a rude, comical imitation. The third ransacker promptly knocked off his cocked hat and replaced it with the silver chamber pot.

"Lucky for you, soldier, it is empty," said a firm, resonant voice. The threesome turned and snapped to attention with looks of pure terror. It made them look even more laughable.

Commanding General Winfield Scott sat staring down at them from astride his huge black horse. As usual, he was in perfect full-dress uniform with its yellow-plumed fore-and-aft hat. With him was young Captain Robert E. Lee, attired immaculately in the more somber dark-blue field uniform of an engineer, trimmed in black.

"Gentlemen, General Scott has orders against foraging," Lee declared, his deep voice mildly scolding in a soft Southern accent. He looked amused.

" 'Tain't 'foraging,' sir," ventured the man wearing the chamber pot in a thick Irish accent. He saluted and looked ludicrous. Scott and Lee suppressed a laugh. "Private Roger Hogan, Company I, Fourth Infantry, sir, and his mates was merely taking inventory of your captured valuables."

"Then you are relieved, Private," commanded Lee with authority. "Put down the valuables."

The threesome began taking off the clothing and dropping it. Two more ransackers emerged from the tent carrying Santa Anna's strongbox and stopped short at seeing Lee and Scott. One, a corporal, rolled his eyes knowingly.

"Open it, Corporal," commanded Scott, "and I use that rank in the most temporary sense."

The twosome put down the heavy box and the corporal opened it, revealing thousands of shining U.S. gold dollars.

Scott grunted in surprise while Lee straightened in the saddle, always struggling to control emotions.

"The corporal and private were merely securing it, General," the corporal asserted in a German accent. "Why, there are thieves around here!" Lee turned in his saddle, failing to hide a smile. He saw Captain Merrill and a squad marching past herding a flock of hapless Mexican prisoners.

"Captain," Lee called, halting Merrill. "For General Scott, please safeguard these valuables and their 'liberators.' " Merrill and four privates surrounded both booty and ransackers as Colonel Harney rode up with a small escort of Dragoons. Harney glared at the souvenir hunters.

"Corporal Johann Rose, Company F, Sixth Infantry," offered the corporal in a search for mercy. "The corporal has always soldiered well, sir."

"And you shall again," said Scott gently, "if you want to regain the stripes you just lost." He nodded at Merrill, who started marching his group away.

"Hold, Captain," commanded Harney. Merrill stopped. Harney saluted Scott and nodded at Lee's salute. "Ten lashes are prescribed punishment for theft, sir, at an officer's discretion," he urged respectfully. "You cannot command immigrant rabble like this without the lash, sir."

Merrill saw indignant looks cross the faces of the ransackers. Rose and Hogan were seething. They scowled at Harney. Merrill sidled up to Rose as Harney walked his horse to Scott and Lee.

"Be a good soldier, Corporal," Merrill whispered urgently, "and mind your tongue." The corporal quickly sized up Merrill as a fair-minded officer.

"They treat us like we were the enemy, sir," he whispered.

"Not all, Corporal," whispered Merrill, "not all."

"Colonel Harney, today you handled infantry superbly, sir,"

Scott said, adding with a twinkle, "for a horse soldier." Lee held his right hand up to his face quickly, hiding a smile while pretending to cough. "You do not, I trust, lash the horses in your regiment of Dragoons."

"No, sir!" Harney protested, shocked at the thought. "Just the men, sir."

"I shall make this army less bestial, Colonel," Scott explained firmly. "Less lash, more leniency."

Merrill looked up at Scott with reverential respect. When Scott nodded at him, he gave a sword salute and put the men in motion.

"You see, Corporal?" Merrill whispered. "With time, things can improve."

"Yes, sir, the corporal sees," Rose said. "The trick is surviving the wait."

"I am sure, soldier, that things are worse on the other side," Merrill said. Remembering Riley, Merrill recognized the familiar, restless look in the corporal's eye. He had seen Hogan agree with a smirk. Rose and Hogan got Merrill's meaning and marched on in silent dismay.

Lee eyed Scott in admiration. His mentor tempered justice with mercy, a trait Lee aspired to emulate, should ever he obtain the chance.

Scott turned his horse to view the field, where tiny bits of paper, torn from cartridges, flitted on a breeze across the dead like macabre confetti. American medical staff treated wounded where they lay. Troops arranged Mexican and American corpses in rows for mass burial in separate pits already being dug. Hundreds of Mexican prisoners huddled in a holding area. To Scott, it was only victory that made the ugliness of war palatable. Scott knew Lee felt the same.

"Colonel Harney, I should present the senior officer of my engineer staff, Captain Robert E. Lee," Scott said. They exchanged nods. "Captain Lee scouted and secured the mountain trail used in our surprise rear attack."

"My compliments, sir," said Harney, impressed.

"Providence provides," said Lee, sincerely humble. "Some Mexican guides showed us a hidden path."

"That's what you get," groused Harney, "when you demand patriotism at the point of a bayonet—traitors and more than three thousand prisoners." Harney gestured contemptuously toward the holding area where captured Mexicans milled about.

"This victory is an embarrassment," Scott declared. "We haven't even the means to feed them, to secure them. I have no choice but to parole them."

"Greasers don't know what 'parole' means, sir," Harney protested. "After the Monterey parole, we fought the same soldiers again at Buena Vista."

"What would you have me do, Colonel? Shoot them?" Scott said in mild rebuke. "It would be more merciful than starvation." He eyed the open strongbox. "Santa Anna will find it hard to inspire patriotism with no payroll. Disarm them and let them go."

Harney grit his teeth in disappointment. He saluted, wheeled about, and rode away with his escort. They trotted past two medical stewards carrying the corpse of a Mexican teenage girl. They carefully laid her beside a row of dead Mexican soldiers and other soldaderas. Scott and Lee watched in silence.

"I cannot understand why they keep fighting," Scott said, welling with emotion. "It is such a futile, tragic waste."

"Their cause is lost, sir," agreed Lee. "Perhaps their honor lies in fighting beyond hope of victory, in duty faithfully performed."

"Our cause can only be shamed by continuing this slaughter," said Scott. "We must secure another secret path, Captain," he said, "one that stops the killing. It must lead them with honor

121

intact to peace." Scott squinted to stare again across the battlefield. He idly wondered if this is how Cortez felt as he followed the defeated Aztec warriors up this same road toward their ancient citadel. Recalling his secret meeting with Polk in what seemed ages ago, Scott felt a soldier's jubilation at victory but tempered now with a sense of loss and guilt. The distant road crowded with refugees looked to him like a black snake crawling through a dust swirl toward Mexico City. "Captain Lee, please take down this message," he decided. "Address it to 'His Excellency, General Santa Anna.' "

An hour later, Santa Anna sat astride his black stallion atop a small hill on the distant road seen earlier by Scott. Flowing around the base of the hill on that road was a seemingly endless stream of broken soldados and the shattered remnants of his army. Walking wounded held filthy bandannas to bloody injuries. Oxcarts carried others too severely hurt to walk. Women of all ages bore cast-iron cooking pots, utensils, blankets, and baskets on their backs like beasts of burden.

Officers and enlisted men, most without weapons, walked aimlessly in dazed, confused, and informal groups. Cavalry galloped beside the choked road and trampled any who strayed into their path. Teamsters cracked whips and spewed profanity at mules and oxen moving too slowly. Their curses joined a creaking, moaning din of misery rising to the seemingly deaf ears of Santa Anna.

He stared above it all through a spyglass focused back on his captured camp. Ten yards behind him were the disheveled remains of his staff. General Micheltorena stood hatless, his uniform coat ripped and hanging unbuttoned. He beckoned to various high ranking officers passing on the road to join them.

Moreno was ambling on foot beside a cart full of wounded when Micheltorena caught his eye. No other San Patricios were in sight. He paused to light a cigar and then climbed the hill.

Moreno passed through a gauntlet of Hussars, posted in a sentry line between the routed army and the officers. The nervous Hussars had their musketoons at the ready. They traded threatening looks with passing soldiers. The defeated men glared up at imperial Santa Anna, who apparently now had more to fear from his own people than the U.S. army.

But Santa Anna remained oblivious. General Micheltorena showed Moreno a crumpled note written in English as he ushered him forward urgently.

"They want him to persuade our government to negotiate!" said Micheltorena. Moreno looked stunned. "The norteamericanos want peace!" Micheltorena's hopeful enthusiasm failed to excite Moreno.

"It is of no matter," he replied warily, "unless Santa Anna wants peace."

As Moreno strode to Santa Anna, he straightened his uniform. Arriving, he snapped to attention. The general stared down at him.

"Colonel Moreno," Santa Anna said, sounding weary. "Speak English, so none can comprehend and spread rumors." Moreno nodded. "Where is Major Riley and your excellent regiment?"

"Excellency, I do not know where my horse is, let alone my regiment," Moreno confessed, choking back emotions. "Perhaps destroyed."

"I do not know where my army is!" Santa Anna snapped, pointing in contempt at the streaming survivors. "All is not lost, though," he continued, straightening in the saddle, "unless we lose our self control."

His words sounded brittle, as if he himself might shatter. He was sweating profusely and his hand trembled as he wiped his forehead with a handkerchief. Santa Anna nodded toward the captured camp. "They ask me to barter peace for them."

"We have nothing left with which to fight them," said Moreno.

Santa Anna offered an enigmatic smile. "Time is our only ally," he replied. "Their government is under pressure to end an 'unpopular' war." Santa Anna looked back at the other officers, who remained out of earshot. "I want you to personally deliver my reply in spoken English, nothing written." Moreno felt honored but suspicious.

"I am gratified by your trust, Excellency," Moreno said.

"I trust no one," Santa Anna replied icily. "But I admire your discretion, Colonel, and your ability to communicate with the 'gringo mentality.' " Moreno bowed at the compliment. "Tell General Scott I will be pleased to urge our government to negotiate, if the norteamericanos reward me for my talent to persuade."

Moreno barely hid his outrage: Santa Anna again wanted money. "It has been my experience," said Moreno carefully, "that the 'gringo mentality' detests bribery." Santa Anna frowned but Moreno forged ahead. "They vilify Riley and the rest. And what did they do but take what amounted to a bribe from us?"

"Yes, Colonel, but Riley's band became notorious," said Santa Anna. "This must remain secret." Moreno nodded. "Tell them I want ten thousand dollars immediately and one million more, once a treaty is in place."

"As you request, Excellency," said Moreno tight lipped, barely containing his anger. But he felt military respect must supercede his personal outrage.

Santa Anna perceived Moreno's discomfort and looked at him sympathetically. "You must be careful not to confuse 'honor' with 'practicality,' Colonel," he said. "They just captured six thousand dollars of my money. I want it back. And I want more, for my services, so I could then pay what I owe our soldados."

"That would be an honorable thing to do, Excellency," said

Moreno, sincerely surprised. "At least, they could go home with some small shred of dignity." Moreno felt his anger quickly subside, replaced by a sense of purpose.

"They shall get exactly what they deserve, Colonel," said Santa Anna, turning his horse. "Nothing less will do." He spurred his horse and galloped past the staff and guards, who scrambled to mount and follow him down the hill. At the bottom, a limping soldado crossed his path, forcing him to rein back his horse. "Out of my way, coward!" Santa Anna screamed. He whipped the man with his riding crop, the soldado covering his head and staggering out of the way. "Cowards!" Santa Anna screamed at other stunned soldiers. "You should all die for my shame!" He pushed his horse through and galloped toward Mexico City.

A few miles away, Riley ambled alone through the deserted streets of Jalapa with his musket in one hand, his flask in the other. Broken pottery, pieces of clothing, smashed furniture, and cast off military gear littered the street. No one was in sight. He paused beneath the torn welcoming banner from the parade only days before. He raised the flask in a toast.

"Viva Battalion of Saint Patrick," he said. Riley took a healthy swig. "Rest in peace." He walked on with a little laugh. He tried to fight an overwhelming sense of self pity but decided it was more gratifying just to wallow in it. Somehow, it felt good.

He rounded the corner into the plaza and saw Dalton, seated alone on the ground. His distinctive sombrero was pulled low over his eyes, his back against the fountain. He was blowing smoke rings. His musket rested across his lap. At the sound of Riley's approach, he cocked his musket instantly and looked. Then he relaxed and eased off the hammer. Riley plopped down beside him. Both were filthy with dust and black powder grime. They looked exhausted.

"Harney's Dragoons may come back," said Riley, taking

another swig. He handed the flask to Dalton.

"Let them. I ain't moving," Dalton said, drinking. "I am getting too damn old for this line of work."

"Where are the lads?" asked Riley.

"Everywhere," shrugged Dalton. "Somewhere, I suppose. Probably on a road going nowhere."

"Just come from there," Riley said. " 'Tain't worth the damn trip." Dalton sat up and looked at Riley.

"When we got split up by the mob," he said, "I was sure t'was the last I'd see of you. And I'm blessed if I didn't say good riddance."

"Without no army, there ain't nothin' left to desert," Riley replied. "Where's the fun in that?" Dalton and Riley shared a weary little laugh. Riley eased back against the fountain. He idly caressed the gorget around his neck.

"Don't fret," Dalton said. "She is still warmer than that brass trinket." Riley bolted upright. "She and Bel both, I seen them make it to the road."

"During the fight when I thought she'd gone up," Riley said, sounding relieved, "my heart stuck in my throat. I couldn't speak."

"And for that we are all eternally in her debt," Dalton said.

"Took an oath then and there," Riley continued. "If ever I saw her again, I'd tell her plain how I feel."

"You at last sorted it all out from the blarney, have you?" Dalton scoffed.

"Learnt to ask questions afore telling myself lies," Riley said. "What would I be worth without her?"

"Three hundred acres," muttered Dalton. Riley managed a tight little smile. "Now that it don't matter no more, what with there being no more army," Dalton said, "would you have gone over the hill again?"

Riley stared at him with a gleam in his eye. "And if I had and you'd seen," Riley countered, "would you have pulled the trigger?"

Dalton merely grinned, blew a smoke ring, and rolled his eyes. Before Riley could respond, scuffling feet and clanging accouterments shattered the quiet. Riley and Dalton sprang to their feet. They crouched behind the fountain with muskets cocked and ready, expecting to see American troops.

Instead, Mejia and six survivors of his company pushed a terrified Mexican prisoner into the square. He wore leather trousers and leggings, a parrot-green vaquero jacket with red cuffs, a black sombrero with a red silk scarf tied as a hatband, and the white buff saber belt of the U.S. Dragoons. His hands were tied behind him and his bearded face was matted with blood from a beating.

" 'Tain't no greaser uniform," observed Riley.

"Must be a recruit," joked Dalton.

The prisoner stumbled when pushed into the square and fell to his knees. Mejia kicked him hard in the ribs. The man doubled over in agony.

"Mercy, please, in the name of our Blessed Virgin of Guadalupe!" he begged in Spanish.

"You are not fit to speak her name, you son of a whore!" Mejia yelled. "The best part of you dribbled down your mother's legs!" Mejia spat at him and nodded at two of his men. They drug him whimpering toward the fountain.

Riley and Dalton stood and stepped out from behind. Mejia immediately snapped to attention. His squad presented arms as Riley and Dalton walked to them, each returning a salute. The hapless prisoner took hope when he saw the two Anglos.

"Help me, please!" he pleaded in Spanish. "I have done no more than you!"

"What's he saying?" Riley asked Dalton, who shook his head.

"I only know bedroom greaser," Dalton said cockily.

127

"This piece of pig shit his country is betraying," explained Mejia.

"Ah, a deserter," crooned Riley, looking at Dalton. "Can't be all that bad."

Mejia shook his head. A curious smile crossed his lips. "He is a bandit," Mejia explained, "who is joining the other side. The gringos have a company of them." He ripped off the man's sombrero and removed the silk scarf. "The green coat, the red scarf, is being their uniform." He handed the scarf to a sergeant, who shoved the man in front of the fountain and blindfolded him with it.

Riley and Dalton looked stunned. They stared hard at the man as he stood shivering in fear, pitifully alone. The six riflemen formed a line fifteen feet in front of him. Riley and Dalton traded grim, knowing looks of foreboding. Sooner or later, they felt that they could be standing in his shoes.

"Can't just kill him," said Riley. He felt as if someone had just traipsed across his own grave.

"You still are not speaking the greaser, are you, Major?" asked Mejia. He turned to his squad. *"Preparen!"* he shouted. The men brought their rifles up and cocked the hammers.

"I have a family!" the man pleaded in Spanish. "I joined for gringo gold to feed them!" Riley stared at Mejia for a translation. Mejia just shrugged.

"He is a bandit with no soul," he explained. "He says he did it for the money." Mejia turned to his squad. *"Apunten!"* he said, and they aimed.

"Faith he's nothing but another 'professional,' " chided Dalton, firing his pipe. "Sure and he owes his allegiance only to the shilling in his palm." Dalton looked accusingly at Riley, who felt curiously embarrassed by his old words.

"Don't recall seeing that uniform in the fight," Riley said, averting Dalton's piercing glare. The professionalism he once took such pride in had lost its sheen. But Riley would never admit that to Dalton.

"They do not have the courage for manly fighting," replied Mejia scornfully. "They only sneaking as spies, scouts, and guides." He looked at the man and shouted in Spanish, "May your flesh burn in hell for murdering your country!" Mejia raised his arm, preparing to fire.

"In the name of the Blessed Virgin," the man pleaded in Spanish, "please forgive me!"

"Even I understood that," snapped Riley. "Ain't we had enough killin' for one day?!"

Mejia stared at Riley as if he were an idiot. "His band showed the gringos our hidden mountain trail!" he exclaimed.

Riley's eyes opened wide. He suddenly realized that this man's mercenary treason had lost the war for Mexico, had lost the dream for Riley and his men, and possibly all their lives. Mejia started to give the command but Riley grabbed his upraised arm, stopping him. Riley's bright-blue eyes hardened into their battlehue of cold, blued steel.

"*Fuego!*" Riley bellowed. The squad fired a volley that blasted the man backward and into the fountain. His blood rapidly stained the water red as his upper body floated, legs dangling lifeless over the side.

"I'm blessed if your grasp of the greaser ain't becoming purely elegant," said Dalton soberly. Glaring at him, Riley suppressed a rising urge to vomit. He waved the group forward, leading them out of the square and toward Mexico City.

CHAPTER 5
MEXICO CITY
APRIL 23, 1847

It seemed to Riley that Mexico City shimmered in the heat like a mirage on a hot, humid coastal island, something tangible but unattainable. He had seen such visions from aboard ship on his way to Afghanistan as a young British soldier. He had hoped this adventure would end better. The elegant, compact complex of Spanish Colonial architecture was hemmed on three sides by shallow blue lakes and a rugged range of mountains on the fourth. The towering, snow capped summit of Popocatepetl volcano loomed above it all from forty miles away. Narrow causeways with elevated roads and aqueducts crossed the lakes. Hundreds of scurrying refugees swarmed like ants along them toward perceived safety in the city of the Aztecs. Riley feared that it too would prove to be just another mirage: it was evident just ahead.

Pandemonium reigned at the causeway gate. Civilian and military refugees surged toward the open portal beside an elevated Spanish aqueduct supported by masonry buttresses. Some weary travelers rested beneath a roadside grove of trees that shaded a wading pool and fountain fed by the aqueduct. The arched gateway, ornate with eighteenth-century Spanish volutes, a large cartouche, and urn shaped finials, was congested with soldiers rolling cannon into place and building barricades. The result was a noisy traffic jam as refugees pushed past.

Riley and Dalton arrived on the scene dangling their weary legs off the back of an oxcart piled high with tobacco and clay jugs of aguardiente. Each with several days' growth of beard, their faces and hands were black with grime and dust. The civilian teamster was too busy cursing in Spanish and cracking his whip to notice Dalton casually stuff his jacket with tobacco as Riley refilled his flask. They looked amused by the bedlam rising from Spanish yells and oaths traded among refugees trying to enter the city and soldiers trying to defend it.

"If nothing else, Ireland and Mexico share the gift of eloquent profanity," joked Riley. He took a swig from his flask just as something caught Dalton's eye by the grove of trees.

"Profanity and the magic!" Dalton declared jubilantly, pointing.

Beneath the branches, Bel stood with one shapely leg resting on a side of the fountain as she washed off the dust and battle grime. She was smoking a cigareet. Seated on the ground with her back against the tree was Luzero, her head bowed and resting in her hands, exhausted. Riley could not see her face, but she still wore his rose in her hair.

Riley and Dalton hopped off the cart, slinging their muskets. Dalton started toward the grove but Riley hesitated.

"Ain't you coming?!" Dalton urged.

"Can't recall a word of what I'd planned to say," Riley said, worried. He felt his heart pounding like a blacksmith's hammer.

"Praise be," Dalton grumbled, lighting his pipe. "Maybe now you can cut to the heart of the matter." He pulled Riley along with him toward the fountain.

"I can always find work at a cantina," Bel said idly to Luzero. She rinsed off her other leg. "You can stay with me in a room there, until you find something."

Luzero looked up to reply but was stunned silent to see Riley standing in front of her, staring. He managed a slow, apologetic, fragile smile that seemed to her to ask an unspoken question. Luzero mustered a smile through tears. Riley helped her up and embraced her so tightly she thought she could not breathe.

Dalton had crept up behind Bel and swept her off her feet and into his arms, twirling her around. "Buenos dios mi darlin'!" Dalton shouted.

"Alive you are!" Bel squealed in delight just before he tossed her into the fountain. Dalton and Riley roared with laughter as she staggered dripping to her feet. Bel's shapely figure showed in exquisite detail through her clinging wet cotton clothing. The taut nipples of her breasts pushed against her semi-transparent cotton camisa. Her doused cigareet hung bent in her mouth.

"You clumsy donkey!" she screamed. "See how wet I am!"

"Indeed," Dalton leered. "And I've spoilt your smoke entirely. So, I'd best help you out of them wet things." His twinkling eyes asked a question. She smiled at his notion as he gave her a hand out of the fountain.

Riley still felt at a loss for words, to his own astonishment. Luzero's eyes were red from crying; her hair wet, from washing dust off in the fountain. Tears traced down her cheeks. He felt embarrassed as an unfamiliar tear traced down his own. Riley produced a bandanna and began wiping her face gently.

"All my things, family pictures, clothes . . ." Luzero barely managed, welling with emotion. "I have lost everything," she choked out, her eyes searching his for an answer to her own unasked question.

Riley lifted her chin with one hand and slowly pulled the rose from her hair with the other. He held it in front of her face. "You found something what I'd lost," he said softly. She stood considering his eyes with a slight smile. "You may not be wanting it no more," he struggled. "After all, 'tis gettin' a bit wilted with age."

"Growing older but wiser?" Luzero teased, encircling him

with her arms and burrowing her head into his chest. His brawny arms enfolded her in a gentle bear hug. He shrugged a laugh as she squeezed him tightly and pulled away to look laughingly into his eyes. "Thankfully, you merely look like you could be somebody else's father."

Riley looked aghast before bursting into laughter with her. But the roar of a musket volley jerked their heads toward the road.

Surviving San Patricios and Mexican guards stood astride the causeway, pointing their smoking weapons into the air. Riley was shocked at how few were left, less than forty, barely enough for a company. But he was relieved to see his most familiar faces.

"*Retiren!*" shouted Mejia and both Anglo and Mexican troops lowered weapons from shoulder to chest level. Morstadt, Conahan, and Ockter stood together at one side. Moreno, mounted again, walked his horse to the front of the formation as a hush fell on the jostling crowd.

Riley and Dalton led Luzero and Bel to the roadside. Moreno saw them and nodded at their salute. Riley was gratified to see that he looked pleased, and perhaps a bit surprised.

"Lieutenant Mejia misplaced us back a ways, sir," opined Dalton. "It gladdens my heart to see his smiling face once again."

"Reporting for duty, Colonel darlin'," Riley said with a reassuring nod. "Any report you heard 'bout my having gone missing must surely be treacherous Yank blarney." Moreno almost smiled but quickly recovered his control to focus on the task at hand.

"Brave citizens of Mexico City," Moreno bellowed in Spanish, "there is no need for panic. His excellency, General Santa Anna, is pleased to announce an armistice."

Titters and murmurs of excitement ran through the crowd as

all exchanged hopeful looks. Riley and Dalton looked at Luzero urgently for translation, but she could not believe her ears. She waved them off impatiently to let Moreno finish.

"There shall be no further military activity while discussions for a treaty of peace are considered," he continued carefully in Spanish. The crowd erupted into cheers, screams, yells, and tears of joy. Men embraced one another. Women picked up their children and hugged them tearfully. Some fell to their knees crossing themselves.

Luzero looked in wonder and sheer delight at Riley. Dalton was already being smothered in a clinging hug by Bel, in tears and speechless.

"There is peace!" Luzero uttered breathlessly, almost like a prayer. Riley and Dalton were racked with shock and disbelief, but they eyed one another in cautious hope. "It is an armistice," she continued. "No more fighting!"

"Viva darlin' Mexico!" Riley roared. He flung his cap into the air with a shout, then gently engulfed Luzero in a jubilant embrace.

"Faith if the nightmare ain't ended," Dalton said, staring at Riley. A wide grin spread across his face as he looked again at Bel. He yanked his pipe from his mouth. "Harroo!" he howled at the sky and whirled Bel squealing off her feet, round and round.

Conahan poked Ockter and pointed gleefully at the foursome. He pulled up his fiddle and put it to his chin. But Morstadt gently placed his huge hand across the strings. Conahan glared up at the giant German.

"Your brutish paw is barring my way, Morstadt," Conahan observed with an edge to his voice.

"I am having a request," Morstadt replied, his tone indicating more.

"Perhaps a command performance is in order," Ockter suggested to Conahan, who shrugged sheepishly.

"Enough of the Irish," Morstadt grumbled. "For this moment of deliverance, we should like 'Ode to Joy' by Beethoven." The surrounding German squad grunted, a few shouted "*Javol!*" with militant enthusiasm.

"Gladly I'd oblige, gentlemen," Conahan blurted quickly, "but 'Soldier's Joy' is 'bout as classic a tune what I know."

Morstadt frowned and reluctantly released the strings. Conahan ripped into the rollicking Celtic reel. Riley, Luzero, Dalton, and Bel improvised a few turns of a dance. Mexican civilians in the road joined in.

"In place, rest!" Ockter shouted. The jubilant San Patricios clapped, laughed, and hollered while remaining in ranks.

Amidst the general ongoing jubilation, Moreno sat astride his horse quietly contemplative. He lit a cigar as the sound of ringing church bells began in the city. First one, then another, and finally an entire chorus of churches were ringing their bells as the news spread. Mejia sauntered up to Moreno.

"What do we do with them?" Mejia asked, pointing at the San Patricios.

"Encamp at the San Cosme Convent," Moreno replied, watching Riley and Dalton still frolicking with their women. He peered down at the suspicious Mejia. "We will keep the streets safe for Santa Anna," Moreno said caustically, "and then merely wait." Mejia nodded with a knowing smile. Both had been through this drill before. But Moreno still harbored a hope, fragile as a flickering candle.

That evening, the San Patricios were feted as celebrities in the torch lit courtyard of the ancient Spanish convent. Bonfires blazed in front of their tents pitched against the walls. At one fire, Conahan played a romantic Mexican ballad in a fiddle duet with a Jesuit priest. One of Mejia's guards sat playing harmony on a wood flute. Upper class Mexican men and women mingled with the Irish gringos. Tables and benches from the convent were covered with food and drink, much of it carried in through the open gate by arriving citizens. The joyous church bells still clanged. Amazingly, they had never stopped.

Morstadt sat preoccupied on the ground near Conahan's musical trio. Ockter walked up and peered over his shoulder. Morstadt was drawing a crude diagram in pencil on a sheet of linen parchment bearing the crest of the convent. The shape was a rough square divided into smaller squares, each labeled in German either "barley" or "hop vines." An unlabeled cluster of buildings in the center looked as if drawn by a child.

"You will build a good German brewery on your three hundred twenty acres?" Ockter asked in German.

"For making good German beer," Morstadt replied. "There is none of that here." He labeled a large building "brewery" in German.

"Where will you sell it?" Ockter asked.

"In my tavern," Morstadt asserted, labeling another building appropriately.

"Do not get too drunk on your dreams," joked Ockter. Morstadt looked up at him. "You must take out the next street patrol." Both laughed as Ockter walked away. He crossed the bustling courtyard to a tiled, torch lit walkway fronting the main convent building. Riley and Dalton stood there watching the festivities with Bel, Luzero, and a Mexican nun.

"Thank you for your gracious hospitality, sister," Luzero said in Spanish as Ockter walked up. He saluted with his usual strict formality.

"Enjoy it while it lasts, Ockter," Riley warned, returning the salute with Dalton, who chuckled. " 'Bout done with this army, maybe . . . any army."

"Even acting as police, we are still soldiers," Ockter replied, "though many now are thinking more like farmers."

"And what will farmer Riley be growing?" Dalton asked with a mischevious smile, lighting his pipe.

Riley looked at Luzero. "Potatoes, watermelons . . . and *niños*," he said. Luzero squealed in mock outrage, nodding with a frown toward the nun.

"What, farmer Dalton, you will be growing?" said Bel with a sexy look.

"Tired," Dalton replied dryly. Riley laughed while prudish Ockter looked affronted. Both women giggled and hid their smiles with their fans.

"We had better go to our rooms," Luzero said to the nun in Spanish. "Pleasant dreams, 'gentlemen,' " she said mockingly. She turned with Bel to follow the nun into the convent. Riley watched her leave, a look of longing on his face but an ache in his heart. Peace, he felt, brought hard decisions.

"Not to put the blight to your potato patch," said Dalton, "but she don't strike me as nothing but the marrying kind. God help her, she will need commitment."

"And that be the blessed rub," Riley sighed, trying not to think about his deepest secret. He averted Dalton's eyes and looked at Ockter. "Street patrol going out?" Duty to him always provided safe harbor, he thought.

Ockter nodded, pointing at the torch lit open gate where Mejia stood with a six-man squad: Four were San Patricios, including Morstadt; two, Mexican guards. Distant bells were still ringing. Mejia saluted as Moreno walked up.

"I shall spend tonight with my family," Moreno announced, sounding weary but joyful. "It has been a very long year."

"But such a short war," said Mejia, waxing almost nostalgic. Moreno looked at him knowingly.

"You have done well enough," Moreno said. He flicked the fringe on Mejia's gold epaulette. Mejia shrugged.

"The man who sees a saddled horse often decides he needs to take a trip," Mejia joked.

Moreno smiled, revealing a hint of sadness. "You may yet ride that horse farther," he said. Mejia stared at him suspiciously. "Not all of the criminals are in the streets." He followed Mejia and the patrol out the gate.

Across the festive city and inside his plush headquarters office, Santa Anna stood staring out an open window at the regal Grand Plaza below. The wide, cobblestone expanse was dominated by an ornate Spanish cathedral. Hundreds of people were celebrating by torch light and bonfires. Joyous Mexican folk music and dancing abounded. The cathedral bells were still ringing.

"Peace at any price is not the Mexican way," Santa Anna said with dismissive arrogance. He turned to face into his office. "Is it all here now?"

General Micheltorena nodded. He stood at an ornately carved Spanish table with two grenadier guards. They set down a military strongbox marked, "U.S.," beside another one already open, full of gold U.S. dollars. Micheltorena nodded at the two men who saluted, turned, and left the elegantly appointed room. On one wall hung a Mexican tri-color richly embroidered in gold; on another, equally sized oil portraits of Santa Anna and Napoleon in full dress uniform. Santa Anna walked to the open strongbox and ran a hand through the coins.

"Now when our soldiers go home," said Micheltorena, "they will have money with which to start their lives over."

Santa Anna looked at him as if he were beholding an idiot. He could not understand why he could never find staff officers who fully appreciated his greatness, who could grasp the brilliance of his grand schemes. "General, I can draw out this 'treaty negotiation' for several months," he said. He took a step back toward the open window and cocked his head to the ringing sound of the ancient cathedral bells, richly resonant with golden, deep tones. "Would that be time enough," he mused, "to melt down the bronze bells to forge new cannon?"

Micheltorena stared in mute, horrified astonishment.

CHAPTER 6
WASHINGTON CITY
SUMMER 1847

Cows swished their tails at swarms of dung flies infesting the parched brown meadow between the Capitol and the Washington Monument. Diversion of federal funds to the war effort had halted construction with only its base completed. In the sweltering, humid heat, this stubby cube of marble looked more like a grave marker than an inspiring white obelisk intended to honor the republic's most indispensable founding father.

Inside the Capitol, the physically failing son of another founding father sat sweating in his drenched frock coat in the stifling House of Representatives chamber. The crowded room stank of tobacco juice, cigar smoke, and body odor. As he listened to the impassioned plea of an eloquent colleague, John Quincy Adams doubted if the rancor of this war was what his father and his contemporaries had envisioned for their new democratic republic. And he wondered if he would live long enough to see it survive the storm.

"Mister Chairman!" Abraham Lincoln's shrill voice sang out, his now familiar Illinois twang making the title sound more like "cheer-man." "Months ago, I demanded that President Polk reveal the exact spot where American blood was shed upon American soil," Lincoln said.

He paused to allow the inevitable hostile murmurs to die down. "Those were his words, his expressed pretext for sending American troops into the disputed Rio Grande territory and provoking this war."

Hot, sweating congressmen fanned themselves and craned their necks backward to see Lincoln, standing tall at his desk near the rear of the chamber. A shaft of brilliant sun had thrust through the skylight and bathed him in a smoky glow. Adams and his steadfast, anti-war caucus dubbed the "Immortal Fourteen" sat clustered around him. Adams looked peaked from the heat.

"To date, he has refused," continued Lincoln, his voice rising. "His efforts to blame this conflict on Mexico, therefore, amount to nothing more than the half insane mumbling of a fever dream!"

Derisive shouts and boos erupted from the clear majority of congressmen, countered by some mighty cheers from Lincoln's surrounding comrades.

Adams looked pleased in an almost fatherly manner. He took comfort in the knowledge that were it time to pass his mantle of leadership, Lincoln as his protégé could be trusted with it.

"In blaming this war on Mexico, the Democrats have given me a clear choice," Lincoln resumed, "either to tell the truth or tell a lie, a foul, villainous and bloody falsehood!" Again, boos interrupted him until the chairman's pounding gavel restored order.

"I must vote for the resolution placed on the floor by our esteemed sixth president, the son of founding father and second president, John Adams," Lincoln took care to remind them, "and your colleague in this chamber for seventeen years, the honorable John Quincy Adams!" Reserved, polite applause rippled through the reticent ranks of legislators while the "Immortal Fourteen" indulged themselves in wild cheering and shouts of "Huzzah!"

Adams squirmed in his straight back chair and nodded humble acknowledgment. He had never been comfortable with public displays of emotion, whether for or against his position.

His hallmark was bedrock belief in the power of reason, argued with persuasive rhetoric. Adams felt that inflammatory speeches appealing to prejudice and fear were what got the nation into this war; that, and the machinations of President Polk.

"We must vote to withdraw our forces from the gates of Mexico City and negotiate peace in good faith"—Lincoln paused dramatically, knowing what was coming—"from the banks of the Rio Grande!"

Overwhelming boos, guffaws of laughter, and shouts nearly drowned out the pounding of the chairman's gavel as he called for a recess.

Lincoln emerged from the chamber wiping his sweating forehead and face with a homespun cotton bandanna. He tried to adjust his necktie, inevitably askew, but gave up in defeat. He joined Adams and his colleagues near a refreshment table where pages served iced water from silver-plated pitchers.

Adams's thirst seemed unquenchable. He downed several full glasses, yet seemed to have stopped sweating altogether. The others traded discreet looks of concern. Lincoln eyed Adams with anxiety tempered with almost paternal affection.

"The blood fever is upon us," Lincoln said to Adams, as if admitting defeat. Others nodded to agree.

"One fever at a time is enough for me, I must say," quipped Adams, sounding short of breath. "But despite all this 'hot air,' you stated our case superbly." He drank another glass of water as Lincoln bowed in gratitude.

"Our troops are winning," continued Lincoln, "so Congress wants to continue the war, right or wrong be damned. It seems that might always does make right."

"Had Mexico beaten us just once, perhaps at Buena Vista, we could have mustered enough votes to end the fighting," observed Adams.

"And now this stalemate of a false truce drags on," said Lincoln. "We are in the predicament of a man who has a wolf by the ears." The others traded knowing, amused looks in anticipation of another Lincoln fable. "It is dangerous to hold on . . . but it may prove fatal to let go."

Adams joined the group in a much-needed laugh, which died out as Adams poured himself more water and appeared a bit wobbly on his feet. Someone brought up a side chair and he gratefully eased into it.

"Mexico makes an ugly enemy," Adams said. "She cannot fight anymore. But she will not surrender. So now many in there want us to gobble up all of Mexico, simply because we can."

"Back home, it seems they want to gobble me up too!" Lincoln cracked, a bitter grin spreading across his craggy face. "They won't nominate me for a second term, not after a newspaper editor in my district dubbed me 'the Benedict Arnold of Illinois.' "

The others traded amused looks but Adams looked concerned. He did not want to lose Lincoln. He was one of the few legislators who understood the danger that slavery presented to survival of the republic, which was Adams's cornerstone issue. Adams knew that victory in this Mexican War would revitalize the South's "peculiar institution."

"I fear, President Adams, that my speech has only stirred up that nest of snakes against you," Lincoln surmised.

"We have no hope of winning this vote on my resolution," Adams conceded with an almost nonchalant air. Some of his colleagues looked perplexed. "But that, gentlemen, can no longer be the point."

Inside the chamber minutes later, mustering every ounce of his waning strength, John Quincy Adams stood at his desk delivering a ringing, impassioned plea, a departure from his usual lowkey style.

Occasional rude remarks, boos, and catcalls could be heard, but he ignored them and rode in fine grace over all opposition. Lincoln led the "Immortal Fourteen" in supportive cheers and applause.

"Some among you would annex all of Mexico," Adams said, having concluded a brief history of the war. "Mexico is to us the forbidden fruit! The penalty of eating it would be to subject our institutions to political death!"

The chairman had to pound his gavel for order, the explosion of emotion too intrusive for Adams to continue. Every congressman knew that this was Adams's veiled reference to his belief that the war was a southern crusade to seize more land for the extension of slavery. Most disagreed with his view that it could only lead to national self-destruction. Lincoln, he knew, fervently believed that the acquisition of western lands would lead to a sectional rift. It could even lead to civil war.

"Rather, I urge you, remove the temptation!" Adams pleaded, his ringing voice finding a surprising reserve of energy. "This war was unconstitutionally begun and unnecessary. We must withdraw our forces from Mexico, negotiate a new boundary, and give up all territorial desires!" Lincoln led his hearty group in sustained applause.

"Disregard how your colleague might vote," Adams chastised. "Ignore the ignorant ranting of your constituents who are perplexed and bewildered by a biased press."

Low, hostile murmurs began spreading throughout the chamber like a contagious fever of resentment.

"Always vote for a principle, though you may vote alone," Adams urged, his voice rising to a spellbinding crescendo. "You then may cherish the sweet reflection that your vote is never lost!"

Lincoln and the anti-war group stood to cheer and applaud but were nearly drowned out by abusive hoots, howls, boos, and catcalls, all underscored by the frantic chairman as he pounded his impotent gavel.

Suddenly, Adams straightened momentarily to stiff attention as his right hand rose to his temple and touched it, as if in deep thought or, possibly, a salute. Some thought that he was, indeed, saluting the chamber. But then his eyes rolled back in his head and he dropped to the floor like a sodden bag of meal.

Lincoln and the others toppled their chairs to reach him quickly as a hush descended. Pages scurried down the aisle, tipping over a few squalid spittoons in their rush to pick up Adams's limp form. Lincoln and the others followed the pages up the aisle as they carried Adams from the floor. They gently laid him on a settee and waited for a doctor.

"He is lost to us," Lincoln agonized, hovering over the dying Adams, voice tight with emotion. "And with him, I fear, dies any hope for peace."

CHAPTER 7
AZTEC RUINS
JUNE 1847

Riley and Luzero walked their horses along a dark jungle path shaded by thick, green tropical foliage. Oppressive humid heat enveloped them amid wild animal cries and the incessant drone of insects. Riley looked anxiously in the direction of each strange sound. Luzero calmly led the way, looking angelic in a new skirt, blouse, and rebosa of embroidered white cotton. Riley rode in his shirtsleeves and blue vest, his coatee tied behind his saddle. She urged her horse through the overhanging leaves of a huge banana tree into a clearing awash with sunlight. Riley followed and reined up short, staring.

"What kind of heathen place have you brung me to?" Riley wondered, quickly crossing himself as he looked around.

"An ancient place of magic," Luzero replied softly. "If we had your leprechauns," she teased, "they would be living here."

" 'Tis a damn spooky bush to be pokin' around," he said with a nervous laugh.

She smiled and led him through a maze of tumbled columns, stone blocks, and statues encrusted in creeping jungle vines. Riley frowned at carvings of hideous winged serpents, warriors beheading enemies, and priests wielding knives to disembowel sacrificial victims.

They stopped at the base of a dozen high, overgrown stone steps leading up to an Aztec temple. He helped her off the horse and reveled in a fleeting glimpse of her moist cleavage. She looked up too quickly and caught him.

146

Embarrassed, he averted her eyes and she could only giggle. As she untied a wicker picnic basket, he looked around with a note of caution. The jungle noises had suddenly fallen silent.

"The quiet could make you deaf," Riley said.

Carrying the basket, she bounded up the steps with youthful energy and waved for him to follow. "Come on!" she whined. "This place is special to me."

"I'll be scaling th'walls a bit slower," he cautioned, a hand to his lower back as he climbed. " 'Tain't like I'm a pony soldier used to riding twenty miles."

"Be thankful this is the top of the pyramid," she taunted. He darted a questioning look at her. "My people say hundreds of steps lay buried." He looked down in disbelief. "The superstitious say to dig them up is to unleash demons from deep in the earth." He gingerly hopped up the steps to her side. Laughing, they climbed together toward the top.

Later inside the dark temple, Riley and Luzero finished her picnic lunch spread atop a sculptured stone altar. She poured more aguardiente into two wood cups. Riley stared at her in undisguised lust as she handed him one. The sunlight filtering through the open archway behind her left little to his imagination. He could not help staring at the thin, damp cotton camisa clinging to her body.

Luzero knew what was on his mind. It had been on hers, as well, and this seemed the perfect time and place. Smiling, she held up her cup in a toast.

"To being supremely alone together at last," she said. Riley looked at her longingly, downed his glass in one shot and held it out for more. Luzero poured again, laughing. "Is it the climb up that makes you so thirsty?" she teased, leaning into him until her soft, full breasts pushed warmly against him.

"That must be it," he gasped. Seizing her gently, Riley kissed her long and tenderly. Her lips softened and parted and her sweet tongue flicked and swirled around his. He responded in kind eagerly. "If I am to be damned," he whispered in her ear, "t'would best be for a demon like you." He placed nibbling kisses along her neck and felt her go limp in his arms as she moaned softly. He found himself kissing the inviting mounds of her chest that peeked out teasingly over the top of her camisa. She moaned more. Emboldened, he ran his tongue along the topmost edge and began to tug the blouse down, exposing more of her breasts. Suddenly, she reached and gently squeezed his hand, stopping him.

"I love you, but stay patient," she gasped, looking suddenly conflicted.

He could not hide his disappointment but then felt ashamed, a unique emotion for Riley. "Meant no disrespect," he stammered, suddenly realizing that he sounded very "Mexicano." "Must've been the magic of this place, making me think my heathen prayers had been answered." He hoped they still would be.

"What else would you pray for, besides sin?" she smiled, nuzzling.

"A lasting peace so's Dalton and the lads could get their land," Riley confessed sincerely, "and I could, for once in my worthless life, deliver that which I'd promised." Riley sensed that what he was feeling must be remorse, for him another new sensation. He began to realize that this young woman had, indeed, changed him into someone he himself no longer recognized.

"So you could then leave us?" she ventured, an edge to her voice.

"Not anymore, darlin'," he admitted. "So I could stay with you in clear conscience," he affirmed.

He ached to unlock his mental footlocker and reveal his deepest secret, but he lacked the moral courage, as usual with him when it came to the full truth. He was becoming more comfortable with something close to honesty, at least.

"Sometimes, I am thinking, the answer to a prayer must be no," she said sadly. "Here the Aztec prayed and sacrificed to stop the Spanish soldiers under Cortez. But the Aztec were destroyed. The Spanish marched here using the same road as the gringos."

"Leastwise the one God give us an armistice and this time alone together," Riley offered. "Maybe the heathens just run out of sacrifices," he joked.

"Before the magic could work," she laughed lightly, running her hand along the top of the altar stone, "maybe they ran out of time."

"Seems I've heard that clock tickin' in my head forever," Riley admitted, "time to go . . . time to go. So, I've bashed or blarneyed to get what I wanted, only then just to leave it behind, along with a bit of myself. At times, I've been thick as my own arm," he added. "Now it seems wrong if ever I were to leave you."

"Maybe this is why our one God also gave us the gift of confession," Luzero whispered suggestively. Something seemed to change within her, she felt her resistance melting. She faced him solemnly, taking both his hands in hers. She stared steadily, lovingly into Riley's amazed eyes as she lifted his hands to her breasts and softly squeezed them through his, moaning and closing her eyes. Then she used his fingers to gently pull her camisa down.

Riley caught his breath at sight of her perfect beauty. Her young, light tan breasts curved up and out from her brown chest to form tender, inviting points of rose. He easily lifted her up and onto the top of the short altar.

He knelt before her as if in worship, consumed in reverential respect but fired by lust as he kissed her breasts. She moaned out loud something in Spanish. Riley gently caressed with his hands what his lips could not reach quickly enough. He sensed her hips beginning to rotate slowly. He pushed her back down so that she lay facing the ceiling, alive with sunlit carvings and paintings of Aztec gods, demons, and sacrificial victims. Her long, bare, shapely legs dangled off the side, as if just waiting to be wrapped around him. He pushed her long skirt up and began kissing the tan, smooth velvet of her thighs. She began babbling more Spanish louder and louder, but nothing he could understand. He slowly kissed his way up her thighs, fighting his urge to move faster but knowing he must take his time. Riley inhaled the oddly sweet, wildly exciting perfume of her body. She exuded the now familiar fragrance of cinnamon with something new, he thought . . . marigolds?

"I like how you touch me," she whispered breathlessly, "as if I am fragile and might break in your hands."

Oddly, Riley found himself suddenly thanking his mother for teaching him to be careful with her only precious object, one tiny sugar bowl of willow pattern Spode china, so paper thin that a harsh look could shatter it.

She grabbed his head and began tugging it upward faster while moaning over and over, "No . . . no . . . no." Riley thought she seemed to be fighting her own rising passion. Then, suddenly, she yanked on his hair and jerked his head hard and straight up. He stared in wide-eyed shock.

"Ouch!" he yelped. She sat up, smiling warmly at stunned, confused Riley. She pertly pulled her camisa up to cover her breasts. Riley moaned in a sad little whine.

"Enough sin for one day, por favor," Luzero declared softly with a smile. "Soon I make the waiting worthy of your patience."

"Tell me something, darlin'," Riley gasped, struggling to his feet and looking down into her flashing black eyes. "If an Aztec's prayers weren't answered in one god's temple, could he trot over to the next and give it a go?"

"I know they believed each god had his own magic," she replied with a delightfully sexy little laugh, sounding to Riley like many a tart he had known in various brothels. Was it something she had learned or were all women born with this tantalizing ability to torture, no experience required? "Something of that lingers in my people still, even as Catholics."

"There's more heathen Celt in me than holy Saint Patrick," he admitted meekly. Riley ran his hand across the flat stone top of the altar. "Were this a place of marriage?" He felt on the verge of admitting the truth, as if her innocence might rip it from his heart. She laughed, shaking her head no.

"Here they sacrificed virgins," she replied, eyes twinkling.

He vowed then and there to confess all on the ride back to Mexico City, though he feared his deepest secret might lose her in the end. But he felt he had to risk it, to at last empty his mental footlocker: he owed her at least that much. Riley did not want to build his new life upon the cornerstone of yet another lie. If he did, he felt sure that it would crumble as it had so many times before.

CHAPTER 8
MEXICO CITY
JULY 1847

Riley, Dalton, and Moreno led their daily patrol down a typical crowded, narrow street in Mexico City. One- and two-story Spanish Colonial stone houses and shops lined the narrow cobblestone way. Most had gabled tile roofs with balconies; others, wood shingles. Riley felt gratified to see Mexican citizens of all classes move aside with admiring glances as the San Patricios passed. Folk music and Spanish dancing could be heard from inside a cantina to the hoots and howls of patrons. Riley nudged Dalton and nodded toward the swinging doors.

" 'Tis a sad fate you rescued herself from," Riley said, a gleam in his eye.

"Mind your filthy tongue," Dalton snapped, puffing his pipe. "Bel prefers to be dancing now only for the likes of me."

Further along the street, canvas awnings shaded vendors who squatted between buildings. They hawked their wares in Spanish as the relaxed San Patricios ambled past. One old man with a streetside display of apples beamed at their approach.

"Gracias!" he shouted, tossing an apple at Dalton, who caught it in surprise. He held it out to an amused Riley.

"No thanks, Dalton," Riley said with a dour look. "Got my fill o' fruit back at Monterey."

Overhearing, Moreno turned away, unable to hide a smile. Brightening, Dalton bit into his apple with vigor.

"*Gracias, mis valientes amigos!*" the old man continued. He tossed an apple to each of the six San Patricios on patrol. They

152

caught the fruit with nods of thanks and a few shouts of "Gracias!" Other Mexican vendors and civilian shoppers clapped politely in tribute.

"You have won their hearts, gentlemen," Moreno explained.

"But we ain't never won a fight," Riley said, looking puzzled.

"Neither has the bull," he replied. Moreno smiled as he lit a cigar.

Riley felt the unaccustomed rush of sudden understanding. He nodded an appreciative look of thanks at Moreno for the education. Moreno bowed slightly in tacit acknowledgement.

"Deserters!" Dalton suddenly cried, pointing just ahead. The squad snapped muskets to a ready position.

Hogan and Rose, the ransackers arrested at Cerro Gordo, stood filthy and bearded in tattered U.S. uniforms at the back of a freight wagon piled high with watermelons. Startled by Dalton's cry, Hogan dropped one with a splat. Rose started to run carrying a watermelon under each arm. The imprint of his lost corporal chevrons still was evident on his faded sky-blue jacket.

"Dummkopf!" snapped Rose. "Come on!" He headed for a nearby alleyway as the sound of scuffling feet from the squad approached.

"Faith they're white men!" exclaimed Hogan, pointing behind.

"Halt or your sorry arses will be shot!" bellowed Riley, waving a fist. The squad stopped and took aim.

"And with a brogue!" Hogan added in amazement. He ran to catch up with Rose. They disappeared down a dark, crowded, pestilential alleyway.

Riley and Dalton arrived at a run just behind the squad. Dalton led them down the alley. Riley remained at the watermelon wagon with Moreno.

"Every day we're finding more," panted Riley. "Yank deserters hiding in th'streets." He pulled out his flask and took a swig. "If the fighting weren't over, we could recruit a new regiment of 'volunteers' just from his worship's jails."

"Much like the regular army," observed Moreno with a sly smile.

"White boys stealin' like street niggers," crooned a familiar voice. Riley turned to see Sandy, the runaway slave he had met the night he deserted and again in Matamoros. Sandy stood in an open doorway to a small warehouse. "It feels more than tolerable to be the one gettin' stole from," he added. Sandy looked the image of a profitable merchant, festooned in a tailored black frock coat, gold and black checkered silk vest, red cravat , and red and black plaid trousers.

"All niggers ain't black," recalled Riley with a laugh. He bounded over to Sandy and grasped his shoulders. Three laborers, two black and one Mexican, emerged from the warehouse.

"Unload the wagon," Sandy snapped in perfect Spanish, "before we lose all our day's business. Be quick!" The three hustled to heft the fruit into the warehouse. Riley stared in amazement as Moreno ambled up beside him. "Mexicans do like their watermelon fresh," Sandy explained. He flicked both of Riley's gold epaulettes, arching an eyebrow.

"Your rise in rank, as it were, will be more lasting than mine," Riley said. "With peace, I'll soon enough be barterin' my potatoes to the likes of you." Sandy and Riley shared a light laugh. Moreno remained stoic.

Dalton and the breathless squad arrived at a trot without Rose and Hogan. Dalton grabbed Riley's flask and emptied it, quenching a mighty thirst.

"Scurried away like rats, they did," Dalton panted, handing back the flask. Riley shook it with a frown.

"We'll nab 'em the next time," Riley said, staring mournfully at his flask.

"You can get your fill of that tonight," offered Sandy, nodding at the flask, "at the celebration."

"Treaty been forged, has it?" Dalton asked hopefully, looking at Riley. He eyed Moreno anxiously. Moreno shook his head.

"It is a time of tribute," Moreno said, holding something back, "second in festivity only to Christmas." Riley and Dalton brightened at the prospect as Moreno and Sandy traded knowing looks. Riley stared at Sandy curiously.

"You've learnt the Queen's English better than herself since last we spoke," Riley observed, "and the greaser to boot." Riley tossed a mirthful glance at Moreno. "Slower to learn, thick sot what I am," he added. Moreno smiled.

"To learn Spanish," Sandy admitted with a sheepish smile, "I had to first 'unlearn' bad English."

That night, the Grand Plaza was crowded with rows of vendors who promoted the paraphernalia for what looked to Riley like a cult of death. Riley and Luzero walked the crowded aisles with Dalton and Bel. Riley began to feel an uncontrollable gnawing anxiety. He squeezed Luzero's warm hand tighter.

All classes rubbed elbows to buy amulets, food, and drink themed to the grave. Blazing bonfires and torches enhanced the deathlike images with flickering shadows and a hellish orange glow. The two Irishmen looked unnerved by what they saw and the two women were amused by their reactions.

At one stall, a puppeteer wearing black Jesuit robes and a wood mask carved like a skull worked marionettes for small children. The puppets were skeletons made of animal bones that clattered as they "danced." A lower class Indian mother pulled her two children from the macabre show to the next booth, where she bought sugar skulls emblazoned with their names. The children laughed with glee as they walked away eating the grisly morsels.

"This be the stuff of nightmares," Riley opined, nodding at the tikes.

"Part of looking death in the face," Luzero said with a smile, "is learning to laugh at it." Riley exchanged looks with Dalton.

"I'll be laughing with a full stomach, I will," said Dalton. He paid another vendor for a long loaf of bread baked and sugared in the shape of a skeleton leg bone. He held it up and Bel bit off one end while he devoured the other.

"It is the 'pan de muerte,' " whispered Luzero, "the bread of death." Riley's eyes grew wide. "It has a different purpose," she added, leading him on.

Riley grew more anxious as the images of death slowly seemed to engulf him. Children ambled by dressed in black cotton costumes painted with white skeletons. Adults danced past in a maudlin parade led by a flutist and drummer playing an eerie Mexican death march. They wore carved masks painted garishly in blood, tears, and gore. Hanging papier mache skeletons adorned booths.

It seemed to him that everywhere Riley looked, he saw the face of death. Perhaps, he thought, it bothered him because he had seen that face too many times on too many grisly battle-fields. Or was it all a dark omen? He wondered.

Luzero paid a vendor for a candle in a black ceramic holder with a cross at its base. The vendor's face was heavy with white and black grease paint in the image of a skull.

"Holy Mother Church blesses this?!" asked Riley, noting the cross. Luzero shrugged no.

"The church chooses not to see," she said, "like with anything Aztec. They honored the dead with festivals of flowers." She put the candle in her picnic basket. "Somehow, Aztec parts and Church parts got all mixed up!" she laughed.

"Like bones in a crypt," Riley said with a straight face.

"We usually celebrate this Day of the Dead on All Souls Day

in the fall," Luzero said, "to show there is no difference." Riley frowned and quickly crossed himself as they resumed walking. She saw the dark mood descending upon him. "Since peace is now upon us," Luzero continued, "they decided to hold the fiesta today, to honor so many sacred dead from the war."

" 'Tis a terrifying blend of savage and sacred," Riley observed.

"But that is Mexicano," she said matter of factly. Riley looked at her. "And now, so are you."

Riley straightened at this blunt assessment of his new self, not sure if he should be pleased or insulted. His ingrained prejudices had left a tough stain on the fabric of his judgment: perhaps a bit more lye soap, he mused, taking a swig.

" 'T'aint regulation but it sure smells good!" blurted Dalton from behind.

Riley and Luzero turned around to behold Dalton with a massive wreath of yellow and orange marigolds laid like a new hatband around the base of his sombrero, its tin serpent head peeking through the blossoms. Dalton drank from an earthen jug of aguardiente.

"Hang it he will tonite on the door of my room," confided Bel to Luzero, "after the good sisters retire," she added in a whisper. They both giggled. Bel started to lead Dalton away.

"I already have mine," Luzero said to Riley, who looked puzzled. She opened the lid of her basket to show more marigolds.

"The whole plaza smells like a field of marigolds," he observed, wrinkling his nose at the curious blend of the pungent and the sweet.

"The *flores de los muertos*," she smiled, "the favorite flower of the dead, said the Azetcs." Riley instantly reacted in horror, his Irish superstition surfacing. He spied Dalton, fast disappearing into the crowd with the passing parade.

"Get them damn deadly weeds off your head!" Riley hollered, waving at him. " 'Tis bad luck to you!" Luzero looked confused by the outburst.

"You got to clear the weeds to 'plow' a fertile field!" Dalton yelled, nodding at Bel. He waved goodbye and vanished.

Riley stood silent, staring at the spot where Dalton disappeared. He took out his flask and downed a heavy hit. " 'Tis a warm night to be feeling a chill," he mumbled. "Banshee must be crossing a grave."

"Irish are as 'spooky' as Mexican," Luzero teased. She smiled and hugged Riley. "We both confuse life and death as two sides of the same coin."

"Or two sides of the same flag," he said softly. She took him by the hand.

"We go now," she said, pulling him along.

"What a grand notion," Riley sighed. "Seen enough of this blessed carnival o'corpses."

"We cannot be going home," Luzero pleaded. "You have not yet seen the celebration!"

"This ain't the damn wake?" Riley asked, hopeful for something more uplifting. She grinned, shaking her head no and dragging him along. "Why didn't you say so, darlin'!" he laughed, following now more eagerly.

They passed along the front of the Palace of the Governors on one side of the plaza. The ornate facade of the Spanish edifice was dark except for one wide window and balcony shining brightly on the top floor.

In that office, Santa Anna stood at the head of his conference table idly dabbing opium powder to his tongue from his gold snuff box. Micheltorena unrolled a large map painted on oilcloth. He spread it across the table as Santa Anna's two lovely mistresses entered, followed by Moreno.

The teenage girls carried trays of Day of the Dead candies and breads, which they set down on a sideboard. Moreno carried a small burlap bag. He snapped to attention, nodded at Santa Anna, and walked to the sideboard, where General Rincon already was sampling the pastries. Rincon was barrel chested, swarthy and sported a thick, curling mustache. His medals marked him as a veteran of many campaigns. From the Grand Plaza below, the eerie Mexican dirge music and crowd noise floated in through the open window.

"Why does he call this emergency meeting?" Moreno whispered urgently.

"Because he can," Rincon replied grimly. "With no more fighting," he added with a smirk, "he has nothing to do."

"With what is left of our army," Moreno said, "perhaps he finds himself staring at a saddled horse." Rincon nodded to agree as the mistresses glided out of the room, closing the door behind them.

"Before the others arrive, gentlemen," Santa Anna said, waving them over, "I impart tasks of discreet importance to you." As they stepped to the table, Santa Anna nodded at Micheltorena. "Commence," he ordered.

"General Valencia marches here today from San Luis Potosi with four thousand veterans," Micheltorena said. "General Alvarez, from the south with twenty-five hundred . . ."

"Mark it," Santa Anna interrupted. He flipped his hand at the map.

"I have nothing, Excellency," Micheltorena replied.

"I must see my soldiers," Santa Anna insisted. "They are not here and I must see them!" Micheltorena, Rincon, and Moreno looked concerned as Santa Anna again indulged in his opium. He appeared delusional.

"Excuse me, Excellency," ventured Rincon, "but are we not to avoid military activity during this 'armistice?' "

"General Rincon," Santa Anna replied icily, "how can the Napoleon of the West avoid military activity? Can the sun avoid the dawn?!" He eyed Micheltorena. "Find something."

Micheltorena walked quickly to the sideboard and began searching through drawers. Moreno looked embarrassed for him.

"Once General Micheltorena finds my soldiers," Santa Anna resumed, "we will show you where to begin building fortifications for them." He added flippantly, "In case the armistice fails."

"Yes, Excellency," Rincon replied with measured contempt, "though, as a soldier, I need only to see a map."

"You must see things as I do!" Santa Anna snapped. Rincon bowed stiffly at the reprimand. Santa Anna pointed at several large rectangles of sky blue painted on the map. "After three months of doing nothing in Jalapa and Puebla," he raved, "even I would go mad!" He pounded his fist atop the map repeatedly as the others traded nervous looks. "That is why their deserters fill our streets," he said. "Soon they must march on us or see their army melt away," he dreamed aloud, staring at the map as if into a crystal ball. "Colonel Moreno," Santa Anna resumed in a tone markedly more mellow, without looking up from the map, "you will have Riley recruit from norteamericano deserters you have caught. Fill two companies. We have no cannon yet, so arm and uniform them as infantry."

Suddenly, six-inch-high carved wooden figurines appeared in Santa Anna's drug-affected field of view atop the map. As Micheltorena would point, Moreno firmly planted a figure. Santa Anna's jaw dropped when he realized the figurines were skeletons. Rincon barely hid a smile. Santa Anna glared at Moreno, who calmly lit a cigar.

"It is the day, Excellency," Moreno shrugged innocently. "I bought them for my children," he added, pulling a final skeleton from his burlap bag. "Where is the last point of defense?"

"The bridge and convent at Churubusco," Santa Anna said

in a monotone. He eyed Moreno suspiciously.

"Excellency, can you see your soldiers now?" Moreno asked. With a hard thud, he covered "Churubusco" with the figure of a skeleton. Santa Anna glared at him, unsure if insolence was intended. Moreno puffed his cigar.

Later, when Riley at last arrived in an ancient cemetery with Luzero, he felt such a chill that his mother would say someone just walked on his grave. He eyed a fresh interment covered in bananas, apples, bread baked in the shape of bones, sugar skulls, earthen jars of aguardiente, and bouquets of marigolds. It was awash in the soft, eerie light from candles burning atop actual human skulls. Untrained voices sang a Catholic hymn in Latin to guitar and concertina music. As Riley and Luzero walked past, Riley paused to gape, astonished.

"Some say Aztecs dug up their dead for the festival," Luzero said. Riley looked horrified. "It was a true 'family reunion,' " she added, smiling.

"That would be taking a wake too damn far," Riley said somberly, staring at the skulls. She yanked him along the path.

They strolled past grave after grave, crowded tightly together in the lower-class cemetery. Each was a variation on a theme. Some bore painted miniatures of the deceased; others, flowers in the shape of crosses. Most had flickering candles. Mourners sat or knelt beside graves in prayer. Some burned incense in blatantly Aztec burners; others, in Catholic vessels with crosses.

"We are here," Luzero said quietly. She knelt beside two graves covered in old bricks and marked only with two simple wooden crosses. She dug into her basket. "Clean it off, por favor," she said, handing Riley a small straw broom.

He knelt beside her and whisked dirt as she laid two crosses formed from marigolds atop the bricks. Riley watched intently as she set out her candle, lit it, and placed one loaf of bread and a small jug of wine between the two graves.

"They shared everything," she said. He smiled and placed his arm around her for a gentle squeeze.

"Thank you, darlin'," Riley whispered, "for sharing something what must be so private and personal."

Luzero kept staring down at the graves as her lips finished a silent prayer. She crossed herself and looked at him with a sly smile. "You shared something with me so very private, I had to bring you tonight," she said. "To honor my father, I promised him as my dowry to go to my marriage a virgin. So, I had to let him meet you." Riley gaped dumb struck, a rare sensation for him.

They turned to leave, walking through the cemetery. It seemed "alive" now, Riley thought with his usual black humor, with inebriated celebrants and musical groups. Riley pulled out his flask, feeling confused. "At home they'd stone me for this," he said, taking a drink, "but here I'm just one of the drunks."

Luzero giggled, grabbed the flask and took a drink. "Are you . . . disappointed?" she asked tenuously. He looked offended.

" 'Tis the grandest honor a man can be given," Riley exclaimed, pausing long enough to bow grandly with a sweep of his arm. "But you know my situation now, how are we gonna? . . ." He caught himself, straightened, cleared his throat and looked sadly into her eyes. "And if the peace don't hold?" he asked.

"My father will find a way," Luzero said confidently, pulling him along. "He just told me so." Riley gave her a dubious look, taking another swig.

"Now we go to the rich people cemetery," Luzero said brightly. "Their decorations are more beautiful, like at Christmas!"

Riley looked aghast but walked with her toward the cemetery gate. But something kept naggng at him. "Birds of a feather, darlin' . . ." he began, then stopped. "Got to ask . . ." he blustered, but she put a finger to his mouth. She looked as if she had heard what he was about to ask too often for it to matter.

"By having friends who are whores," Luzero explained, "I stay safely hidden in their crowd. And . . ." she unleashed a coy smile, "while I do nothing, from them I learn much."

"If them soldados knew th'truth, 't'would be Katy bar the door," he teased.

"It would be like waving the red cape at ten thousand bulls!" Luzero said.

Riley laughed as they neared the cemetery gate. He sobered when he saw a fresh, lonely grave in the shadows. A wrinkled, leather faced Indian woman burned incense in an Aztec urn painted with a fierce warrior visage. Candles burning atop a skull lit the grave among a pile of yellow and orange marigolds. The battered shako of a Mexican soldado hung atop a wooden cross. Against its base leaned a painted oval miniature of a proud, young Indian soldier. The old grandmother stared long at Riley as he passed with Luzero. The haunting music of a lone Indian wood flute drifted lightly in the heavy air.

" 'Proud of itself is the city of Mexico-Tenochtitlan,' " the old said, reciting an ancient poem in Nahuatl, the Aztec language: " 'Here no one fears to die in war. That is our glory.' " A tear traced down her cheek. As she watched Riley disappear out the gate, the old woman crossed herself. So did Luzero, who understood enough of the ancient language to feel chilled by the words.

CHAPTER 9
MEXICO CITY
AUGUST 1847

One month later, a grimy, flea infested civilian jailer led Riley, Dalton, and Mejia down a dark corridor in a dingy, dank city prison. The filthy stone floor was alive with cockroaches. Rats scurried squealing into the shadows at the approach of their heavy footsteps. Riley and Dalton peered through tiny barred windows as they passed each cell door.

"Hotel's empty, it is," said Riley, pulling back from a window.

"Sure and it is the maid service," said Dalton, stomping one leg to shake off a few cockroaches.

Mejia gave a laugh and nudged the jailer. "Where are the prisoners?" he asked in Spanish.

"The last cell," the jailer replied. He scratched a flea bite.

"Not the gringos," Mejia said. "I meant the usual criminals."

The jailer laughed. "All who could walk were taken by soldiers," the jailer said. "And they are now soldiers too!"

Mejia appeared troubled, drawing looks from Riley and Dalton. They reached the end of the corridor and faced a double wide wood door strengthened with iron plate. The jailer fumbled for the right key and began to unlock it.

"Santa Anna into the army throws the prisoners," Mejia said, frowning.

"So for weeks we been nothing but recruiting for him, as it were, in every hellhole and piss pot in town," mused Dalton. He lit his pipe, scowling at Riley.

" 'T'would feel a damn more like peace with criminals loose

164

in th'streets," joked Riley. Dalton grunted. The jailer swung open the heavy, creaking doors.

Inside, a dozen wretched U.S. regulars sprawled and sat on filthy straw in a dark cell with one high window. Rose, heavily bearded, sat up as the door opened. Bearded Hogan squatted bare ass over a rancid bucket in one corner. As Riley, Dalton, and Mejia entered, he quickly stood and pulled up his trousers.

"Now there is a unique salute," Riley said deadpan.

"Sure an' it's all you deserve," crooned a graying Irish private seated beside the door. Riley and Dalton looked around Mejia to see the grizzled veteran glaring up at them. "Least the stink of your own hides buries what Hogan was makin' in the corner there."

"We come to make them 'landed gentlemen' and they thank us with insults," observed Dalton.

"Must be a Protestant," Riley said, loud enough to be heard.

"I'll not put on your tawdry greaser rags," the man snarled.

At this, Mejia dropped with deft agility to one knee, producing a gleaming dirk held to the surprised man's throat. *"De la carcel sales,"* Mejia snarled with a fierce grin, *"perode la tumba no."* Riley smiled as Dalton arched an eyebrow.

"What's he sayin'?!" the old Irishman gasped, frozen with eyes wide.

" 'Men walk out of jail,' " Riley translated, " 'but never from the tomb,' you flamin' ignorant arse." Dalton looked in surprise at Riley. "I added the last grand flourish myself, I did," Riley said proudly. "Luzero been teaching me."

Mejia stood and smiled at him while sheathing his dirk. "Bueno," said Mejia. "You speaking the greaser now, Major."

"We are two good soldiers," Rose said, his German accent adding a touch of arrogance as he stood. He cast a quick look at Hogan, who nodded. "We would walk out of here with you."

"We was proud regulars, we were," said Hogan. "And then

we even lost that, when ol' Fuss 'n Feathers gave the damn volunteers sky-blue uniforms."

Riley and Dalton looked stunned, both feeling a nostalgic bit of outrage. Sky blue always set the regulars apart, a cut above the like of militia rabble.

"So all the disgraceful volunteers look like regulars now, do they?" Riley said. "I'll wager they don't fight like them."

"What if the uniform makes them rise to the occasion, as it were?" worried Dalton. He eyed Hogan more carefully. "Busted from corporal, I see," Dalton said, noting the chevron imprints on his sleeves. "You hold promise," he added.

"I'm blessed if I ain't tired of runnin' like a rat in these streets," said Hogan in his thick brogue, "and you chasin' us."

"I tell you plain," chimed Riley, "as deserters, the rest of you lads face a worse fate." He paced slowly around the room, hands behind his back and looking down at each grimy, bearded face. "This war is done but for signing of the treaty. Then you'll be exchanged to the Yanks . . . and shot."

The men traded grim, worried, frantic looks as Dalton refired his pipe, leaning to Mejia with a twinkle in his eye. "Damn if the old faker ain't good," Dalton whispered, "when he believes what he is saying."

"Speaking the greaser betters the blarney," Mejia joked softly.

"Join my Battalion of Saint Patrick," Riley continued, "and you become a jailer instead of the jailed." A few deserters chuckled. "The fighting is ended, so's you won't have to agonize over shooting at your old pals, like some of us already done." He darted a look at Dalton. "You keep the streets safe from the likes of yourselves," he joked, drawing more chuckles, "and when your time is up, you start life anew with two hundred acres as thanks from old Mexico." The deserters exchanged surprised, approving shrugs and nods of tentative agreement.

"Dummkopfs only would choose to stay here," Rose observed,

urging the others to stand. All but the aging Irishman rose. Riley and Dalton stepped over and stared down at him as Mejia finished rolling a cigareet.

"Go I will," the prickly man warned defiantly, "but I'll not fire on my old mates." Riley and Dalton merely nodded, with no fighting imminent. Mejia struck his match. "So help me up, damn your eyes," he said. Dalton extended a brawny arm.

Weeks later in the convent courtyard, the defiant old Irishman, Rose, Hogan, and eighty other newly recruited U.S. deserters stood in ranks, freshly scrubbed and with new Brown Bess muskets at shoulder arms. The beards were gone but for mustaches, chin whiskers, and sideburns in curious blends of Mexican and Irish hirsute tradition; seen in the veteran San Patricios, as well. The recruits wore the newly issued uniform for the Mexican Territorial Infantry: dark-blue coatees faced in red with yellow piping, sky-blue trousers with red seam piping, and barracks caps—of course, with the Irish harp.

"*Altas armas!*" shouted Dalton beside the men. Conahan echoed the command. Both still wore their once glorious, now faded "Mexicanized" artillery uniforms.

The new company snapped the gleaming muskets from their shoulders to the vertical position of tribute. Moreno gave a nod of approval to Dalton as he passed, slowly walking the line to inspect the troops with Riley. Morstadt stood with the flag at one end, flanked by Conahan and Ockter.

The veteran San Patricios watched in informal groups throughout the camp. All still wore their old artillery uniforms, much repaired and augmented with civilian attire. A few looked up from tending fires, cooking, or playing cards, dice, or dominoes. Some lounged on the convent verandah with nuns who were sewing patches on ripped and worn out bits of uniform. At a well near the verandah, Luzero and Bel scrubbed shirts. They stopped long enough to watch Moreno walk to the center of the line and face the troops, Riley beside him.

"*Orden armas!*" Dalton shouted, with Conahan echoing the command. The men lowered muskets to their sides with butts on the ground.

"In but a few weeks," Moreno declared, "you have grown ready to defend your new home." Riley cocked his head slightly and eyed Moreno. This was a curious twist, he thought, if we were so surely teetering on the brink of peace: was this armistice like blarney, "Irish truth" teetering on the brink of a lie? Dalton also noted the ominous tone, exchanging a look of concern with Riley. "Whatever duty Mexico may demand," Moreno concluded, "I know you will prove equal to the task, as have others before you." He waved at the veteran San Patricios, who stood. Moreno nodded at Riley.

"Let no man dare to say," Riley bellowed, strutting proudly and admiring their splendid martial appearance, "that it ain't Hibernian whores and Dutchman drunks what soldier the best!" Chuckles passed among the men. "*Ropan filas!*" Riley bellowed.

"Viva!" the troops shouted in unison as they instantly broke ranks and walked toward their tents.

"Viva Mexico!" shouted the veteran San Patricios, who clapped, cheered, and waved their caps for Riley and Moreno.

Riley gestured Dalton to him as he joined Conahan, Ockter, and Morstadt. Riley watched Moreno stride to the open gate, where two of Mejia's guards stood as sentries.

"Maybe he's waiting for news of treaty," Morstadt observed hopefully as he slowly furled the green flag around its staff. Riley looked doubtful. He took out his flask and downed a swig. Dalton arrived.

"Hate to say it," Riley confided, "but it may again come to a brawl. Will these new lads throw a punch?" Dalton lit his pipe as Ockter, Conahan, and Morstadt exchanged crestfallen looks of disbelief.

"So, you think it may take a bit longer," sighed Conahan, "to track down little 'Rosarita of Alabama'?" He was clearly crestfallen.

"To fight again," moaned Morstadt, "make my stomach churn. Cannot we end this with good German beer around a well-tuned piano?"

"Is it as infantry that we must fight?" whined Ockter, missing his cannon.

"Any wench knows, 'tain't the size of the weapon what counts but how you use it," Conahan chuckled. They all tried to enjoy a laugh, but it faded as quickly as their dreams.

"Any Mexican knows, 'tain't what you say but how you say it," Dalton mused, nodding toward Moreno pacing at the gate. He looked at Conahan and arched an eyebrow. "So, if there is another storm heading our way . . ."

"They'd fight for their skins, if for nothin' else," Conahan surmised.

" 'Tain't likely they'll be blessed with time enough to find nothin' else," Riley observed. "In that alone, we been blessed."

"Twice over," Dalton added, blowing smoke in the direction of Luzero and Bel, still washing clothes.

Riley and Dalton traded knowing looks: They needed to pry the truth from Moreno. "The good colonel and us, we need a little chat, we do," Riley said. Dalton nodded, puffing his pipe like a bellows. They started walking toward Moreno at the gate, leaving the three sergeants.

"One more night in Jalapa," mused Conahan wistfully, "and Rosarita would've been me own, she would."

"Only after grandmother finished with you," Morstadt cracked.

"And then 'harmless' you would have been," joked Ockter.

Conahan laughed as they walked toward the tents. Morstadt

casually toted the furled green flag on his shoulder.

At the gate, Moreno paced while smoking a cigar. The two guards presented arms as Riley and Dalton arrived. Moreno glanced at them and salutes were exchanged, but he returned an anxious eye to the cobblestone street.

" 'T'was inspiring what you said to the new lads, sir," Riley chimed sweetly. "Dalton and me are more curious, though, about what you didn't say."

"I do not speak my suspicions, gentlemen," Moreno said. "That only adds my fears to those of everyone else." Their attention suddenly was drawn down the street to the unmistakable sound of marching feet and clattering tin cups, canteens, and military gear.

"Your fears seem to be heading our way, Colonel," Riley said.

"Sounds like army broghans," added Dalton, lighting his pipe, "tramping the treaty to dust." Moreno gave them an implacable stare.

Rounding the corner and coming toward them was a column two abreast of grim, determined, and grimy Mexican infantry, all elite rifle companies. The tattered tri-color battle flag of the Eleventh Regiment was carried at the front flanked by several drummers and fifers. They struck up the jaunty Mexican marching tune, "La Cachuca." The veteran troops wore green faced uniforms like Mejia and his guards, who marched behind the first company with General Rincon on horseback. The soldados wore blanket rolls on their shoulders and carried brass trimmed British Baker rifles. They are all business, Riley thought grimly.

Behind the troops, Sister O'Gara rode in a wagon beside a frail but distinguished Anglo man with graying mutton-chop sideburns. He wore a silk cravat, colorful silk vest, and dusty black frock coat, topped with a Scottish cap. Behind them, several small mule-drawn carts carried more nuns and stacks of stretchers, cots, blankets, and boxes of medical goods.

As the music continued, Mexican citizens came out of their homes and small shops. They waved at the troops and began to shout "Viva Mexico!", "Viva La Republica!" and "Viva Santa Anna!"

One upper class gentleman and presumably his son emerged on the balcony of their home. Each carried a flintlock hunting musket.

"We will go with you!" cried the old man in Spanish. He raised the musket above his head.

"Gringos cannot have our city without a fight!" his son vowed to others below. They cheered.

More men of all ages and classes joined his impromptu call to arms. They brought out blunderbusses, fowling pieces, and shotguns from their homes and businesses and flourished them at the passing troops with cries of "Viva!"

The head of the column tramped past Moreno, Riley, and Dalton and into the courtyard. Inside, startled and curious San Patricios gathered to gawk, stare, and wonder. Luzero and Bel exchanged worried looks, put down their laundry, and started walking toward the crowd.

"We all have questions," Moreno said. He removed his cigar, tossed it down, and ground it with his boot heel. "Perhaps General Rincon has answers."

Moreno, Riley, and Dalton saluted Rincon as he rode past and into the courtyard. Mejia gave the threesome a proud sword salute as he led his squad. Directly behind was the wagon with Sister O'Gara and the Scots gentleman. Riley doffed his cap and Dalton his sombrero to the nun in the wagon.

Minutes later, the Mexican troops sprawled in the courtyard, resting from an exhausting march. Many clustered around the well, drinking and filling empty canteens. San Patricios wandered among them sharing canteens and food and swapping rumors, all in Spanish. The Irish had learned the lingo, Riley observed with some satisfaction. He felt proud and thankful that he had been among the first, thanks to Luzero.

Riley helped Sister O'Gara down from the wagon as other San Patricios did likewise with the remaining nuns on mule carts. Dalton, Luzero, and Bel waited beside the Scotsman.

" 'Tis an ill wind I fear what's brung you this far south, sister," Riley said, "though 'tis always grand to see your shining face." The nun laughed and looked at Luzero.

"Such a master at the blarney, and you haven't married him yet?!" O'Gara said. Riley and Luzero traded uncomfortable looks of embarrassment.

"He is more 'complicated' than he looks," Luzero said with a shy, sad little smile. "Perhaps later we may talk?"

"I see," said O'Gara, giving Riley a stern look. "I also see our flag still flies," she observed, gesturing at the green banner planted at Moreno's wall tent. He stood in front conversing with Rincon.

"It flies higher than our hopes, good sister," Dalton said with a hapless shrug directed at Bel.

"I know little for certain," O'Gara said, "except we couldn't stay in the north with General Valencia saying they were short of medical folk here, and him coming this way."

"Doctor James Humphrey, at your service," said the Scot, presenting himself with a small step forward and slight bow. He continued in his thick Scots accent, "I'll be openin' a hospital here for your regiment." Riley and Dalton bowed in respect to him, Mexican style. "We foreign nationals in Mexico City canno' ignore our duty to her, can we?" Humphrey smiled.

"Duty is something none of us can ignore no more," Riley admitted with a wry look at Dalton.

"And don't the Good Shepherd love his found black sheep the best?" Dalton said.

"We want to be helping you," Bel said to Humphrey, "though

shooting the musket I would more be liking to do," she added. Bel darted a saucy look at Dalton, who frowned.

"We both are used to the blood," Luzero added. Humphrey nodded.

"Don't it be cause and effect?" Riley observed. "We get us a hospital and are bound to fill it up, much like diggin' a latrine."

"And should we be giving it a go again," Dalton said sternly to Bel, "you will be bound to stay put here, where it is safe." He yanked his pipe from his mouth and pointed it at the ground.

"A good woman always is doing what her man says," Bel said too sweetly. Luzero broke into laughter joined by all but Dalton.

That night, candle lanterns burned brightly inside Moreno's wall tent. Rincon pointed to a painted canvas map unrolled on a camp table. Gathered around were Moreno, Riley, Dalton, and Mejia. The detailed drawing of fortifications was labeled *"El Plan Convento de San Mateo."*

"It is a strong place that we have made stronger," Rincon explained. His finger traced the map. "Outer earthworks, the wall, the convent building, all give us three levels, three firing platforms."

" 'Tis a lot of line for so few lads, sir," Dalton worried. He lit his pipe.

"We will be joined there in the morning by the Fourth Light Regiment," Rincon said, "veteran riflemen all."

"Already here are the rifle companies of my regiment," said Mejia proudly. "We can all be killing the gringos at farther away!" he asserted.

Riley laughed and took a drink from his flask. He noticed something on the map. "Begging the general's pardon, sir," he ventured, "but my Spanish be puny as a newborn babe. What might this mean?" He pointed to a section of the outer earthworks labeled *"Bateria tres nueve libra."* Rincon nodded to Moreno.

"It is a battery of three bronze nine pounder guns, Major," Moreno said with a wry smile, "newly forged in the British style from the city's old Spanish bells. You have noticed how quiet the city has been?"

"Ockter'll dance a German jig, he will," Riley said. He looked at Dalton. "Now we got us a fighting chance, we do."

Moreno and Rincon exchanged grim looks. Both knew better.

"In the unlikely event that our 'Napoleon of the West' meets defeat elsewhere with the main army," Rincon warned sarcastically, "we must hold the road until his survivors reach Mexico City." Rincon and Moreno stared at Riley, Dalton, and Mejia in fatalistic resignation.

"There never was a treaty," Moreno added bitterly. "It was but a paid pause in the killing to talk about talking about a treaty." He lit a cigar. "Now Santa Anna has had time to catch his breath."

Outside the tent, Dalton fired up his pipe as Riley pulled out his flask, their ritual at times of crises. They stood quietly watching the San Patricios and Mexican infantry enjoy campfire camaraderie. A few Mexican singers harmonized to Conahan's fiddle at one roaring bonfire. Morstadt and Ockter tried to sing with them in Spanish. The song was a melancholy corrido about lost love. Mejia suddenly emerged from the tent, nodded at them, and started to hurry toward the campfires with the bad news.

"Let 'em finish the song, Mejia," Riley called out quietly. Mejia stopped. Riley stared at him and slowly shook his head. Mejia released a sad smile in understanding, turned, and merely walked slowly to his camp. "How the hell do we tell them?" pondered Riley, slowly unscrewing the cap to his flask.

"Straight up," snapped Dalton, "like setting a broke bone."

"Meant the ladies, you sot," Riley said.

"Sure and you have noticed," Dalton said, "the ladies down here are made more of fire than frill. Tell them plain, says I."

Riley nodded as Dalton puffed his pipe, each lost in quiet contemplation. " 'Tis a death sentence," Riley sighed. "And now me with somethin' at last to live for." Riley took a drink and handed Dalton the flask. Riley stared at the torchlit convent in dread, not wanting to shatter Luzero's dreams.

"Well, were I to go up," Dalton mused, "I'd rather it be for something than for nothing." Dalton downed a swig. They started toward the convent building.

Riley entered a hallway dimly candlelit by wall sconces. He stole into a small chapel whose altar was dominated by a carved wooden crucifix painted in full color. Every wound, lash mark, and blood drop on the Christ figure showed as gloriously garish gore. In an alcove hung a beautiful painting of Our Lady of Guadalupe, a rendition of the Virgin Mary that showed her as a dark-skinned Mexican woman. The white plaster walls were decorated with brightly painted borders and scrollwork of obvious Indian origin. A large burning candelabra hung above Luzero and Sister O'Gara as they knelt in prayer in front of the alcove. Luzero lit a votive candle at the foot of the painting as Riley approached. He genuflected and crossed himself.

"We have just given thanks," Luzero whispered happily.

Riley looked in confusion at Sister O'Gara, who crossed herself. "Find precious little this night to be thankful for," Riley said. "What've you heard?"

The nun stood and stepped up to him like a bantam rooster ready for a fight. "Enough from her to know you've been keeping the both of you in agony for no good reason!" she scolded in a loud whisper. She took Riley by the ear and walked him toward the door as if he were back in a grade school classroom.

"Yeeouch!" Riley cried, stumbling after her. Luzero giggled and followed them into the hallway.

Minutes later just outside the chapel, Riley stood like a penitent truant explaining himself to the sister superior. Luzero beamed beside him.

"Ain't never told this to only herself," Riley confessed, "and even then, I'd tricked myself into not remembering, when convenient." Luzero blushed. "But you see, Sister, she was a willing Protestant lass back home with a fullsome Protestant . . . uh, 'disposition,' " he blustered. Luzero hid a smile as O'Gara rolled her eyes. "Being young and full of myself, as it were," he resumed delicately, "I got her in the family way. She brung 'round her minister and so the lad he were not born a bastard. Then I marched away with th'British and never went back."

O'Gara looked at Luzero and nodded, as if confirming what Luzero had told her. Luzero sighed in relief and threw her arms around Riley impetuously, squeezing him tightly. He smiled in surprised, tentative confusion.

"Since you left her flat back home so many years ago," O'Gara said, "she's probably already re-married anyway, as a Protestant might."

"And me sending money home all along," Riley frowned. "Even told old O'Malley back in Fort Mackinac to send it to my mum and sis, when it was them plus the lass and the boy." Riley had started this grand plan in the hopes of returning home, he admitted to himself, but now none of it seemed to matter anymore. Perhaps it was true, he marveled: everything happens for a good reason, even despite ourselves. As usual, you must merely give it time.

"What I'm saying to you, John Riley," O'Gara said sternly, "is that your Protestant marriage is not valid in the eyes of Holy Mother Church. Sure and you've just been living in sin," she added with a wink. "After you get appropriately sore knees in Confession, I am sure you and Luzero can take the blessed sacrament of matrimony."

At first stunned, Riley started to smile but quickly caught himself. He failed to find words. Luzero saw his indecision. Her smile faded into a confused look of fearful frustration. She glared in emotional panic at Sister O'Gara.

"It is the honorable thing you will do for this young woman, it is," O'Gara warned, scowling. "Faith the redeeming of your soul is at stake."

This gave Riley a start. He stared blankly at the nun. Then he almost laughed: it would take a lot, he thought, to redeem his soul.

"Do you want me no longer?" Luzero asked softly. Riley frowned and recovered enough to embrace her as tears welled.

"I'd rather rub burning salt into my wounded heart," Riley managed, "than go stumbling down my crippled path without you at my side." She smiled weakly through her tears. "But I come this night bearing a bit of bad news."

The sound of incessant drums intruded from the courtyard. Sergeants and corporals yelled "Form ranks!" and "Fall in!" in English and Spanish as infantry musicians beat the long roll. Luzero pulled away knowingly.

"That sound I have heard all my life," she sobbed. Sister O'Gara crossed herself. Riley pulled Luzero to him again, cradled her tightly, and left.

Minutes later, the weary Mexican rifle companies trudged out the gate to a steady drum cadence. Rincon rode out with them after giving a parting salute to Moreno and Riley. They stood quietly a moment and traded fast, fatalistic looks. Then Moreno smiled weakly and flicked one of Riley's gold epaulettes. Riley chuckled, then sighed. "Damn I could die laughing but 't'would kill me sure," he said. Moreno looked at him curiously. "The new lads I snared with a lie," he said, "whilst thinking for once I was telling the blessed truth."

"It was not you who betrayed their trust, this time," Moreno said. Riley looked at him shrugging a grateful nod. Moreno lit a cigar and turned around.

Behind them waited the San Patricios, drawn up in marching order. Dalton and Conahan stood with the new company of infantry recruits. Ockter and Morstadt with the flag stood beside the artillery veterans. The flickering orange light from burning bonfires danced across their grim, determined faces.

Luzero, Bel, Sister O'Gara, Doc Humphrey, and other nuns clustered around one of the fires, watching. Luzero and Bel fought back tears.

Moreno and Riley slowly walked beside the column of twos inspecting the men from front to rear. Among the last ranks stood the reluctant Irish recruit beside Hogan and Rose.

As Riley passed, the old man suddenly reached out and grabbed his arm, yanking him around. "Bein' no fool, I'll take your greaser land," he snarled, "but I'll be damned afore I shoot at the old flag!"

Riley yanked his arm away in a rage. He grabbed the man's tunic by the collar and jerked him out of ranks. Lifting him up to his tiptoes, Riley reared back to hit him. But Moreno quickly grasped his fist to stop the punch. Riley glared at him. Moreno merely shook his head slowly in disapproval.

"That is not the Mexican way, Major," Moreno said. "And you are now Mexican." Riley let loose. The surly Irishman gasped for air as Moreno stepped up to him. "You refuse to fight?" he asked. The man grunted a nod. "Then give to me your musket, por favor," Moreno said.

"Purely with pleasure, sir," the reluctant recruit smiled, glaring at the still fuming Riley. Moreno took the musket in two hands.

"When addressing an officer of the Republic of Mexico," Moreno said calmly, "you show the proper respect." He suddenly whacked the man aside the head with the butt of the musket, felling him to his knees. Blood oozed from his ear and scalp. "And you follow orders," Moreno added. He dropped the musket to the ground beside the wobbly man. Riley stared dumbfounded as Moreno sauntered away slowly puffing his cigar. "Start the column, Major," he added with a casual wave of the hand.

"Sure and that is the Mexican way!" roared Dalton.

"Viva darlin' Mexico!" yelled Conahan, waving his cap. The entire column shouted with a mighty roar, "Viva!"

"At the route step," Riley bellowed, with a look at Dalton, "forward, march!" The companies stepped off as Humphrey walked toward Riley and the injured man with Luzero. Sister O'Gara led the nuns toward the convent.

Bel ran to the gate where she grasped onto Dalton and almost pulled him over with a tearful hug. Dalton opened his mouth to protest but Bel hungrily filled the opening with her own mouth in a fiery, grasping, throbbing kiss. Passing San Patricios hooted, howled, and guffawed at this unusual public display.

"Would you curse me with such a permanent kiss goodbye?!" Dalton gently chided, once she let him gasp for air.

"I would be bringing you back," Bel whispered with a tempting smile, "with a taste of what for you here will be waiting." Dalton gently pushed her away and looked deeply into her eyes.

"Long that wait may be," he said firmly. She nodded slowly, knowing the odds. She mustered a grin.

"But whose pipe can I now be lighting?" Bel whined. He laughed.

"Mine," Dalton asserted playfully, "soon as I get home from work!" He gave her a wink, let loose of her, and re-joined the column. Bel wiped her tears, bridled in frustration, folded her arms, and stamped her foot. Dalton laughed as he disappeared out the gate doffing his sombrero. The tin serpent head on his hatband flashed like a firefly in the torch light.

"Now that I have found you," Bel vowed in Spanish, "I will not lose you." She crossed herself.

Beside Riley, Doc Humphrey patiently wrapped cotton bandaging around the woozy old Irishman's head. Riley watched, quietly holding Luzero.

" 'Tis but a wee cut," Humphrey said, "for such a bonnie rap on the noggin'." The Scotsman smiled.

"Irish skulls be hard to bust," Riley said. The injured man looked at him sheepishly, almost with a smile.

"He'll be able to stand to," Humphrey added. Riley darted him a curious look, recalling the British terminology. "Gordon's Highlanders," he explained.

Riley let loose a laugh, then walked to Luzero a short distance away. They watched the new second company of San Patricios march out the gate.

"Where is it you are going?" she asked, cuddling closer.

"Called 'Churubusco,' " Riley said. "They got an old convent there what's been turned into a fort." Riley always had a bad feeling about being penned up, never having seen it end well. But he kept his fears to himself.

"It is an Aztec name," Luzero said, pulling away to look up at him in some anxiety. "It means 'the place of the war god.' " He stared at her and took a drink from his flask, emptying it. He turned at approaching footsteps.

"We should go," Moreno said quietly as he walked up. The bandaged Irishman stood. Moreno glared and shooed him away like a pesky fly. "Catch up with them!" he commanded. The man trotted to join the end of the column as it passed through the gate. Moreno started walking and cast a beckoning look over his shoulder at Riley.

"*Vaya con Dios,*" Luzero managed with a thin smile. Riley squeezed, pulled away, and looked at her. She reached up and took his face with both hands, gently pulling him down to her for a soft, lingering kiss of smoldering but controlled passion. When she let him take a breath, he stared at her wide eyed.

"It is a kiss of promise," Luzero teased with a smile, "of better things to come." Her wavering voice betrayed her unspoken fear.

"Hold that thought 'til my return," Riley choked out in a whisper, "and this." Riley handed her his flask, turned, and started walking to join Moreno.

Luzero stared at the inscription on the flask. She looked up just before he passed out the gate into the darkness. "Wait!" she cried out, taking a few steps toward him. Riley paused to turn and stare. Luzero ran to him as tears started flowing again. "You cannot go this way, not knowing the truth!" she said.

"Don't be confusing me with more of that at a time like this!" Riley laughed, starting to leave again.

"You must understand, por favor!" Luzero pleaded. "The Aztecs and the war god," she stammered. "You go to his place."

"His place be better than most for a fight, I'll wager," Riley said. He saw Moreno waiting by the gate. "Got to go afore Moreno shoots me for a deserter."

"I was joking when I told you in the temple they sacrificed virgins to the gods," Luzero admitted. "They sacrificed warriors," she said softly. The gorget she gave him still hung from his neck. She kissed the back of her fingers on one hand and pressed them to the gorget's silver Mexican eagle.

Riley's smile faded as he gently pulled away, turned, and marched out the gate. He did not understand why, but he felt a tug to look back. Luzero still stood there, backlit against the roaring bonfire, silhouetted against the flames. How she knew that he would look back again, Riley could only guess. But Luzero waved her hand goodbye in a slow, almost religious gesture, ending with a resolute sign of the cross.

CHAPTER 10
CHURUBUSCO: FIRST ASSAULT
AUGUST 20, 1847

Beneath the oppressive heat of late afternoon sun and a choking pall of smoke, the deafening discord of battle swirled around a walled complex of stone buildings. Behind the Convent of San Mateo's domed chapel and bell tower the Churubusco River flowed, lined with tropical foliage and palm trees. Across a flat plain beyond, the distant buildings of Mexico City shimmered like a mirage at the foot of volcanic mountains.

Rippling toward the complex from the other three sides were sky-blue waves of U.S. regulars in lines of battle. Flags fluttered above their bright bayonets as fifes and drums played "Green Grows the Laurel." In their wake sprawled clusters of dead and wounded among maguey plants and prickly pear cactus.

Three batteries of field artillery massed in one long line fired eighteen guns one after the other sounding like rolling peals of thunder. Each crew stepped lively in turn to re-load with a fever, the scent of victory hanging pungent in the smoky air. During the barrage, a column of Dragoons led by Colonel Harney trotted to a halt beside the batteries.

Harney peered through his brass spyglass to catch glimpses of the fighting. He saw artillery shells burst along the convent walls that bristled with veteran Mexican riflemen of the 11th Regiment. Each soldado loaded and fired independently as rapidly as possible. One squad near the tattered regimental flag finished loading their Baker rifles behind the wall, rose as one, aimed and fired, then dropped back down again to re-load.

A company of U.S. regulars took a resulting half-dozen casualties in the front rank. But officers and sergeants screamed terse commands and the disciplined men closed the gaps, realigned their formation, and continued to trudge forward, carrying their muskets on their shoulders.

"Huzzah! My boys!" Harney shouted, unable to contain his enthusiasm and pride. The long line of artillery beside Harney unleashed another barrage by battalion, in which all eighteen guns fired together in one volley. Their deep roar crackled with a deafening boom and the clay ground shivered. Thick smoke engulfed the guns and grimy artillerymen. Harney again used his spyglass.

Shells exploded above and among the main buildings of the convent, defended by Baker riflemen of the Fourth Light Infantry. The stoic veterans fired as sharpshooters from convent windows, staircases, rooftops, even from the bell tower. They wore distinctive blue coatees faced with scarlet but piped in white with green collars and shako pompons. A shell burst blew one soldado out of the bell tower, shredding a huge Mexican national flag lashed to the belfry.

In its shadow outside the walls and in front of an arched double gate loomed massive, ten-foot-high earthworks. The muzzles of three bronze cannon protruded through gun ports. The green San Patricio flag fluttered above.

"Damn them!" Harney cursed. "But at least I've got one more chance," he added softly.

Inside the earthworks, Ockter looked like a crazed pirate with his eye patch and a bandanna tied around his head. He was sweating profusely, filthy in black powder residue and encrusted dirt. "Ready!" he shouted above the din.

"Fire!" bellowed Riley from atop an observation step beside the gun platform. In an almost prayerful gesture, he jerked both arms from above his head to the sides, as if imploring his guns to hit their mark. His uniform coat hung open, unhooked from above his sword belt to his throat like his vest beneath. His pleated white shirt was brownish gray from powder stains, smoke, and grime. It clung to his skin from sweat.

The three guns erupted one after another in orange fire, white smoke, and a throaty crack. Morstadt's German crew was the first to start re-loading with frenzied precision. Some gunners had removed their uniform coats and worked in shirts drenched in sweat. A few San Patricios lay dead and bloated near the guns from hours in the sun.

Three shells exploded just in front of an advancing line of U.S. regulars. Dozens fell amid screams and flying sprays of dirt, cactus, equipment, and gore. They quickly closed the gaping holes in the ranks at the shouted commands of an officer, who emerged at the side of the troops.

"At last we're in musket range!" Captain Merrill shouted. His beleagured Fifth Infantry veterans responded with an enthusiastic "Huzzah!" "Fire by company!" Merrill ordered, raising his sword. "Ready! Aim! Fire!" he shouted, slicing his blade downward. The disciplined regulars unleashed a thundering, crisp volley that engulfed their ranks in smoke. "Load!" shouted Merrill.

Exposed behind the embrasure as they re-loaded the guns, several of Ockter's crew spun and fell from the volley. Some paused to help the wounded; others dragged the dead out of the way. "Keep to your guns!" Ockter yelled. Morstadt shoved a few back to their posts.

"*Fuego!*" roared Dalton behind his adjacent infantry. The Anglo and Mexican San Patricios unleashed a thunderous volley. Almost immediately, return fire hit some while the rest ducked down. Dalton saw Riley tumble gracelessly off his platform with blood streaming down one side of his head. He lay motionless. Ockter, Morstadt, and others exchanged fearful looks but kept loading the guns. Dalton trotted to him.

Riley moaned and began to move. He sat up, held his head, and found a jagged crease down one side of his scalp. He stared dumbfounded at the blood on his hand. It is always a surprise, Riley thought. "I'll be damned," he muttered.

"Soon enough," Dalton said as he arrived. Riley turned to see him standing overhead, his face clean compared to Riley's.

"See you been hard at work," Riley grunted. Stoic Dalton wrapped a filthy, stained bandanna around Riley's bleeding head. He tied it tight with a jerk. "Ow!" Riley bellowed. "Save 'em the trouble to kill me why don't you?!" Dalton just smiled.

Moreno slipped through the gates and ran a gauntlet of shell bursts as he made his way through the muck to Riley and Dalton. Soldados were blown off the walls and San Patricios tumbled from the ramparts as he passed. He saw Mejia and Conahan behind their companies directing volleys and gestured at them to follow. He reached Riley and Dalton just as Ockter's crews finished re-loading the guns. The Prussian raised his arm.

"Ready!" shouted Ockter, flashing a relieved grin at Riley.

Moreno knelt and looked at Riley with concern.

"Survived worse I have," Riley said, shrugging. Moreno gave a nod of relief as he lit a cigar. Mejia and Conahan arrived at a run and crouched with them. Riley looked at each gun crew and nodded at Ockter.

"Fire!" Ockter screamed. All three guns roared and recoiled. The gunners started sponging out the barrels to Morstadt's commands.

"Ockter!" Riley yelled with a wave. The Prussian trotted over breathless and saluted. Exasperated, Riley barely touched his throbbing head to return the salute and winced in reply. Dalton laughed deliciously and lit his pipe.

"General Rincon requests 'fire by battalion,' " Moreno said, pointing behind them, "in successive volleys."

They looked up to see a solid line of 11th Infantry riflemen standing shoulder to shoulder behind the wall on one side of the gate. On the other, an equally solid rank of Fourth Light Infantry riflemen rose into view. To shouted Spanish commands, all presented their gleaming Baker rifles at the ready.

"Having less range than the rifles, our muskets must be the last to fire," Moreno added, "when the gringos are the closest."

"A 'fourth regiment' our guns could be," Ockter suggested eagerly, "if loaded as shotguns." He looked at Riley, who barely nodded.

Dalton stared at them, puffed his pipe, and peeked over the earthwork. "My own Second, Conahan's Seventh, and himself's Fifth," he observed. He looked at Riley, Conahan, and Ockter. They traded glances of muddled, mixed emotions. "Coming on grand they are," Dalton added, "in the same old way."

Moreno looked at them barely hiding a sense of pity, and some guilt. The pounding drums and screeching fifes of approaching U.S. troops grew louder.

"To recall your Wellington at Waterloo, Major," Moreno said to Riley, "now you must stop them in 'the same old way.' "

"Hell," groused Riley scowling, "just give me the damn range."

Dalton peered out again. A thick wall of regulars with national and regimental flags fluttering above them fired a crashing volley. Dalton ducked hard as musket balls churned up the earthworks and a few more San Patricio infantry fell. Mejia rolled his eyes when Dalton angrily yanked out his smothered pipe to spit dirt.

"Dirty heathens!" Dalton roared, standing and shaking his fist at the oncoming troops. "You've spoilt my smoke entirely, you have!"

"Now they've gone an' done it," said Conahan. "They got

him angry."

"Fire!" a distant Yank voice bellowed while Dalton was still standing exposed. Instantly, Mejia tackled him to the ground as the roar of a volley sent musket balls churning up the dirt where Dalton had just stood.

"Old vaqueros say pace yourself," Mejia said, breathing hard, "so to be living the longer life." He rolled off Dalton as the rest laughed.

"*Ni por relajo!*" Dalton managed, though with a horrible accent.

"Not by a damn sight!" Mejia interpreted to Riley's quizzical look.

Dalton sat up, lit his pipe again, and nodded in thanks. "Seventy yards," Dalton finally said with a frustrated look at Riley.

"I'd pace their lives out to about fifty yards," Riley opined, pointing as he rose shakily to his feet. "Load double cannister," he said with a grim look at Ockter, who saluted smartly. "And the last shall be first," he added to Moreno, who nodded.

"Charge bayonet!" a U.S. infantry captain shouted beside his solid wall of regulars fifty yards in front of Riley's guns. "Huzzah!" the grimy, determined troops yelled as they snapped their muskets to the chest-high position, gleaming bayonets pointing forward.

In the gun embrasures, powder blackened hands ripped canvas covers off the front end of cylindrical tin cans attached to powder bags. Inside the tin cans were twenty one-inch-wide iron balls. The "cannister" rounds were shoved down the muzzles and rammed home with a peculiar, hollow, menacing thunk.

"At the double quick, forward, march!" commanded the same U.S. infantry captain. The men stepped off with precision and moved in a seemingly irresistible wave toward the guns. The tramp of their broghans on the hard dirt sounded like the dull patter of a summer shower on wood shingles.

"Fire!" bellowed Riley, standing on his observation platform beside Moreno. All three guns belched orange fire, white smoke, and thunder. Almost instantly, a resonating metallic clatter followed the barrage as the iron balls sprayed widely from the gun muzzles as if from giant shotguns.

Three corridors were blasted through the solid sky-blue ranks with a pitiful dying moan mingled with shrieks of terror. Bits of shredded bodies, uniforms, and equipment flew skyward in a dusty pink cloud of dirt and blood.

"*Fuego!*" commanded General Rincon. Atop the arched gate, he pointed his sword to the 11th Infantry at his right. The entire battalion fired a crisp, crackling volley. Rings of white smoke swirled toward the Americans.

Clusters of regulars tumbled, riddled with ragged, bloody .72-caliber rifle balls, making wide gaps in another wave of U.S. troops advancing from the right.

"*Fuego!*" Rincon bellowed again, this time pointing his sword at the Fourth Light Infantry to his left. They fired a thundering volley.

Dozens more U.S. troops fell in a third battalion charging from the left at a steady run. Survivors kept coming and gingerly leaped over fallen comrades.

"*Fuego!*" yelled Moreno with his sword upraised, slicing it downward. Dalton, Conahan, and Mejia echoed the command down the entire line of San Patricio infantry. They fired a booming volley.

The stunned survivors of Riley's blast of cannister staggered to a confused stop as more clusters fell in a hail of .75-caliber Brown Bess musket balls. Officers and sergeants screamed to close the thinning ranks. Some hesitated.

Successive massed infantry volleys rotated from the right of

General Rincon to his left and then down again to the San Patricios. Each volley blasted larger gaps in the American ranks.

The brave U.S. troops fired ragged volleys in return, their usual solid, crisp efficiency slackening with their numbers. The charge stalled. A few of the regulars started to run but were shoved back into line by sergeants and officers.

"Fall back in order!" yelled Captain Merrill, pointing behind him with his sword. "Dress ranks!" he barked. "Don't show them your backs!" His company, Riley's old comrades, backed off the field, following the general retreat.

"Fire!" Riley bellowed. The three guns erupted once again with a final blast of the clattering cannister. A shroud of smoke clung like ground fog to the bloody, mottled carpet of mangled corpses and writhing wounded. For a long moment, the only sounds were lonely wind, fluttering flags, mournful moans, and buzzing flies.

"Viva Mexico!" suddenly cried one exuberant soldado on the wall. Instantly, hundreds more took up the cry throughout the convent. Many brandished rifles above their heads in victory. Color sergeants waved regimental flags from the walls in triumph.

In the San Patricio earthworks, gunners and infantrymen slapped one another on the back, clasped hands, and even embraced in the joy of just being alive. Ockter lovingly patted the breech of one of his guns as Morstadt yelled like a lunatic waving the San Patricio flag atop the ramparts.

While some crossed themselves in thanks and others mouthed silent prayers, Dalton, Conahan, and Riley found one another and just stared out in silence at the grisly scene before them, each lost in melancholy thoughts of just who may be lying out there.

Rose, Hogan, and the reluctant recruit, still wearing his head bandage, re-loaded their muskets together on the ramparts.

Rose elbowed Hogan, nodding at the old man. "It was a clean shot to the head you gave that sergeant," Rose teased the Irishman. "His brains fanned out the back of his skull like a spilled pink pudding." Rose gestured graphically as Hogan laughed.

"But you didn't fire on the old flag now, did you Paddy?" Hogan chided as Rose chuckled.

The older recruit finished loading his musket and glared at them. Cheering and general jubilation continued all around them even as the wounded were tended to or carried toward the gates. " 'Tis plain I got t'fight or be killed meself," he growled. "But I'll not cheer me own damnation." The grins on Rose and Hogan faded.

Minutes later just inside the open convent gates, General Rincon was receiving reports from captains of the 11th and Fourth regiments as Riley and Moreno approached. They first stepped to a well, Riley pulling up the bucket and ladle.

"I see this greaser Alamo got itself a back door," Riley joked, pointing to a gate at the rear of the compound. He drank some, pouring most of the cool water on his throbbing head.

"So did the one in Texas," Moreno said as Riley handed him a dripping ladle full. Riley stared at him disbelieving as Moreno drank. "Our lancers caught about sixty breaking out, running in the open," he added. "They did not last long."

Riley stared thoughtfully at the convent rear gate, wondering if the men inside the Alamo had thought of their "back door" as a last gasp for survival. He saw the rifle company captains salute, turn, and leave Rincon, looking grim. Riley and Moreno traded anxious looks and walked to him.

"This go we gave 'em a hard lesson in respect, sir," Riley said to Rincon as he saluted with Moreno.

"Yes, but now the rifle battalions have less than three rounds left per man," Rincon said. He looked questioningly at Riley.

"My guns did good work, but now they're empty as a

drunkard's glass," Riley admitted. "Powder and shot both gone. No more cannister, either."

The three officers looked behind them into the compound. Mexican medical stewards in bloodied gray smocks were giving primitive care to wounded Mexicans and San Patricios, laid in the shade beneath the firing scaffolds. The dead lay everywhere. The surviving ranks atop the scaffolds appeared thin.

"When they come again," Moreno said, nodding at the wounded, "the norteamericanos will be more than we have of either men or of bullets."

"Won't even slow 'em down," Riley predicted. He looked at Moreno. "Maybe if you found his worship," he suggested, "he might could send us something more useful than his elegant words." Rincon and Moreno saw merit in Riley's sarcasm.

"He directs defense at the fortified bridge," Rincon said. "Take the river road," he urged Moreno, nodding toward Riley's back door, "and my horse." Rincon waved at an aide holding a richly caparisoned horse in the shade of a brush arbor. Moreno darted a half smile at Riley, puffed his cigar, and walked toward the horse being led to him. He quickly mounted and spurred out the back gate at a trot. "Leave your empty guns, Major," Rincon said to Riley. "Pull your men inside."

"I'll be careful to close the gate behind us, sir," Riley joked, saluting.

"That should keep them out, Major," Rincon said, laughing as he walked away.

Riley's false bravado wilted to a look of resigned determination as he strode across the compound. At the open gate, he paused, braced himself with a sigh, and walked out to confront his men with their desperate situation.

Minutes later, through his spyglass Santa Anna watched the last of the San Patricios shuffle through the archway and into the compound, followed by Riley. The gates swung shut behind them. "Had I a few hundred more like them," he sighed, turning in his saddle to Moreno, just arrived, and Micheltorena, "I could have won this battle."

"Excellency, I did not realize we had already lost," Micheltorena ventured.

Moreno puffed his cigar and stared in cynical disappointment at Santa Anna as he methodically collapsed his spyglass. They sat their horses astride a crossroads; one led to the convent, the other, to a bridge behind them. Mounted Hussars waited nearby as Santa Anna's escort.

Santa Anna frowned. "But what can one expect?" he mumbled. "You see what I am left with?!" he snapped, pointing beside them. Moreno looked out of politeness; Micheltorena, out of intimidation.

A high earthen embankment with firing steps had been built across the bridge road. The ramparts were manned with a motley mix of dismounted Tulancingo cuirassiers, grenadiers, infantry recruits in white uniforms, "walking wounded" from a dozen different regiments, and civilians, including a few women. Most tried to relax by smoking cigareets and sharing canteens. The dead lay everywhere. A Mexican flag hung limp atop the wall in the humid heat.

"They pushed the gringos back, did they not?" Moreno said in Spanish.

Santa Anna grunted. "This morning near Contreras," he replied in English, lowering his voice and leaning to Moreno, "General Scott attacked with the other half of his army, his volunteer divisions. Trying to stop him, General Valencia destroyed my real soldiers." He grimaced in pain and popped open his snuff box. "This rabble cannot learn the truth," he said, dabbing opium powder on his tongue, "so speak English." Moreno nodded. "I had ordered Valencia to retreat and join me here," Santa Anna seethed. "But Valencia stayed to fight!"

"It is possible," suggested Moreno sarcastically, "that he thought fighting was his duty, Excellency." Micheltorena looked at Moreno as if he had just committed suicide.

"The insubordinate dog deserves to have his brains blown out," Santa Anna fumed, oblivious.

The sounds of a rolling, heavy vehicle, horse hooves, and tramping feet drew Moreno's attention. Coming across the bridge was a freight wagon full of wooden cartridge boxes and guarded by ten mounted cuirassiers. Moreno recognized the driver as Sandy, Riley's black acquaintance. His two black employees rode in the wagon bed armed with muskets. Marching with them was a company of civilian militia led by a teenage lieutenant in the blue cadet uniform of the Military Academy at Chapultepec; marching near him with a musket, Bel.

"Real soldiers are not always the best patriots," Moreno observed, staring at Bel as they marched past. She saw and smiled. "But why are you here?"

"I could not stay away!" Bel exclaimed excitedly to Moreno. "Where is my Dalton?! I come to light his pipe!" she added with a pert smile.

"Quiet in the ranks!" shouted the teenager in Spanish, his voice cracking.

"Is he not cute?!" Bel giggled, pointing at him and marching on.

"Take them with you," Santa Anna snapped, "and the ammunition wagon. I have no use for them." He started riding to the bridge, muttering to himself. "I must leave to organize the final defense of the city," Santa Anna mumbled. "There are new regiments to raise, reserves to bring up . . . so much to do."

"The only regiments we have left," Micheltorena whispered to Moreno, "are in his mind. *Vaya con Dios,* my friend," he said, clasping Moreno's arm. Micheltorena waved the Hussars to follow him and fall in behind Santa Anna. Moreno watched in unnerved fascination as if beholding a madman.

"You must hold long enough to buy me enough time," Santa Anna called out over his shoulder, adding, almost nonchalantly, "even to the death!"

"Viva Santa Anna!" cried the old man from the passing militia ranks who had cheered from his balcony the day before. His son beside him yelled "Viva Mexico!" Others of varying ages and classes took up the cry. Santa Anna did not turn to acknowledge their cheers. He merely removed his red, white, and green feathered bicorn to wave it casually as he rode over the bridge out of sight.

Moreno slumped in his saddle. He struggled to separate doing his duty for that faithless leader from doing his duty for Mexico. It seemed to Moreno that was the only way to find the strength to continue fighting, to return to the fortified convent and to face Riley and his now doomed men.

CHAPTER 11
CHURUBUSCO: THE PAUSE
AUGUST 20, 1847

A ragged human corridor of sweat soaked, grime covered soldados and San Patricios cheered lustily as the mounted cuirassiers, ammunition wagon, and militia passed into the courtyard
through the rear gate. The fiddle strains of "Temperance Reel"
floated above the raucous noise from Conahan playing near the
well, where Morstadt and Ockter stood drinking.

"For the cannon, there looks to be nothing," grumbled
Morstadt, peering into the wagon bed as Sandy drove it past.
Ockter's brow furrowed.

"Nothing but more musket balls than time to shoot them,"
Ockter mused. He nudged Morstadt to follow. "Bring a gun
crew," he said, walking toward the front gate. Morstadt looked
at Conahan, who turned his palms out in a gesture of helpless
curiosity.

"At finding balls of iron, only a wanton wench be better than
Ockter," Conahan cracked. Morstadt laughed.

The young cadet lieutenant stiffly marched his civilian militia
to General Rincon, who watched in amusement with Moreno,
Riley, Dalton, and Mejia.

"Now Santa Anna sends us book soldiers," Rincon noted
wryly, nodding at the young martinet. "He is from our military
academy at Chapultepec."

"It always starts with the books," noted Riley.

"But always it ends here," Moreno added.

"*Alto!*" the cadet sang out. The civilians managed a jerky, bumbling stop. A few even chuckled at themselves. These included Bel, whose infectious giggle was instantly recognized by Dalton. His jaw dropped open when he saw her. He jabbed Riley hard in the ribs.

"What is herself doing here?!" Dalton whispered angrily.

"Being alone, I hope," Riley replied, searching the ranks and relieved at not seeing Luzero.

"My general, I bring citizens who wish to fight," the cadet announced proudly. He snapped a crisp salute, returned by Rincon and the others.

"I am sure their wish will be granted, Cadet Lieutenant," Rincon said wryly. Rincon eyed a low stone wall beside a convent walkway that faced the front gate. "They might do some good there," he said, pointing.

The youngster looked disappointed. "Give us a position of honor, sir," he said with youthful bravado. Rincon, Moreno, and Mejia traded bemused looks. "What can we do in such a place?" he whined.

"When the gringos come charging through that gate," Rincon said with grim humor, "shoot them." The young cadet nodded eagerly, saluted, turned on his heels sharply, and faced his militia.

"Follow me!" he ordered, leading the civilians toward the wall.

Bel smiled and waved airily at Dalton as she left, but he only scowled. She pursed her lips in a pout and stomped away in a childlike tantrum. Rincon and Moreno left the others and walked toward the wagon.

"A sorry man it is," snickered Mejia to Dalton, "who cannot be controlling his woman."

Riley chuckled as Dalton grunted and walked toward Bel, his pipe puffing like a chimney. "With a bit of the luck," said Riley watching, "we can hold long enough now to cover Valencia's

skedaddle—and then beat it out the back door our own selves."
Mejia and Riley eyed each other; trading looks of doubt.

"Major, Lieutenant . . ." Moreno called, "please to join us,
por favor." He sounded worried. Riley and Mejia joined Moreno
and Rincon at the wagon.

At the wall beside the convent porch, Dalton stood frowning
at a petulant Bel. Behind them, the cadet lieutenant patiently
positioned the civilians, even showing some how to work their
muskets.

"Going up is private and only one to a person," Dalton
fumed. "Could you not show me that much respect?! Let me
die unfettered of worrying about the sweet likes of you!" He
grew more furious when she lost her scowl and smiled at him
warmly.

"More Mexicano every day you are sounding," Bel purred.
He threw up his arms and looked at the heavens.

"Give me strength," he muttered. Dalton frowned at her, but
his anger quickly faded. "I only wanted you safe and in the
clear," he said tenderly.

Bel nodded in understanding. "They are one, my heart and
yours," she said. "Were yours to stop beating, so must mine. So-
o-o," she whined, "with you I may as well be staying." He sighed
in submission and enfolded her in his arms.

At the wagon, Moreno held a handful of musket cartridges
above a full wooden box with its lid pried off. He slowly let the
ammunition slip through his fingers. "It is all .75 caliber, too
large for the Baker rifle regiments," Moreno said flatly, watching the cartridges clatter back into the box. He looked at Riley
and Mejia. "It fits only your few Brown Bess muskets."

Rincon, Moreno, Riley, and Mejia stared at one another in
silent, grim resignation: what little hope there was just died.

"And here I fretted if my lads'd have enough to go around,"
Riley opined, nodding at the cartridge boxes. His attention was

drawn to the front gate as it swung open. Ockter, Morstadt, and a gun crew wheeled in one bronze cannon. "Excuse me whilst I go thrash an idiot," Riley said, bowing curtly and striding toward Ockter.

"He will fight to the end," Rincon surmised.

"Like the bull," Mejia observed, exchanging wry smiles with Moreno.

"Those of us not killed will be paroled when captured," Moreno said, looking intently at Rincon. "His brave men will be hanged." He arched an eyebrow in a question. Mejia nodded to agree. Rincon considered for a moment.

"Unload the wagon, Lieutenant," Rincon said to Mejia, who saluted smartly. "Fill it with wounded and send it back to the city, Major, with a strong escort of 'volunteers.' " Moreno understood and nodded in thanks.

Ockter guided Morstadt and six veteran San Patricio gunners in wheeling the big gun around to face the front gate.

"Shut the gate!" Ockter yelled in Spanish at two soldados who swung the gates closed again. Riley approached. "Depress the muzzle," Ockter told Morstadt. "Zero elevation." Morstadt began turning the screw.

"Ain't but one place for an empty gun and this ain't no courthouse lawn," Riley observed caustically. Ockter snapped to attention and saluted. Riley waved it off. "This ain't nothin' but a waste of sweat."

"A box of those cartridges unrolled would give us loose powder and lead balls," Ockter replied, nodding at the wagon. Riley cocked his head, surprisingly liking the idea. "It could be enough for one parting shot from a proud artilleryman," Ockter added solemnly, saluting once again. Riley understood. He slowly braced himself to attention and gave Ockter a formal salute.

Suddenly, distant drums began beating a march cadence,

swelling into a loud, irresistible wave rolling ever nearer. "All the gringos in the world are coming!" shouted an amazed soldado in Spanish from the bell tower. He pointed excitedly in three directions. Rincon and Moreno trotted toward the tower, highest spot in the convent. Mexican officers and sergeants shouted orders. The garrison scrambled up ladders to defend the walls.

The milling San Patricios looked toward Riley. He turned to Morstadt and pointed at the center of the yard.

"To the color!" Morstadt bellowed, trotting to the spot and holding the flag aloft. The men ran to form ranks on either side of him.

"Grand notion, Ockter, but them heathen hooligans ain't giving you th'damn time!" Riley said bitterly, slappingOckter on the back consolingly. Riley trotted to catch up with Moreno, already climbing the bell tower stairs.

Disagreeing, Ockter nudged a gunner and nodded at the wagon being unloaded by Mejia and his guards. Ockter and the gunner ran toward the wagon.

Through a spyglass, Moreno saw a column of dusty sky-blue infantry trudging along the river road to the steady drum cadence. The blue regimental flag read "Eighth Regt. U.S. Infantry." Moreno lowered his glass and looked in resignation at Rincon, who looked elsewhere through his own spyglass.

"They must be arriving from Contreras," Moreno said to Riley, looking anxious. The drums grew louder as more joined in.

Rincon watched as another column of infantry marched over a hill on a road heading straight for the convent. The flag read "Third Regt. U.S. Infantry." The drums grew even louder as another column appeared on the brow of the hill behind them. Rincon lowered his glass and turned to Riley, who was looking in the direction of the fortified bridge.

"Two more regiments," Rincon said. "But they do not yet deploy."

"They do at the bridge," Riley said, pointing. "That'd be where the rest are headed."

Moreno and Rincon turned toward the bridge. A third column of infantry trotted into a line of battle ten companies wide. In the center its flag read "Sixth Regt. U.S. Infantry." More drums joined the continuing rolling thunder. "They will take the bridge first," Rincon predicted, lowering his glass, "to cut us off."

"The wounded and their 'escort' should leave," Moreno said, staring intently at Rincon. He nodded, turned, and quickly descended the stairs. Riley looked suspiciously at Moreno as he lit a cigar. The continuing drums were joined by a chorus of fifes piping "Green Grows the Laurel."

"Shit an' I'm sick of that damn song," growled Riley.

"If nothing else," Moreno said deadpan, "it has added a colorful new word to our language."

"You'd best cough up whatever you're chokin' on, Colonel," Riley glared in reply.

"Back in Matamoros," Moreno admitted, "I gave you less choice than you truly had." He smiled thinly, took a deep drag on his cigar, and exhaled. Riley frowned and cocked his head. "And several times more since," Moreno added, looking pained. "It was my 'duty,' " he said.

"Making it my own duty to pass on the blarney, as it were," Riley said. His frown slowly relaxed into a wry, amused grin. " 'Tis a fitting end for my entire tortured life of the same."

"My duty now," Moreno pressed, "is to give you a choice." The drums suddenly stopped. The only sound was wind whipping the tattered Mexican tricolor on the tower. Riley gave him a quizzical look.

Minutes later, the deserter companies stood in formation in

the courtyard a few yards from Sandy's wagon, now full of wounded soldados and San Patricios. Morstadt held the green flag, which fluttered gently in the hot breeze.

The cuirassiers stood beside their horses in a column of twos in front of the wagon, pointed toward the rear gate. A cuirassier sergeant shouted a command in Spanish. The troopers mounted up. Two soldados swung open the rear gate. Mexican troops watched from the walls, the convent windows, the flat roofs, and the tower. Bel watched with the militia behind the low stone wall. All eyes were on Riley, pacing in front of the serried ranks of his battalion.

" 'Tis by many a road at first you come," Riley declared. "But I bullied and blarnied the lot of you onto my own twisted path. That road runs out here!" Dalton stared stone faced, puffing his pipe. "Whatever demon drove you to shed your life on the other side," Riley continued, "today is your chance to spit in its eye." He stared grimly into the faces of Conahan, Ockter, and Morstadt. "Those what stay got no chance other than that," he added grimly. Riley paced down the line. "If you choose to go out with the wounded," he resumed, pointing, "there's th'back door. For th'first time in my damn life, I've found a reason not to use it."

He stared at Moreno, standing with Mejia and the guards to one side. Moreno gave him a discreet nod of respect, signifying a bond of mutual understanding.

"So long as I can fight," Riley continued, "I'll keep safe what matters more to me now than my own worthless hide." He reached the end of the ranks, turned, and looked down the line of grimy, rigid faces. "Either way, you got my eternal thanks. May the road you choose rise up to meet you. And at its end, may the pot of gold you come looking for be there to greet you."

The San Patricios looked stunned. They began exchanging

curious looks, talking in whispers while trying to maintain military decorum.

"You take with you my personal respect," Moreno declared as he pulled out a cigar, "and the undying gratitude and love of the people of Mexico." He lit up. "Feel free to talk in ranks."

The men openly started discussing the turn in events as Riley ambled toward the wagon. He caught Sandy's eye. The old black man gave a jaunty, casual salute with a touch to his black sombrero.

Dalton looked over his shoulder and saw Bel, leaning on her musket behind the stone wall. She saw his look and nodded with an enigmatic little smile. He turned to the front again, puffing his pipe, frowning.

At the wagon, Riley started shaking the hand of every wounded San Patricio lying in its bed. The sound of an artillery barrage erupted in the near distance, startling everyone. Riley darted a look up at the sentry.

"The gringos attack the bridge!" the soldado cried in Spanish, pointing. The roar of artillery continued unabated.

"Those who go must leave now!" Moreno said urgently. "Fall in behind the wagon!" Mejia lit up a cigareet and watched intently.

Dalton braced, sighed, clenched his pipe tightly, and stepped out of ranks to the surprise of all. He paused and stared at Riley a moment, who looked at him in a curious blend of surprise and relief. Dalton strode purposefully to Ockter's gun, which was pointed at the gates. He turned to face the formation, leaned casually against a wheel of the gun carriage, and blew a smoke ring.

"No friend of mine asks me to quit the grandest fight of my life," he asserted, folding his arms defiantly. Riley just shook his head and doffed his cap.

"Viva!" cried Bel, laughing and clapping.

"Silencio!" ordered the young cadet. She gave him a stern look that might have come from his mother.

"You must learn manners," she said in Spanish, "or I will put you across my knee!" Other civilians chuckled.

Ockter, Conahan, and Morstadt exchanged quick looks and stepped out briskly, walking to join Dalton. Morstadt planted the flag by the gun.

The reluctant Irish recruit adjusted his head bandage as he leaned forward in ranks to look up and down the line. The San Patricios were mostly silent now, staring at either Dalton's group or the wagon, staying or leaving. The unmistakable rattle of musketry joined the ongoing bombardment at the bridge. Rose and Hogan, standing on either side of him, exchanged looks.

"You'd best take your chance whilst you got it," advised Hogan sincerely. "For myself," he admitted, "I've found th'better brawls were always behind barred doors."

"If I live long enough to work my own land," Rose vowed, "not one will be saying I did not earn it."

"Sure an' I'll not be made th'coward here," snapped the old Irishman. He stepped out first and walked toward Dalton. Surprised, Rose and Hogan trotted to catch up. The three fell in behind the fluttering green flag.

As if by unanimous, silent assent, the remaining San Patricios broke ranks and walked individually to Dalton. They formed an uneven, rambling line behind the flag and gun. In a variety of defiant, grim attitudes, they stared at Riley, looking dumbstruck. The roar of the bridge battle grew.

"Viva San Patricio!" bellowed Mejia to Moreno's surprise. The lieutenant waved the tattered survivors of his guard company to follow him over to Dalton. They joined the Anglos as resounding cheers of "Viva!" and "Viva San Patricio!" from the watching Mexican soldados drowned out the din of gunfire.

Riley stood silently staring at his battalion, overcome with emotion. Tears traced his grimy cheeks. "For once," he said huskily, "I got nothing to say." He stepped to the waiting wagon of wounded.

"Looks like I'm waitin' on nobody," Sandy said from the driver's box.

Riley recovered, cleared his throat, and turned to extend his hand up to him. Sandy clasped it warmly. "Leastwise, not since you swum the river," Riley said, pulling a wry smile from Sandy. "I hope it was worth the baptism."

"The only word Mexicans got for us is *'negro,'* " Sandy replied, " 'black.' " He sighed a satisfied smile. "At last, I'm called by just what I always am," he added, "and not what somebody else wants me to be."

"Where'd the 'black Irish' help get off to?" Riley joked, pointing at the wagon bed. Sandy nodded at the low stone wall. The two young blacks stood with the militia near Bel and the cadet lieutenant. "You'll be looking for some new help," Riley warned.

Moreno arrived and waved urgently at the cuirassier sergeant. "Move out at a trot!" Moreno snapped in Spanish. The sergeant issued commands and the cuirassiers started forward.

"At the hospital convent," Riley said to Sandy, "a señorita might be asking after me. Tell her for me," he added softly, "I found my leprechaun's gold when first I looked into her eyes. But I was too damn angry and drunk to know it."

"Vaya con Dios, mi simpatico amigo," Sandy said, his smile fading with a respectful nod. He cracked his whip above the mules. The wagon lurched forward and followed the trotting cuirassiers out the rear gate. It was swung shut and barred behind them with a solid thud, sounding to Riley like the closing of a coffin lid.

Riley and Moreno faced the gathered San Patricios, standing beside the gun and the flag. The roar of the fight at the bridge raged in the distance. Riley looked at the grim, grimy, determined faces, feeling he needed to say more. But he could not find the words, a unique failing for him. He stood there looking sheepish, shifting on his feet.

"For once," Moreno said softly, observing Riley's discomfort, "it is appropriate you say nothing."

Riley assumed a wide stance, determined to muster words of gratitude. He cleared his throat. But suddenly the sound of a close artillery barrage preceded several explosions just outside the front gate, spewing dirt and debris on them all.

" 'Tis a relief!" Riley bellowed, dusting himself off. "The damn wait's been worse than a banshee's wail!" The serried ranks of San Patricios chuckled anxiously. "So now a grand reunion with our old regiments be heading our way!" Riley said.

General Rincon strode up urgently, pointing at the front wall. Mexican officers were leading troops from the left side to join those on the right, leaving half the wall empty. "They re-train their guns from the bridge to get our range," Rincon said. "You will hold the left. With our strength doubled on the right, we can fire longer."

" 'Til your rifles go empty, as it were, sir?" Riley said in a foreboding tone.

"God has His own purposes," Rincon said, resigned. "May He protect you today in this place." He nodded, turned, and left as the others saluted.

"From better places than this," said Mejia, "I have been thrown out and gone." Dalton and Riley joined Moreno in a laugh as Mejia lit up a cigareet.

"To welcome the new 'landlords,' " said Dalton, "let us make it a tough eviction." He strode toward the wall and climbed the scaffold ladder. Mejia followed, waving casually at his guards to follow him up.

"Don't stand here like a bunch o'wallflowers," taunted Conahan, urging the San Patricios toward the wall. "Th'ball's startin' up there!" They took off at a trot and scrambled up the ladders to the sergeant's continuing harangue.

Riley and Moreno started to follow but noticed Ockter, Morstadt, and a crew remaining behind in a cluster by the gun. Morstadt had picked up the flag and stood flanked by two gunners holding their caps in their hands reverently.

" 'T'ain't yet a funeral mass," Riley said, nodding at the held caps.

Ockter merely smiled and stepped aside to reveal one cartridge box lying open on the ground amid a pile of ripped and empty cartridge papers.

The two gunners held out their caps. One was bulging with loose musket balls; the other, spilling over with loose powder. Ockter looked questioningly at Riley, like a child seeking approval.

"A one-eyed Prussian can make murder out o' mush," Riley said, smiling.

"Remember, Major?" Moreno said. "Mexicans make do."

"Bring the banner, Morstadt!" laughed Riley, walking with Moreno to the wall. "May as well piss 'em off good and proper." Morstadt fell in behind with the flag.

"Load!" Ockter bellowed. The gunners took up their implements. One scooped powder from another's cap into the paper bag of a luminaria and stuffed the resulting cartridge into the tube. A third San Patricio poured his capful of musket balls down the yawning barrel with a clatter.

Now all that remained, thought Riley as he watched, was the fight. He marveled at how combat, once begun, always seemed easier than waiting, a kind of terrifying satisfaction. But unlike all those others in his storied career, Riley sensed he already knew how this fight would end. And yet, he felt deeply at peace with it; first, his reformation, he mused; then, reclamation. His once bulging mental footlocker at last felt refreshingly empty.

CHAPTER 12
CHURUBUSCO: FINAL ASSAULT
AUGUST 20, 1847

The line of U.S. cannon belched orange flame and with a muffled, throaty roar, as if the billowing smoke rings curling out from the muzzles somehow strangled their thunder. The gunners sprang to re-load as a cluster of mounted officers trotted to a halt behind the guns. A column of dragoons deployed into line behind them. Conspicuous in the group of staff officers were General Scott and Captain Robert E. Lee, both of whom pulled out spyglasses to observe effects of the bombardment.

Colonel Harney rode up beside them. Lee saluted. Harney nodded and saluted Scott. They saw the front wall and gate of the convent disappear momentarily in dust from the artillery explosions. Still, the brilliant green flag of the San Patricios could be seen fluttering atop the wall through the smoke.

"Missed the gate," muttered Harney, lowering his spyglass. He turned in his saddle to Scott and Lee. "The troops got no ladders, sir. With respect," Harney urged, "blast the gate or we'll never get that damn traitor flag."

"This assault is commanded by General Twiggs, Colonel," Scott said patiently. "I am sure he has made provisions." Harney nodded curtly.

"I believe that General Twiggs expects your dragoons to deploy behind the convent," suggested Lee tactfully, "to cut off any escape to the river." The roll of infantry drums and tramp of marching feet grew near as a column of regulars swung past. Harney bridled impatiently, watching.

"For General Scott, hip hip . . ." cried a passing crusty sergeant, waving his cap. The entire column shouted "Huzzah!"

Scott smiled graciously, removed his bicorn, and waved it grandiosely. "Take them boys!" he bellowed, rising in the saddle. "To the halls of Montezuma, take them!" More cheers resounded as troops responded to shouted commands and deployed from their column into line of battle. They advanced at the loping jog called "double quick" with equipment, canteens, and tin cups clattering in rhythm.

"The very existence of that flag is a stain upon our honor, sir," Harney growled. "It shall not pass by me!" He saluted, wheeled his horse, and shouted to the companies of dragoons in line behind them, "Battalion!"

"Company!" the officers responded, awaiting orders.

"By fours, right!" Harney bellowed, pausing to hear the command echoed by officers. "March!" he commanded and took off at a trot. Every four troopers wheeled as a unit to the right and followed him in a long, jingling column.

"Hard justice rides with Harney," mused Scott, watching him trot off. "It is my judgment, Captain Lee, that the better officer tempers his steel with mercy."

"Should I ever turn my back on our flag," joked Lee, "I shall remind you of that, sir." Scott scoffed as Lee chuckled.

The three batteries of eighteen guns cracked again as each gun fired one after another down the line. The yellow flags of the Third and Fourth U.S. Artillery fluttered barely visible through heavy smoke. A mounted artillery officer near the flags moved forward on his horse and looked through his spyglass. The sound of cheering men, beating drums, and musket volleys grew loud in the near distance.

"Cease fire!" he bellowed, lowering his spyglass. The command echoed down the line. He turned to an aide. "Our boys are already on 'em," he said amazed. "The damn greasers haven't fired a shot!"

In front of the Mexican earthworks, a series of relentless sky-blue waves rolled forward beneath the flags of six regiments. Onrushing ranks of U.S. regulars cheered lustily as they scrambled up the dirt ramparts through heavy, drifting smoke from the artillery bombardment.

"Fuego!" bellowed Rincon, standing defiantly atop the arched gateway. The Mexican regiments and the San Patricios fired a unified, crisp, roaring volley into the faces of the oncoming U.S. regulars.

The front rank atop the abandoned earthworks was decimated as hundreds of soft lead balls found their mark to shred uniforms and flesh at point-blank range. But as soon as the first wave crashed, the next rolled up from behind. More U.S. troops charged forward over the bodies of their comrades.

"A su discrecion, fuego!" bellowed Rincon. Officers echoed the command along the wall. The general pulled his belt pistol, took aim, and fired down at the pool of sky-blue regulars now flowing toward the base of the walls. Others loaded and fired at will as fast as they could.

"Pour it into 'em, lads!" bellowed Riley, walking the scaffolding with Moreno behind the men. "Don't bother to aim, just load and fire!" he yelled. "At this range, even the likes of you can't miss!"

Moreno looked amused, pulled his belt pistol, and fired with almost casual aim into the throng below. A U.S. lieutenant fell like a rock with a hole between his eyes. Riley stared at Moreno dumbfounded but impressed.

"I grew to manhood fighting duels, Major," Moreno shrugged. "It is a curse. Either I joined the army or, someday, someone would kill me."

" 'Tis a blessing you chose a safe trade!" Riley laughed.

"Company, stand!" bellowed Dalton, uplifting his arms. His

men rose from behind the wall. "Now angle down and blow 'em to hell!" he roared. The San Patricios fired straight down into the faces of the U.S. troops as they reached the base of the wall. Dozens crumpled and fell. More pressed forward from behind to take their places as the front survivors started to fall back. Confusion reigned as officers and sergeants tried to regain control.

When Riley and Moreno reached Dalton, the San Patricios were keeping up steady, independent fire all along the wall. "What ignorant arse said 'greasers' can't shoot?!" Riley joked, casting a look at Moreno. His sweating face was aglow with the pounding rush of the combat that he loved.

"Your own self should know!" Dalton yelled, just as invigorated. He heard U.S. commands and looked down at the earthworks. "Like looking in a mirror, ain't it?!' Dalton observed.

Companies of U.S. regulars had halted atop the abandoned ramparts, were dressing ranks and preparing to fire volleys. They appeared oblivious to the effects of Mexican fire even as comrades fell among them.

"An old looking glass what got cracked," muttered Riley. He spied Mejia down the line with his dozen guards. They had just finished re-loading. "Mejia!" Riley hollered. "Give them a lesson in respect!" he yelled, pointing.

"Sí, mi major!" Mejia hollered. He turned to his squad of surviving guards just as Conahan trotted up breathless. He had Rose, Hogan, the old Irish recruit, and several other San Patricios in tow.

"Duets are sweeter than solos!" Conahan shouted. Mejia nodded thankfully and pointed at an empty space on the wall, its scaffolding covered with a half-dozen dead San Patricios and guards. Conahan rushed his men into line.

"Preparen!" Mejia bellowed, Conahan echoing the command. The eighteen Mexican and Anglo San Patricios raised muskets chest high and cocked the hammers. *"Apunten!"* Mejia yelled, pointing his sword at the nearest U.S. troops on the ramparts. The men aimed. *"Fuego!"* he roared. The volley boomed, bathing the wall in smoke.

A dozen U.S. troops below tumbled and fell, leaving gaps in the formation as their company was preparing to fire its own volley. "Close it up!" bellowed their hapless lieutenant. "Ready!" he yelled. The veterans raised their muskets.

"Hold!" yelled Captain Merrill, bounding up beside the lieutenant. Company K filed into line beside the others. "Look!" Merrill yelled, pointing to the left of the gate.

While the San Patricio side of the gate remained ablaze with ongoing musketry, the Mexican side of the wall showed only a spattering of rifle fire. "Fire by battalion!" Merrill bellowed. "Left oblique!" Two companies atop the earthen ramparts aimed their muskets at an angle toward the left.

As General Rincon walked the scaffold there behind members of the Fourth Light Infantry and Eleventh Regiment, he saw they looked brave but nervous as they waited behind the wall. A few fired some final rounds, reached anxiously into their cartridge boxes, and found them empty. One young soldado fumbled desperately searching for a cartridge. He looked up pleadingly at Rincon as he passed. "How can we fight with no bullets?!" he cried.

Rincon, aware that many other eyes were upon him, picked up the rifle of a dead soldado. "With cold steel!" he bellowed, thrusting its muzzle end with gleaming bayonet over the wall. "Viva!" cheered the soldados. "Viva Rincon!" The young soldado smiled thinly, braced himself, and affixed his bayonet.

At the distant cry of "Fire!", two U.S. companies atop the earthworks below unleashed a volley up toward the Mexicans. A dozen men were hit, tumbling into the courtyard. Rincon beheld the young soldado staring vacantly at the sky with a bloody hole in his forehead. Rincon reached down and closed his eyes. Cheers from the base of the wall outside suddenly drew Rincon's attention.

U.S. troops were forming human ladders by climbing up onto each other's backs, holding muskets between two men, and allowing comrades to step up onto the muskets. With a stretch, each man could pull himself up to the top.

"They climb like ants!" Rincon scoffed as he leaned over the wall. He turned to his men and shouted, "Kill these insects!"

Mexicans bayoneted many as they reached the top of the wall, some using their muskets as clubs. U.S. troops tumbled back down onto others milling below. More began climbing. Cries of "Huzzah!" competed with "Viva!"

More volleys were fired by U.S. troops atop the earthworks, creating gaps in the Mexican line as soldados pitched forward off the wall. Finally, some Americans leaped over the top. Some were bayoneted immediately by charging soldados. But many more jumped onto the scaffold. Numbers prevailed.

"They've breached the wall!" cried Merrill, atop the earthen rampart. He pointed his sword at the Mexican side of the gate. Americans still huddling at the base of the San Patricio side, seeking shelter from their ongoing fire, heard his cry and looked. Unable to climb in the face of blazing musketry, men skirted the wall to follow officers and sergeants toward the other side of the gate, now vulnerable.

But for an instant, it looked like victory to the San Patricios. "Viva!" they cried over and over as Conahan, Rose, Hogan, and the old Irishman fired parting shots at what looked like the retreating Yanks. Mejia and his guards beside them cheered and brandished their muskets as they stared over the wall. The ground in their front was now empty, though littered with dead and wounded.

Moreno peered cautiously over the wall toward the gate and

saw a teeming throng pushing forward relentlessly. Fierce U.S. troops were climbing hand over hand on top of one another, scaling the walls without ladders. "Huzzah!" resounded from hundreds of voices. Moreno staggered back, stunned, haunted.

Riley grabbed him. "You hit, Colonel?!" Riley yelled.

"It is the same . . ." Moreno mumbled, idly running a finger down his jagged cheek scar, lost in a nightmarish memory.

" 'Tis always the same!" snapped Riley. "Only us make a damn difference!"

"Nothing can stop them," Moreno said in resignation. "At the Alamo, nothing stopped us. Unlike others, my battalion had no ladders, climbing up upon one another . . ."

"Sure and we can slow them a bit coming over the wall!" urged Dalton. He pointed with his pipe. Riley and Moreno looked. Rincon and his men were fighting furiously in vicious hand-to-hand combat on the scaffold. They momentarily stemmed the surging tide of Americans at a high cost. U.S. regulars shot at a range so close the wool Mexican uniforms ignited into flames.

"Fall back from the wall!" Moreno bellowed, pointing his sword down at Ockter's gun and crew in the courtyard. Rincon heard, whirled, and stared. "We will cover your retreat!" Moreno screamed.

"Form on the gun!" cried Riley. Mejia, Conahan, and Dalton urged the San Patricios toward the ladders. They began scrambling down.

Outside the walls, a company of the Third U.S. Artillery serving as "redleg infantry" stormed over the earthworks. They fired a volley at a section of the wall above just as the Mexicans pulled back. The artillery officer spied the two remaining bronze guns. "Gun crew, forward!" he hollered. Five artillerymen trotted to him from the ranks, now re-loading. For just such an opportunity, they carried leather "pass boxes" containing one artillery cartridge each. "Turn that gun," the officer snapped, "and load!" The men ran to the gun nearest the gate.

More and more U.S. troops pressed up against the walls, scaling them hand over hand in a surging, irresistible wave of sky-blue. U.S. and regimental flags finally reached the top.

"*Fuego!*" yelled Dalton behind one San Patricio company, now standing in line beside Ockter's gun. The men fired a volley up at the scaffold now awash with U.S. troops rushing toward Rincon's survivors. U.S. flag bearers fell but the banners were instantly picked up.

"Viva!" shouted Rincon's veterans as they scrambled down and straggled past the San Patricio line, heading for the convent behind. Rincon ran up. "We now form with the militia!" he yelled, pointing at the low stone wall.

"Save room for us!" Moreno shouted, puffing on his cigar. Rincon grunted a laugh and joined his men.

Dalton looked back to check on Bel, standing ready with her musket. She was smoking a cigareet and looked as determined as the men. She smiled at him and blew a smoke ring. Dalton gallantly doffed his sombrero.

"*Fuego!*" yelled Riley, standing behind the second San Patricio company. They unleashed a sharp volley at the scaffold they had just left. U.S. troops now trickling over that wall tumbled and fell. More took their places.

"*Fuego!*" bellowed Mejia. His guards fired at a few U.S. troops leaping into the courtyard over a side wall. Some fell but more clambered over the top.

Riley, pumped with the rush of battle and sweat soaked, darted looks in all three directions. He saw hope in the U.S. troops pausing, stunned by casualties. The walls were momentarily free of sky-blue soldiers. Some knelt and returned fire from the scaffolds. A few San Patricios fell but the line looked solid.

"Steady lads!" Riley yelled. "Keep up th'fire! Got enough lead to pick 'em off 'til the banshee blushes!" But Riley saw more U.S. troops springing over the walls, the trickle becoming a steady stream. San Patricios took more casualties. Riley gaped crestfallen at the onslaught. In his mind, he saw a slope in Afghanistan where thousands of Muslim warriors overwhelmed his British battalion. He had been among a few who escaped, later feeling guilt about surviving. Perhaps, Riley feared, this was Fate meting out tardy justice.

"Our bullets will outlast our men," Moreno said, frowning at the mounting toll. He almost casually fired his pistol up at the scaffolding. A U.S. regular tumbled to the ground. "We should fall back to some cover." Moreno nodded at the convent, where Rincon was manning the low stone wall with his survivors beside the militia. A few of Rincon's men fired final sporadic shots.

"We're walking dead men anyway," Riley snarled with a bitter nod at the walls. "Don't matter none where we fall."

"It matters 'when,' " Moreno replied firmly. "To hold as long as possible is our final duty to Mexico."

"Then we'd best get to gettin' gone," Riley snapped, "afore simple arithmetic does its final duty." In the face of yet another lost cause like that distant fight in Afghanistan, Riley felt a growing urgency to save as many San Patricios as possible.

Outside, the U.S. artillery officer in the earthworks bellowed "Fire!" The captured bronze gun belched smoke with a mighty roar. The gate instantly disintegrated with a sharp, clattering explosion.

"Huzzah!" cheered hundreds of U.S. troops huddled outside. They surged toward the open gate, running through falling wood splinters and heavy smoke.

Inside the courtyard, startled San Patricios covered themselves as jagged chunks of wood and metal flew past like shrapnel. Smoke momentarily blinded them as charging U.S.

troops rushed through the gate in a screaming horde.

"Fuego!" bellowed Ockter. He personally touched off his lone gun. Its roar reverberated throughout the courtyard walls with splattering musket balls sounding like lead rain. The first U.S. troops through the gate evaporated in a smoky spray of gore and dust. The rest staggered and stumbled back outside in a hasty retreat. For a long moment, there was silence.

"Viva San Patricio!" bellowed Morstadt, waving the flag behind Riley's cheering company. Moreno and Riley stood near him surveying the situation.

"Don't mind dying a soldier's death," Riley said. "Do mind them getting personal with my flag." He pointed at the rear gate with a questioning look.

Moreno got the point. "Now is the only moment you will have!" Moreno replied urgently, pointing to the brush arbor behind them.

"Morstadt!" Riley bellowed, waving him to follow with the flag.

Dalton did not see Riley and Morstadt as he walked behind the San Patricio line, trying to look calm, urging his men to fire faster. Every few feet another fell. Dalton reached the gun where Ockter and his men were firing. One German gunner took a shot to the head, spraying Ockter with blood and brains as he spun and fell across the gun carriage. Dalton knelt beside Ockter. Each was soaked with sweat, filthy with gun powder, dirt, and blood, but looked invigorated.

" 'Tis a wonderful ugly thrill, ain't it?!" Dalton said breathing hard, barely managing a knowing, tenuous smile. The battle roared around them.

"It surely is no longer the romance!" Ockter puffed, breathing just as hard and returning the same curious look. He brushed bits of gore off his tunic.

"Beating the odds buries the damn guilt," Dalton said grimly.

"Until we are the ones being buried," Ockter added. He saw something down the line and nodded. Dalton looked. Riley, Moreno, and Morstadt were trotting back to the brush arbor, where Morstadt had planted the flag.

" 'Tain't the end what counts," Dalton said, "but the telling of the tale."

On the flank of Riley's company, Mejia's soldados loaded and fired furiously, urged on by Mejia. Three musket balls hit one and he dropped dead.

A young soldado stared stunned at the bloody, wide-eyed corpse. "Keep shooting, you dog!" Mejia bellowed. He slapped the youngster in the back of the head hard, knocking off his shako. "Kill them! Kill them all!" he yelled, pointing his sword. "Would you have them spread the legs of your sisters?!"

The youngster looked enraged at the thought, aimed his rifle, and fired. As he re-loaded, Mejia nodded proudly and replaced the youngster's shako.

"Teniente Mejia!" called the distant voice of Moreno. Mejia turned and saw Moreno waving him over. "Bring your men!" Moreno added.

"Follow me!" Mejia sang out. He trotted to the arbor with his squad close behind. Bullets spit up after them as they ran. Arriving at the well, Mejia saluted.

"Take our colors to safety," Moreno said quietly, nodding at the rear gate.

"I would rather fight!" Mejia asserted, his own battle blood surging, out of breath. He looked at the flag. "But this to me it is giving honor," he added, "though not much hope." He tossed a sad look toward his tiny group.

"Conahan!" Riley yelled. "Volunteer me a color guard!" Riley flashed a quick look at Mejia. "Be right back with your best hope," he added, trotting toward Ockter's gun in the firing line. "And put away that damn useless sword!" Mejia sheathed his blade in its scabbard, wondering.

Conahan flitted along behind both companies, tapping original San Patricios to fall in behind him. Near the end of the line, he found Rose, Hogan, and the old Irishman. "Come with me," Conahan snapped, "or stay here as holes in th'line just waitin' to happen!" The three traded looks and fell in with the other four behind Conahan. They trotted back to the well and arbor beside Morstadt.

Riley reached the gun and knelt beside Dalton and Ockter. He picked up the musket of the dead gunner lying there and removed the blood-spattered cartridge box with shoulder sling. "Bury our bodies they may," said Riley breathlessly, "but they'll not be braggin' on it with our flag!" He pointed back at Morstadt and the others.

"Not with a few left to tell the proper tale," Dalton said to Ockter.

"Come on!" Riley said. They both trotted back with him, Riley carrying the musket and cartridge box.

Under the arbor, Rose, Hogan, and the old Irishman traded anxious looks watching Riley, Dalton, and Ockter run just ahead of a spray of musket balls spitting up dirt. Riley thrust the musket and cartridge box into Mejia's hands.

"Sometimes, old tools do the best work," Riley gasped in terrible Spanish. He turned to the waiting San Patricio color guard. "Go with Lieutenant Mejia, lads," Riley said. "Break for the river whilst we hold 'em a bit longer."

"Upriver there is a ford," Mejia asserted, "behind the trees."

"I see we got the best man for the job, we do," said Dalton, gripping Mejia's hand in farewell.

"Ni por relajo!" Mejia replied, clasping his tightly in return. Dalton smiled as Mejia hefted the musket and nodded in thanks at Riley.

"You speaking the greaser well today, Major!" Mejia said.

"As you said to Dalton, 'Not by a damn sight!' " Riley asserted. U.S. drummers began beating the attack cadence outside the front gate. "Now get your greaser arse out that back door afore I kick it there!" Riley joked. Mejia laughed as he deftly slipped on the cartridge box.

"Control your nature, Lieutenant," Moreno said. "Run rather than fight."

"If I were destined to be a tamale," Mejia replied, "I would see corn husks falling from the sky."

"Take this," Moreno added, "please, to my family." He handed Mejia a letter folded and sealed in wax. Mejia looked at him with a solemn nod, tucked it inside his tunic, and waved his squad of guards to follow.

Conahan, Morstadt, and the others paused, looking at Riley, Dalton, and Ockter, who clasped Morstadt's arm. Bullets splattered noisily onto the well.

"Keep a mug of beer at your tavern cool for me!" joked Ockter in German. "God go with you."

"He is best left with you, friend," Morstadt replied in German. Morstadt saluted Riley and Dalton firmly, then trotted with the flag after Mejia's group, at the back gate. Four other San Patricios followed. But Riley caught Rose, Hogan, and the old Irishman trading hesitant looks. Hogan stepped forward.

"You promised us better than runnin' with th'rats, sir," he said. "I'll fight any blaggard what says John Riley ain't a man of his word." They gave a quick, parting salute and trotted to catch up with the others. Riley looked touched. Dalton saw and nodded approvingly, puffing his pipe.

Conahan alone remained, staring at Dalton, Riley, and Ockter. Choked with emotion, he struggled to find words. "For myself, 'twas music what always said it best," he said, patting the battered fiddle hanging at his side.

"Make Morstadt happy," said Ockter, grasping Conahan's

shoulder. "Learn some Beethoven!" He turned and trotted back to the firing line.

"They say we Irish are mad," Riley said softly with a thin smile, remembering a waltz that now seemed a century ago. "For all our wars are merry and all our songs are sad." Riley grasped Conahan's hand and patted his fiddle. "That's how to tell the tale," he added.

"But add a bit of a lilt for me," said Dalton with a puff of smoke. He grasped Conahan's hand. "Now be gone with yourself," he said.

Conahan nodded, doffed a little salute, and ran after the others. U.S. troops on the walls fired as he caught up with the last of the color guard. Bullets spat up dirt all around him. One San Patricio was hit several times, spun like a top, and dropped dead near Conahan.

"Cover them, damn you!" Dalton roared, running to the sparse line with Riley and Moreno. Some stared sullenly at those sent to safety with the flag.

"Viva San Patricio!" shouted others as the flag and color guard ran out the back gate. Most kept firing at U.S. troops on the walls, stalling their advance.

"Huzzah!" shouted more U.S. troops who suddenly rushed through the shattered gateway in a solid column of twos. They smoothly deployed into a line of battle as they poured through. Each company began firing as soon as it got into line. The column seemed endless. A solid rank of U.S. troops along the scaffolds and both side walls fired constantly at the San Patricios. More U.S. troops scrambled over the walls in a torrential downpour of sky blue.

"Fall back!" commanded Moreno, pointing to the low stone wall behind them. "Behind the wall!"

"Fire as you go, lads!" roared Riley, brandishing his sword as he backed up with his company. "The more you shoot at them, th'less they shoot at you!"

"Steady! Steady!" yelled Dalton, doing the same behind his company. "Don't be greeting your sainted mother with a bullet in your back!"

As the column charging through the gate deployed across their front, the San Patricios fired, loaded, and backed away, taking heavier casualties.

At the right end of the stone wall, General Rincon found the eager young cadet. He stood behind a wood beam on the convent porch, lined with doors and shuttered windows. Bullets peppered the stone and splintered the wood. A volley disintegrated a wood shutter as Rincon arrived. The youngster looked unnerved but determined. Rincon was amused at the slim protection offered by the beam.

"No matter where you hide," Rincon said, "your bullet will find you."

Embarrassed, the lad stepped out and cleared his throat. "I thought it my duty to stay alive," he said meekly, "until you needed me."

"Now is your moment, Cadet Lieutenant," Rincon said, hiding a smile.

"Sí, mi general!" the cadet replied with a salute. He turned to his militia, huddled behind the wall. *"Preparen!"* he commanded.

Bel and the others rose to a kneeling position and raised their muskets waist high. On one side of Bel were Sandy's two black workers; on the other, the old aristocrat and his son. She saw Dalton, Riley, and the others backing up toward them through the choking, heavy smoke, firing as they retired.

"Hold your fire!" yelled the young lieutenant, also seeing. "Our men are still in the way!" Rincon patted him on the back and strode to his own men.

Anxious moments passed as the battle escalated. The jittery

militia grew more nervous as bullets thudded all around them. One civilian was hit in the head and fell dead. A large pool of blood spread quickly onto the ground tiles. Some stared transfixed, as if disbelieving the reality of what was engulfing them.

Bel looked at the dead man with fatalistic resignation, lit up a cigareet with shaking, nervous hands. She then braced to face the oncoming troops.

The old aristocrat beside her saw and traded looks with his son. "This is not what we expected," the old man said. Bel and one young black beside her stared curiously, eyeing their fine, upper-class clothing and personal jewelry.

"How do you handle the blood so well?" the son asked her, shaken.

"I think of things one such as you could never know," she said softly. "I think of babies I have helped be born and soldiers I have helped bury." She exhaled and smiled at their astonished looks. The young black leaned into her.

"I think of clothes," the black whispered. Bel looked at him quizzically. He postured his lower-class attire comically, forcing her to smile. "These are mine, not given to me by any 'massa.'" He stared anxiously out into the deadly courtyard. "They will never take me back," he vowed.

"Look at that!" cried the son, pointing.

The end of the San Patricio line backed out of the field of fire to reveal a chilling, awesome formation. Four sky-blue companies stretched in line almost across the entire courtyard. Space for one more company remained directly across from them.

"*Apunten!*" the wide-eyed cadet shouted with questionable authority. Bel and the others traded anxious, frightened looks, but raised their muskets shakily to their shoulders and cocked the hammers. "*Fuego!*" he yelled, his voice cracking.

Bel fired with the rest in a ragged, sputtering volley. The recoil of the musket nearly knocked her over. She already felt a bruise rising in her shoulder.

Riley saw the front ranks of deploying U.S. troops take heavy casualties and falter in momentary surprise. To shouted commands, the companies facing him closed their gaps and re-aligned themselves. He saw an opportunity and nudged Moreno beside him, who nodded.

"Battalion!" Riley bellowed to the entire line. They looked at him. He pointed his sword behind them. "Run for it!" The San Patricios broke ranks and sprinted the final yards back to the left end of the low stone wall. Some lifted and carried wounded comrades. Riley, Moreno, Dalton, and Ockter leaped the wall and hurriedly placed their men lying and kneeling behind it. They resumed independent fire.

Captain Merrill led Company K at a trot through the gate and into place as the fifth company in line, facing the militia across the plaza. They were still shrouded in smoke from their own volley, but he could see they were civilians, including women. Some were frantically trying to re-load. A few had succeeded and were firing random shots. Merrill looked pained by what he must do. He stepped out in front of his company and to the side, in full view of the entire line.

"Fire by battalion!" Merrill bellowed, pointing his sword at the militia. The command echoed down the line of companies. Two hundred regulars angled their muskets with the precision of a machine at the hapless civilians, still fumbling to re-load. "Ready! Aim! Fire!" Merrill commanded quickly. The troops responded with a thundering volley that echoed in the courtyard. Merrill saw the civilians vanish in the cloud of smoke unleashed by his men. He heard screams, wails, and moans. "Load!" Merrill shouted, turning away, sickened by what he had to accept as his duty.

Outside the convent, Mejia led his men at a trot across open, wide ground approaching the river. The sound of raging battle inside the convent could be heard plainly. A thick tree line was in the near distance. Mejia pointed at it with his musket.

"Just beyond the trees is the ford!" Mejia called out, breathing heavily. "We catch up with our breath when hidden!"

"My chance at hero and they boot me out," chuckled Hogan, jogging beside Rose and the old Irishman.

"Cannot we be heroes if alive?" asked Rose, puffing as he trotted.

"Heroes got t'be dead, else you get to know 'em too damn good," the old man said with a grim laugh. They looked at him. "An' then you learn there really ain't no heroes."

Between the Anglo and Mexican squads Conahan and Morstadt trotted with the flag. Conahan struggled in taking two steps to each of Morstadt's. "Faith we might make it," Conahan gasped, "if my legs don't go puny!"

Morstadt looked ahead and scowled. "And we getting them out of way," he puffed. Conahan looked.

Emerging from the trees was a skirmish line of mounted U.S. dragoons, glistening sabers already drawn and tucked against their right shoulders.

"Alto!" Mejia snapped, coming to a stop as he glared. He turned to his soldados. "We run no more," he said.

"Get me that damn traitor flag!" Colonel Harney declared, waving his dragoons forward. He stared coldly at the tiny group of San Patricios.

"Yes, sir!" said a captain beside him, saluting. "Forward, guide right, march!" he commanded, trotting up to the line. They walked their horses forward a few yards. "Trot! March!" he yelled. The line lurched into the faster gait.

Harney watched anxiously. He turned to look behind him at a second rank. "Draw carbines!" he snapped. The men produced their short Hall's rifles, unique to the dragoons as fast-firing percussion weapons. They held them ready.

Morstadt stood behind a tight skirmish line flanked by Mejia and Conahan. Rose, Hogan, the old Irishman, and three other Anglos were in front of Conahan; six Mexican guards, in front of Mejia. All stared in stoic fatalism at the oncoming dragoons.

"Preparen!" shouted Mejia, raising and cocking his musket.

"Gallop! March!" the dragoon captain could be heard yelling. The line broke into the faster gait, closing the distance and bearing down on them.

"Apunten!" spat Mejia, a snarl spreading across his mouth. He and the rest raised rifles and muskets to their shoulders. Mejia drew a bead on the captain.

"Charge!" the captain bellowed. He lowered his sword to the front and right, twisting the blade out and down. The line of dragoons shouted and broke into a full run with sabers forward. They thundered ahead at full speed.

"Fuego!" Mejia cried, squeezing his trigger. The hammer fell, the flint sparked, the pan flashed, and his musket fired. The captain flew backward off his horse to hit the ground dead with a dusty thud.

The entire squad fired with Mejia. Two horses tumbled with their riders as three more dragoons fell from the saddle. The remaining eight galloped around the flanks of the squad and sliced with their sabers.

As one Mexican guard fell with a gash to his forehead, Mejia ran screaming at the slashing dragoon. He pierced the horse's chest with his bayonet and grabbed the bridle, pulling the horse over as it reared from the wound. When the dragoon tumbled with his horse to the ground, Mejia bashed in his skull.

An Anglo San Patricio beside Rose cried out and dropped to his knees, clutching a mortal slice across his throat as if to stem the gushing blood. He toppled over. Rose, Hogan, and the old

Irishman had just finished re-loading. They aimed together at the back of the dragoon as he rode past and fired. Three lead balls slammed into his back. He flopped dead.

"Better a backache than a pain in the arse," said Conahan, stepping up. He saw the momentum of their charge carry the surviving six dragoons well behind them. "Our only chance is now!" he cried, darting a look at Mejia.

"To the trees before they come back!" Mejia yelled. "Run!"

The squad broke ranks and ran fast toward the trees. Behind them, the six dragoons slowed, turned around, and started galloping after them.

Unseen inside the tree line, Harney fumed in his saddle as he waited. He drew his horse pistol from a pommel holster. "Now we've got them," he growled, cocking the pistol.

Inside the convent, General Rincon traveled down his line of Mexican regulars huddled behind the stone wall. They looked enraged at being helpless with no ammunition. Dead and wounded were sprawled everywhere. As he crouch-walked, more men were hit almost with every step. He came upon one squad of the Fourth Light Infantry lying behind the wall with an opened box of the oversized cartridges, which lay scattered about.

"Pound it down!" insisted a grizzled corporal. He had inverted his Baker rifle with the ramrod stuck in the muzzle. He slammed it down hard into the ground tiles, indenting them.

"Mother of God!" cried one of his squad, pounding feverishly. "Make it fit!" His ramrod bent in a final blow. Defeated, he collapsed in despair.

Across the courtyard in front of them, a solid phalanx of sky-blue regulars continued to fire volleys by company. Thunder and smoke rolled down the line.

Rincon looked again at his men, unable to fight and falling in clusters. He stood and strode fully erect, oblivious to his danger, toward the San Patricios at the end of the wall. Bullets spat up stone and dirt behind him.

"Stay low and keep firing lads!" Dalton yelled. He looked anxiously over his shoulder at the far end of the wall, where stood the militia and Bel. Rincon's men were between them and the San Patricios and heavy smoke obscured his view. Dalton could barely discern dark shapes moving from the wall toward the convent building behind it. "Shit!" he mumbled, biting on his pipe. He saw Rincon arrive and walk to Riley and Moreno. Dalton ran to them.

"We will not be shot down like wild dogs!" Rincon declared. He pointed his sword at the Mexican line and raised it. "Stand and die like men!" he roared. The entire line of battered survivors from two regiments unleashed a mighty "Viva!" They rose to their feet and remained steady even as more fell from ongoing fire. *"Enguardia!"* Rincon yelled. They thrust their rifles forward waist high, sword bayonets gleaming. "Viva!" they shouted. Rincon stared at Moreno as if offering a challenge, daring him to do likewise.

Riley, Dalton, and Moreno exchanged fatalistic looks as they scanned the sky-blue legions in front of them. The regulars stepped off to slowly advance toward them from the shadows of the far side of the courtyard. A line of bayonets waist high stretched almost wall to wall and shimmered across the gloomy, smoke enshrouded plaza as they moved. The flags of six regiments fluttered above the relentless ranks.

"Battalion, rise!" Moreno bellowed. The troops scrambled to their feet. Ockter materialized breathless out of the smoke before Riley and Dalton. He handed each a musket with bayonets affixed.

"Old tools for old professionals!" Ockter asserted.

With proud looks of thanks, Riley and Dalton sheathed their useless swords and grabbed the muskets. They trotted with

Ockter to positions behind each company.

"Enguardia!" Moreno yelled, pulling his belt pistol with his left hand while holding his sword in the right.

"Viva!" the San Patricios cried as they snapped their muskets to the lethal, waist high position, bayonets forward. A few more took hits, spun and fell as fire continued from the walls.

"Empeñarse!" Rincon bellowed, stepping atop the low stone wall and pointing his sword at the oncoming sky-blue legion of regulars.

Unleashing a primal, careening yell, the San Patricios and Mexicans ran full speed straight into the stunned U.S. line. They collided in mid-courtyard with a sickening, crunching dull thud as muskets hit muskets, bayonets hit bone, and musket butts cracked skulls. In a swirling melee of bodies and blood, the lines dissolved into personal combat obscured by mushrooming dust and smoke.

Outside the courtyard near the river, the six dragoons thundered down hard on the running heels of Mejia, Conahan, and the color guard. The safety of the trees loomed invitingly just ahead.

"Keep going!" Mejia yelled at Conahan, waving on the San Patricios with the flag. Mejia nodded at the pursuing dragoons and turned to his soldados. "These tamales will find their corn husks today," he growled. As he raised his musket, the others snickered and did likewise. *"Fuego,"* Mejia muttered. They fired in unison, sounding as if one rifle.

Four dragoons fell to the ground amid plumes of dirt. Two survivors veered away. Satisfied, Mejia turned and trotted with his men toward the trees.

"Fire!" roared Harney, hidden in the shadows. His dozen mounted dragoons unleashed a sharp volley. Their horses jerked and pranced in line spoiling their aim. But the first two San Patricios entering the tree line dropped dead.

Conahan grimaced and yelled as four balls slammed into both his legs, tumbling him over in agony. He hit the ground hard, his fiddle crunching flat beneath him.

Morstadt was stunned to see his friend crumple and lie bloody and motionless. He shook it off and took command. "Through them and into the cactus!" he bellowed, pointing the way with the gleaming brass spear point of the flag. A formidable forest of tall prickly pear grew thick beneath partial shade trees just beyond the dragoons.

Rose, Hogan, and the old Irishman charged yelling into the gaps between the mounted dragoons, their prancing horses creating spaces. They lunged at the horses with bayonets as the dragoons struggled to regain control and pull pistols. The old Irishman knocked past his dragoon and ran into the high, meandering bed of prickly pear looming like a thorny wall of safety.

"We can't follow 'em into that shit!" roared a dragoon sergeant. He fired his pistol at the old Irishman but it only exploded an ear of cactus near him. "Damn!"

As Morstadt ran between two dragoons, one reached for the flag. Morstadt yanked it away and pulled the man off his horse with a mighty tug. With his musket in the other hand, Morstadt bayoneted the dragoon lying on the ground. He left his musket sticking up from his body as he ran with the flag toward the cactus beds.

"Stop them!" roared Harney. "Get that damn flag!" He trotted out and took deliberate aim at Morstadt with his pistol.

"Fuego!" yelled Mejia. His squad fired from the edge of the woods.

Two dragoons fell from the saddle and Harney's horse reared, tossing him painfully to the ground. His pistol fired harmlessly in the air.

"Viva!" the Mexicans shouted as they charged into the swirling melee of men and horses. Dragoons fired and dropped two.

Harney rose to his feet and pulled his sword just in time to impale the youngster among Mejia's charging guards. The soldado slumped to the ground with a confused look of surprise on his face. Harney put his foot to the dying boy's chest and coldly shoved his torso off his blade.

"Help me," moaned Conahan, squirming on the blood-soaked ground. Pitiful and delirious, he clawed in the dirt trying to reach some cover. "I can't move my legs!" he cried.

Nearing the cactus, Morstadt turned at the sound. He saw two dragoons trot their horses toward Conahan with pistols drawn.

"He cannot be dying like that!" Morstadt bellowed. He ran back to Conahan screaming at the top of his lungs. The startled two dragoons turned at the sound and reined up.

Morstadt arrived and at full speed thrust the spear point tip of the flag into the heart of the nearest dragoon. Gasping a dying moan, he toppled back off his horse with the flag stuck in his chest. He landed dead beside Conahan with the banner sticking upside down and draped bloody over his body like a green shroud.

Rose was bashed on the head with a horse pistol and slumped dazed to his knees with blood gushing from scalp and an ear. Hogan bayoneted the dragoon as he cocked his pistol to finish Rose. Two other dragoons circled Hogan and pointed their pistols at him.

"Take them alive!" demanded Harney, striding up. He was glaring at Morstadt, kneeling over Conahan beside the flag. The second dragoon held a pistol to his head. "I want something more to show for this," Harney muttered, sheathing his sword. "More than this traitor rag," he added, yanking the banner out of the dead trooper.

Dragoons herded Rose and Hogan to Morstadt. He rose tall

from the swirling dust with Conahan's frail figure in his arms. Harney held the bloodied green banner aloft, turned, and led his Dragoons and prisoners away.

"Let us go," Mejia said sadly, feeling guilty over what he saw as his failure to save the flag. The old Irishman rose from behind another cactus and crossed himself as he watched, then turned to go with Mejia. Two surviving Mexican guards appeared from behind more cactus. They all sneaked away toward the river using the impenetrable prickly pear for cover.

Inside the compound, thick smoke enshrouded much of a dark, savage melee unfolding across the convent grounds. Fighting went on in scattered, furious duels of no quarter between individuals and groups. Screams, shrieks, moans, and gunfire echoed throughout the shadowed complex as the sun set.

Five battered, bloodied, exhausted San Patricios backed through an open door into one of the convent rooms. They fired their muskets as they went inside. The shutters of a window were thrown open and two more aimed their muskets out and fired, dropping two regulars point blank.

The U.S. artillery captain and crew from the earthworks had turned Ockter's abandoned gun, loaded it, and aimed it at the room. The gun roared and blasted out the front wall of the room amid screams. The convent porch was sprayed with debris and smoking body parts as the room erupted in flames.

Near the rear gate, General Rincon and battered survivors finally were backed into the corner. An overwhelming mass of infuriated sky-blue regulars pressed against his troops in bayonet fighting. Among his men were San Patricios. Rincon saw no hope. He whipped out a white silk handkerchief, stuck it on the end of his sword, and thrust it high into the air as he bowed his head in disgust. His troops tossed down their rifles and raised their hands sullenly. U.S. troops rushed in and roughly pushed and poked San Patricios away from the Mexicans. Some regulars spat in the faces of the defiant Irish and Germans. They herded them into a separate group as fighting continued elsewhere.

At the end of the stone wall in front of the convent, a semblance of a "last stand" took shape. Moreno, Riley, Dalton, and Ockter led tattered, blood covered San Patricios across the space between the wall and porch.

They stepped over bodies of militia as they backed up firing. On the porch, some took cover behind the slim support columns. Most remained completely exposed as they re-loaded feverishly. A line of U.S. regulars rushed to the wall, knelt, and fired. Caught in the open, clusters of San Patricios fell dead. Less than one company was left standing.

Riley looked about frantically and saw no way out. He traded looks with Dalton and Ockter, who agreed to his unspoken question with grim nods. Moreno fired his pistol and read their mood as he deftly re-loaded. He also nodded.

"You're damned well already, lads!" Riley roared, holding up his musket. "So take it to them like you don't give a damn!" Riley leaped off the porch with a wild, careening Celtic yell. The rest followed with a shout and ran headlong at the wall. They bashed, bayoneted, and shot U.S. regulars in a whirling fight.

One young regular lunged at Riley, who parried the thrust expertly and smacked him aside the head with the butt of his musket. The teenager flew back against a side wall and dropped. Riley slammed his foot down onto his chest and pressed the point of his bayonet against his throat.

"Sweet Jesus . . . you're just a pup!" Riley whispered, breathing hard, staring fiercely into frightened, barely seventeen-year-old eyes. "Just lie there 'til this is over," he warned, easing off. " 'Twon't be long."

"At least," the boy gasped, closing his eyes in relief, "I'm bested by a white man and not a damn greaser!"

Instantly, Riley felt enraged, not even understanding his own fury at the lad's bigotry, a sin not unfamiliar to himself. "Wrong boy-o!" Riley snarled. "I'm just another greaser!"

Riley saw terror fill the boy's eyes when they popped open. Riley braced to thrust his bayonet through his throat, then stopped. Eerily, Riley thought he caught a fleeting glimpse of innocent young Parker's hopeful eyes in the young man's face. Riley unleashed a straight left punch, knocking him out. " 'Stead of wakin' up dead on the morrow, lad," he said, "you'll just wake up . . . and thank a greaser for the damn privilege." Behind him, more San Patricios fell at the low wall in the melee. But the surprised regulars began to fall back.

Dalton raised his musket and stepped atop the wall as Riley ran up breathless beside him. "Keep going 'til you can't go no more!" Dalton bellowed at his men. His face glowed ruddy red, pumped with the rush of battle.

Riley peered into the courtyard, growing dim as dusk fell and shadows grew long. The sun had sunk behind the convent building. A pall of smoke added an unearthly sheen to the glow from the burning, blasted rooms. In the gathering dark, he saw the pan flash of a musket. Instantly, he dove behind the low wall just as the musket roared. A ball splattered into the rock near him.

"Drop!" he bellowed. The San Patricios flopped down as fifty more muskets flashed in the darkness. Balls thudded, whizzed, and splattered all around them. Dalton sprawled on one side of Riley; Ockter and Moreno, on the other. More muskets flashed across the courtyard, pinning them down.

During this cacophonic bedlam, Dalton amazingly rolled onto his back and calmly re-lit his pipe. "About now, weren't your most recent 'brilliant plan' for us already to be gone up?!" he asked, cooly exhaling smoke.

"Professionalism got the better of me," Riley grinned sheepishly. "And just what does it take to get killed around here?!"

Dalton laughed. "Leastwise Bel ain't here," Dalton replied, breathing easier. He nodded down the wall. Riley looked and saw grisly militia corpses sprawled among surviving San Patricios, ducking low from the ongoing musketry. Sandy's young black worker lay dead, curled on his side. Beside him, the aristocrat's son stared wide eyed up at the darkening sky. Draped across the wall was the young cadet lieutenant, hand still clutching his sword.

"Wherever Bel is, she's better off than the spot we're in," Riley said.

"Perhaps more than our color guard found a way out," added Moreno, hugging the ground beside Ockter. He fumbled in a pocket for a cigar, failed, and let loose a resigned sigh. "This is a bad omen."

Ockter lay on his back and adjusted his eye patch. He saw something on the porch. "Maybe they hide inside," he suggested, pointing.

They peered into the descending darkness and saw a wooden door smashed open halfway down the building. It was silhouetted by an eerie orange light cast from the burning room just beyond.

"Another 'back door'?" Moreno asked, smiling thinly. "Some 'Alamo,' " he added, trading looks with an amused Riley.

The roar of musketry suddenly increased. The darkness was illuminated by the flashes of hundreds of muskets. Lead balls buzzed overhead and spat up dirt and rock on the wall. San Patricios hunkered down farther, some covering their heads from flying rock chips.

"Seen more concern on a corpse than you," Riley snapped, looking at Dalton, on his back unconcerned and still puffing his pipe. Riley's head wound had opened again and blood trickled down one side of his grimy face. He adjusted the filthy bandanna to stem the flow and frowned at Dalton.

"Whatever comes my way now don't matter none," Dalton exhaled. Riley stared at him quizzically. "She will remember me fondly, she will," Dalton mused wistfully. "That's as close to being in heaven as the likes of me shall get."

"My thoughts on Luzero ain't hardly been 'heavenly' of late," Riley admitted. "True hell for th'likes of us is to go up knowing nobody gave a damn."

Suddenly, the din of crackling musketry stopped. Riley and Dalton traded worried looks, then eyed Ockter and Moreno, equally concerned. An ominous, heavy stillness descended on the dark, smoky courtyard as surviving San Patricios pondered the meaning.

"Maybe we're dead and already been forgot," Riley offered.

Moreno cautiously peered over the wall. His countenance fell momentarily, though he quickly recovered. He got to his knees slowly, his sword in one hand. He looked at Riley with a sad little smile. "Our duty is at last done, my friend," Moreno said. He lowered his sword.

Riley frowned and looked. A hundred grim faced U.S. regulars stood shoulder to shoulder a few yards from the wall with muskets leveled waist high and pointing right at them. He recognized Captain Merrill, who stepped forward and gave Moreno a slow, respectful sword salute. A white silk handkerchief was tied to his blade's point. "End this butchery, Colonel," Merrill pleaded softly.

Moreno bowed graciously and dropped his sword onto the bloody floor tiles with a hollow, metallic clank. He felt disgraced, ashamed, and helpless. Then he faced Riley, understanding he would be feeling much worse.

Riley looked up at Moreno, who nodded in resignation. Riley slowly stood, followed in turn by Dalton, Ockter, and the rest, all with hands upraised; sullen, defiant, battered, and, curiously, relieved that it was all at last over.

"Death to traitors," snarled one grizzled regular from the ranks, triggering dozens of others to whisper "Kill the poper scum," "Irish whores," "Damn Mick greasers," "Shoot th'traitor bastards," and more.

"Sure and it's poor 'Juan O'Riley,' " chimed one grizzled Irish regular, "soon to be a victim of ragin' 'hemp fever.' " Snickers rippled through the ranks. "I got a lead pill here that's th'sure cure." He cocked his musket.

"Silence in the ranks!" shouted Merrill. Instantly, the regulars fell quiet but glared in seething hatred. Merrill stepped to Riley and just stared at him, more in pity than anything else. "You've come a long way from Fort Mackinac, Riley," he said with choked emotion, "just to end here in such disgrace."

Riley managed to muster a tired, cocky look with no hint of apology or regret. He slowly lowered one grimy hand and flicked the powder-encrusted fringe on one of his gold epaulettes. "Why, Captain Merrill," Riley said, "no salute for me?"

CHAPTER 13
CHURUBUSCO: AFTERMATH
AUGUST 20, 1847

Along the winding banks of the laconic Churubusco River, Mejia led his tired guards and the old Irishman. Their shoes and trouser legs were soaked from fording the shallow stream. At a bend, Mejia paused to look back with the others.

The sun was sinking below the mountains and bathing the ancient convent in warm, rich light. Columns of sky-blue infantry trudged past the smoking complex to the sound of distant drums. The Mexican tricolor fell and floated down from the bell tower after an officer used his sword to cut it from the halyard. A lone, tinny bugle played "To the Color" as the U.S. flag was raised.

"How much like a painting it looks," said the voice of Bel. Mejia and the others turned to see her rise from a field of tall corn beside the riverbank. "It is too far away to smell the death, to taste the fear." She walked to them smoking a cigareet, carrying her musket with a cartridge box slung across her chest. Her blouse was smeared with blood and soaked with sweat; her sandals and bottom of her skirt, wet from the river.

"How did you get out?!" asked Mejia, stunned as if beholding a miracle.

"Through a back window of the convent," she said absently, staring at thick black smoke spiraling upward from the domed chapel. It reminded her of a massive funeral pyre.

"Are there more?" Mejia asked, barely hoping.

"You can come out now!" Bel shouted. "They are ours!"

237

Twelve exhausted, battered San Patricios rose from the tall corn with as many more soldados of the Fourth and Eleventh Rifle Regiments. Sandy's surviving black worker held the old aristocrat, who was wounded but bandaged in strips of white, lacey cotton. The San Patricios, many nursing superficial wounds, walked to the amazed old Irishman, exchanged bear hugs, some crossing themselves.

"I prayed I weren't th'only one," sighed the old Irishman. "Some say only shirkers survive legendary slaughters." A few managed weary smiles.

"Surviving there are more, *ja!*" said one survivor of Morstadt's crew in a thick German accent. "The corn it grows high for miles," he added with a sweep of his arm. "Can hide many!" A few chuckled.

"We need some flamin' orders, sir," said the old Irishman.

Mejia suddenly realized that he was the only surviving San Patricio officer. "Follow the river," he managed, pointing upstream from the convent. "More may find us still."

The banty old man started walking. The other San Patricios and the soldados fell in behind in a strung out, casual column. Mejia waited with Bel, who seemed distant, dazed, reluctant to leave. She stared at the convent in the fading twilight. She rolled a cigareet and lit it, exhaling.

"Our medical corps found you first?" Mejia asked. Bel looked at him confused. "The bandages," he added, "on the rich one." He pointed at the wounded aristocrat.

"Oh, that," she said almost flippantly, smoothing her skirt. "I just tore up my last petticoat."

"They take everything, these gringos," Mejia joked.

Bel ignored his humor, staring at the convent. She did not intend being rude, but her thoughts were with Dalton. "Not everything . . . not what we can remember," she said.

Intrigued by her thought, Mejia looked at the ragtag group

heading upriver. "Not the honor," he said, turning to her. "You make a good soldier, for a woman," he added sincerely.

She glared at him for an instant, then brushed off the familiar prejudice. "You make a good officer," she countered, "for a half breed."

Mejia scowled quickly, then detected her slight smile. He grinned. They turned together to watch the jubilant, victorious sky-blue columns marching past the convent, pressing forward irresistibly toward Mexico City.

"He is still there," Bel said, her voice sounding almost mystical. "I feel my Dalton he is alive," she added, "here," touching a hand to her heart.

"If he is," Mejia warned, "he must feel as if already he is dead." She darted a pained look at him. "For you, he knows that it is time to move on. He would wish it."

They began walking with the others into the mournful setting sun, turning their backs on the smoking, shattered ruin of the once ethereal stone edifice.

Inside that dark convent courtyard, torches lined the walls as squads gathered dead Americans in the twilight. Left lying where they died were Mexicans and San Patricios, looking like grotesque flickering shadows.

One pair of grizzled regulars laid another corpse in a long row of U.S. dead near the gate, each covered in a blanket or rubberized poncho. They heard approaching horses, looked up, and immediately snapped to rigid attention, saluting. Slowly riding past were General Scott, Captain Lee, and General David Twiggs, a ruddy fifty-six-year-old regular from Georgia.

"You may have won more than a battle here today, General Twiggs," Scott said, sadly eyeing the rows of corpses as he passed. "Santa Anna sends a truce delegation tomorrow."

"I pray this carnage proves not to be in vain, sir," Lee said hopefully.

"Highest damn casualties of any fight yet," Twiggs snapped gruffly in his Southern twang, glaring at guarded Mexican prisoners seated on the ground to the left of the gate. They stretched almost to the stone wall in front of the convent.

"The Mexicans fight harder," observed Lee to Scott, "the deeper we invade their homeland." To him, it seemed only natural. "I would do the same."

"Viva Mexico!" cried one defiant soldado from the seated ranks as the officers rode past. A few others echoed, "Viva!" Most just glared sullenly.

"Damn greasers can't fight worth a pinch o'shit," snapped Twiggs, staring at the soldados. Lee looked offended. Scott frowned with imperial displeasure.

"The Mexican soldier fights as well as any soldier ever does," Scott said firmly. "His leaders have betrayed his valor."

"Respectfully, sir, I blame this bunch that betrayed us," Twiggs said.

He reined up his horse in front of the convent and spat tobacco juice toward the porch, where more than sixty captured and wounded San Patricios lay sprawled and seated. In the orange glow of torch light, their haggard, blackened faces looked up at the uniformed finery of Scott and Lee in sullen defiance. None stood, remaining silent and resigned.

"Present arms!" shouted Captain Merrill. A squad of guards along the low stone wall gave honors as the officers arrived. Merrill offered a sword salute, acknowledged by nods from Scott and Lee.

"We know those men, sir," whispered Lee, pointing to Hogan and Rose seated near the wall. Rose's head was bandaged. Barely conscious, he stared vacantly into space. Hogan looked up, chewing tobacco.

"The Cerro Gordo ransackers," Scott recalled with a fleeting look of amusement. Hogan grunted and looked away. Scott frowned.

"Once proud soldiers," said Lee. "And now look at you."

"Still proud," Hogan asserted, spitting tobacco juice, "and still soldiers."

"But you have lost your country," said Lee, struggling to understand.

"So that's why my 'country' come lookin' so hard for me," he joked bitterly. Hogan gave a grim little laugh and eyed Lee. A few others snickered until drawn to the sound of horse hooves clattering across the courtyard tiles.

Trotting through the gate were Colonel Harney, a dragoon aide who carried the bloody San Patricio flag, and ten flamboyant Mexicans in cavalry gear. They wore short, parrot-green jackets trimmed in red like the one worn by the man executed by Riley in Jalapa. Around their broad-brimmed felt hats and sombreros they wore red bandannas, many painted in white letters, "Spy Co."

At their head rode fierce Manuel Dominguez, who looked to be as ruthless as he was rotund. Dark skinned with a long, twirling mustachio, Dominguez was clad smartly in a U.S. officer's jacket sporting the gold oak leaf shoulder straps of a colonel. A filthy straw sombrero drooped atop his head.

"Traidor!" yelled one soldado prisoner as they rode past. Others quickly took up the cry. Some stood and shook their fists. Others threw rocks and debris, pelting the riders. A few cried, *"Yankedos!"*

"You wear your shame on your hat!" yelled one soldado in Spanish. Another soldado next to him leaped past a guard and spat into the face of a rider.

"It should say, 'Gringo whore,' " he cried in Spanish, "like your mother!" Two U.S. guards used their muskets to roughly shove him back as other soldados laughed and cheered his bravery. The outcry threatened to become a riot.

Moreno leaned against a wall beneath a scaffold strewn with Mexican bodies. Smoking a pilfered cigar, he had been quietly watching in the dark from the rear of the Mexican prisoners. Rincon squatted dejectedly beside him.

"It is Dominguez and his gringo 'spies,' " Moreno snapped contemptuously. "Still, we must stop this."

"Yes, for I must kill Dominguez myself," Rincon vowed. He stood and strode toward the convent, pushing soldados aside. Surprised, Moreno followed.

Harney and Dominguez joined Scott, Lee, and Twiggs at the low stone wall, exchanging hurried salutes as the outcry grew. The other spies formed a line along the wall between the San Patricios on one side and the Mexican prisoners. Lee appeared calm and confident, in control. He nodded at Captain Merrill on the flank of the crowd.

Merrill already had formed a double rank of infantry with the front row's muskets pointed in the air. "Fire!" Merrill commanded. The muskets roared. Silence instantly fell on the crowd. San Patricios pointed, stared, and whispered.

"Thank you, Captain," Lee said. He turned to Harney with a barely suppressed smile. "You certainly have a way of making your presence known, sir," he said. Scott and Twiggs chuckled. Harney saw no humor.

Dominguez wiped his sweating brow, relieved. "I beg to report, Excellency," said Dominguez too sweetly, "the nationals run back all the way to the city."

"By the beard of Jehovah," cursed Harney, "today you scum kept us from ending this damn war!" He shook his fist at the San Patricios, drawing a few snickers. Harney nodded at his aide, who tossed the blood stained green banner atop a pile of captured muskets. The San Patricios shook their fists and glared. Harney smiled.

In a dark corner of the porch, Conahan lay white as chalk and propped up against a wall. Gathered around him were Riley, Dalton, Ockter, and Morstadt, who held a torch above a Mexican medical steward. He wiped Conahan's fevered brow. Both his legs were bandaged heavily with stick tourniquets. Riley and Dalton kept looking over their shoulders at the commotion.

"I can do no more," the steward said.

"Then go back now with my thanks to General Rincon," Riley replied.

"*Sí, mi major,*" the steward said, standing. He gave a solemn salute. "*Vaya con Dios,*" he added, leaving. Riley looked at the others.

"Once the Yanks square away their own," growled Riley, "the heathen blaggards will finally get little Conahan a doctor."

"They wouldn't want him to miss his own hanging, now would they?" said Dalton, sharing an amused look with Riley. Conahan mustered a weak smile as the others chuckled. Dalton and Riley walked to the edge of the porch. Dalton lit his pipe as Riley sagged against a post beneath a torch.

"There's the damn scoundrel son-of-a-whore-bitch now!" Twiggs yelled at sight of Riley, easily recognizable from his officer uniform. "Private John Riley, Company K, Fifth United States Infantry," he snarled, "and traitor!"

"That'd be Major John Riley to you," Riley growled, straightening, "Army of the Republic of Mexico and proud citizen thereof!" The hapless San Patricios mustered a weak cheer. A few shouted "Viva!"

"You brazen, treacherous Irish puke," snapped Twiggs. "How dare you take that tone with me!"

" 'Tis better than you deserve, you shithouse adjutant," Dalton said in a low, omionous snarl. He blew a smoke ring toward Twiggs. A few more San Patricios chuckled. Twiggs could merely bridle his rage in his saddle.

"Let me at that traitorous dog!" Rincon suddenly roared in Spanish. He charged at Dominguez from among the prisoners. Moreno restrained him from leaping onto the spy company leader, who quickly backed up his skittish horse.

"General Rincon!" exclaimed Scott, taken aback by the raw, dangerous emotion surfacing around him. "You must control yourself, sir!" Scott looked at Twiggs and Harney. "We all must!" he added. They nodded grudgingly. Rincon ignored him.

"Dominguez, you bloated vulture!" Rincon yelled in Spanish. "Were you any part of a man, I would slap your fat jowls!"

"We did no more than your Irish Patricios," Dominguez seemed to spit in Spanish, "except that our side won!" He leaned back arrogantly in his saddle.

Suddenly, Moreno snapped. He lunged at Dominguez and almost pulled him from his horse. Captain Merrill and a guard raced to restrain him. Moreno yanked his cigar from his mouth and pointed it like a pistol at Dominguez.

"If I still smell your stench in Mexico when the gringos leave," Moreno said in Spanish, "I will find you and crush you like a cockroach." He tossed down the cigar and slowly ground it with his foot, as if it were the insect.

Dominguez looked unnerved, turned, and looked pleadingly at Merrill and his company for protection, then to Scott and Lee. "You will protect me?!" Dominguez asked, shaken. Scott and Lee traded wary looks. "I want to stay here! I love my country!"

"America considers you a hero, sir," Scott said soothingly. "You and your men have given her good service." Dominguez regained his composure.

"And she has given us good gold," Dominguez said with an oily smile, sneering down at Moreno and Rincon.

"You could not love your country," Moreno said in English,

for all to hear, "any more than a whore can love one who pays her."

Merrill looked at Moreno as he turned away disgusted, beside Rincon. Merrill seemed wracked by conflicted feelings. A ground swell of Spanish abuse grew as Merrill cautiously walked to Moreno. "Colonel Moreno," Merrill said quietly. Moreno faced him. "Riley did no more than Dominguez, did he?"

"No, Captain, he did much more," Moreno said softly, "more than even he understands." Moreno managed a thin, pained smile. He and Rincon exchanged knowing looks, intrigued by Merrill's curious gaze. Rincon glared up at smug Dominguez.

"You are a dead man, Dominguez," Rincon said in Spanish. Dominguez blanched and crossed himself. "The brand of the traitor falls beyond the reach of mercy," Rincon added. The soldado prisoners jeered and hurled Spanish curses at Dominguez and his spies.

"I don't know what these damn greasers are yelling about," snarled Harney, glaring at Riley and Dalton. "But I'll say it plain. Hanging is too merciful for you!"

"Do your worst," Riley taunted, trading wry looks with Dalton, who blew smoke toward Harney.

"Might not flogging do him some good, Colonel Harney, sir?" Dalton taunted, eyeing Riley as if sizing him up. "See what it done for me since you graced my back with the lash down in Florida?" He flicked one of his own epaulettes and bowed, drawing chuckles from the San Patricios.

"I can't be expected to recall every Mick criminal," snarled Harney.

"Sure and my scars remember you as a blackhearted butcher," Dalton said. "Remember the Seminoles impaled on stakes around your camp down there?!" San Patricios unleashed derisive guffaws. Mexicans continued their tirade in Spanish. The noise grew into a bilingual cacophony of abuse as San

Patricios yelled at American officers and soldados berated the Dominguez Spy Company.

"Curb your spleen!" roared Twiggs. "You immigrant trash turned your backs on the country that took you in!"

"Aye t'that!" roared Hogan, leaping to his feet. "Th'native born needed more floors scrubbed!" He shook his fist at Twiggs.

"And more wars fought!" added Rose, standing groggily but managing to yell. A few San Patricios cheered, pulling Rose back down before he fell over.

Hogan hopped backward gingerly as a U.S. regular stepped up and threatened to give him a butt stroke. Some San Patricios pushed forward, looking ready for a brawl. Merrill's regulars barred their way with upraised muskets.

Ockter and Morstadt emerged from the porch shadows to stand beside Riley and Dalton. Morstadt carried Conahan, looking like a limp rag doll.

Holding the torch, Ockter frowned. "Quiet, damn dumm-kopfs!" he bellowed. "The fighting is finished!"

"Dying Conahan a complaint he has," Morstadt announced gravely. He turned sideways so Conahan could see the restive crowd, now quieted to listen.

"I'm blessed if a dyin' man can get any sleep around here!" Conahan managed, mustering all his strength. "But I suppose there'll be plenty o'time for sleep soon enough," he added with a weak smile. "Now shut up, damn your eyes!" He sank back into Morstadt's chest as San Patricios laughed, clapped, and cheered their impish jester.

"Fools!" snapped Twiggs, fuming. "They scoff at their own doom."

Lee traded looks with Scott, who sighed in exasperation. "With respect, sir," Lee said firmly to Twiggs, "I do not know how anyone can soldier without humor." Moreno overheard and looked up at Lee pleasantly surprised.

"My compliments, Captain," Moreno said with a polite nod. Lee looked at him curiously. "As we say, 'The man who laughs at death conquers his fear of it.' " Understanding, Lee nodded with a slight, courteous smile.

"Ain't this just grand?!" roared Riley suddenly with an overly broad, sarcastic grin, looking a bit theatrical. Heads turned at his booming voice. He outstretched his arms almost religiously, as if taking on all comers. He nodded at Conahan. "Ain't none of them knows whose 'traitors' are the better 'patriots!' "

Conahan managed a smile. Dalton laughed, joining Riley in what amounted to gallows humor. Ockter and Morstadt's chortle grew quickly into contagious, irrepressible guffaws, belly laughs, and horse laughter, spreading through the rest of the San Patricios and echoing across the courtyard in raucous, grim glee.

Helpless to stop it, Twiggs and Harney looked even more infuriated. They stared in a potentially lethal rage at Scott and Lee, who seemed bemused.

"We cannot shoot them for laughter, gentlemen," said Scott, surmising their wishes. Moreno and Rincon overheard and smiled.

"In good conscience, sir, how can we justify rewarding their traitors while hanging our own?" Lee asked. "It seems hypocritical."

"By the book, Captain Lee," replied Scott firmly, "strictly by the book." Scott scanned the sullen Mexican prisoners as the laughter died out. He looked at Captain Merrill. "Begin paroling the Mexicans, Captain," he said. Merrill saluted, wheeled, and left. Scott looked at Rincon and Moreno. "Take your men home, gentlemen," Scott said sincerely, "to what I pray is peace." Moreno frowned and took a step forward.

"Thank you for the gracious gesture, sir," said Moreno, "but those are my men, also!" He pointed vehemently at the San

Patricios. "One and all, they are Mexicans!" he added, quickly stooping to pick up the bloody, fallen green banner. The U.S. troops exchanged looks of astonishment as Moreno thrust it aloft. San Patricios clapped, cheered, and cried "Viva Mexico!"

Riley and the others exchanged proud looks on the porch. As the cheers petered out, Riley took a step forward and bowed with a gracious sweep of his cap. "Gracias, Colonel darlin', and it's as Mexicans we will surely die," he said lyrically. "But with a bit of a brogue!" Riley snapped Moreno a jaunty salute.

The San Patricios burst into hoots, guffaws, and shouts of "Erin go bragh!" The Mexican soldados joined with cries of "Viva Mexico!" and "Viva San Patricio!" Their jubilant defiance engulfed the frustrated U.S. officers and guards along the stone wall. Truly moved, Moreno bowed respectfully, furled the green banner, and, kissing its folds, gently laid it atop the surrendered muskets.

As Riley watched, he felt tears trickle down his grimy cheeks and into his beard stubble. His eyes became blurry with ghostly images of young Parker, the frugal Scot, the blustery Price, the inveterate tobacco chewer, and so many other nameless dreamers now dead whose hopes drove them to desperation and desertion, trying to start over "someplace else," as he had himself. And now it seemed a futile waste with impending doom awaiting the survivors. At least, he felt, he had known some fleeting happiness with Luzero, and she remained safe. As for himself, Riley accepted, the pain and frustration would be ended soon enough. As usual, he would merely give it time—until time itself at last thankfully would run out.

CHAPTER 14
SAN ANGEL
AUGUST 29, 1847

Inside a stark white plastered room, the resounding cheers of Churubusco rang distant and hollow in Riley's mind. He sat sweating with a week's growth of beard at his court martial. Facing him were thirteen U.S. officers ranging in rank from lieutenant to colonel and arrayed in glittering full dress attire. Riley wore his tattered, grimy, stained Mexican uniform, not brushed clean since the battle. Seated at several heavy, ornate Spanish colonial tables, officers fanned themselves, shooed flies, drank water, and sweated profusely in the oppressive heat. A U.S. flag hung limp on its staff behind the ranking colonel, none other than Colonel McIntosh, Riley's former commander in the Fifth Infantry. As Riley surveyed them, he saw hateful faces looking jaded with minds already made up, even as Captain Merrill sat testifying.

"His character was very fair," said Merrill carefully. "I don't recollect ever having to punish him in any way."

"Then why, Captain Merrill, do you suppose Private Riley chose to desert and join the enemy?" asked McIntosh. "He cannot deny the uniform he wears."

Merrill eyed the court and felt pressure not to defend a traitor. He looked at Riley, seated stiffly and staring at him with armed infantry guards on either side. Then Merrill stared unblinking at McIntosh, his own regimental commander and the man who had denied Riley promotion. "For reasons beyond my command, he could not advance in rank to the level he felt that his skills warranted, sir," Merrill replied.

McIntosh frowned, refusing to accept or possibly even remember his own culpability, Riley thought. McIntosh merely traded looks of disgust with the other officers. Riley barely hid a smile, the verdict in his mind a foregone conclusion. But he nodded a look of thanks at Merrill, nonetheless. Merrill remained stoic.

"Do you have anything to add to your defense, Private Riley?" McIntosh asked, wafting a six-page, handwritten letter through the heavy, sticky air.

"My rank is major now, sir, nearly as elevated as your own self," Riley insisted politely. The officers exchanged contemptous, amused looks. "As I wrote you in that letter you see fit only to fan yourself with," Riley said, "once captured after attending Holy Mass, I thought prudent to accept of the commission they offered, for fear of being immediately shot." He mustered a wry grin. "So I accepted of it, I did," he added with a flick at one of his gold epaulettes.

"The court will retire to consider a verdict," McIntosh snapped. The others looked weary as they stood and started to file out. Merrill rose, nodded at Riley, and walked toward the door.

"Thank you kindly, sir," Riley said sincerely as he passed. "You always were fair with me."

Merrill paused to look at him. "You could have been top soldier," he said, still probing for an explanation that made sense to him.

"Don't you see, Captain," Riley said wearily, "with them what matters most to me now, I am top soldier."

Merrill considered the possible consequences, then drew a gasp from nearby U.S. officers as he straightened to attention: He offered the proper salute due Riley's rank as a major.

Touched to the point of tears welling in his eyes, Riley pushed back his chair, stood slowly, braced to ramrod straight attention, and returned the salute. Merrill turned on his heels and left.

After the courts martial, the captured San Patricios languished for days in a muddy, adobe-walled corral littered with straw and cow dung. Some lay beneath tattered blankets propped up on gathered sticks as shelters from the steaming sun. Ockter and Morstadt walked among the grimy, lice infested, unshaven men, offering words of encouragement. U.S. regulars stood guard around the wall at ten-foot intervals. Just beyond the corral, more guards surrounded a two-horse adobe stable with wooden roof and barred doors. The deserters could hear faint fife and drum drill calls from nearby U.S. encampments, sounding now like a distant martial memory.

In a corner of the corral, Rose reclined against a muddy heap of gathered straw. He held his bandaged head as if it ached. Hogan was propping a blanket up over him for shade. He saw something, nudged Rose, and pointed toward the wall with a scowl.

A grizzled corporal of the guard stared at them with a smug look of disgust. He nudged a private beside him, nodded toward Hogan and Rose, and slowly drew one finger across his throat. Both men uncoiled sinister smiles.

Hogan and Rose exchanged mutual looks of chagrin. Hogan slowly raised one hand and extended his middle finger, wiggling it with a satisfied smile.

Inside the horse stable, dusty rays of sunlight filtered down onto Riley and Dalton through a ramshackle roof. The sky-blue uniforms of guards walking outside showed through holes in the adobe walls. Dalton sat leaning against a stall, idly smoking his pipe as he wove a hangman's noose from straw gathered from the floor. A pile of finished nooses filled the crown of his sombrero, upside down on the insect infested floorboards.

Dalton looked as wretched as Riley, leaning against an opposite wall.

"Sixty-eight courts martial and sixty-eight guilties," Riley sighed, staring transfixed at Dalton's weaving. "Damn shameful waste of words."

"So much for kissing the blarney stone," Dalton said.

"With no loose ends left hangin' so to speak," Riley replied, "a doubting man might wink at such 'perfect' justice."

"Some of ours got over the back wall," Dalton observed, wrapping the final knots in his straw noose. "If any ever gets the land," he said, eyeing Riley, "all sixty-eight will go out winners." He tossed the noose into the hat, scattering a few dung beetles.

"Quite a hat full," said Riley. "Think they got enough rope?"

"Maybe we'll share," Dalton suggested wryly, "and go in shifts."

"Hate to be hanged with a used rope," Riley grimaced. " 'Twould be bad luck on me, sure." They both laughed.

"As if we got any luck left what ain't already run out on us," said Dalton.

" 'Tain't luck but the good Lord His own Self what's run out on us," Riley almost whispered, "don't it seem?" Riley nodded toward the door. Dalton looked and saw a carved wooden crucifix above it. Riley crossed himself more out of superstition than reverence. "We're surely damned," Riley said in cautious fear, "sacrificed in the place of the war god."

"We spend our lives trying to take somebody else's dirt," Dalton said, aghast, "and you think that fighting for our own dirt this once evens up the score?!" He folded his arms and looked above. "Forgive the wretched arrogance of the man," he said, crossing himself.

Riley confronted the logic and felt penitent. " 'Tis times like the present, though," he said, "what give you pause to at least wonder." He eyed Dalton, who gave a considered nod to agree.

"All that praying and for once from the same pulpit," Riley continued, "so you'd think it'd win us at least one good fight."

"To lose having glimpsed what we might have won," Dalton sighed. "Seems more the pity. Bel and me, a little mud ball cabin on my own land . . ." His voice trailed off, lost in reverie. He slowly exhaled smoke.

"Young Luzero and me," mused Riley, gently fondling the tarnished gorget around his neck, "rolling around in a floppy feather bed 'til my old ticker finally goes tock . . ." They each mustered the tired smiles of a lost dream.

"I suppose He got His reasons," Dalton pondered. "He ain't in the habit of telling the likes of us, you know."

"I suppose He don't got to tell," Riley sighed, leaning back. "But He might could ease the dying with a bit of a hint."

Late that night on the plaza of nearby San Angel, a dusty, lone rider loped his weary horse up to the two-story adobe government house. Low stone and adobe buildings lined the dirt square, dominated by a small church. Torches and street lanterns burned brightly, revealing a sparse stand of trees in front of the church. A patrol tramped past two guards outside the government house, dark but for one lit window. Captain Robert E. Lee dismounted stiffly, tied up his horse, and dusted himself off. He saluted the guards, who presented arms as he walked inside.

In a sparsely furnished office dominated by a U.S. flag and a street map of Mexico City, General Scott labored in shirtsleeves and vest by candlelight. His large rough-hewn desk was cluttered with two stacks of handwritten court transcripts—one tall, one short. Scott was reading Riley's six-page letter from the court martial when Lee rapped at the open door. Scott looked up and waved him in as Lee saluted. He walked straight to the map, Scott watching.

"We scouted two causeways, sir," Lee said wearily, tracing a route. "By one, you take the city with no real resistance." He fingered a second road. "By the other, you face fortified troops at Chapultepec Academy and an old factory near there called Molino del Rey."

"So long as he has an army," Scott sighed, "Santa Anna will keep fighting until his country crumbles around him." Lee walked to the desk and plopped down exhausted into a chair facing Scott. "We go after the army," Scott decided, "not the city." Lee eyed the two stacks as Scott handed him Riley's letter.

"I see that one pile remains pitifully small," Lee observed.

"If I had my way, I would pardon them all," Scott sighed, slumping behind his desk. He still felt pangs of guilt whenever the memory of his and Taylor's clandestine meeting with Polk crossed his mind. Of course, Lee did not know of that meeting. "Santa Anna forces my hand," Scott confessed.

"With this latest truce broken, our men must fight again," Lee said, holding up the letter. "The deserters can have no hope for mercy."

"But the deserters can have justice under the law," Scott asserted. He rested his hand on a thick book of army regulations. "And on occasion," Scott said, "mercy survives the ravages of both." Lee sat up straight, looking intrigued.

"Reporting as ordered, sir," announced Captain Merrill. He stood saluting in the open doorway. Scott nodded and waved him in, gesturing at a chair beside Lee. Merrill sat down stiff and uncomfortable. Scott eyed him wearily.

"This is no court, Captain," Scott said. "You may speak plainly here and in confidence."

"Yes, sir," said Merrill, still wary. He eyed Lee, reading Riley's document. Merrill recognized it. "If you cut through Riley's 'Irish,' " Merrill said, "you can see that he thought he had little choice."

"Soldiers seldom do," said Lee, tossing the document onto the desk. "They must derive satisfaction from duty faithfully performed."

"Once a soldier determines where that duty lies," Merrill suggested. Lee looked at him askance, as if the notion of conflicting loyalties was blasphemy.

"When, exactly, did you last see him?" Scott asked. "In our uniform, I mean," he added hastily.

"April 12 last year, a Sunday," Merrill recalled. "I should have suspected when he asked for a pass to Mass," he added, "Riley not being especially devout."

Scott eased back into his chair, satisfied. He looked at Lee and tapped his fingers on the book of army regulations.

"Another one," Scott said. "That's a baker's dozen gone before war was declared." Scott took out a sheet of official army stationery, dipped a quill pen, and began scratching an order. Merrill looked cautiously hopeful.

"This one is Riley, sir," Lee said, trying to avoid a disrespectful tone of admonishment. "In the coming assault, it could have a bad effect on our men."

Scott frowned, putting down his quill. "In the coming assault, I would rather be put to the sword with my whole army," he said, "than execute Riley or any of his men unjustly." He eyed Merrill approvingly. "I know where my duty lies."

A few days later, Ockter, Morstadt, Hogan, Rose, and others stared dumbfounded as the surviving dozen original San Patricios were culled from the corral by guards. More deserters gathered around pointing and whispering as the twelve were shoved through the gates and held in a tight bunch.

"They must being the first to be hanged," Morstadt surmised grimly, "the first to having deserted."

Ockter watched the corporal of the guard march with a squad

toward the adobe horse stable. He suspected Riley and Dalton would be next. "At least Conahan will die in hospital," Ockter said.

Morstadt crossed himself. "For him, that is better than 'dancing in air,' " he said with a rueful look.

"And now they take the last of 'the first,' " Ockter said, pointing at the stable.

Inside, Dalton slumped half asleep with his sombrero over his face. Riley sat against a wall slapping away flies. Suddenly, the door creaked open and bright sunlight flooded the stall. Riley shielded his eyes against the blinding rays as Dalton sat up groggily. The corporal stood silhouetted in the doorway.

"Riley!" the corporal barked. "Come with us, you swine!"

Riley and Dalton exchanged a look of final goodbye as both rose to their feet shakily. They clasped hands.

" 'Twas quite a merry spree," Dalton said, "I'll give you that." He lit his pipe.

" 'Twill be one hell of a hangover," Riley said, taking a deep breath. He turned to face the door.

"We'll share a toast above," Dalton added, looking skyward.

"Stow th'blow and come on," snapped the corporal. "Your traitor arse ain't gonna swing," he said, disgusted.

Riley and Dalton stared in stunned disbelief.

"We been pardoned?" Riley managed, cautiously hopeful.

"We been cheated," countered the corporal, shaking his head no. "Seems we can't kill you because you skipped before the war actually started." He spat tobacco juice. "But we sure can make you howl some," he warned. "Let's go."

Two regulars stepped inside and shoved Riley to the door. Confused, he looked back at Dalton, who was staring with an agonized look of betrayal.

"Ain't this rich," Dalton said coldly, puffing a cloud of smoke.

"I didn't know!" Riley pleaded, struggling. "I swear!" He felt as if his revived sense of self esteem just took a sucker punch, his recently emptied mental footlocker instantly filling with a rush of guilt and evil deeds. As the regulars pushed him through the door, he pulled away frantically to face Dalton. "On my mother's grave, Dalton," Riley swore, "I had no hand in this! I did not know!"

Dalton slumped to the floor and leaned against the wall, staring up in tortured dismay. "The Lord must love a black joke, boy-o," he said bitterly. "When I prayed for one of us to get out alive, I never dreamt t'would be you—instigator of it all." He glared at Riley with a dismissive wave. "Get out! The sight of you makes me sick."

Riley was yanked outside. The door slammed shut with such force that clods of mud fell from the rafters, filtering through widening rays of sunlight.

Next morning, screams of agony mixed with the sharp crack of bullwhips in the San Angel square. A crowd of horrified Mexican civilians watched Riley and the twelve original San Patricios receive fifty lashes each from hard-bitten Mexican mule drivers, determined to earn their pay. In the shadow of the cross atop the church, the screaming deserters were tied to trees and lamp posts. They stood stripped to the waist, bare backs resembling bloody, pounded raw meat. With each crack of the whip, a man lurched, pulling himself in futility against leather thongs as he yelled. Barking dogs danced excitedly around the tortured men. Flies swarmed. Mexican women and young girls, wrapped modestly in rebosas, wailed and wept. A line of U.S. regulars kept the hostile crowd back. Another company stood in ranks, muskets ready.

Stoic General Twiggs watched on horseback with several mounted staff officers. An artillery wagon forge was parked nearby. A burly army blacksmith tended the glowing coals atop which rested several white-hot branding irons.

"*Aa-a-agh!*" cried Riley as the lash cracked again. He sagged against his rawhide ties. Sweat and tears of pain trickled down his face. He looked ready to pass out from pain and loss of blood.

The Mexican muleteer held up his next stroke, trotted up to Riley, inspected his tortured, pale face, and then turned to Twiggs. "He is dying!" he said. The other floggings continued unabated with loud screams and the cracking of bullwhips.

"I won't let him," Twiggs growled, pointing at a wooden bucket of water and nodding at Riley. The nearby blacksmith ran to Riley with the bucket and splashed him. Riley jerked awake and moaned. "Now," said Twiggs, "you left off at forty-seven. The sentence is fifty." Twiggs glared at the muleteer, who nodded and again cracked his whip. Riley screamed in agony.

"Sir, if you don't mind my saying," ventured the returning blacksmith, "me an' plenty more would've gladly done this work." He pointed at the busy line of Mexican bullwhackers. The whips kept cracking and the screams resounding in the plaza.

"Riley and his ilk are not worthy to be whipped by a United States soldier," snarled Twiggs. He looked at the forge. "But keep your irons hot, master ferrier," he added. The blacksmith nodded in a shared understanding, doffing a salute.

Minutes later, the hiss of burning flesh and curling black smoke was punctuated by hideous shrieks. The San Patricio tied next to Riley was being branded on his right cheek with a two-inch letter *D*, forever marking him as a despicable deserter.

Two regulars held him tight and grimaced at the acrid stench as the blacksmith applied the red-hot brand. The man fell limp, unconscious. The other San Patricios already branded were being cut down and carried to waiting ambulance wagons as the blacksmith and two regulars walked to Riley.

"You didn't stand up well to the whip," said the blacksmith. The two regulars grabbed Riley and held him up straight on his now wobbly legs.

"Ain't none of you worth impressing," Riley gasped, breathing heavily. Riley glared as the two soldiers snickered. He tried to spit in the blacksmith's face but was so weak he only managed to dribble saliva down his chin. "Shit," he muttered. The blacksmith and two guards laughed.

"Master ferrier!" Twiggs called out, walking his horse closer to Riley. The blacksmith turned to look. "Be careful to apply that brand properly," he said.

"Of course I will, sir," the blacksmith replied, sounding offended.

Twiggs frowned, realizing the ferrier did not get his implied point. "If not done properly," he stressed, "it might have to be done again."

"Yes, sir!" the blacksmith replied smartly, at last understanding.

"Yee-ow-w-w!" Riley screamed, eyes wild with pain and terror as the glowing *D* brand seared into the smoking flesh of his right cheek. The two guards held him upright on his feet, head bowed and breathing hard, when Twiggs sidled up on his horse.

"Let me see," Twiggs snapped. The blacksmith grabbed Riley's hair and yanked his head back painfully. Riley's right cheek showed an ugly, seared *D* but applied upside down. "Too bad," Twiggs said. "It is backward. Do it again."

"May you roast in hell, you shitfaced, heathen bastards!" Riley croaked.

"Today, only Poper scum traitors are roasting!" gloated the blacksmith. He seared the smoking brand deep into Riley's left cheek. Riley screamed in renewed agony, sagging into unconsciousness.

★ ★ ★ ★ ★

Days later, the screams, moans, and whimpers of dozens of wounded men filled the crowded halls and rooms of a U.S. army hospital inside an expansive adobe hacienda. In the near distance, the roar of guns and rattle of musketry swelled, ebbed, and flowed from a raging battle.

Two stretcher bearers carried a moaning, writhing, terrified regular with a bloody shredded arm past the rooms of wretched patients. Some lay on the floor; others, on cots and in beds. A few occupied household chairs and divans. Discarded bandages stained with blood and pus littered the tile floor, glistening with pink water.

"The butcher's bill is runnin' high," puffed one of the stretcher bearers as he navigated the maze of patients.

"Damn greasers puttin' up a stiff fight," said the other, "for them," he added in a disparaging tone.

"Don't bring me here!" cried their patient. "Let me die whole!" He pushed himself up on his one good arm, twisting the stretcher to the side. The wounded man rolled off and hit the filthy floor hard with an agonized yell.

In the next room, two army surgeons cut, sawed, and sewed using carved Spanish doors slung between chairs as operating tables. One surgeon had just finished sawing off an unconscious man's leg. He dropped it to the floor, slippery with entrails, fingers, hands, arms, legs, and bloody pink water. The surgeon folded the flaps of fat and skin over the bloody stump and began sewing them with gutta percha thread.

"This one's gone," sighed the other surgeon angrily, sagging from exhaustion over the corpse of Captain Moses Merrill, Company K, Fifth U.S. Infantry. He saw the two stretcher bearers waiting with their frightened patient, now back in place. "Our good captain here is beyond caring," he said. "Take him out back."

Two stewards removed Merrill's stretcher as another washed off the door with a tossed bucket of water, splashing onto the floor. The surgeon waved impatiently. The two stretcher bearers plopped down their ward.

"Don't take my arm," the man whimpered. The surgeon gave a quick look at the bullet riddled arm and frowned.

"I have no choice. Bite on this!" he snapped, shoving a tooth-marked stick into the man's mouth. Two stewards pushed him down as the surgeon picked up a bloody bone saw and wiped it on his stained apron.

The stewards carried the body of Merrill into a back room past two armed guards. As they walked down a narrow aisle toward a guarded rear door, a few San Patricios flogged in the plaza looked up from their cots. The distant battle could still be heard but not above the sounds of men hammering nails and sawing wood just outside.

In a cot beside a window, Riley stared in shock and dismay as he saw Merrill's corpse lugged past. Propped on feather pillows with his cheeks and back bandaged, he painfully moved his arm to cross himself, and then salute.

"The best of the crop be harvested first," Riley sighed. "Leastwise, the good captain weren't killed at the hands of me . . . or mine."

" 'Tain't th'way of things at all," chided the weak voice of Conahan.

Riley grimaced as he turned his head stiffly to one side. In a bed next to him, Conahan looked as gray as the soiled sheet covering the flat space which once would have held his legs.

"If so," Conahan said in jest, "why th'hell weren't the rest of me 'harvested?' " He looked down at his two stumps. His face and forehead were dripping with sweat from a raging fever.

" 'Tis my sinful ways cursing me with long life," Riley said. " 'Twas enough to make a lesser man doubt his course, the look on Dalton's face," he moaned.

"Faith the only 'lesser man' here is me!" Conhan declared, frowning. The sounds of distant battle and nearby construction rattled on.

"Sorry mate," Riley shrugged contritely. "I joked someday you'd grow, Conahan," Riley said. "Never thought you'd be growin' shorter."

"My wounds went sour," Conahan said. "Something started eatin' my flesh. So, they cut on me to stop it." Riley sniffed at a foul, sour stench.

"Tossed them rotten parts outside, did they?" Riley surmised.

"No, you're smellin' what's left of me right here," Conahan said sheepishly. "It keeps eatin' at me still and now they can't cut off no more," he sighed. "I'm a goner."

Riley stared at him, then rolled over painfully and looked out the window. On a low, rocky knoll, he could see soldiers in shirtsleeves pounding nails, sawing logs, and tying ropes to fashion long, primitive gallows. In the distance, a stone castle-like fortress loomed atop a steep hill above the swirling dust and smoke of the ongoing battle at the old factory below called Molino del Rey. The Mexican flag flew from the ramparts above.

"Leastwise you can go up knowing you cheated th'damn hangman," said Riley, staring with a haunted look at the gallows.

"And you didn't?" Conahan scoffed. "Sure and life with scars is better than no life at all."

Riley stared at Conahan with a mute, tortured look of doubt. He had been trying to toss the memory of Dalton's face of betrayal into his mental footlocker, along with all the other sorry and regrettable misdeeds and bad memories of his sorry and regrettable life. It had been emptied but now it had all come rushing back with a fury. He feared it would grow to overflowing. Riley felt that Dalton's accusatory look of condemnation would haunt him for the rest of his days. The most damnable part of it, he understood painfully, was that he had in fact done nothing this time around to deserve it. But, of course, Riley had started it all in the first place. Perhaps, he surmised, a remorseful life with scars was indeed the good Lord's just punishment.

CHAPTER 15
MIXCOAC
SEPTEMBER 13, 1847

In the golden glow of early morning light, Riley and twelve other surviving, original San Patricios stood in shirtsleeves digging a long, shallow trench. It stretched atop a windswept, rocky mound just outside the tiny village of Mixcoac. They worked slowly, painfully. Though their facial brands had scabbed over, the bandaged wounds from their brutal floggings had re-opened. Blood soaked through the backs of their grimy white cotton shirts. Their spades crunched into the earth as the familiar rumble of battle drifted across to them from two miles away on a cool breeze.

Riley could see smoke creeping up the stone castle of Chapultepec Military Academy like the spectral hands of a banshee, rising like Death itself from the steep hillside highlighted by orange flashes from musketry. The Mexican flag flew atop the tower and jutted into a brilliant purple horizon of snow capped mountains. U.S. flags fluttered among dusty sky-blue troops at the base.

"That's deep enough for traitors," snapped Colonel Harney from horseback beside the pit, only about three feet deep. He stared down smugly at Riley as he stopped digging. Breathing hard, Riley leaned on his shovel, the two purplish *D* brands on his cheeks glistening from dripping sweat. "Seeing you like this makes keeping you alive tolerable," Harney gloated.

" 'Twould only be worth it to me," Riley glowered, "were I to live long enough to cook the goose what got fat eatin' grass on your grave." Harney ignored him with the arrogance of the victor. He reached behind him for his spyglass case as the sound of battle grew more intense. Riley felt a twinge of satisfaction at hearing a familiar deep chuckle from Dalton, who had not even acknowledged him all morning.

"And will you be tending our graves as well?" Dalton asked loudly. Stung, Riley looked up with an agonized face obviously in pain but also racked with guilt. Dalton sat facing backward on an artillery limber, staring down at him. Two nooses dangled in front of him from the rough, overhead gallows Riley had seen built from his hospital bed. "Faith you started digging them a year ago," Dalton added. He looked to his left in disgust.

Beside Dalton, Morstadt and Ockter sat on a board across the back of a Mexican mule cart, nooses dangling in front of them. Beside them, Hogan and Rose sat similarly across the back of an army wagon, nooses dangling. To their left beneath the long gallows waited twenty-four more captured San Patricios, all in their tattered Mexican uniforms. Nooses twisted in the breeze in front of them as they stared grimly at Chapultepec. Hands tied behind their backs, they sat two at a time on boards across the backs of varied livery hitched to horses and mules. Army teamsters sat in the wagon and cart boxes; three artillery drivers, astride the horses of Dalton's limber.

"Dragoons, to your posts!" yelled Harney, twisting in his saddle. He turned back to face Chapultepec and extended his spyglass.

Mounted dragoons glided in between each wagon and waited ominously next to the doomed men. Some dragoons refused to look at the San Patricios. Others stared in pity or contempt. A few looked quietly ashamed.

Riley and the gravediggers watched as a mounted squad of dragoons walked into line at each end of the gallows. They drew sabers and tucked the gleaming blades upright against their right shoulders, waiting for something.

Suddenly, the jingling rattle of a bouncing, two-wheeled army ambulance drew Riley's attention. He and the others stared curiously at the oddly bright blue conveyance. It jerked to a jolting stop under a shady pepper tree behind the far line of dragoons. Two medical stewards rode the ambulance.

"Why waste an ambulance on us?" wondered Rose, staring.

"Sure an' to patch us up," snapped Hogan, chewing tobacco, "so's we can go through it all again!" Anxious San Patricios on either side grunted small, nervous laughs.

"Silence!" roared Harney. He held the spyglass to his eye and peered toward the battle. Focusing on a corner of a stone tower, he could see sky-blue regulars storming up ladders and over medieval looking battlements. Mexican soldados fought fiercely but were killed or fell back, overwhelmed. Six academy cadets, distinguished by their dark-blue jackets and carrying a Mexican flag, backed up fighting into a corner. A U.S. volley cut down five. The sixth teenager wrapped himself in his flag and dove to his death off the tower. Cheering, U.S. troops charged into the fort.

"It won't be long now," warned Harney, voice pregnant with anticipation. He lowered the glass with a look of sublime satisfaction. "Put on the nooses!"

The dragoons yanked off the San Patricios' hats and tossed them into the burial pit. They slipped a noose over each man's head and adjusted the knot behind the right ear. Dalton's flamboyant sombrero sailed slowly into the pit and landed almost at Riley's feet. He stared at it, stooped down, and picked it up with reverence, feeling as if it might be a sacred relic. His hands crumpled the soft felt brim as he rose to look up at Dalton, who averted his eyes.

Harney wheeled his horse and galloped to the center. He reined up and faced the condemned. "You'll live just long

266

enough," Harney yelled, pointing at the battle, "to see the flag you betrayed fly over that last greaser fort!"

"Then may we all feast on Riley's cooked goose!" shouted Dalton.

Anxious, sweating, grim San Patricios broke the tension with light laughter. It rippled quickly down the gallows and just as quickly faded.

"I said be silent!" screamed Harney, glaring at Dalton.

"And what more could you do to them if they ain't?!" bellowed Riley, taking a step forward in the grave so Harney could see him. Riley heard a few more San Patricios share nervous laughs. Even Dalton grunted with a slight, tight smile, watching Riley glare at Harney in one final, futile act of defiance. Riley half hoped Harney would jerk a horse pistol and put him out of his misery. He felt he had lost everything: his love, his best friend, his battalion and the men who had trusted him, his profession, and his self respect. Riley wondered if perhaps he had even lost his soul.

Harney stared hard as flint at Riley, then scanned the long line of haggard, fearful faces beneath the gallows. "Talk as you will," he said begrudgingly, turning his back on them to resume watching the battle.

Riley took heart in this tiny final victory. He half smiled as he took a few steps closer to the gallows. Both the grave diggers and the condemned eyed him curiously, as if he were a stranger they had never seen. Gone was the cocky, strutting, commanding professional soldier. Riley looked more like a penitent sinner as he stood there, head bowed, slowly wringing the brim of Dalton's sombrero in an act of contrition.

"I were the sorry spinner of this tale," Riley called out, "but this ain't the ending I had dreamed. Somehow, it all got away from me." He looked up at Dalton, staring stone faced. "But a friend of mine says the good Lord He got His reasons. That may be, but if I could have my own way, lads, I'd swap my own neck for yours."

"So would we!" yelled Dalton. Again, nervous laughter tittered down the line of the condemned. A few looked beyond their own fear with compassion at Riley, choked with emotion and teary eyed. Dalton's tense smile faded when he looked down and saw Riley staring up at him imploringly, silently begging for forgiveness. Suddenly, the roar of battle died away to a few sputtering shots, then deafening silence. Dalton and Riley both looked at Harney.

"Though you deserve none," Harney yelled, drawing his saber, "are there any last requests?!" He pointed at Chapultepec. The Mexican flag was being lowered as a brisk wind picked up and whipped across the hillock.

"I am having one!" Ockter called out. Seated beside him, Morstadt turned his head to look at him curiously.

Harney trotted over. "What do you want, Dutchman?" Harney asked contemptuously.

"Dutchmen make good soldiers!" Rose blurted out, taking exception to Harney's tone. Half a dozen other Germans shouted *"Ja!"* and *"Jawohl!"*

"Well?!" Harney said impatiently, frowning at Ockter.

"I am an artilleryman," Ockter asserted proudly. Harney looked confused as San Patricios exchanged amused looks. "Not Dalton but me should be hanged from that artillery limber!" Ockter alone started laughing, proud of his jest.

"Bah!" Harney blurted, turning his horse in disgust.

As more San Patricios mustered laughs down the line, Morstadt gaped at Ockter as he darted looks all around, enjoying the grim merriment. "No jokes you make the entire war," Morstadt said, "and now you decide it is the time?!"

"Jawohl!" Ockter yelled, laughing even louder. His eyepatch rode up and down on his crinkling cheeks with his belly laugh,

To the Color

making him look like a piratical lunatic. He almost sounded delirious. Morstadt joined in the laughter, but it died out quickly.

Dalton's grin faded when he looked down at Riley, who brushed a few tears off his grimy cheeks and turned away. Dalton sagged with a cavernous sigh, then darted a frown at Harney.

"Could you grant a favor to a dying man, sir?" Dalton shouted.

Harney trotted to Dalton and pushed his horse up painfully hard against Dalton's dangling legs. Harney's red hair seemed to glow in the rich morning light. He smiled in smug enjoyment as Dalton grimaced in pain.

"Make it quick," Harney snarled. He held his saber upright and tucked tight against his right shoulder.

"Could you take my pipe out of my pocket, sir," Dalton said loudly, "and light it with your elegant flaming hair?!"

Riley could not help himself but to whirl around laughing, joining the rest. Harney exploded in rage and smashed the hilt of his sword into Dalton's grinning mouth with a sickening dull crunch. Dalton spat out bloody teeth.

"Bad luck to you!" Dalton bellowed, undaunted as blood sprayed from his ripped mouth and dribbled down his chin. "You've spoilt my smoke entirely! I shan't be able to hold a pipe in my mouth as long as I live!"

At first horrified, Riley and the rest again burst into rowdy laughter. Harney looked furious but he was frustrated and helpless, making him even more lethal. He suddenly became aware of the dangling noose and the empty space beside Dalton on the limber seat. He grabbed the noose and yanked it fiercely.

"Where is the man for this noose?!" Harney demanded.

"Holding it!" boomed Riley, drawing more laughs and a gratifying, bloody grin from Dalton.

"My orders are to hang thirty traitors today," Harney seethed at Riley, "and twenty-one more tomorrow. And I will do no less!" Laughter faded as San Patricios exchanged questioning, sobered looks. Dalton stared at Riley, who shrugged.

"He's in here!" cried a medical steward from the ambulance at the end of the gallows. Enraged, Harney galloped its entire length past his dragoons to the parked vehicle. He reined to a stop and glared at the intimidated steward. "Doctors kept him, sir," he pleaded, "but they wanted you to see for yourself that he's dying." He pointed laconically at the back of the covered ambulance.

"Damn right he's dying!" Harney bellowed. "At the end of that rope!" He pointed his sword at the gallows. "Get him over there!"

The shocked steward snapped his reins. The ambulance lurched forward and rolled to the other end of the gallows. The two stewards carried the limp form of Conahan out of the ambulance to Dalton's artillery limber.

"God in heaven!" Morstadt exclaimed in German as boos, guffaws, and curses flew from the San Patricios, both condemned and gravediggers.

"Your heart comes from the depths of hell itself," grumbled Riley, watching in horror, "if you've got a heart at all." Even the Brits would not have lowered themselves to this level of savagery, Riley thought.

The stewards perched Conahan precariously on the seat beside Dalton, who looked sickened. Barely balanced, Conahan wobbled while seated on pus-saturated, bloody stumps. He looked like a breathing corpse, eyes sunken and shadowed with jaundiced skin. He started to topple over. The mounted dragoon beside him grabbed Conahan and held him upright. Conahan looked at him groggily in thanks.

"Your sainted mother would be smilin', she would," Conahan gasped with a weak smile, "if ever you'd had one."

"It'd kill you hatin' so hard as himself," the dragoon whispered in a thick brogue. The dragoon muffled a laugh and tossed a sneer toward Harney as he trotted back to the center. Conahan looked surprised not only at the empathy but the brogue as the dragoon dropped the noose over his head, adjusting the knot.

"Thought only th'native born could be dragoons," Conahan replied, screwing his face into a cockeyed question around the hemp.

"That's only the First Dragoons, Harney's own regiment," he replied. "I'm Second Dragoons, the newest regiment an' open to one an' all." He smiled reassuringly. "This ain't personal," he added.

"Thank God," Conahan gasped. "At least I ain't bein' sent up by a native-born bastard."

"My quota is to hang thirty traitors and I won't be one traitor short!" Harney bragged, expertly making his horse prance at the center as if on parade.

"Don't you mean 'one short traitor'?!" Dalton snarled through a bloody smile. He jerked his head toward wobbly Conahan weaving beside him. More San Patricios snickered in derision.

"Quiet in th'damn ranks!" Conahan surprisingly shouted with a mighty effort. "Or is it now th'ranks of th'damned?! No matter. I can still dance in the air with th'lot of you—and better!" he gasped loudly, drawing more laughter and some cheers. A few shouted "Viva!" sounding like a Mexican taunt at their executioners.

Riley smiled broadly as he stared, struggling with raging feelings of pride, remorse, and guilt. He had seen comrades die in horrific fights his entire career. But coupled with his sense of loss and sadness was the comforting knowledge that they had exercised a fighting chance. With a soldierly, fatalistic acceptance of Fate, Riley had shaken off his mourning and marched on in quick time. This was different, he sensed. This was sadistic and vengeful murder. And he could only stand and watch while feeling impotent rage.

Harney pointed his sword at Chapultepec. The U.S. flag was climbing up the tower mast at a torturous pace. A distant bugle began to play "To the Color."

"Drivers, ready!" Harney bellowed, raising his sword. Teamsters raised their whips and gathered their reins.

The grim humor evaporated as the condemned saw the flag slowly rise and heard the haunting, oddly joyful bugle call. Some silently mouthed prayers. A few whimpered with quivering lips; most just stared in fatalistic acceptance.

Riley glanced over his shoulder and saw that only moments remained. He scanned the length of the gallows, desperate to burn images and faces into his memory. His trusty mental footlocker felt bulging, as if some treasured images would fall out before he could safely lock them away. He felt a sense of panic, as if he could not gather them all in quickly enough before they disappeared forever.

Hogan sat chewing tobacco with a look of defiance on his face. He spat a glob that splattered on Harney's prancing horse. Harney did not see. Hogan nudged Rose and they shared a childish sense of joy in this small, secret revenge.

Morstadt sat humming Beethoven's "Ode to Joy" louder and louder as he watched the flag rise higher and higher.

Eyepatch slightly askew, Ockter stared stoic, proud, and straight as a ramrod, softly reciting The Lord's Prayer in German.

Conahan was weaving on his seat, eyes half-closed and wearing a sad little smile. The Irish dragoon held him up with an arm around his shoulder.

Dalton stared straight at Riley, who choked back tears.

"Don't make me remember you as a blubbering sot, boy-o," Dalton complained. "It will disturb my long sleep."

"Some sot," Riley said, voice husky with emotion. "Ain't had a drink since parting with Luzero." He managed a weak smile.

"You pick one hell of a time to go dry on me!" Dalton cracked. "For the sake of us all, promise to go and find her! And get them three hundred twenty acres that we are dying for!" Dalton fired a fierce look at all the gravediggers. "That goes for the lot of you! Demand that the dream come true! Give this damn nightmare some meaning!"

Riley could only nod yes in tearful reassurance. Dalton looked up at the flag, now nearing the top of the mast. He braced himself, took a deep breath, looked at Riley, and flashed a bloody, toothless grin.

"So, now 'tis goodbye! Remember me—and that no friend of mine ever stretched a rope in my place!" He added quietly, "I do forgive you."

"I . . . I don't know what to say, Patrick," Riley said in a hoarse voice, choking back his emotions.

"Thank God!" Dalton boomed. "Every damn time you open your mouth, somebody dies!"

Black laughter rippled along the gallows until all saw the United States flag billowing atop the pole at Chapultepec Castle. Riley realized the end had come.

"I'll toast you above, Patrick," Riley whispered with a thankful nod, crossing himself. "I'll toast you all!" he shouted. The final notes of "To the Color" faded away.

"Drivers!" Harney commanded, sword held high. The San Patricios seemed to take a collective, deep breath, looking in surprising disbelief at the flag.

Dalton jerked his head to his left, breathing hard and sweating. "For Ireland and old Mexico . . . !" he bellowed at the top of his lungs.

"Now!" yelled Harney, viciously slicing his sword down. Whips snapped, drivers whistled, and the wagons, carts, and limber lurched forward.

"Viva!" the San Patricios roared in a resounding, mighty shout as they slid off their seats. Their necks cracked with a sickening, dull crunch that sounded to Riley like army hard crackers crushed on a wood barracks floor. The dozen grave-digging survivors stood silent and staring. Some gagged. A few dropped to their knees in prayer. Most wept. One turned away, doubled over, and vomited.

Riley sagged in surrender like a captured battle flag, hanging limp on his shovel. He held Dalton's sombrero in one hand. Tears streamed down his grimy cheeks as he gazed long and thoughtfully at the contorted faces and swaying corpses. But he managed to muster a cockeyed, proud smile. He felt the weird, twisted agony only a combat veteran could feel when comrades he loved died while he, of all people, somehow survived. The only sounds were the strangely sympathetic moan of a gentle, warm wind and the rhythmic creaking of taut, swinging ropes.

Sunlight poured brightly through a high barred window into a cramped, dank prison cell. Riley sat on a stool at a rough-hewn table writing a letter. He wore his dark-blue Mexican military trousers and vest, a clean white shirt, and the gorget given to him by Luzero. He was freshly shaved. After nearly nine months in prison, his two *D* brands showed on his cheeks only as bright-pink skin. The scabs had fallen away. And Riley was bald, his head having been shaved clean per U.S. Army regulation treatment of convicted deserters.

Dalton's sombrero lay on the table top. The shining tin serpent head hatband glinted in the dusty rays of sun. The sound of hundreds of tramping feet and lusty voices singing "Green Grows the Laurel" floated in through the open window. Riley finished writing, dropped the quill pen, and sealed the letter. His final act while under United States control was to wipe the slate clean with an old mentor in Mackinac, Michigan.

"To my honorable judge and friend, Charles O'Malley," Riley heard himself recite in his mind's voice. "Upon my release today, I take pen in hand to relate to you the end of my adventures, since it was with yourself they begun . . ."

A U.S. regular swung open the cell door and gestured for Riley to rise and leave. He stood, put on his Mexican major's tunic and Dalton's sombrero, and carried the sealed letter with him out the door. The sound of the music and marching troops continued haunting him from the street.

Riley knew that, at last, Santa Anna had signed what was called the Treaty of Guadalupe Hidalgo. It ended the war and gave President Polk what he had envisioned as his country's manifest destiny: California and a huge expanse of western lands that stretched unbroken to the Pacific Ocean. Today, the occupying U.S. troops were marching to Vera Cruz to board ship and sail for home.

Most did not know that their victorious commander had left with no pomp or ceremony in a carriage the night before, facing political retribution in Washington City. Riley had learned from smuggled notes and Mexican newspapers that General Winfield Scott had fallen victim to President Polk's political jealousy, as had Taylor before him. Polk apparently could suffer no heroes from the opposing political party, even though they had won his unconscionable war. Scott faced an inquiry on trumped up charges. He had been relieved of command and departed with his headquarters flag furled. Riley owed Scott his life and felt that he was indeed an officer of courage and integrity. Last night, he had seen U.S. officers in the street stand at attention with their caps over their hearts as he was driven past. Riley himself had braced to attention in respect as he watched through the cell window bars.

". . . I suppose from the accounts in the United States papers," Riley's voice continued in his mind, "that you have formed a very poor opinion of Mexico . . ."

Grim, stoic guards and a fifer and drummer marched Riley down a long, dark, stone prison corridor. The musicians played "The Rogue's March," regulation for drumming a deserter out of the service.

Riley recalled Conahan fiddling the tune for the captured Kentuckians just before Buena Vista. Now it sounded discordant, bouncing off the walls as the strains of "Green Grows the Laurel" floated in from outside.

". . . But be not deceived by the prejudice of a nation that was at war with Mexico, for a more hospitable or friendly people there exists not on the face of the earth. That is to a foreigner and especially to an Irishman and Catholic . . . ," Riley heard himself recite from his letter.

The detail halted at the main prison door, which was swung open. Riley was shoved out roughly onto a narrow Mexico City street. The door slammed shut with a resounding clang of finality. He inhaled deeply and felt his lungs expand to that delicious point where he thought they might burst with joy; not only was the air fresh, but he was at last free.

The column of U.S. troops swung past like a romantic painting come to life in new, pristine sky-blue uniforms, volunteers and regulars alike. They looked just as Riley had first seen them a long and painful two years ago, singing "Green Grows the Laurel" to the jaunty accompaniment of fife and drum. U.S. flags hung from the Spanish styled stone buildings. But the Mexican citizens lining the street watched in silence, depressed and hateful. Riley stared a few long moments, scowling and remembering, proud and remorseful.

Near him stood six Mexican veterans, several with crutches and missing an arm or a leg. They instantly saluted him, the first refreshing sign of respect he had enjoyed since imprisonment. He formally returned the honor, recalling with a poignant smile how this would have made Ockter proud.

Moreno had smuggled a letter to him confirming that he could retain his commission in the Mexican army if he wished. He had decided to continue soldiering. After all, he mused, it was more than what he knew best—it was, in fact, all that he knew.

". . . It grieves me to have to inform you of the death of fifty-one of my best and bravest men," Riley's inner voice continued bitterly, "who have been hung by the Americans for no other reason than fighting manfully against them . . ."

Suddenly Luzero stepped out of the crowd and into Riley's view. She looked stunning, lusciously arrayed in lacy Spanish-accented attire. Riley thought at first that he was seeing just another fantasy of her, one of many that he had imagined for months. This was their first meeting since before the fight at Churubusco. Her long hair was styled up with comb, mantilla, and a red rose. Riley gaped, unable to believe his eyes.

She glided to him with tears tracing her smile. They embraced long and tenderly, even as U.S. troops continued tramping past. She gently pushed away to produce Riley's shining silver flask, recently polished. Luzero had kept it safe with an almost religious reverence.

Surprised, he grasped it eagerly with a thirsty smile. He wrapped one arm around her and they walked away from the troops. With his other arm, Riley thrust the flask toward the heavens in the promised toast to his friends above.

With a loving look at Luzero, he silently vowed that he would complete the rest of his promise: He would obtain Mexico's promised land grants not only for himself, but every one of his surviving San Patricios.

". . . As they say down here and as I have come myself to believe," Riley's voice concluded in his letter, "history is but a cruel joke played by the living upon the sacred dead."

EPILOGUE
JALAPA, MEXICO
SPRING, 1876

The old Mexican spied the buggy brawling up the dirt road. He pulled himself up ramrod straight, leaned on his hoe like a musket, and watched. Sweat glistened on his bearded face, shaded by a battered felt sombrero with a broad brim. In the hot reflected glare of morning light, the gold cross atop the ancient cathedral of Jalapa glistened above stone and adobe houses plastered in weary pinks, reds, and yellows. Already they were basking in the muggy heat and seemed to flow together like wet watercolors, he mused. Then the dust cloud trailing the buggy blurred his view. His blue eyes squinted until at last he could see the driver plainly. Instinctively, his brawny bronze hands clenched the hoe tightly. He felt emotions long buried rise like bile in his stomach. He grunted and resumed hacking vines off watermelons, but now with a vengeance.

The buggy rolled to a stop across the road in front of a two-story adobe plastered in pale green. Its wood balcony was festooned with clay pots bristling with red roses. The porch below was stacked with watermelons and burlap bags of potatoes. More watermelons were piled in a small cart hitched to a donkey, tethered to the railing. Flies buzzed around the lazily swishing tail of the donkey.

"Hello inside!" hailed the driver, a mustachioed lieutenant in the elegant undress uniform of the Seventh United States Cavalry. His dark-blue blouse was trimmed in black braid and his sky-blue trousers striped bravely in bright yellow. The gold bullion edging on his yellow shoulder straps gleamed in the blazing sunlight. Using a white silk scarf draped rakishly around his neck, he pushed back his straw "boater" hat to wipe his forehead, starkly white above his tan line.

Fanning herself beside him was an alabaster skinned young woman, her face smooth, pretty, and innocent like that of a china doll. She sweltered in bustled burgundy Victorian finery under a dusty tan parasol, once white. Perched precariously atop her piled mound of blonde hair was a fashionable bird's nest hat. She was working her fan double time, thought the old Mexican.

"Anybody home?!" the young officer persisted. He tossed a quick look of irritation over his shoulder at the old Mexican, again noisily chopping vines and ignoring them, it seemed to him.

"Here comes someone," his wife said hopefully, nodding at the sound of footsteps inside the house. Her thin, doll like lips grew taut with impatience. She nudged her husband. He pulled his gaze from the old Mexican back to the porch.

A strikingly attractive, older Mexican woman stood in the open doorway with broom in hand. She wore a floor length skirt of deep green, a simple, white blouse, and an apron. Streaks of silver played in her long black hair, worn up with a Spanish comb and one red rose. Her wide, full lips formed a curious, cautious smile. The young officer appeared instantly captivated.

"She must have been beautiful in her day," the officer observed idly. This insensitive comment drew a pout from his wife.

"In my day, she looks more comfortable than me in this heat," she whined.

"Pardon me, madam," the officer ventured, doffing his hat.

"May we buy a watermelon?" He tacked on a condescending smile.

The woman merely stared at him either in non-comprehension or stunned disbelief. She looked past the buggy or right through it, perhaps at something in the distance.

Unnerved, the lieutenant looked over his shoulder across the gently sloping valley and cultivated fields to the snow-capped mountains beyond. There was nothing exceptional to see but the old Mexican in sandals and soiled canvas trousers. He had stopped chopping to tug up his bloused cotton shirtsleeves, exposing surprisingly beefy forearms for an older man. The lieutenant gawked at the whiteness of his skin, but shrugged it off. He had seen plenty of white-skinned "creoles" in Mexico. He returned his gaze to the woman.

"It's so very hot down here," he pleaded.

"We're on our honeymoon," his bride revealed, her tone suggesting that they were doing something delightfully naughty. "We're celebrating our nation's first one hundred years by sightseeing our way through your beautiful country, from Vera Cruz to Mexico City!" She wafted her fan in prickly agitation. "Then we must return home. My husband's regiment leaves for a campaign against the Sioux."

"My own father marched this way with our army thirty years ago," the officer added proudly, gesturing with an imperial sweep of arm at Jalapa.

The Mexican woman's piercing black eyes suddenly flashed with the hot glow of someone much younger than her forty-nine years.

"No entiendo, mi teniente 'turista' gringo," she said mockingly, barely suppressing a leering, haughty smile. With a swish of her broom, she sent a small cloud of dust curling toward them. She stepped back inside the adobe and shut the wood door with a solid thunk.

The stunned couple stared in silent shock at one another. The only sound was energized buzzing from the profoundly irritated legion of flies.

"Why are these native people so rude?!" the girl blurted in a loud whisper. She heard the old Mexican across the road unleash a light, airy laugh.

"Because you Yanks marched home with half of Mexico in your pockets and on your flag!" he boomed in a tired Irish brogue. He felt a warm wave of satisfaction and crowned their looks of astonishment with a wry grin. The old Mexican dropped his hoe, picked up a watermelon, and walked to them. "Now take this and be off with you," he said, gently plopping the green melon into the lap of the now giggling girl.

The young officer caught himself staring at the old man's ruddy face. A pink scar in the shape of a *D* could be seen high on one cheek where his graying brown beard thinned. A second *D*, but upside down, disfigured his other cheek. The young officer's civil facade faded to a suspicious frown.

"You've done well for yourself down here, 'Paddy,' " he said suggestively. "Beat the hangman, did you?"

"Some may think so," the old Mexican said softly, his smile fading. "And the name is Riley," he added, mustering a proud challenge. His taut face skewed into a cocky attitude of defiance, still intimidating for a man of fifty-eight years. Piercing blue eyes locked the officer in an uncomfortable, dangerous stare.

"How much do we owe you?" the lieutenant said stiffly, his earlier suspicions now confirmed. He thought to break this trance by producing a wad of greenbacks.

"Not be owed nothing by the likes of you," Riley said in a low whisper. He turned to the girl, looking confused and a little frightened by these two men who seemed to share a dark, somehow threatening secret.

"Darlin', 'tis a price paid by better men than me too long ago," he struggled to say, his voice growing husky. Riley's look softened into a gentle, almost wistful smile. "And now only me cares to remember."

He took her gloved hand, bowed low, and kissed it with a flash of his old Irish charm. As she giggled, she noticed that his stained felt sombrero sported a peculiar hat cord. Tattered, faded green silk was coiled around the crumpled crown almost like a serpent ready to strike. The cord was tied on one side with its ends encased in rusty tin, hammered into the head and tail of a rattlesnake.

Riley shook off his reverie, let loose of her hand, took a step back, and smiled. "As we say down here, when a man sees a saddled horse, he must take a ride," he said. She could not help but smile. The old saying had become religious dogma to Riley. He slapped the butt of their horse. It bolted and the buggy lurched forward, the surprised young officer gathering the reins quickly. His bride squealed. As they rattled down the road, they heard Riley laughing.

Luzero emerged again from the house to glide down from the porch with the saucy elegance of her much younger self. Riley eyed her with fond remembrance, thinking that she had not changed all that much. Thirty years, the war, and two revolutions later, and he still felt his loins stir at the sight of her.

She joined him in the road and smiled at the familiar twinkle in his eye, playfully poking him in the ribs with her elbow. He produced his flask engraved with the Irish harp and thrust it skyward in a silent toast, so routine now that they both understood its meaning without a word. They each downed a healthy swig.

Arms around one another's waist, they watched the buggy push west beneath gathering storm clouds, rapidly taking the shape of bruised, brawling fists. Riley unleashed a fatalistic laugh. He had seen this sleight of hand by Fate too many times before. It always had meant trouble. Maybe this time, he hoped, it would be for someone other than himself: Perhaps the lieutenant, he idled.

Soon the buggy was consumed by its trailing cloud of hot, swirling dust, glowing blood red in the rays of the tropical sun. Distant thunder rumbled like the muffled roar of rolling cannon fire, Riley thought. Suddenly, he felt surprised and even a little embarrassed. He found himself inexplicably longing for that faded reality, wishing he could once again feel the burning surge of energy from battle, taste that acrid smoke, and savor the raw power as he touched off a booming salvo from the guns of his gallant San Patricios.

But, of course, they all were gone long, long ago. He let loose a resonant sigh. Staring up into his distant blue eyes, Luzero knew. She understood root and branch. She squeezed her arms more tightly around him, as if to keep him and their memory from vanishing into the mists of time.

BIBLIOGRAPHY

Though *To the Color* and its prequel, *Changing Flags,* are works of historical fiction with storyline, narrative, characterizations, and dialogue by Ray Herbeck, Jr., every major character and many minor characters existed. If their actual words survived as part of the public domain historical record via speeches, letters, etc., they were incorporated whenever appropriate. And when known, the real names of characters were used and their historical actions truthfully portrayed, drawn from the following sources:

United States National Archives: Department of War, RG 94, Adjutant General's Office, Miscellaneous Papers Relating to the Mexican War, Box No. 7 (Riley's letters)
"The Other Side, or Notes for the History of the War between Mexico and the United States, written in Mexico and Translated from the Spanish," Ramon Alcaraz, John Wiley, New York (1850)
United States National Archives: Department of War, RG 153, Judge Advocate General's Office; Proceedings of General Court Martial at Tacubaya, Mexico, 1847; Proceedings of General Court Martial at San Angel, Mexico, 1847
"Shamrock and Sword: The Saint Patrick's Battalion in the U.S.–Mexican War," Robert Ryal Miller, Univ. of Oklahoma Press (1989)
"El Soldado Mexicano (The Mexican Soldier) 1837–1847,"

Nieto-Brown-Hefter, Mexico (1958)

"My Confession: The Recollections of a Rogue," Samuel E. Chamberlain, Harper & Brothers, New York (1956)

"Sam Chamberlain's Mexican War: The San Jacinto Museum of History Paintings," William H. Goetzmann, Texas State Historical Association, Austin (1993)

"Chronicles of the Gringos: The U.S. Army in the Mexican War, 1846–1848, Accounts of Eyewitnesses & Combatants," George Winston Smith & Charles Judah, The University of New Mexico Press (1968)

"The Highly Irregular Irregulars: Texas Rangers in the Mexican War," Frederick Wilkins, Eakin Press, Austin, Texas (1990)

"Rip Ford's Texas," John Salmon Ford (Edited by Stephen B. Oates), University of Texas Press, Austin (1963)

"Army of Manifest Destiny: The American Soldier in the Mexican War, 1846–1848," James M. McCaffrey, New York University Press (1992)

"The View from Chapultepec: Mexican Writers on the Mexican-American War," Translated & Edited by Cecil Robinson, University of Arizona Press, Tucson (1989)

"A Country of Vast Designs: James K. Polk, the Mexican War, and the Conquest of the American Continent," Robert W. Merry, Simon & Schuster, New York (2009)

"So Far from God: the U.S. War with Mexico 1846–1848," John S. D. Eisenhower, Random House, New York (1989)

"The Mexican War: Changing Interpretations," Edited by Odie B. Faulk and Joseph A. Stout, Jr., Sage Books, Swallow Press, Chicago (1973)

"Essays on the Mexican War," Wayne Cutler, John S. D. Eisenhower, Miguel E. Soto, Douglas W. Richmond, Texas A & M University Press, College Station (1986)

"Mexico Under Fire, Being the Diary of Samuel Ryan Curtis, 3rd Ohio Volunteer Regiment, During the American Military

Occupation of Northern Mexico 1846–1847," Edited and Annotated by Joseph E. Chance, Texas Christian University Press, Forth Worth (1994)

"The Mexican War Journal and Letters of Ralph W. Kirkham," Edited by Robert Ryal Miller, Texas A & M University Press, College Station (1991)

"The Truth About Santa Anna," Walter Caruth Emerson, Cardinal Press, Dallas (1973)

"Eyewitness to War: Prints and Daguerreotypes of the Mexican War, 1846–1848," Martha A. Sandweiss, Rick Stewart, Ben W. Huseman, Amon Carter Museum, Fort Worth, Texas, Smithsonian Institution Press, Washington, D.C. (1989)

"The Mexican-American War 1846–1848," Text by Philip R. N. Katcher, Colour Plates by G. A. Embleton, Osprey Publishing, London (1976)

"The President's House: A History," William Seale, White House Historical Association, National Geographic Society, Washington, D.C. (1986)

"Brassey's History of Uniforms: Mexican-American War 1846–1848," Ron Field, Colour Plates by Richard Hook, Brassey's (UK) Ltd (1997)

"The Mexican War, 1846–1848," Jack Bauer, Macmillan Co., New York (1974)

"The Old West: The Mexican War," David Nevin, Time-Life Books, New York (1978)

ABOUT THE AUTHOR

Author **Ray Herbeck, Jr.,** is a journalism graduate of California State University–Long Beach and a student of Texas, Mexican War, Civil War, and Old West history. His stint as a copy editor/reporter at *Billboard* and editor of *On Location*, a film/TV production magazine, led to a twenty-year film career that married his writing with his hobby. Among his credits are historian and technical advisor ("North & South–Books I and II," "Gone to Texas"); associate producer ("Alamo: The Price of Freedom"—IMAX, "Glory"), and writer and producer "("The True Story of 'Glory' Continues," "The Wild West"). He also wrote film scripts for National Park Service historic sites. A resident of Prescott Valley, Arizona, Herbeck is a member of the Western Writers of America.

The employees of Five Star Publishing hope you have enjoyed this book.

Our Five Star novels explore little-known chapters from America's history, stories told from unique perspectives that will entertain a broad range of readers.

Other Five Star books are available at your local library, bookstore, all major book distributors, and directly from Five Star/Gale.

Connect with Five Star Publishing

Website:
gale.com/five-star

Facebook:
facebook.com/FiveStarCengage

Twitter:
twitter.com/FiveStarCengage

Email:
FiveStar@cengage.com

For information about titles and placing orders:
(800) 223-1244
gale.orders@cengage.com

To share your comments, write to us:
Five Star Publishing
Attn: Publisher
10 Water St., Suite 310
Waterville, ME 04901